INVENTED LIVES

Andrea Goldsmith originally trained as a speech pathologist, and was a pioneer in the development of communication aids for people unable to speak. Her first novel, *Gracious Living*, was published in 1989. This was followed by *Modern Interiors*, *Facing the Music*, *Under the Knife*, and *The Prosperous Thief*, which was shortlisted for the 2003 Miles Franklin Literary Award. *Reunion* was published in 2009, and *The Memory Trap* was awarded the 2015 Melbourne Prize. Her literary essays have appeared in *Meanjin*, *Australian Book Review*, *Best Australian Essays*, and numerous anthologies. Her shorter articles and reviews are posted at www.andreagoldsmith.com.au. Andrea Goldsmith lives in Melbourne.

INVENTED LIVES

ANDREA GOLDSMITH

SCRIBE
Melbourne • London

Scribe Publications
2 John St, Clerkenwell, London, WC1N 2ES, United Kingdom
18–20 Edward St, Brunswick, Victoria 3056, Australia
3754 Pleasant Ave, Suite 100, Minneapolis, Minnesota 55409 USA

Published by Scribe 2019

Typeset in Bembo by the publishers

Printed and bound in the UK by CPI Group (UK) Ltd, Croydon
CR0 4YY

Scribe Publications is committed to the sustainable use of natural
resources and the use of paper products made responsibly from those
resources.

9781947534902 (US edition)
9781912854820 (UK edition)
9781925713589 (Australian edition)
9781925693492 (e-book)

Catalogue records for this book are available from the National
Library of Australia and the British Library.

scribepublications.com
scribepublications.co.uk
scribepublications.com.au

To the Porters:

Jean, Chester, Maudie and Josie

'Exile itself has become an emblem, no
matter whether it is experienced by
someone in his own country, his own room,
and in his own language, or outside and far
removed from them. The moment we are all
experiencing is convulsive. The theatre of
the world is convulsive … no matter where
we live. We are all exiles.'

Norman Manea, *The Fifth Impossibility*

'I am like a pelican of the wilderness:
I am like an owl of the desert.'

Psalm 102

1

DEATH AND RECKLESS BEHAVIOUR IN LENINGRAD

Galina Kogan completed the documents to record her mother's death. She filled out forms to stop wages, cancel benefits, and nullify identity papers. She parted with a week's pay for a coffin, and when told that transport from the state mortuary to the cemetery would be delayed several days, another fistful of notes solved the problem. A few more roubles here, a few more there, and her mother would be laid to rest the following week.

It was now official: Lidiya Yuryevna Kogan had died at 8.37, on the morning of Wednesday, 27th November, 1985.

Galina gathered up all the documents. The bag was bulging with her mother's belongings, so she shoved the papers down a side pocket. She fixed her mother's watch to her own wrist, surprised to see it was already four o'clock; this day of her mother's death had passed without her noticing. She hefted the bag over her shoulder and hurried along the corridor to the stairs. She made a brief phone call in the hospital foyer to say she was on her way home, and finally emerged through the doors into the fresh air outside.

Winter had powered in during the last weeks of her mother's illness, weeks stretched by death's determined assault against her mother's steadfast grip on life. Fully occupied by the struggle

1

playing out before her, Galina had given no thought to the weather. But now as she entered the street, she slammed into the cold. Her winter coat was still packed away in the trunk—the rest of life so callously undisturbed while her mother lay dying—and her jacket, the one she had worn every day since her mother's stroke, was no match for the weather. Yet, despite the chill, and despite there being a trolley bus in sight, she needed time to think, to collect herself, to pull together a life that had just lost its centre.

She wrapped her scarf about her head and knotted it at the neck, thrust her hands deep in her pockets, and set off through the sombre streets. The smell of the hospital lingered, and she wondered if she'd ever be rid of it. She quickened her pace, but her legs resisted; she tried to order her thoughts, but her brain had turned to slush.

She was heading home, although her mother's death had already stripped it of homeliness. There'd be relatives and friends waiting, and food and drink and an explosion of memories. But Lidiya had provided a sense of home that went beyond their flat, beyond the old books and the new TV, beyond the table where they ate and worked, beyond the sallow green stairwell with its human reek, beyond the building itself, only twenty years old and already frayed and weary. Lidiya had been sanctuary.

And what now for the future—*their* future, which had just shrunk to *her* future? What now for emigration? They knew when they submitted their papers they were signing over the right to change their minds—not that it mattered then, as they had no intention of doing so. And in the months since, despite Gorbachev's *glasnost* and *perestroika*, despite his heralding new freedoms and greater prosperity, they'd not wavered. Her mother had scoffed at Gorbachev's promises. The trouble with Russia, she'd said, was that nothing fundamentally changed. Thaws were followed by crackdowns, crackdowns were followed by thaws, so why should it be any different on Gorbachev's watch?

'We've an opportunity to leave. Best to go when we can.'

Officially they were emigrating to Israel, the only permissible destination for Soviet Jews, yet they had no Zionist yearnings nor religious stirrings; in fact, they lacked all but the most rudimentary knowledge of how to be Jewish. But given the push and snarl of Russia's chronic anti-Semitism, not a day passed without a reminder that ethnically they were Jewish. This was such a common aspect of life in the Soviet Union that Galina had accepted, with neither rancour nor resentment, that the bribes she'd had to pay for her mother's funeral were more numerous and hefty than those extracted from Russians. It was, simply, the way things were.

They had planned to change their destination from Israel to America once they got to Vienna. Or was it Rome where they were to make the change? Galina's head had fogged up. Vienna or Rome? She couldn't remember. Her mother had died, and it seemed that memory and reason had cut and run. How was she going to manage? Whether here or elsewhere in the world, how would she manage the future alone?

Her breath was drawing short and harsh. She stopped by a canal, pulled the air into her lungs, and forced out a slow exhalation. She felt faint, and leaned against the iron railings for support. The metal was sharp and cold against the bones of her hips; she pressed in harder. The surface of the water was an oily, dark opalescence — strangely beautiful, she found herself thinking. Garbage bobbed against the canal walls, ducks poked about looking for spoils, a barge and a smaller boat chugged past. She closed her eyes and slipped into a gentle, muted world where life seemed to have stopped. It was a brief respite, however, for intruding into this twilight zone came her own clear voice: *You're twenty-four years old, Galina Kogan. You're an adult, and you're on your own. So pull yourself together.*

She opened her eyes, took one last deep breath, pressed her hands to her chest as if that would squeeze the terror out, and set off again.

It was not yet dusk, but with the low, swarthy clouds it might have been night. Street lights glowed with that frosted halo that hinted at snow; noises were smudged as if coming from a great distance. There was no wind. Galina felt weirdly disconnected from the world, a world that had moved into the future while she sat in limbo with her dying mother. And yet she'd made an attempt to keep up with events, had read *Leningradskaya Pravda* to her mother every day, and when her mother no longer responded, had read to pass the time. A volcano had erupted in Colombia, killing twenty-five thousand people—and why, she wondered, was her own single death so much more weighty than all those dead Colombians? She'd read about bomb attacks in Paris, and hijackings in the Mediterranean. Then, a week ago in Geneva, General Secretary Gorbachev and President Reagan of America had met for the very first time. It had been rumoured that the situation of Soviet Jews was on the agenda, along with arms control. There was no way of knowing whether Soviet Jews had, in fact, been discussed. As for arms control, it simply made no sense, not after years of being told of the necessity of a great Soviet arsenal as security against the war-mongering, untrustworthy Americans. But then so much in the Soviet Union made no sense. It gave traction to her mother's joke that Soviet citizens, while starved of the comforts of life, were gourmands when it came to swallowing absurdities.

No more of her mother's jokes now.

They had been told regularly of the Soviet Union's superiority in nuclear weapons—it was anyone's guess as to whether this was true or not—but what every Soviet citizen knew without a skerrick of doubt was that America was the land of plenty, the émigré's El Dorado. They were told that poverty was endemic in America, that education and housing were in a parlous state, that only the very corrupt or the very rich could afford to be sick, that photographs of shops full of goods were not real shops, but rather staged sets for the cameras. Yet despite the official line, every Russian knew there was plenty of food in America, and huge stores filled with clothes and household goods. It was not just the American films they saw, the Soviet Union's thriving black market was proof of the quality and range of American goods.

There had been a photograph in the paper of Gorbachev and Reagan standing together surrounded by their advisors, the Soviet team clearly distinguishable from the American, and film of the meeting had been shown on the *Vremya* news, so that aspect of the report — that the leaders were meeting — was true. Gorbachev, stylish in his Italian suit, looked like a Westerner. As to what had been discussed, she'd learned from her mother always to be suspicious of reports in the official press.

A year ago, such a meeting between the two leaders would have been inconceivable, but then a year ago it was equally inconceivable that her mother would suffer a massive brain haemorrhage. Some changes, like having the bathroom tap fixed at the communal apartments or being allocated your own flat, seemed to take years. Other changes, like the gas explosion in the block near her old school, or the death of her fifty-seven-year-old mother, were shocking in their suddenness.

It wasn't that she wanted her mother alive again, not in the dreadful state the stroke had rendered her. She wanted life as it had been before the stroke, their papers to emigrate submitted, the two of them sifting through their possessions trying to decide what to take, and both of them managing to save as much as possible because as soon as their request to emigrate was approved, they knew they'd be forced to leave their jobs (and if their application was refused, they'd lose their jobs anyway). In short, they were living for today while making preparations for tomorrow: a new life in America, where everyone was equal, where her mother, a translator and teacher of languages, would find work that matched her experience and abilities, and where Galina, herself, could draw what she liked, confined only by her own artistic limitations and not by the state. She was a Soviet Jew and a Russian illustrator. The irony had long struck her: both the Jew and the artist were censored here.

Galina pulled her hand from her pocket and brushed her face. Just when she thought things couldn't get worse, it had begun to snow, only a few wet flakes at the moment, but gearing up for more. If she believed in a god, she'd think she was being punished. But for what? Nothing in her twenty-four years would warrant the illness and death of her still-young mother, nor the twenty-year absence of a father she couldn't remember, nor an impending blizzard on a day when it already took all her energy just to remain upright and moving.

She tugged at her scarf, shoved both hands deeper into her coat and continued on her way. And suddenly she was on the ground, pitched forward on the uneven brick paving. A sickening pain filled her knee.

She needed to move, she couldn't move.

Galina is lying in a stink of urine and ancient filth. She wants to fade out, she wants not to be here. Where is oblivion exactly? she is wondering. And what is it about Leningrad paving that prises the bricks from their cement beds? Might there be tiny earthquakes occurring all over the city?

A strange man is hovering over her. His hands are flapping, and a barrage of Russian mixed with English is spilling out of him. Life as she has known it stopped this morning, and now, in full view of everyone, she's the target of a hysterical foreigner.

'Please.' She manages to find some English. 'Please, I am all right.'

The man is crouched over her, she can smell onions. 'Please, sir, move away. I need air.'

He utters a stream of apologies, grabs a scarf from his neck, rolls it into a sausage and places it under her head. He stands back, his face bright red. He's clearly embarrassed, and so he ought to be. Not that she cares; and it occurs to her she doesn't really care about anything anymore. She turns her back to him, closes her eyes, and curls up small. The whoosh of tyres, a blitz of car horns, the stop-start wheeze of a bus come to her muffled, as if through water. It's not unpleasant, a sort of holding bay for life, and she tries to insert her mother—her healthy, vibrant mother. But the bed-ridden figure of the past terrible weeks, with the face shrivelling over the skull, the twisted mouth, the perpetual drool, refuses to be dislodged. And suddenly the abysmal thought: it might never be.

You're on your own, she tells herself again. You're lying on the filthy ground, a blizzard could be on the way, there's a foreigner fussing over you, and you're on your own. And as much as she wants to stay right where she is, she makes herself move. The stranger is watching her. The flush has left his face; his skin is smooth and unmarked—healthy skin, which for some reason makes her think of oranges.

He steps towards her. 'Let me help you.'

Tall and unmistakeably Western, he is dressed in Levis and a sheepskin jacket; his blond wavy hair, clean and lush, is swept back from his forehead, he wears no hat. She guesses he is much the same age as she is, although Westerners always look younger than their years. It's impossible to know who or what he is, whether friend or foe. Not that it matters. In kindergarten, in school, in the Pioneers, in the Komsomol, at university, at work, wherever you are in the Soviet system, you're told that all foreigners are suspect, and all are to be avoided. Although now, at this moment, if anyone is watching her—and all prospective émigrés can expect to be watched—she's simply too exhausted to care.

Life without her mother is not about to wait any longer. She shoves her pains aside, stretches out her hand, and the foreigner grasps it. As he leans down, she sees the skin of his throat. It is

7

bronzed and unblemished, and there is a scent about him—not the onions, but something fresh and spicy; she breathes it in. He keeps his arm about her until she has regained her balance. His apologies are profuse, his touch gentle, and to her horror, she feels tears; she swallows hard, takes her time to find a steady voice, insists she is not hurt. But no amount of reassurance will placate him.

'I could have caused you a serious injury,' he says.

'You have not hurt me.' She is surprised at the ease of her English when everything else is in tatters. 'It is not your fault. The paving is a mess, and I was not watching where I was going.'

'Neither was I.' The man pauses a moment before adding, 'I'd stopped to look at the snow.'

Not simply a foreigner, but a mad one to be lingering in freezing temperatures gazing at a few miserable snowflakes.

'I've only seen snow once before.' His face is again bright red.

'In your entire life?' This man is clearly no spy, no enemy of any kind.

He nods.

'Where on earth are you from?'

She hears him say Austria. But no, he repeats it, Australia, the big country at the bottom of the world. 'Not much snow down there,' he says. And after a moment he adds, 'Most Australians respond to snow as you Russians do to kangaroos.'

She feels the muscles around her jaw protest: it has been a long time since she smiled. Her very first English-language book, which was also her mother's first English book, was called *Babies at the Zoo*; and of all the baby animals in the book, the kangaroo was her favourite. Accompanying each illustration was a short poem written by the great Samuil Marshak. She can still recite the one about the kangaroo.

And suddenly she sees her mother, pre-stroke Lidiya, sitting with her younger self, and the two of them are reading this book together. She is so tempted to prolong the image, to grasp her mother's aliveness, but knows she can't, not right now. But tomorrow and next week and next year this image, and she desperately hopes others too, of a healthy Lidiya will come back to her. For the moment she distracts herself with busyness. The bag has spilled its contents; she thrusts them back, smooths herself down, twists her hair under her scarf, and starts on her way.

'Can I walk with you?' The Australian speaks in a rush, like someone out of practice.

Galina supposes she is suffering from shock, or perhaps this is how grief and mourning feel, and she knows she needs to think about the future, but it's beyond her at the moment. She glances at the Australian, he really does seem innocuous, and besides, with night falling and the weather deteriorating, there'll be few people to observe her fraternising with a foreigner. And again it strikes her: she doesn't care who is watching because she doesn't care what happens to her now that the worst has happened. She shrugs and nods. It's permission enough and all she has energy for.

'Tell me about yourself,' she says, knowing she'll manage better if she doesn't have to speak.

There's more blushing, and his hands knot together in a white-knuckled grip. He's clearly very uncomfortable, or perhaps he's shy. A shy Westerner: it seems such an unlikely combination.

He tells her his name is Andrew Morrow, that he is twenty-five years old, from Melbourne, Australia. He speaks hesitantly, and there's a long pause before he adds, 'I've come to Leningrad to study mosaics.'

'You are an artist of mosaics?'

He shrugs. 'I try to be.'

Of all the artistic students at her *gimnaziya*, and later at the art college, none had wanted to be a mosaicist, yet mosaic was such a Russian art and, given the Australian's presence here, clearly famous across the world. He tells her he has been in Leningrad for a month. He says he has permission to view a range of sites, but most of the next three months will be spent with the mosaicists who are restoring the Church of the Resurrection of Christ. 'The Church on the Spilled Blood, as you call it.' He pauses. 'You know it, of course?'

She nods. Like most Petersburgers, she has a special fondness for this great Russian-style church in the centre of Baroque and Neoclassical Leningrad. Resilient, like the Russian people, it has survived against the odds.

He's looking at her expectantly. What's she to do? Talk or not talk? And does it make any difference now? And it occurs to her that nothing makes any difference now.

'This church where you will be working has a chequered history.' Her throat is dry and she gulps down some air. 'At one stage it was used as a store for theatre props. Later, during the Great Patriotic War, it was used as a mortuary, and after the war when it was a warehouse for vegetables it became known as "The Saviour on Potatoes".' And then a wayward comment escapes. 'Whether palace, church, or person, we fight for our survival in the Soviet Union.'

The terrible words freeze in the quiet, still air. What on earth is she thinking to speak so carelessly? And to a foreigner, of all people? But then she isn't thinking. That's the problem.

'Your church has been saved now,' the Australian says, seemingly unaware of her blunder. 'Soon it'll be restored to its former splendour.'

She looks around, there's no one in hearing distance; she's been lucky this time, but unlikely to get a second chance. She has to be more careful. The man is prattling on about the Church on the Spilled Blood; he thinks it will be one of the most beautiful churches in the world when it is finished. And perhaps he's right, but she and her mother, like so many Petersburgers, have watched the church being brought back to life while their own miserable apartment blocks have been left to crumble. Millions of roubles have been spent on the restoration; it's been hard to admire without envy. The cupolas are now complete, six or eight of them all clad in brilliant blue and sun-coloured ceramics, and real gold, too, so it is said. More recently—she knew this even before the Australian told her—work has shifted to the mosaics that originally covered the entire interior of the church.

'I love Russian mosaics.' The sentence catapults from him. 'Such variety in the materials—glass, porcelain, even jewels—and the detail, and the size of the projects.' She hears a jerky riff of laughter. 'Russians seem to be drawn to bigness.' There's a pause so long she is framing another question when he starts up again, in short bursts, like machine-gun fire. 'Your Boris Anrep'—the name is vaguely familiar to her—'Boris Anrep, born here, Leningrad, St Petersburg, in the 1880s, became one of Britain's most celebrated mosaicists. His work's in the National Gallery, it's in Westminster Cathedral. He and your Anna Akhmatova were,' there's a pause, 'they were close.'

And now she remembers why she's heard of Boris Anrep, although this foreigner, either due to his own modesty or in deference to hers, cannot bring himself to say that Anrep and Akhmatova were lovers.

He is walking more slowly, and his speech, too, has slowed. 'I'd stay here longer if I could, there's so much to learn, and my fellowship money would stretch for a couple more months. But I have to be home after our summer break, when the new term begins.'

'Most foreign students come here in *our* summer. In fact,' she adds, 'most visitors of any sort come in summer.'

'I've come when I was free to come. And actually, I'm not a student. I teach at an adult-education institution.' Then more softly, 'I love the idea of winter here.'

'I guarantee you won't love it in a few weeks' time.'

'Perhaps you'll see for yourself.'

It sounds like an invitation, and just as she is working out a non-committal response—the last thing she needs is a lonely foreigner dragging her down—the clock tower sounds five. Andrew

11

suddenly stops, checks his wristwatch in the light of a street lamp, and excuses himself.

'So sorry. I've a meeting at 5.30.' He thrusts a card at her. 'Sorry,' he says again. 'Have to rush.' He nods at the card. 'Russian contacts one side, Australian on the other.'

She points him in the direction of the nearest Metro station, and watches him dash to the corner. He pauses, then turns around. 'Your name?' he shouts. 'What's your name?'

If she hasn't already been noticed with a foreigner, she certainly will be now.

'Galina,' she shouts back. 'Galina Kogan.'

Nothing matters anymore.

The foreigner disappears from view. She shoves his card into her pocket and continues on her way. Snow is falling more energetically, yet she makes no attempt to hurry. It is as if life without her mother will begin once she is home. Until then, her limbo state will continue.

Most girls of Galina's age have loosened their attachment to their mother, but since her father vanished twenty years earlier there had only been the two of them. Her paternal grandparents withdrew soon after her father disappeared, and the maternal grandparents, Lidiya's own parents, were long gone, both of them arrested in the desperate days of 1937 when Lidiya herself was a child.

For years after her father's disappearance, in the hours before her mother came to bed, Galina would make up stories about him. She needed to explain his absence and, more importantly, she needed to believe in his eventual return. One of her stories had him working on the Russian space program, another saw him based in a remote region engaged in secret weapons work; one of her favourites made him the admiral of a submarine whose mission was to stay below the surface for several years. She would imagine his joyful

12

homecoming, his pride in her schoolwork and his praise for her art, and she imagined most especially his promise never to go away again. Day after day, month after month, year after year, she fantasised how happy the three of them would be: mother, father and daughter together again. While she and her mother were still living at the *kommunalka*, she used to imagine that on his return her father would be rewarded for his secret work with a flat for his family: a kitchen, bathroom and toilet all to themselves. As it happened, when she and her mother were finally allocated their own flat soon after her twelfth birthday, she was so worried her father wouldn't find them, she didn't want to move. It took considerable persuasion on Lidiya's behalf to convince her that, should her father turn up, the authorities would be sure to tell him their new address.

It was the enduring hope of her childhood that her father would return, for he truly had disappeared. One day, around the time of her third birthday, he simply did not return home after work, nor the next day did he turn up at the Ministry of Education where he was employed as an overseer of resources. Later, she would concede her father was not qualified for any of the secret work she gave him in her fantasies, but as a young girl the fantasies were essential, particularly in their old home in the *kommunalka*. Here she and her mother had two rooms, and fortunately were allowed to keep both after her father disappeared. (It was Soviet bureaucratic specificity that had intervened, and the only time it had worked to their advantage: because the partition between their rooms did not reach the ceiling, it was officially designated as a single room.) They shared a bathroom and kitchen with seven other families, twice the number who had lived here when the rooms were first allocated to Lidiya's parents. It was crowded and it was noisy, and everyone knew everyone else's business. Galina learned at a young age that fantasies, make-believe of all sorts, provided the space and other luxuries absent in your real life.

Her father disappeared and no one knew what had become of

him, neither friends nor colleagues, not even his own parents—or so she and her mother believed at the time. Later, when the story of his absence emerged, they guessed his parents had known his whereabouts all along, for within months of his disappearance they obtained permission to move—to Georgia, of all places.

With her father gone, there were just the two of them in the communal apartment. In a strange way, the crowd and bustle that surrounded them seemed to connect them ever more tightly. She and her mother often joked that their home of two rooms—between themselves, they always referred to their *two* rooms—three storeys above the street, with their own south-facing window, was like their own floating island.

In the *kommunalka* they used to share a bed, but by the time they were allocated their own flat, two divans were more practical. Hours would pass with her mother sitting on her divan, typewriter firmly arranged on a square of wood, dictionaries to one side and the book she was translating perched on a stand. And on the divan closest to the window, her back supported by the wall, Galina would do her schoolwork, and when that was finished she'd draw and paint, paper clipped to a board, paints and pencils on the windowsill. Sometimes her mother would read aloud from the novel she was translating—it cultivated Galina's own interest in both English and Italian—or she might recite Russian poetry.

Yevtushenko was one of her mother's favourites. He was a great defender of Russian Jews, she said, and his 'Babi Yar' was one of the most important poems ever written. She said that even if Yevtushenko wrote doggerel—which, she added, he'd been known to do—she would still buy his books, and she would still wait in line, for hours if necessary, to hear him read his poems. Lidiya was a woman of strong passions, or rather had been a woman of strong passions—not that Galina was ready to relegate her mother to the past just yet. She doubted she ever would be.

It was six years ago that news came of her father. He had died

14

in Tbilisi, Georgia, where he'd been living since leaving Leningrad. A small box addressed to Lidiya had been found by his new wife (although not so new, given there was a half-sister only a couple of years Galina's junior), and she had sent it to their new flat. Lidiya wondered why Osip had bothered. The box contained the tie-pin she had given him as a wedding gift, an English pipe she had bought on the black market that had cost a small fortune, an envelope addressed to her in Osip's handwriting containing a bundle of roubles so small it would not cover food for a week, and Lidiya's well-read copy of *The Twelve Chairs*, inherited from her own father and inscribed with his name—the only item, apart from the money, that she kept. There was a scarf that Lidiya could not remember seeing before, and neither apology nor explanation.

There was, however, one positive outcome of Osip's certified death. If he'd been alive, or, more particularly, if they'd been unable to prove his death, they would have needed his written permission as husband and father for their exit papers from the USSR. With his death now official, the only permission required was from the sole surviving grandparent, Osip's mother. She'd had no contact with them for years and, as a stubbornly loyal Soviet citizen, they guessed she'd want nothing to do with two would-be deserters of the Motherland. In the end they took a calculated risk: Lidiya had not changed her name when she married, and Galina was a Kogan too, so any connection with Osip's family should be impossible to trace.

'What about your brother,' Galina asked her mother. 'What about Mikhail?'

'He's been gone a lifetime,' Lidiya said. 'And unlikely to turn up now.'

So they embarked on their plan to emigrate. It was exciting, it was nerve-racking, it was all-consuming. The easing of exit visas for Jews, begun in the late 1970s, was continuing, but for how long was anyone's guess. The crucial requirement, they'd been told, was to be an insignificant Jew. Physicists and other scientists, dissenters and writers were likely to be lifetime refuseniks—not because the Soviet Union wanted to make use of their skills (it was common knowledge that most had been forced into menial jobs and some into internal exile), but because of the security risks of letting these people go. For ordinary people like themselves, people who were of little use to the Soviet Union and posed absolutely no danger to Soviet power, applications were being processed relatively quickly and successfully.

They made enquiries, they tapped into the information networks, and they filed their papers to migrate to Israel. But it was the paradise of America that was their true destination. They talked endlessly about American food and clothes, American TVs and stereos, American toasters and mix-masters; they talked about their American apartment, its central heating, the garbage chute, the reliable water and electrical supply, and a bedroom for each of them; they talked about the American 'melting pot' of Europeans and black people, of Latinos and Asians, of Catholics and Jews, all in together, everyone equal, everyone with the same opportunities. America thrilled them, America sent them into raptures. America was the destination of their dreams.

America, think about America, Galina tells herself as she walks through the darkening streets. But she is unable to think of an America without her mother. Tears again threaten, and she stops to collect herself—no time for tears, no place for weakness—presses the palms of her hands against her eyes, slows her breathing, steadies her nerves.

A short time later, she turns into her street. The snow has eased, but the sky is still heavy; a small elliptical smudge of cloud, slightly lighter than the rest, marks the location of the moon. She finds herself wishing for some sort of religion, not specifically involving God, but an afterlife, with her mother whizzing through the cosmos liberated from her stroke-struck body.

She may as well wish for wings.

She crosses the street and walks the last few metres to her building. She pauses at the threshold, then trudges up the stairs. She hears the slap of each step, she smells the ubiquitous *karbolka*, she feels her way through the dark stretches where the globes have been stolen. When she reaches the flat, she stands outside her no-longer home, unable to make the next move.

The door opens — might she have knocked? — and immediately she's drawn inside and embraced by well-wishers. Everyone is sad, everyone needs consolation, but everyone knows a daughter's loss is greater than theirs. More people arrive, and soon the flat is jammed with friendly faces and rousing memories. Despite the cold, the door to the balcony is open to draw out the cigarette smoke and the heat of so many bodies. There's plenty of food and several bottles of Georgian wine, and no shortage of vodka despite Gorbachev's absurd prohibitions. ('Not even Lenin himself would dare separate a Russian from his vodka,' Nadya, her mother's best friend, says.) People share stories about Lidiya; there's laughter as well as sadness, but with the passing hours, it's the laughter that dominates. The night deepens, the food is eaten, the alcohol is drunk.

It's close to eleven o'clock when everyone finally leaves. Nadya helps with the tidying up, then makes them some fresh tea. They sit at the table where she, Galina, and her mother have spent so much time, and where Nadya and her mother have spent so much time, but never before has it been just her and Nadya sitting here together. And it occurs to her that it is these small everyday happenings that will drive home the fact that her life has cruelly and irrevocably changed.

Nadya tucks a fresh a cigarette between her lips, and reaches for Galina's hands. As soon as Lidiya is laid to rest, she says, Galina will be going back to work, even earlier if she is up to it. Work will help, she says, work will distract. She takes a deep drag of her cigarette, ash falls to the table. 'And, Galya, no more talk of emigration. It is better to remain in the country you know. Where you yourself are known.' And when there is no response, she adds, 'Life must go on, Galinochka. And life here is not so bad. Not like it used to be.'

Nadya continues to talk about the future, but Galina is not listening. She is caught by Nadya's face, a face so familiar she's not really looked at it before. It is as if a hessian sack has been stuck to the skull and neck, leaving holes for the eyes and mouth. This rough, mustardy fabric-skin, falling in folds and creases, is the map of Nadya's life. It reveals poor nourishment and too many cigarettes, too little money and too much vodka, too much work for too little satisfaction. She loves Nadya, but now, suddenly, looking at this woman she has known her entire life evokes a terrible fear: might this be the face of her own future?

What is left for her here? Even if it were possible to withdraw her emigration papers without penalty, even if she were permitted to remain in her job as a book illustrator, she will never be promoted beyond her current position. There'll be nights and weekends spent in the flat—that's if she were permitted to stay here alone—painting pictures that will never be seen by anyone other than herself. She supposes there'll be a husband and a child or two whose own future would be as strained and stained as her own. As a Jew, she'll never know the freedoms of other Soviet citizens, much less those experienced in the West. Gorbachev's reforms, like all those that have preceded them, will not last. If she stays, this—what she has now—is the best she can hope for, this life stretching ahead to her own death.

Nadya must have realised that Galina's thoughts were elsewhere because finally she stops talking. She pours more tea for them both, lights another cigarette, and when she speaks again, her voice is gentle, it is kind.

'So, Galya, what do you plan to do?'

'I'm still going to emigrate.' The words come of their own accord.

Nadya stares at her. Sadness and pity are etched in the crumpled face, and suddenly she is apologising. It was wrong of her to have raised the subject of the future. It's far too early to make decisions. Lidiya has only just gone, Galya is in a state of shock.

Now Galina reaches for Nadya's hands. She holds them gently between her own. Her voice, however, is firm.

'I'm going to emigrate … to Australia.'

The word fits uneasily in her mouth. She has decided to move to a country whose name has never before passed her lips.

Australia.

2

IN TRANSIT

In February 1986, within two days of each other, Galina Kogan and the Australian mosaicist, Andrew Morrow, left Leningrad.

Andrew was returning home. He had a myriad of ideas for his own work, and was impatient to begin, but at the same time a queer foreboding he might never return to Russia made him reluctant to leave. Only a small portion of the interior mosaics of the Church on the Spilled Blood had been restored so far, and he could not bear to miss seeing the finished glory. Nothing on the face of the earth would compare.

Then there was the girl he had knocked down in the street, the girl who had never called, the girl who, if he were to be realistic, was never going to call. But in the three months since their meeting, he had spent so much time thinking about her, she had become part of his Leningrad life. Her striking presence back when they met had inflated to giddy proportions now. Not just her height—so appealing, given his own six feet—but the dark eyes and olive skin, the lush figure, and the caramel-coloured hair that reminded him of palomino horses. He had crafted their second meeting and all the ones after that. He had scripted conversations with her; he had imagined holding her and kissing her, he had even imagined making love to her. In short, he had managed to make her an intimate, and typical of a shy bloke, to fall for an imagined woman—although gratifyingly easy to transport her home.

He arrived at Pulkovo airport very early on the day of departure, having learned that despite all the rules and regulations circumscribing Soviet life, rarely did things proceed as planned. It was minus ten outside, with an Arctic wind blasting across the flats. The Intourist driver had dropped him off a good fifty metres from the terminal entrance (that in itself was against regulations), rightly guessing she'd not receive much of a tip from a foreigner with a backpack. Russians, he had learned, had a great sense of entitlement when it came to Westerners; they were also shrewd punishers. By the time he entered the terminal, the cold had carved into his bones, his lungs had stiffened, and his face, foolishly uncovered, was flayed by that unique blend of sting and burn that is the province of extreme cold.

He found a space away from the doors against a small patch of wall. His breath still refused to come, and his hands and feet were blocks of pain. This will subside, he told himself, in just a few minutes, his hands and feet will return to normal, and his lungs will resume their usual work. He forced his attention outwards, beyond his beleaguered body.

It struck him as typically Soviet that a relatively new international airport should have such a small waiting area. Much the same size as a basketball court, there were very few seats and, as far as he could see, only one food-and-drink kiosk. There was a single tourist outlet, with two shop assistants talking animatedly to each other, while travellers browsed shelves of matryoshka dolls and embroidered peasant shawls. On his left, so incongruous at this international airport, was a *babushka* seated on the floor surrounded by bundles; and huddled together on a single seat, was a young couple who looked so dazed they might have been on Mars. Apart from a large family who had spread themselves across an entire row of seats, the rest of the people in the waiting area appeared to be foreign businesspeople, predominately male

21

and mostly European. He was the only traveller with a backpack.

Ten minutes later he had recovered sufficiently to move. He collected his luggage and approached the check-in counter. His pack was heavy, certainly heavier than when he arrived. Would he be liable for excess baggage? And what would they do to him if he couldn't pay the fee? He put his backpack and shoulder bag on the scales, lowering each as gently as possible—as if that might lighten the load. He watched the needle swing vigorously across the dial and stop at twenty-four kilograms.

The woman at the counter looked at him, she held his gaze. He was four kilograms over the luggage allowance, but something in her expression, together with a just-perceptible shrug, suggested there might be room for negotiation. In his pocket was a small purse shaped as a map of Australia which contained the last of his American dollars—enough to buy a meal in the transit lounge in Vienna, but would, he decided, be put to better use here. He reached for the purse and offered it as a gift to the woman. He pointed to the word 'Australia' on his passport, and told her in Russian he was Australian. She took the purse, had a quick look inside, and indicated he was to remove his shoulder bag from the scales. The dial now indicated nineteen kilograms. She wrote nineteen on his form, pocketed the purse, and waved him through. Two hours later Andrew was in the air, two hours after that he was in transit in Vienna, and another twenty-four hours saw him arrive at Melbourne airport.

No gift would help him here. He was passed to two customs officers who combed through his pack. They checked the toes of his shoes and turned out all his pockets; they leafed through notebooks and dismantled his ballpoint pens; they unscrewed the lid of his talcum powder and stirred the contents with a metal prong; his deodorant stick wasn't worth keeping after they were finished with it. And they unwrapped every single mosaic piece he had packed so carefully. He was among the last to exit customs. Beyond the doors were his parents, Sylvie and Leonard, whose anxious faces burst into smiles when he appeared.

Andrew Morrow was home.

In contrast with Andrew, Galina Kogan was leaving home, heading towards a country that if the paucity of reference books in the library was a reliable guide, barely existed. Yet she had not wavered over her choice of destination. She had settled on Australia the day her mother died; it was an omen, and she was convinced that to change her mind would bring bad luck.

She carried a single suitcase, a small valise and, safe in her pocket, two train tickets. The first ticket would take her via Kiev to Lvov in western Ukraine; the other covered travel from Lvov through Czechoslovakia across the border into the West, terminating in Vienna. So many times had she and her mother imagined the moment of crossing from east to west — like moving from a dingy flat into a palace, or from black and white to full technicolour — but the excitement they'd anticipated together had now disappeared. Every aspect of this trip made her anxious.

She'd heard of other émigrés loading tables, chairs, divans, cupboards, beds, carpets, crockery, pianos and paintings into huge containers, packing up long-established Russian lives and shipping them to far-off destinations. She had dithered for weeks over the contents of the flat — full-time dithering, given that when permission to emigrate came through, she was, as forewarned, dismissed from her job. (Grief, she decided, must give irrationality a free ride, for she truly had believed that because of her loss, the authorities would show sympathy and waive the usual termination of employment.)

Like all sensible Russians, she and her mother were hoarders — with shortages a fact of life, you never knew when something might become useful — so their flat was choked with stuff, and not simply stuff for now or stuff for an uncertain future, but also stuff from a dangerous past. There was the collection of maths books belonging to her grandfather, a man arrested and shot more than forty-five years earlier, and the four volumes of Dahl's *Explanatory Dictionary* belonging to her grandmother, who died of neglect in a Siberian labour camp a year after her husband; there was a pre-revolutionary embroidered *challah* cloth with matching table napkins made by Lidiya's grandmother, her own great-grandmother, and a lacquered cigar box, courtesy of her cigar-making great-grandfather.

In the long days and weeks of decision-making, Galina weighed up each object, and she bartered: this of my grandfather's, but not that of my grandmother's; this of my grandmother's, not that of my grandfather's. It was hard, it was stressful: these things that survived when their owners had not had acquired an odd sort of power — like relics. And with her mother now gone, the choices became even weightier. What to do with Lidiya's clothes, her mementos, her trinkets? And what about the books she had translated and the books she had loved? All these things emerged from her mother's life, were evidence of that life. How could any of them be left behind?

As the days and weeks passed, Galina was making herself sick with choice. In the end, practicality and limited funds forced her to be tough. She decided to restrict herself only to what could be fitted in the trunk that she and her mother had used to store their winter clothes and bedding. She packed the Dahl dictionary, together with the Italian and English books Lidiya had translated; she included two settings of the crockery Lidiya had herself kept of her own parents' possessions, two sets of cutlery, and Lidiya's stained and tatty copy of *The Book of Tasty and Nutritious Food*; she added four photograph albums, including one belonging to the maternal grandparents she had never known; and she packed her mother's best gloves, her ring and pendant, her favourite shawl, and her embroidered *tapochki*—the prospect of wearing her mother's indoor slippers in far-off Australia appealed to her. She wavered over Lidiya's type-writer and in the end settled for her fountain pen, but it was the bulky Cyrillic typewriter she really wanted. To prevent herself from changing her mind, she gave it to Ivan, an engineer by day and a poet by night. She packed eight English novels, including *The Time Machine* and *War of the Worlds*, both long-time favourites of her own; among the French books, she chose *The Count of Monte Cristo*, *Around the World in Eighty Days*, and Zola's *The Masterpiece*—another enduring favourite, and she also included Lidiya's precious Dante. The Russian books presented her with the hardest task: she wanted to keep them all. When she could delay no longer, she took all those with her mother's signature inscribed on the inside cover, a good selection of Dostoyevsky, Tolstoy, Gogol, Turgenev, Yevtushenko and, of course, Pushkin. She slept only fitfully in those weeks of choosing; plagued by future regrets, she must have changed her mind a hundred times.

It was an easier job with her own possessions. She packed her new winter coat and her hard-wearing winter boots. She chose two Chagall posters, a set of Kandinsky postcards, a selection of her own illustrations, a collection of Krylov's tales, and all her illus-trated children's books, many of which had belonged to her mother as a child. These were the books that had ignited her own artistic ambitions; doubly precious, she couldn't leave them behind. With a small amount of space left to fill, she packed a teaspoon with an enamelled handle and a clock in a handpainted wooden frame that had belonged to Lidiya's Baba Marya, along with the embroidered *challah* cloth and matching napkins that had come down through the Kogan family. With little interest in cooking, she selected a small samovar, some tea glasses, a set of serving platters also from Lidiya's family, and a single pot and pan.

She sent the trunk to a Jewish organisation in Rome, and wor-ried, increasingly as the weeks passed, that despite the huge price she had paid, she would never see it again. And while she told herself these were only things, that memories were far more durable, it was to no avail. These objects she had so carefully selected to take to her new life, these things that would connect the unknown future to the familiar past, these things were like solid memories, and she could not bear to lose a single one.

On a February morning in 1986, Galina left Leningrad. In the wintry dark, there were no farewells to this city she would never see again, no last glimpses of favourite landmarks to cement into memory, nothing to distract her from the fierce anxiety that was now a constant presence in her days.

The train to Kiev was not the express she had expected, and each time it drew into a station she steeled herself for the official who would enter the carriage, inspect her documents, find them wanting, and haul her off the train. She tried to reason herself into a state of calm. After all, what was the worst that could happen? She'd be sent back to Leningrad with no job, no place to live, and no possessions. Friends and family wouldn't leave her stranded, or at least some wouldn't; others would go out of their way to avoid a self-declared traitor to the Motherland. But even if the worst happened, she would manage. And besides, the worst in known and familiar Leningrad was not nearly as intimidating as the worst in utterly unknown Australia. So she reasoned, but reason transported her nowhere close to a state of calm.

With her limited funds she'd had no choice but to settle for the cheapest compartment, the *obshchiy*. She had counted on the blur of the passing countryside to tranquilise her during the journey, but discovered she'd not been allocated a window berth despite having requested it. There were no doors to the *obshchiy*, she had no view, she had no privacy. She wanted to insist, she wanted to demand, but had to stifle her protests, knowing she mustn't draw attention to herself. There were three other places in the compartment, and she hoped her fellow passengers would make the journey bearable. But when a husband and wife and their daughter, an overdressed girl of about twelve, arrived, she quickly realised there would be no joy from them. After a brief nod when they took their places, they ignored her. With neither window nor distracting company, she rummaged in her bag for her mother's copy of Chekhov, her literary equivalent of comfort food.

Soon after the journey began, the family laid out real food—so much expensive food that she wondered why they were travelling in an *obshchiy*. There were hard-boiled eggs, pickles, cheese, bread, sausage, smoked fish—a huge array, and far too much for the three of them. They ate slowly, tauntingly, or so it seemed to Galina. She was hungry, very hungry; with so much to think about, it had not occurred to her to prepare food for the journey. She knew she could buy food at the stations, but she didn't want to get off the train just in case it departed without her, leaving her stuck in the middle of nowhere, with no possessions and hardly any money. And why, she wondered, was she dogged by these worst-case scenarios? As if she didn't already have enough to be anxious about.

She put her book aside and watched the family eat. She willed them to share their food, but she might as well not have existed. When they were finished, they cleared everything away except a tin of *montpansiez* placed where they could all easily help themselves. The bright, fruity sweets fanned her hunger. She swallowed over and over, surprised that the body, usually so adaptable, would keep up saliva production when the enterprise was so obviously futile.

The tin of sweets gradually emptied, the train rattled through the countryside, the air grew hotter and stuffier, the man's feet stank. Galina tried to read, but couldn't concentrate, just stared at the page. With each stop she hoped the family would disembark, and when finally they did, she had barely enough time to be relieved when their place was taken by another equally unfriendly family.

It was as if she gave off a message: *I am emigrating; I am a traitor to Mother Russia.*

The train picked up speed, the new family spread their bodies, and Galina stepped into the passageway — not too far, so she could keep an eye on her belongings. And there she stood, her body rolling with the train, the time passing, she couldn't say for how long, when she felt a touch to her shoulder. She sprang around. There was a woman about her mother's age asking whether she would like to join her and her husband. The voice was friendly, the smile warm, and alone and miserable and at the end of her tether, Galina refused to allow her usual suspicions to dominate.

She moved her belongings into their compartment, and the three of them travelled all the way to Kiev in a space reserved for four. The couple shared their food, they shared their tea, and over the next several hours she and her new friends read, dozed, and conversed about safe topics: work (both were teachers), family (a married son, no grandchildren), the passing scenery, the books they were reading. It was only when they arrived in Kiev that they mentioned their connection to Lvov.

Being careful is a way of life in the Soviet Union, and a feature of being careful is to be sensitive to nuance. The code word here was Lvov. Who other than emigrating Jews would be travelling with large suitcases from Leningrad via Kiev to Lvov? Yet the couple's name was Russian, not Jewish. Galina would never have guessed.

On the journey from Kiev to Lvov they opened up. The woman told her they were emigrating to America, along with their family. 'Our son and daughter-in-law are already in Rome. We'd intended to travel together, but something unexpected happened.' She raised her eyebrows and shrugged, as if to acknowledge that Galina would understand without her having to elaborate. 'We thought it prudent they leave early.'

Galina wanted to ask whether they really were Jewish, but knew she could not. If the best way of emigrating was to be Jewish,

28

it would be a narrow-minded or stubbornly anti-Semitic Russian who did not take the opportunity. The irony of it did not escape her or any Jew: there was so much anti-Semitism in the Soviet Union, but with the relaxation on Jewish emigration, people were suddenly rushing to be Jewish.

Whatever the couple's ethnicity, she was glad for their company; she even found herself regretting she was not going to America with them. She did, however, welcome them on the journey, and she needed them too, for Jewish or not, they'd done their homework. In Vienna, they knew to look for the representative from HIAS, the Hebrew Immigrant Aid Society. She'd never heard of this HIAS, and her anxiety flared again as she wondered what else she might not know.

'HIAS look after any Soviet Jew, no matter where they're going—unless it's to Israel, another group looks after them.'

She'd been nervous of asking too many questions, but now, anxious to learn as much as possible before the couple left her, she did not hold back.

'No,' they said in answer to her question as to whether they had relatives in the US. 'We've *arranged* to have relatives.'

Through a friend of a friend who had already emigrated, an American had been found with the same surname as theirs, an American who was willing to be a sponsoring cousin.

'At the moment you don't actually need a sponsor, but we were told it speeds things up.'

No sponsor was required for Australia either, but now that she'd learned she could be accepted into the US without a sponsor, Galina was again tempted to change her destination just to stay with these people.

By the time they arrived in Vienna, she was more confused than ever. Torn between her choice of Australia and her overwhelming desire not to be alone, the situation had become impossible. She couldn't manage it by herself. All she wanted was to be looked after.

And the couple did exactly that. They took her with them to speak with the man from the Jewish Agency for Israel. It was as they had foretold, for when he heard their destinations — their loudly stated America, and her mumbled Australia — he referred them to the HIAS representative. Both she and the couple would be going to Rome, the HIAS man said, where all the requirements for emigration and immigration would occur, including the issuing of a special document, a passport substitute for stateless people, without which they would be going nowhere.

And suddenly it hit her. What she had done. She was stateless. She was alone and she was stateless. She was no longer a Soviet citizen, she was no longer Russian. She was Jewish, that's all she was. But being reduced to Jewishness was like the crippled boy in her block of flats, the boy with three thoroughly good limbs being reduced to his withered leg. She was Jewish and stateless and terrified.

And what would happen if she were refused this passport substitute? Would she be condemned to a foreign no man's land for the rest of her days? And what would she do for money? Stateless, alone, penniless: it was hard to conceive of a more wretched prospect.

She managed to collect herself sufficiently to ask the representative how long all this might take. He said the US immigrants were being processed very quickly, a matter of weeks, but the Australian ones were taking a good deal longer, as much as several months.

So go to America, she told herself. After all, what did it matter where she ended up? It wasn't Leningrad, and it was without her mother. Mindless superstition was no way to select where she was to spend the rest of her life.

It was the man from HIAS who put her back on track. He had visited Australia a couple of years earlier. His brother had settled in Melbourne.

'Beautiful city,' he said in English, 'and wonderful climate. I was there for a week in autumn, and every day the sun was shining.

Good coffee, excellent cakes. This city is greatly cosmopolitan. And the southern coastline!' She saw the wonder cross his face. 'You have made a very good choice.'

'But the long wait,' she was thinking aloud. 'How will I support myself?'

When he discovered she spoke a passable Italian, he said she'd have no trouble finding work as an interpreter.

She never knew his name. She would have written to him and thanked him, for if not for this man, she might have fastened herself to the couple all the way to America. She would discover in time that Australia was the right place for her.

In the years to come, those months spent in Italy were a fog. She interpreted, but couldn't say for whom she interpreted; she translated, but could not remember what she translated. She lived in two different hostels, but she, who could draw her flat in Leningrad down to the light switches and doorknobs, could not describe either place. She was simultaneously immigrant, emigrant, and traveller-in-transit; and to new arrivals she was information and liaison officer as well. So many definitions, so many identities, but to herself she was a stranger: stateless, homeless, and alone.

The only clear memory from that time was the disaster at Chernobyl. Every day brought a new doomsday possibility, every day brought greater distress. And it was so disconcerting to learn about her own country via Western sources: her familiar Soviet Union suddenly seemed very foreign. Soviet officials were neither denying nor confirming a nuclear accident, they simply refused to be engaged on the issue. But according to the Western press, there could be no doubt: soaring radiation levels had been registered in neighbouring countries, and a satellite had photographed an explosion in Ukraine. The evidence seemed to be incontrovertible. The only other explanation—a Western conspiracy to undermine the

31

great Soviet state—was not credible, not from this side of the East-West divide.

While the Soviet Union remained silent about Chernobyl, Western politicians, scientists and journalists hypothesised endlessly about the effect of a nuclear accident on human health and agriculture, both in the Soviet Union and the rest of Europe. Cut off from all those who were important to her, Galina felt squeezed between freedom and disaster. Far from feeling relief that she had escaped the danger, her own safety increased her fear for those who remained.

By the time Gorbachev officially acknowledged the disaster, a full two weeks after the explosion, the West had already guessed most of it. Gorbachev made his announcement in what, for a Soviet leader, were uncharacteristically sombre terms; that he requested foreign assistance and expertise was incontrovertible evidence that the situation was dire. Galina wanted to do something, anything. Russia was being poisoned under a nuclear cloud, and her friends were at risk of radiation sickness, cancer, and premature death. She wanted to write to them, warn them, tell them what she knew, what the West had told her. But she held herself in check: to receive letters from an émigré would only make things worse for them.

As she waited and worked and worried in the safety of Rome, her days were overlaid with the disaster at Chernobyl, while night after night her mother and Chernobyl clashed together in a stormy sleep. Bereaved both for mother and motherland, she felt the grief as a physical pain deep in her body. It was there every morning when she woke, and it worsened during the day. She was surrounded by food—how eagerly she had indulged when first she arrived, but now she struggled to eat. She lost weight as the nuclear cloud thickened over her country. Hadn't the Russian people suffered enough? Hadn't they had more than their share of disasters? Every day she read about the sufferings of the Soviet people, every day she read about the ineptitude of the Soviet leaders, every day was ringed with sorrow.

Chernobyl was front-page news for weeks, and then other, non-Russian disasters took precedence. She found it no less distressing not knowing what was happening in the aftermath of the meltdown as it had been knowing. She was making herself ill. Her joints ached, she had a continual headache, she wanted to stay in bed all day. *Unidentified Russian girl found dead in Rome*. She imagined the headline.

She turned to her new country for distraction. She read books about Australia, she was alert to anyone with a connection to the country, and, most significantly, she saw a documentary about Italian migration to Australia. According to this film, there were so many Italians living in Australia, they had built a mighty hydro-electric scheme, started the tobacco-growing industry, owned most of the market gardens, and supplied the main labour for the building industry. Australia, it seemed, was built on the backs of immigrant Italians. The main urban precinct for Italians was located in the city of Melbourne in an area called Carlton—she grabbed a pen and wrote down the name. In the film, the Italians of Carlton were shown in cafés, eating pasta and drinking espressos, talking and laughing and smoking. Students from the nearby university sat at adjacent tables also eating, drinking, chatting and smoking. Everyone looked happy and relaxed. In the street, Italians and students clustered on the pavement, or strolled along against a backdrop that appeared to be delightfully cosmopolitan—exactly as the man from HIAS had said. This, she decided, was where she would live in Australia, this location of Carlton.

❧

Nine months after Andrew Morrow returned home, Galina Kogan's plane descended towards Melbourne airport. The estimated arrival time was only minutes away, and her terror was such that she might have been heading into a KGB interrogation. The land below was mostly uninhabited. There was an occasional house, a few clumps of cows, muddy ponds, and grass that looked as dead as the winter grass at home. The nothingness stretched unconstrained to the horizon. Galina looked around at the other passengers. Were they seeing what she was seeing? Was her view of nothingness their view of home?

She understood Melbourne to be a city of millions. Might she have been mistaken? Might Melbourne be the Australian equivalent of a Siberian outpost? With a jolt and a roar, the plane touched down. Still no people, no vehicles, no buildings. *No city*. The plane turned, and the air hostess announced they were taxi-ing towards the terminal. Galina stared out the window. There was still nothing to see, just the brown, empty, dried-out land. She could not possibly have mistaken the size of Melbourne. She leaned forward to take in the view through the windows on the opposite side of the plane, saw the same bristly grass, the same grim flat land, the same empty sky.

And then—the relief of it—some buildings, airport buildings, many of them, and many international planes lined up at the gates. Only a big city would have a large and busy airport, and she sank back in her seat, closed her eyes, and tried to breathe the terror away. But it had settled in. Reason told her that in a year or two she would have marked out her new life, rendered it known and navigable. But for now, she wished she could leap across the next year or, better still, slip into a long sleep from which she would awake and find herself at home.

The future pressed down on her—how to find an affordable flat, how to find work—but first the immediate issue of customs and immigration. Would they recognise this travel document for foreigners, this *Titolo di Viaggio per Stranieri*? It was stamped by the Australian Embassy in Rome, but would they know what it was here? And would they accept it as legitimate?

A short time later, she handed the document to an official. He looked at it and said something to her. She didn't understand what he was saying. He repeated himself. She still didn't understand; this English was unlike any English she'd ever heard before. The man continued to speak, and at last a few recognisable words surfaced. She wanted him to slow down, speak more clearly, but wouldn't dare ask this of an official. With a few words here and a few words there, she understood enough to respond. And she must have passed, because he waved her on to another official, a woman this time, but with the same incomprehensible English. And again she must have passed because the Italian travel document was stamped, and the official wished her 'good luck'.

She exited through the doors into the airport, and immediately located a card bearing her name. She was not home, but neither was she stranded.

3

THE RIGHT JOB FOR A SHY MAN

Andrew Morrow nods to the technician to place the last carousel on the slide projector. There's an air of expectancy in the hall. The woman in the front row is still knitting; her hands seem to move of their own accord as she gazes up at him. (The organisers had warned him, 'She comes to all our public lectures, she always sits in the front row, and she always knits.') With her fluffy cardigan falling tent-like from collar to calf, she looks like a soft pink pyramid. Only two people have fallen asleep: an elderly man whose head has slumped sideways to rest precariously close to the chap next to him, and a beautifully groomed woman sitting behind the knitter. Given this is overwhelmingly a mature-aged audience, and it is late afternoon on a hot day, Andrew thinks that two sleepers out of approximately eighty people is acceptable.

He has titled his lecture 'Paradise on Earth', and in the past forty minutes has guided the audience on a mosaic journey beginning in ancient Greece, passing through the Middle East, lingering in the Byzantine era, moving on to Renaissance Rome and Ravenna, and concluding here in Melbourne.

'Melbourne,' he tells them, 'is Australia's mosaic capital.'

He shows them slides of the Block Arcade, of St Paul's Cathedral, of the magnificent floor at 333 Collins Street. Each image draws appreciative recognition from the audience. He then projects a slide of the façade of Newspaper House. This art-deco mosaic, with its near-naked figures set among symbols of scientific progress and its inspiring caption, 'I'll put a girdle around the earth', this mosaic located in central Melbourne is unknown to all but a few. He hears gasps and murmurs: how can they not know of this beauty right here in their own city?

He pauses for exactly thirty seconds—he calculated this break when rehearsing at home—a pause long enough to absorb the shock of not knowing the Newspaper House mosaic, but not so long that people will start thinking of the post-lecture wine and cheese. He looks out over the hall, slowly he moves his head from left to right as if to gather everyone in his gaze—also rehearsed at home—before arranging his features into a light smile: he has something special for them, he says. Keeping his gaze on the audience, he clicks the remote control and the first slide appears. It depicts the exterior of Leningrad's Church of the Saviour on the Spilled Blood, seen at a distance from along Griboyedov Canal. With its cupolas of gold and gorgeously coloured ceramics, the church looks like a fairytale castle.

Click.

Closer now, and the external mosaics are visible with their divine figures sparkling with gold. Also seen are the small, multi-coloured tiles capping the mini towers and arches, and the elaborate plaster mouldings around the shapely windows and panels. It is as if the art of the entire world has been incorporated on this single building.

Click.

'This,' he says, 'is the Church of the Saviour on the Spilled Blood in Leningrad, where I spent several months during the last European winter.' He allows a brief pause. 'While the exterior of the church is magnificent, as you can see, it was the interior that brought me to Leningrad.'

Click.

'Reconstruction on the interior started only recently. In its completed state, all the walls, the ceilings, the massive columns, all the surfaces will be covered in mosaic. The church is gargantuan, with soaring ceilings and nine domes. Nine, imagine it. There are side chapels and apses, corridors and a huge central nave, and all this will be clad in mosaic. But the finish is a long way off; some say five years, but the more realistic whisper fifteen. However, you, all of you here, don't need to wait. You can see and experience the church in all its magnificence now, today, without leaving your seats.'

Click.

A full-colour impression of the interior seen from just inside the entrance appears on the screen. Like all the slides he will show, it is based on drawings used by the mosaicists to recreate the interior.

'Let me take you through the church.'

He pitches his voice a little lower, and brings his mouth closer to the microphone. His words, intimate and mesmerising, fill the hall.

'The size of the church is what first impresses. It is overwhelming, truly awesome. But a few steps into the church, it's the beauty that takes over: it literally stops you in your tracks. Here is mosaic so abundant, so decorative, it's hard to believe that mere mortals, just like you and me, could create anything so beautiful.' He shifts his gaze to the rear of the auditorium. 'You know how great natural wonders—mountains, oceans, vast deserts—make you feel small, insignificant, yet at the same time inspire wonder? The same can happen with man-made beauty. You enter this dazzlingly beautiful church, and it fills you with wonder.'

Click.

'Huge rectangular columns rise from the floor to fuse with gorgeously patterned arches in the distant ceiling. And on every panel of these columns, rising from eye level to the very top, twenty metres away, stand gigantic, halo'd men clad in flowing robes.'

Click.

'Let's stand at the base of a column together.' He pauses briefly.

'At the lowest level, on a par with your eyes, are a pair of feet, feet larger than life, and somehow—these are feet, after all—they seem imbued with the sacred.'

Click.

'Lift your gaze higher, and you see velvety cloaks hanging in loose folds. These cloaks are formed from hard mosaic, chips of stone, yet they look so soft, so *touchable*. And see how the bare skin of feet and arms glitters. This mosaic figure shimmers with life.'

Click.

'And there are not just human figures here, but animals and exotic birds, flowers and forests. All of God's creations cover the columns and walls of this vast space.'

Click.

'And the myriad of colours. They're sublime. Reds, oranges, greens, yellows, pearly whites, stunning blues. And one blue in particular, not a wishy-washy Western blue, this is an intense Russian blue, with tints of sky and ocean that draw earth and heaven together.'

Click.

'Surrender to this miraculous place, don't analyse it, don't try to understand it, immerse yourself in this colour and light, saunter among these glittering figures, marvel at the gold, the jewels, the semi-precious stones. You are actually inside a work of art.'

The screen goes dark. The hall is silent. The knitter is poised between stitches. Andrew gazes out at the audience; he thinks the lecture has been a success. And when the applause begins, loud and prolonged, he knows it has been. If only he could leave now with a job well done, and avoid the agony ahead of him.

Andrew accepts another top-up, his third or maybe his fourth, he's lost count; it's still too early to leave and the alcohol helps. He tries to concentrate on what the woman is saying. She's one of several people gathered about him, and while most of them have stories to tell, she's not inclined to relinquish the floor. She's describing a trip she made to Ravenna — 'a mosaic wonderland,' she calls it — and with an admirable memory for detail she's unlikely to finish any time soon. Not that he's concerned: people like to talk about themselves and their experiences, and his preference always is to listen.

Another fifteen minutes and he should be able to leave.

The alcohol has softened his nerves, but with his face still burning he expects he looks like a ripe tomato. And why his body should turn traitor in this way has always confounded him. The blushing, the revved-up heart, the sweating, the wayward eye contact, the trembling hands, the stammering, a swag of betrayals that never run out of steam. Even in a situation like this — he's the guest of honour, his lecture was a success — his body doesn't let up. He likes praise as much as anyone, but unless it comes in the mail, he's never free to enjoy it.

Lecturing and teaching are different. Far from the anarchy of these social occasions, they're performances, he's in control, there are no surprises. He expects he might have succeeded as an actor if he hadn't chanced on mosaic first. He's good at following scripts.

The woman is winding down. She reconfigures her facial expression and leans in towards him. 'So,' she says, 'do you have any plans to return to Leningrad?' She's so close he can see shreds of food lodged between her teeth.

He shakes his head and steps back. Then, drawing on his customary lifesaver, answers her question with one of his own: 'Have you been to Leningrad?'

And she's off again, and while others eager for their turn might be annoyed, Andrew is not: keep the other person talking, is his tried-and-true solution. Although the best solution is to avoid these situations altogether. Usually he tells his hosts he'll need to dash off after a lecture, but it's a challenge to come up with a prior engagement when an invitation is issued months in advance.

The foyer is crowded; he expects the post-lecture conviviality is as much of a drawcard as the lecture itself. The cheese and cabana disappeared quickly, but the wine, donated by one of the sponsors of the lecture series, is in good supply. There's a jostling of bodies, a clamour of voices, wafts of powder and perfume, and from his height advantage, a bobbing of bald heads and neat grey hairstyles.

One of the larger groups is congregated around him, and now that Ravenna woman has finally been elbowed aside, a lively chatter ensues. Everyone is having a good time, yet all he wants is to be out of here. Though that's not correct: he wants to be here, in this room with these people, but he wants to be enjoying himself, and not crushed by this utterly useless self-consciousness.

'I am all thumbs at life,' Rilke, favourite poet and life companion, wrote. I am too, Andrew intones silently.

He manoeuvres himself into his out-of-body experience, a private and reasonably reliable device he has never mentioned to anyone for fear of being judged crazy. And it seems to be working. He hears his voice — he sounds quite sensible — and he sees himself from a distance, a man who looks to be at ease, a man at the centre of a group and in control of the situation. He just needs to maintain this for a few minutes longer, but a woman intrudes with an unexpected question, and wrenches him back into his own wretched body.

He knows these toils of his are camouflaged, that others see a reserved, slightly bashful man — the sort of demeanour one would expect of an artist. He knows his tomato face is ascribed to the heat in the room, and any hesitancy in his speech is attributed to his being a considered and thoughtful conversationalist. But knowing he is alone in his agony does not lessen it, not one bit. O to be mellow. O to acquire the gift of mellowness.

'It strikes me as curious,' the woman is saying, 'that the anti-religion Soviets would be spending a fortune on restoring the Church of the Saviour on the Spilled Blood.'

41

The group is looking to him for an answer. His heartbeat ramps up, his throat has constricted, but before he can collect his words, Ravenna woman is answering. *Thank you, Ravenna woman.* She refers to changes under Gorbachev; she says that despite religion being outlawed, there are plenty of Russians who remain loyal to the Orthodox Church. And these restored sites, she continues, are important to the nascent tourism industry — she, herself, visited just two years ago — with its influx of foreign currency and other benefits. What other benefits? someone asks. Jeans, cosmetics, books, music, practically any material goods are wanted, she says. Andrew nods and smiles. Encouraged, she keeps talking, while he follows the conversation, rehearsing some sentences just in case he's called upon, and monitoring his demeanour — mustn't appear aloof or disengaged or, god forbid, arrogant, and to dispel any possibility of this he broadens his smile, only to feel his mouth quivering, as if the muscles have gone into spasm.

O for a more muscular sensibility, he is thinking, but at what cost? Rilke, when considering psychoanalysis, famously wrote to his lover, Lou Andreas-Salome, that while psychoanalysis may well drive out his devils, he was afraid that his angels, so essential to his art, would be driven away too. Andrew knows he is far from being mosaic's counterpart to Rilke, but still, he wonders if his social squeamishness in some way feeds his art, that a more muscular sensibility would have seen him as the engineer his parents wanted him to be. The fact is, this sensibility of his, this crippling millstone in public, is ideal for the solitary work of the artist.

A man is offering to refill his glass. Now is his opportunity. He'd love to stay, he says, but he has another engagement and, he adds, after consulting his watch, he's already late. He says goodbye to the people around him, he finds the organisers and thanks them, he strides to the door, springs down the stairs, sprints to the entrance, and finally he is outside in the warm steamy dusk. Blessedly alone.

Twenty minutes later, Andrew Morrow arrived home. Godrevy greeted him with much leaping and licking. It was worthwhile going out in order to receive such exuberant love on your return, although, given Godrevy quietened down immediately his dinner appeared, Andrew was in no doubt which commanded the greater canine devotion: love of food or love of human companion. He tossed his satchel on his desk, took a beer from the fridge, would have smoked a joint if he'd had any dope, kicked off his shoes and flopped into his armchair. Goddy, his dinner finished, flopped on the floor next to him, his head resting on Andrew's feet.

The dog snuffled and snored, there was a hum of traffic coming from the street, and the intermittent squawk of rainbow lorikeets flying overhead. Andrew sat in the darkening studio, eyes closed, sipping his beer; the thud of his heart softened and the squeeze in his head eased.

He needed to cut back on these events, on teaching, too. They took too much out of him and, besides, were no longer the financial necessity they once were. He was mentally sifting through his upcoming engagements, counting off those from which he could withdraw, when the phone rang. He guessed it would be his mother, ringing to check how the lecture had gone; he let the call pass to the answering machine. Soon he'd prepare a meal, just a few more minutes in the peace and quiet, when the phone rang again. Yes, definitely Sylvie. She'd be checking on him when he was sixty.

He had not wanted a phone, and with a public telephone box just up the road, he didn't need one. But Sylvie had insisted, his friends, too. The public phone was all very well, they said, but what if they wanted to call him? He'd always hated the telephone. As a child he'd watch his mother with the receiver jammed to her ear, exclaiming and gesticulating, grimacing and laughing; he'd see how exposed she was, and he would cringe for her. And the other person on the end of the line, they might be laughing at you or making fun of you; they might be bored and itching to finish the call; if the cord was long enough, they might even be using the toilet. You can't read people if you can't see them, which made the telephone an unnerving and risky prospect. Not that he'd said any of this to Sylvie, he simply explained logically and coolly why he didn't need a phone.

There was, however, to be no discussion, his mother had said. He lived alone, he worked alone, and his place was located on the opposite side of the city from her and his father. (This was more than a mere statement of fact, it was a complaint.) 'I need to be able to contact you,' she said. 'And you may need to contact us. You could be seriously injured, you could be unconscious.' In which case, a phone would be of little use; but realising how worried she was, he relented.

Now the phone rang a third time. He slipped his feet from under the sleeping dog and picked up.

Sylvie's familiar voice came down the line. 'I knew if I hounded you long enough, you'd answer.'

Perhaps it's the fate of all only children to have over-protective parents. Or perhaps it's only the shy ones and the not-quite-right ones, but all too often his parents seemed to forget it was the free-wheeling 1980s, that their son was a man of twenty-six, that he'd travelled alone overseas for prolonged periods, and had been making a reasonable living for years, that their son was a man who was, in fact, a man.

'How did the lecture go?'

Sylvie typed his lectures for him, which gave her an acceptable excuse to enquire, but he knew her real reason for ringing was to check he hadn't collapsed in an attack of nerves. It was of no matter that he'd never botched a lecture, she was convinced he still might. Ever since his senior years at school, she had typed his papers; she was quick and convenient and she enjoyed the work. But maybe, he was now thinking, it was time to find a more detached typist.

He assured her the lecture had gone well, that the audience had travelled with him inside the church, that they experienced something of the wonder he, himself, had felt. But still she persisted.

'Sylvie!' He spoke more sharply than he intended. Then more quietly, 'Mum,'—he never called her 'Mum'—'I'm fine, and the lecture could not have gone better.'

And before she could say any more, he told her his dinner was getting cold, and he would speak with her later in the week.

He wished that a meal really was ready. It was foolish not to have bought a hamburger on the way home. He could never eat before these events, and he was now very hungry. He went to the kitchen to investigate. The choice was limited; he could cobble together fried eggs on a single slice of toast, with a banana for dessert. And set about preparing it.

For the first half of the century his kitchen had served as tea-room for the staff of Simon & Sons, manufacturers of men's suits, and apart from a new stove and oven, this area remained largely unchanged; even the blackboard for the tea-room roster was still fixed to the wall, although it was now converted to a memo board. His living quarters, about 20 per cent of the entire space, occupied the former company offices with the partitions removed, and the factory floor had become his studio. He had moved in here nearly three years ago, and now couldn't imagine making his home anywhere else.

He ate his dinner in front of the evening news, the plate perched on his knees, and Godrevy on the alert for crumbs. He ate slowly, concentrating on the food not the TV, and when he was finished he took himself to the far end of the studio. Here was a work in progress, an indoor oasis he was creating for himself, and the very first piece he had ever made specifically to keep. He was working freehand, directly onto the floor, creating a mosaic pool at the base of the wall. He had decided, with a nod to Monet, to add a few waterlilies, and on the wall itself, a white-faced heron standing in a cluster of reeds. He wanted to bring nature into his studio, an area of tranquillity within the squall of his life. He slipped a cassette of Joni Mitchell into the tape recorder and settled on the floor beside the half-finished work. As the songs spooled into the room, his pool of blue grew.

People asked him if he was ever lonely, alone in his studio day after day, month after month, year after year. But he'd never been lonely, and certainly not in the act of creation: anxiety trumps loneliness every time, and work is the best cure for both.

He used to hope he would leave his shyness behind with childhood. But while his voice deepened and his body hardened and inches were added to his height, the shyness remained unchanged. He would take its temperature each year with his parents' question: *What do you want for your birthday?* Translated, this became: *What matters to you?* He would answer he didn't want anything in particular. But he always did. There was the year of the basketball and the year of the dog, the year of the sleeping bag and that of the oil pastels. Every birthday, Christmas too, found him wanting something, and every birthday and Christmas, in response to his parents' question, the same dread, the same discomfort, and the same reply: 'You decide. I like surprises.'

He hated surprises, but he hated exposing himself far more.

He managed at school because he was good at sport. He made the first cricket eleven, he played on the wing in the first football eighteen; he learned the role of the sporty boy and performed it well. It brought him friends and followers, it brought him protection. He was also a swot, but in a high school known for its academic standing, his retreating to the library was not considered odd or unusual. That he retreated for respite rather than research was known only to himself.

These days, he no longer hoped for change: no point in wanting what would never eventuate. He wasn't unhappy, he wasn't lonely, he didn't dislike people, nor was he intimidated by them; but being who he was—shy—he had learned not to need them. The exceptions were his parents, a few longstanding friends who accepted him as he was, and the girlfriends—not many, but sufficient to prove he was neither a weirdo nor a virgin. In fact, the girlfriends said he was refreshing, that unlike most males, who were animated only when the subject was themselves, Andrew seemed genuinely interested in other people.

The situation might have been different if he'd become the engineer he started out to be. His parents and teachers had proposed engineering as an excellent career for one who liked science, liked precision, and liked his own company. The fact that he also excelled at art had not figured in their considerations, although it had long been central to his.

He followed their advice: they were so certain about what would be best for him, and being so unsure himself, he found their certainty reassuring. He applied for engineering, and with good results in his school finals he was accepted. But within a month of starting the course he knew he'd made a mistake. There was a soulless quality to engineering, or perhaps he simply lacked the capacity to find engineering's soul.

During that first term, he determined on numerous occasions to tell his parents engineering was not for him, but the right time never seemed to present itself. It would be preferable, he knew, if he could offer them an acceptable alternative.

All through childhood his secret dream job was that of lighthouse-keeper-come-artist. While such a choice might be a cliché for a shy person, his lighthouse-keeper dream had provided him with powerful and reliable escape. He would imagine himself alone with his dog, living in a slender tower perched on a rocky crown surrounded by a rollicking sea. His living quarters, about halfway up the tower, contained a single comfortable armchair, a basket for the dog, a table and chair, charts and logs, a shelf of books, a stereo, easel and paints. Up a few more steps from the living area was the bunk room, and twisting up from there was the long spiral staircase leading to the lamp. He and his dog would climb to the top of the tower several times a day, for maintenance on the lamp and for maintenance of fitness. He loved being up there amid the roar of the ocean, the blustering wind, the whirling rain.

He had just started high school when he learned of Godrevy Lighthouse. One day, while browsing the books on his mother's bookcase, he found a slender volume called *To the Lighthouse*. He'd not noticed it before and quickly pulled it from the shelf. There were no pictures, and there wasn't much of a story either—even the cover painting was of a girl in a red skirt and not of a lighthouse. But slipped inside the book was a postcard. It depicted a sea scene with a cloudy sky, calm waters, and in the rosy light of dusk or dawn, a magnificently isolated lighthouse called Godrevy. The postcard was unused. He took the book and postcard to his mother, and not knowing what to say, simply held both up for her to see. Her face opened into a smile. She told him how she and his father, on their trip to Britain before he was born, had driven down to Cornwall where they saw the Godrevy Lighthouse. This was the lighthouse used by Virginia Woolf in her novel.

'Such a wonderful trip that was,' she said.

She had gazed at the postcard for a long time—Andrew could see the happy memories in her face—before replacing it in the book. Then she had a change of mind, for she retrieved the postcard and handed it to him. 'You keep it,' she said.

Godrevy Lighthouse became the lighthouse of his dreams. Like lighthouses throughout the world, it had been automated for decades, but he didn't let that spoil his imaginings. Later he learned that a number of lighthouses had been converted to meteorological stations, so he considered becoming a meteorologist-come-artist. But what he knew for sure was he didn't want to be an engineer.

It was Melbourne's Block Arcade that gave him the courage

to confront his parents and quit engineering. He had been to the arcade numerous times, but had never taken any notice of the building—with the notable exception of the Hopetoun tea rooms with its famous cakes and desserts.

One Thursday, late in the first year of his engineering course, he was whiling away an hour in the city, wandering through the arcades and bluestone lanes. It was after six when he found himself in the Block Arcade. The shops were closed, human traffic was light, and for the first time he saw the domed ceiling, he saw the glossy wood-and-brass shop fronts, and, most particularly, he saw the floor.

It was covered in mosaic.

This floor, smoothed by the passage of millions of feet, yet retaining its colours and images, was not simply beautiful, he found it utterly compelling. How could all those tiny fragments come together to produce a coherent and seamless whole? All those tiny pieces—tiles? stone?—forming patterns and human figures, and of such variety: some resembled friezes from the ancient Greeks, others looked quite modern. He squatted down, ran his hand over the pieces. He had to know how this wonder had been created. He had to know more.

He left the arcade and rushed through the lanes towards Bourke Street. At the first phone box, he stopped to ring his parents. He explained he was with friends and would not be home for dinner—they'd be happy to hear he was not alone—and bolted up the street to the Paperback Bookshop, open late every night. In the art section he found a book on the world's most famous mosaics, an oversized volume with many coloured plates. With insufficient money to buy it, he settled himself on a bench near the window. He studied the pictures, he read the text.

And so it happened, in a city bookshop an hour after he had seen his first mosaic, Andrew Morrow decided on his future. Page after page of mosaics from Spain and Morocco, Italy and Russia, Turkey and the Middle East; mosaics in stone, glass, pottery, enamel, gold and jewels; geometric patterns, landscapes, interiors, animals, human figures, the sacred and the secular; skin shadings, fancy hair, flowing garments, complex movements. Mosaic, this extraordinary enduring art, was the work he wanted to do.

He decided to complete the first year of engineering before telling his parents of his new career. With a creditable pass, he hoped they would see that his choice not to be an engineer really was a choice.

He studied, he passed with honours, and he made his announcement. His parents were not happy; his father in particular was very unhappy. Finish the engineering degree, Leonard said. Give yourself something to fall back on; after all, he added, very few artists make a living from art alone. Sylvie was worried he would become even more 'socially isolated' than he already was. Those were her exact words, and the first time in Andrew's memory she had described him in such a way.

Andrew ended up doing what he wanted, and his parents continued to worry. He found more books to read, he studied every mosaic in Melbourne, he travelled up to Canberra to surround himself in Napier Waller's great mosaics at the Australian War Memorial. He enrolled in short courses (the major art schools ignored mosaic as pensioner craft and sheltered-workshop activity), and eventually secured an apprenticeship with one of the few established mosaicists in Australia. He had never been happier.

He was just twenty-one when he entered the landscape competition that would change his life. With nothing to lose, he used his entry to explore the sort of mosaic-meshed-with-nature design he aspired to, in lieu of the commissions that were yet to come his way. And to his amazement he won; even the organisers were surprised that a complete unknown had walked off with the prize. He used the money to travel. He went to Spain to see traditional Moorish mosaics, before crossing into France to study some stunning modern pieces. And then he went to Ravenna. He visited church after church filled with mosaics. He examined dozens of glorious images, and discovered an astonishing array of materials. In the vestibule of the Archiepiscopal Chapel at Ravenna, he stood before a wall on which had been transcribed the words of an unknown poet. *Aut lux hic nata est, aut capta hic libera regnat*: 'Either light was born here or, imprisoned here, it reigns supreme.' This would be his future.

Ravenna remained his mosaic apotheosis until his trip to Leningrad and the mosaics of the Church of the Saviour on the Spilled Blood. During that exhilarating winter, he worked alongside the men and women who were restoring those marvellous artworks. And when he came back to his room at night, tired and euphoric, the girl he had knocked down in the street filled his thoughts, and she continued to do so even when he returned to Australia. She had become so much a part of his life that he had told his parents about her, implying she had been his girlfriend and the two of them still corresponded.

On this warm November night in Melbourne, as he worked on his indoor pool, she entered his mind with the ease of a regular visitor. He imagined talking with her about this mosaic he was making for himself, discussing why it was that artists keep unfinished pieces, keep pieces that fail to sell, but rarely, if ever, create a work specifically for themselves.

It was an issue that had been puzzling him for some time. It was not just the money, but something more personal. He was his own harshest critic — most artists are. He knew all too well that last year's successful work can reveal shocking flaws twelve months on. Only a committed masochist could live surrounded by old and accusing mistakes. And besides, it'd feel like bragging to display your own work at home, as if you were saying you admire your art more than anyone else's. But despite these problems he had gone ahead with his pool.

Joni Mitchell sang on, the pool grew, the night moved forward.

Immersed in his work, he was removed from himself, from this world. Work silenced his demons. He knew he ought to protest against nuclear tests in the Pacific, he knew he should rally for a better deal for nurses, but his was not a loud-hailer personality, and never would it be.

It was late when he went to bed, tired yet relaxed, the trials of the day entirely subdued. With Goddy curled up next to him, he fell asleep. He slept through to the morning and woke refreshed, happy with the prospect of an uninterrupted day of work.

4

PROSPECTING FOR HOME

Not far from Andrew's studio, on this warm November morning in 1987, Galina Kogan was marking her first anniversary in Australia. She didn't feel it warranted a full-blown celebration, she was still too unsettled for that, but she did have steady work and sufficient money, and she was now living in her very own Australian home.

Perhaps it was this, she was thinking, that deserved a celebration: that after a mere four months, her odd, unconventional dwelling did feel like home — not home as in Leningrad, but a secure and welcome comfort after the extended bivouac of her first months in Australia.

Her home was a former saddlery shop, located in a lane opposite the Melbourne Cemetery. She was inclined to believe that the very unorthodoxy of the place had been its primary attraction: that in the same way she was an oddball among the Australian people, so too was this dwelling among Australian houses and flats. Decades earlier, the saddlery shop had been converted to a bedsitter, with a shower and toilet closeted off in a back corner. She had placed her bed down one end of the rectangular space. A kitchen was pressed into one of the side walls, and she had put a small table and two chairs nearby; a glass sliding door along the other side led to a courtyard garden, described as tiny by her visitors, though many times larger than the balcony of the Leningrad flat. The northern end of the room doubled as a work and living area. With a mere half-dozen steps from bed to desk, the saddlery, Galina decided, must have specialised in gear for miniature horses. She bought a two-seater couch upholstered in a splashy green-and-fawn floral; it was not a pattern she would have chosen—hard to imagine what sort of person would choose such a pattern—but the couch was in good condition, it was cheap, and it was comfortable. She added a side-table and a well-worn leather pouffe from the same second-hand goods shop.

Her desk was constructed from a door suspended between two banks of shelves, and it was here she was working, just after eight in the morning, drawing slender female figures. These illustrations would be used on packets of sewing patterns sold to the home seamstress. It amused her that a Soviet girl was bringing fashion to Westerners, a Soviet girl moreover, who was a hopeless seamstress. The current crop of patterns depicted the new season's fashions, the 'new season' referring not to the summer about to begin, which if today's weather was any guide had already begun, but rather summer 1988, more than a year away.

She had the whole morning to finish the current batch of sewing patterns before leaving for her other job, her real estate job—in the middle of a day, she suddenly realised, when the temperature was expected to be in the mid-thirties.

'Today will be a stinker,' she said aloud, indulging in the earthy Australian vernacular that both confused and delighted her. She regarded Australian English as an outlaw form: much like the saddlery, much like herself.

This would be her second summer in Australia. Last year had been so stupendously hot, she'd viewed the heat with the same fascination as a scientist might the atmosphere on Mars. The saddlery, a low-pitched dwelling shaded by taller two-storey buildings, fortunately remained quite cool, and despite today's heat she was wrapped in her mother's shawl, and her feet were snug in Lidiya's old *tapochki*.

Her place was located in Carlton, the area she had chosen during her time in Rome for her Australian home. Carlton was on the opposite side of Melbourne from where most other Russian émigrés lived, and where she herself had stayed for the first several months in Australia. She had been tempted to remain there, with people she knew and among streets that had grown familiar, but the decision to live in Carlton had been made, and she was determined not to change her mind.

Being decisive made her feel as if she were in control. She had decided to emigrate despite her mother's death, so she had emigrated. She had decided on Australia because of a chance meeting with an Australian, so here she was in Australia. While in Italy, a film of the Carlton area of Melbourne had appealed, so now she was living in Carlton. The decisions acted as stakes in her new life, holding it in place; decisions, she would admit, that were often made impetuously. Indeed, with each major decision various adults, both in Leningrad and here in Australia, had cautioned her to wait and consider. But she believed that to waver even for a moment would cause her to stumble. Two factors pushed her forward: she was young, and her mother was gone. She could do nothing about her mother's death, but if she had waited for maturity to shape wiser decisions, she probably would never have left Leningrad.

For her first eight months in Australia she had lived with a Jewish couple whose ancestors had migrated from Russia after the revolution. Although both Zara and Arnold managed a halting formal Russian, to Galina they seemed entirely Australian. Their house, the first Australian home she had entered, struck her as very grand. Their 'living room' was just for sitting in, and their three bedrooms were just for sleeping; they had a special room with a dining table that could seat ten people; their kitchen was fitted with every conceivable appliance, and there were two bathrooms, two toilets and a whole laundry room just for themselves. It came as a shock to discover that their house was considered a typical suburban dwelling. Zara and Arnold slept in one room; the other two bedrooms had belonged to their daughters, both of whom had moved to different houses when they married. One of these rooms was now used as a nursery for the visiting grandchildren, the other was given to Galina.

The house was surrounded on all sides by a private garden, with trees and bushes and flowers and not a square metre used for growing food. The beach was a five-minute walk away. This was Galina's favourite place in those early months. She came to believe that the sea, or rather this Melbourne sea, had a mysterious power. She knew that if she were to travel across the water, sweep over the horizon and stay her course, the first land she would see would be Australia's southern island of Tasmania; a few thousand kilometres further on and she would reach Antarctica. But, as she stood on the sand staring out at the horizon, the landmass she felt to be in front of her, although hidden by the curve of the earth, was Russia. There on the beach she would sit, in the burn of her first Australian January and the bluster of her first Australian July, and be transported over the sea to home.

Her hosts were kind, welcoming people and, to Galina's secular gaze, very Jewish. Arnold wore a *yarmulke* and Zara's kitchen was kosher; they attended synagogue every Saturday and they encouraged Galina to join them. They observed a staggering number of special Jewish laws—laws previously unknown to Galina, whose favourite food at home had been *salo*, pork fat, and whose major key to Jewishness was Leon Uris's *Exodus*. She never told Zara and Arnold about *salo*, but she did explain about *Ishkod*, the Russian version of *Exodus*, which her mother, like so many Soviet Jews, had read in *samizdat*.

Ishkod came to Lidiya in the late nineteen-sixties after the Six-Day War in Israel, and following a new batch of anti-Jewish and anti-Zionist measures in the Soviet Union. It was a faded carbon copy on tissue-thin paper; the print was so pale that Lidiya said hers must have been the last of the four sheets when the typing was done. *Ishkod* provided Soviet Jews both then and later with a model of Jewishness, replete with strength and hope and a country, too, although Israel's struggles with her neighbours meant that as a homeland it never appealed to Lidiya, who longed for a life of freedom *and* peace.

Pork fat, Leon Uris's *Ishkod*, and entrenched Russian anti-Semitism had contributed to Galina's Jewishness, so it was not surprising she found Zara and Arnold's Judaism so foreign. After attending a few *Shabbat* services, she'd had enough. 'Perhaps later,' she said to Zara, 'when life here is no longer so strange.' But even as she spoke, she knew she would never embrace their kind of Jewishness. It was too late for her — she suspected it was too late for most Soviet Jews. It wasn't just the revolution's official removal of religion from their lives, Orthodox Christians had experienced that too. There was something else, something specific to Russian Jews that she only realised once she moved to Australia: when you've been the target of anti-Semitism all your life, this actually contributes to the sort of Jew you are. And it doesn't change: despite your having crossed the world, despite witnessing other forms of Jewishness, despite your wishing it were not so.

Living with Zara and Arnold, she acquired the basics of being Jewish; it was not so difficult. Becoming Australian, however, presented a far greater challenge. She walked Australian streets, she shopped at Australian stores, she ate at Australian cafés, she worked alongside Australian workers. And all the while, trespassing on her emerging Australianness was a residual suspicion of other people (would she ever become trusting like the Australians?), a continuing tendency to hoard food and clothes (would she ever develop their easy materialism?), and a fear of authority coupled with the compulsion to determine the power hierarchy wherever she found herself (would she ever acquire their casual anti-authoritarianism?). Even her habit of overdressing intruded on her Australianisation program. Soviet ways, she was realising, were her blood and marrow, her heart thumped to a Soviet tune; permanently removed from the Soviet Union, the Soviet Union had travelled with her. In Melbourne, Australia, despite all her efforts, she was still in large part a Soviet Jew.

She grappled with the arcana of Australian customs and the mysteries of Australian Jewishness, and if Zara and Arnold ever found her behaviour odd or incomprehensible, they never revealed it. They welcomed her into their home, they treated her like family, she owed both her jobs to them. She had no doubt that Arnold and Zara liked her, even loved her; she suspected they would have been happy if she had stayed on with them permanently. But she had decided on Carlton as the place to live, so despite many good reasons to remain exactly where she was, Carlton it was going to be. Although it would not be easy, she realised, when she came to explore the area. There were plenty of Italians and students, as the film she'd seen in Rome had shown, but the students were vying for the same cheap accommodation as was she. The irony did not escape her: half her week was spent working in real estate, but when it came to her own housing, after two months she was no closer to moving from Zara and Arnold's than when she first started her search.

And then luck intervened. Luck: such a delightful concept to one far more accustomed to *sistema*, that Soviet staple of knowing who to contact and how much to pay when there was something you needed. She had been studying the advertisements for vacant rooms posted on the noticeboard of Readings, a big bookstore in Carlton. These were rooms in shared houses, *kommunalki* Australian-style, and while not her preference, it was all she could afford. She was noting down possibilities when she became aware of a man also perusing the advertisements. She stepped aside to allow him a better view.

'What are you looking for?'

It was the man who had spoken, and with no one else nearby, he was clearly addressing her.

She swung around, immediately on her guard.

'I've a place to rent,' he quickly explained. 'A great place.'

It was a former saddlery, he said. He'd lived there for the past four years, but now needed to break his lease. 'I'm moving to Tasmania.' And after a brief pause, he added, 'To follow my heart.'

By the end of the day the saddlery was hers. It came with a higher rent than she had wanted to pay, but she was already employed four days a week, and had been led to believe the sewing-pattern work would increase, so she should manage, and managing was, after all, ingrained in all Soviet citizens.

It brought her great satisfaction to be settled in a place of her own, as if now her life in Australia could truly begin. And four months later, the saddlery did feel like home — when she was inside, with the door shut, and surrounded by her belongings; but the grunt of displacement that had been constant since leaving Leningrad was not much diminished.

More and more she was realising that hers had been an upheaval of seismic proportions. Not that she ever regretted her decision to emigrate. You risked everything for a new life in a new country, not because you were certain that life would be good in the new place, but because of what life had become in the old. While state-sanctioned killing of Jews had ended with Stalin's death, and large-scale pogroms had stopped some years earlier, it didn't mean these were gone forever. All it would take was another autocratic leader and the killing would return. As for the pogroms, they might have ceased, but the hatred that fuelled them was still very much in evidence, particularly in the vast rural regions. Then there was the daily discrimination in employment, housing, health and education, and all the slurs and insults as well. Jews in the Soviet Union, no matter how long they had lived there and no matter how loyal to the system, would never be Russian.

No one willingly chooses exile — exile is the option when choice has run out — but Galina, being of a positive mindset, had tried to make the best of it, despite the permanent undercurrent of anxiety. When she boarded the train to Lvov, she had felt a nervous excitement; when she travelled from Lvov to Vienna, she had felt audacious; when she told the Jewish organisers in Vienna she had changed her mind about Israel and wanted to go to Australia, she felt astonishingly mature; on the train to Rome, she was both eager and fearful; in Rome, while waiting for her travel documents, she felt disoriented, but because of her interpreting work she also felt responsible. It was only eight months later, during the long flight to Australia, that she felt terrified, and the courage, or perhaps the denial, that had stifled her fears to this point was finally depleted. During the first few months in Australia, exiled from home, from language, from everything that was familiar, she felt far more an outsider than she ever had as a Jew in Russia — though a good deal safer.

It was impossible to know the extent to which foreign Australia or the absence of her mother contributed to her alienation. Grief had accompanied her across the world when she travelled to Melbourne, and it had accompanied her across the city when she moved from Zara and Arnold's to the saddlery. Grief followed her to bed, it patrolled her sleep, it was waiting for her in the morning. Grief, it seemed, was relentless, but at the same time migration was tougher than she had ever imagined. There had been the rupture from her language, from work, city, customs, history, habits, procedures, and a break with all the people who loved and accepted her and mirrored who she was. Complicating the situation still further was the way in which the Australians regarded her. Labelled 'immigrant' and 'New Australian', defined almost exclusively by her foreignness, she barely recognised the Galina Kogan the Australians saw.

All migrations, she was coming to realise, were based on hope. And hope, at least for one born in the Soviet system, was just an abbreviation for wishful thinking, or a shorter word for delusion. The Australian press ran glowing reports of how life in the Soviet Union was changing. Politicians, commentators and journalists had latched on to *glasnost* and *perestroika* with a devotion that Gorbachev could only dream of when it came to his own Soviet citizens. The West viewed Gorbachev as a saviour, a strong leader intent on bringing democracy, liberalism and a free market to the Soviet Union. But Galina knew better. Even during his first months in power, it was clear to her that the new general secretary was no saviour, and far less in control of the unruly Soviet Union than he would ever appear to the West. The Soviet hardliners hated his reform type of communism, and the democrats hated him for adhering to communism in any form. For ordinary people, Gorbachev's free-market reforms meant there was less food in the shops, with some essential goods unavailable for months, and his insane alcohol restrictions enraged people already doing it tough.

It was obvious to Galina when she left the Soviet Union—Gorbachev had been in power for nearly a year at the time—that he wouldn't last. A small breath of change like the NEP of the twenties, or Khrushchev's thaw, or Gorbachev's current loosening of the economy might bring better food for a lucky few, a new winter coat, perhaps even a holiday by the Black Sea. But before long, Soviet life always returned to its usual harsh ways. The situation was clear: Stalin, Lenin, and the seventy-year-long revolution swirled in the Soviet blood and would not be eliminated in a hurry.

Not that Galina would voice her opinions to the admiring Australians, nor contradict them on this or any other matter. She was intent on watching and listening and learning the requirements of her new country—which would not have excluded her speaking about the old, but Australians rarely asked her about the Soviet Union. It was not for lack of interest, because they frequently raised the topic themselves, and always had much to say; in fact, they acted like authorities, couching statements as questions. *Life in the Soviet Union must be much better under Gorbachev?* they would say. Or: *We know about the changes, but it's still communism?* Or: *You must appreciate the freedom here?* There were so few real questions about the USSR, but in stark contrast, so many questions about her thoughts and impressions of Australia. Australians loved hearing about themselves.

Such an easygoing, casual people they were, and so comfortable in their Australian skins. Even the popular prime minister, Bob Hawke, fitted this profile. People referred to him fondly as their larrikin prime minister. When she consulted 'larrikin' in her dictionary she simply could not understand how this could be an admirable trait in a national leader. She knew about Mr Hawke's support for Soviet Jews — he was wiser than most Westerners on this issue — and he had won a scholarship to study at Oxford University, so he must be clever, yet there was nothing intellectual about him. But then she had learned from Zara and Arnold that there was a problem regarding intellectuals in this country. They were not on a par with murderers or spies, but neither did they rank anywhere near the sporting stars, pop singers and actors who made up the pantheon of Australian heroes.

No one would die for poetry here.

Intellectuals were, to use an Australian expression, on the nose. Perhaps that explained the satisfied smugness she had observed in the people, and their widespread belief that Australia was the best country in the world: there were no intellectuals to disabuse them. Yet even this was not clear-cut. There existed alongside the self-satisfaction what Zara had described as 'the great Australian cringe', a sort of national inferiority complex, she said, possibly rooted in the country's colonial past. (Maybe that explained all those questions about her impressions of Australia: the Australians were seeking reassurance.)

So Australians were proudly insular on the one hand, yet embarrassed to be Australian on the other. They were fanatical about sports, yet so unfit that the government was sponsoring a campaign featuring the 'couch potato' Norm. They were generous and friendly, but quite a few of them did not like foreigners. *Why doncha learn ta speak bloody English, ya fuckin' wog?* had been hurled at her by one angry man waiting behind her in a queue. Her skin was pale, her features were Caucasian; in appearance, she looked like most Australians. Only her accent singled her out. How much worse if she were African or Asian. As for the Australian Aborigines, she'd been in the country for a whole year, and had not met a single one.

She flipped through the folder on her desk. This was the catalogue of templates for the sewing-pattern illustrations. Each page depicted a different figure: men, women, youths, children, toddlers. In a country with so many Asians, not one figure in the entire catalogue was Asian.

From birth to death in the Soviet Union you knew exactly who you were and how you slotted into the system. Complex processes were simplified and streamlined; there was little need to think for yourself and no rewards if you did. She found the contradictions of Australian life confusing, and the flexibility they demanded of her stressful. While she knew this was all part of the West's freedoms, she was coming to see that freedom was not the safe, happy-go-lucky state she had assumed it would be. And there was something else, something unexpected and unnerving: with so much freedom, it was easy to feel that no one was looking after you.

With the last sewing illustration finished, Galina ate some leftover chicken before readying herself for her other job, her real estate job. Not that there was any hurry; punctuality was far from being an essential quality for workers at Ralph Merridale Graphics.

'We keep artists' hours here,' the boss had said when he hired her. 'We're all part-time, we all have our own art, so don't panic if you're running late.'

Ralph Merridale was, like his employees, an artist, but as he explained at her job interview, with three school-aged children he had bills to pay. His company supplied illustrations of houses for sale to several real estate agents. 'And the number keeps growing,' he said. 'If I'm not careful I could become a painter *manqué*, as well as a merchant prince.' He was not smiling, so neither did she.

She had looked Ralph up in a catalogue of Australian artists. He was mentioned, but compared with other listings his entry was very short, and none of his work had been reproduced. Perhaps he was not much of an artist. Perhaps the real estate business was saving him from mediocrity.

She surveyed her rack of clothes. What to wear? Melbourne's weather was impossible to predict, an idiosyncrasy in which Melbournians seemed to delight. It had been winter when she moved into the saddlery, and so cold in her new home it felt positively Russian. In September (which had been unseasonably warm, according to the Bureau of Meteorology), she put away her radiator. The next month she brought it out again in what was described as an unusually cool October, and while she was tempted to return it to the cupboard today, a cool change was due later that would send the temperature tumbling. But for now, the sun beat down. Even her shaded place was warming up. She opted for her sea-green sundress and sandals, and hoped the cool change would wait until dark.

She stepped outside into blazing heat. Having learned the necessity of conserving energy when it was hot, she walked slowly to the tram stop, and after a short wait was on her way. She liked the Melbourne trams, so clean and uncrowded, and she'd never known one to break down. She liked so much about her new country: the relaxed and easygoing people, the availability of anything and everything; she liked the perfumed bleaches and detergents, and the little price tickets on all the goods; and creative little touches like the plastic greenery in the butchery displays. And Australian shopping was bliss. Her all-time favourite shop was the huge Myer

Emporium. With six upper levels plus a basement, and occupying almost an entire city block, Myer's was a paradise of private enterprise. Everything from furniture to frocks was sold there, in a myriad of styles and colours and sizes. She loved the variety found in the West.

Even the cars here appealed. There were so many brands and in a multitude of shapes and colours, and she loved the fresh, tangy smell of Australian petrol—clearly Soviet vehicles ran on a different fuel. And Australian food. It was so abundant and so easy to buy that once she started cooking for herself, she made sure to allow ample time for shopping. Who would have thought, she wanted to say to her mother, that shopping could be so enjoyable?

When she first moved into the saddlery she had indulged in takeaway food. How greatly she had indulged. Two or three times a week she ate an Australian hamburger made by a Greek man whose shop was just a ten-minute walk away. The hamburger was enormous, with a thick meat patty, fried onions, a whole egg, cheese, lettuce and pickled beetroot, all sandwiched between the halves of a toasted bread roll, and dripping with tomato sauce. She bought hot, salty potato chips cooked by the same Greek man. (The first time she ordered chips, she asked for 'the minimum', expecting eight or ten chips, and was surprised to discover that the minimum was really a meal in itself.) And chicken, she loved the salty oozy Australian chicken cooked on a rotisserie. She could resist most of the cakes—her mother had been an excellent pastry cook—but not the pineapple donuts available from her local milk bar. And as an act of both freedom and defiance, she ate a banana every day: at home, bananas might have been wombats for all she ever saw one. Her favourite dessert was preserved fruit floating in condensed milk.

Within a month of moving into the saddlery her clothes seemed tighter; after two more weeks there was no denying it. If she didn't make some changes she'd soon look like a twenty-five-year-old *babushka*. She cut down on the food, but still she was eating too much and, as Zara pointed out, eating the wrong sort of food. But it was all so delicious, she simply could not resist.

'You need to eat more vegetables,' Zara said on one of her visits to the saddlery, inspecting the fridge and shelves.

Galina bought tinned peas and tiny potatoes: there was something so secure and comforting about canned food. She bought more and more cans until her cupboard was full.

'*Fresh* vegetables,' Zara said on her next visit.

This was, as it turned out, Zara's last visit, and despite numerous invitations, Galina had not been back to her home. She wanted the warmth that Zara and Arnold offered, and she wanted the closeness. But their affection reminded her of her forever-absent mother—a painful reminder that she was alone in a strange place, alone in all the world, and she had to learn to manage on her own.

Every night at half past six she would watch the news on the multicultural TV station, switching to the government broadcaster at seven. It was an evening ritual just like in Leningrad, when she and her mother and two hundred million other Soviet citizens tuned into *Vremya*. In her Australian saddlery, seated on her Australian couch, with the news playing on her Australian TV, Galina, having transposed this familiar habit, would experience a contented hour.

And she read her Russian books. These evoked only the good of her Soviet life. They were her childhood, they were her mother, they were home. Home and language: how very connected they were. Even after a year in Australia, Galina felt like a renter of English, and feared she might always be.

With other émigrés, it didn't matter how little she had in common with them, there was a sense of connection just in speaking Russian together. And yet she felt she must ration her time with other émigrés, in the same way she had with Zara and Arnold. As much as she hungered for Russian, she responded to a fierce and uncompromising imperative that she learn to manage alone.

Nothing was simple, nothing was clear, nothing was easy. She read about Australia's history and geography, its flora and fauna, the Great Barrier Reef, the Aboriginal people; she even read books about Australian cricket and football. So many books, but what she really needed was a manual on how to be an Australian.

Exile, it seemed to her, was a juggling act between past and present, remembering and forgetting—and her emigration *was* a form of exile, given she couldn't ever return. This loss of place was hard enough, but the way in which exile divided her mind was even worse. She needed her past, but not so much of it that it would sabotage her new life. Was this the condition of exile? To want too much of memory while at the same time trying to control it? When it concerned her mother, she wanted to remember everything, except the last illness. As for the rest, she tried to remember particular people, particular places, particular experiences. Demanding of memory yet restricting it, she was rarely satisfied. And there were the black holes, deliberately created in order to manage her new life, but which, at the same time, stifled crucial aspects of who she was. That more people did not collapse under the burden of exile was remarkable.

There was one prominent overlap between Australia and the Soviet Union that she found very amusing: the British Queen Elizabeth was as ubiquitous here as Lenin was at home. The queen's image was on all the coins, it graced a good many of the stamps, it hung in public buildings, it appeared in churches and schools. Queen Elizabeth here, Lenin at home. The plenitude of Lenin ensured that all Soviet citizens were caught in his aura and the Soviet ideological web. So what might the omnipresent queen reveal about the Australians?

Thirty minutes later, Galina was settled at her desk at Ralph Merridale Graphics. Neil, who occupied the space next to her, had been at work for hours. His current artwork, his 'real work', a triptych inspired by Tasmania's old-growth forests, was turning into 'a dog's dinner', and he simply couldn't stare at it for 'another fucking fruitless innings'. Despite the state of his real work, he seemed quite cheery, humming along to some internal music as he drew.

The office was at capacity today: four artists, a typist, a receptionist, as well as the boss, Ralph Merridale, who was always there (and again, Galina found herself wondering how real his 'real work' actually was). When she started here, Merridale's was supplying drawings to five real estate agents; that number had now increased to eight.

'We could work here full-time,' Neil said. 'Live the Australian dream.'

There was not a glimpse of a smile, but Galina was sure he was making a joke, so she laughed. When he laughed in return, she knew she had got it right. Australian humour was a baffling business.

Neil's job today was removing real trees from the front of houses and replacing them with low, picturesque bushes that would show the houses to advantage. Given he was a painter of the Australian bush, there was humour to be applied here—the laconic, dry type in which Neil was an expert. She was wondering whether she might try it herself when Neil got to his feet.

'I'm going to the stationery cupboard. Do you want anything?'

She didn't know what he meant. 'I have never heard of this cupboard.'

He looked horrified. 'You've been here … how long?' He didn't wait for an answer. 'So what have you been using to do your work?'

She explained that she used the pens and inks and stationery she had found in her work space, supplemented with materials she brought from home.

Neil shook his head in disbelief. 'You should've been taken to the stationery cupboard on your very first day. Come with me.'

Down the end of the office next to the kitchenette was a cupboard with double doors. There was a lock, but no key. Galina passed this cupboard regularly, but had assumed it had nothing to do with her work. Now Neil opened the doors to reveal broad shelves rising to a height of about two metres, each shelf stacked with stationery. There was paper of all sizes and thicknesses; envelopes small and large; manila folders and suspension files; thick, thin and medium-weight cardboard; pens, inks, pencils; poster paints, trays of water colours, brushes; rubbers, sticking tape, glue; staplers and staples, paperclips and butterfly clips, and more Letraset than she had ever seen in one place before. It was a spectacular sight.

'This,' Neil said, 'is a stationery cupboard.'

'It looks like a stationery shop,' Galina said.

'Well, yes.' Neil was smiling. 'But we don't have to pay.'

He explained that these materials were for the use of Merridale staff. 'You take what you want.'

'You mean you take what you need?'

'What you want, what you need ...' He shrugged, and smiled again. 'Sometimes it's hard to know the difference.'

The cupboard was full of materials she needed and more materials she wanted. 'You are saying I can take anything?'

He nodded.

'But surely someone will check?'

He shook his head.

'*Anything*?'

Again he nodded. 'Let me help you.' He reached for an empty carton and started piling items into it.

She was uncomfortable, she was worried, it was this business of helping yourself, and Neil must have noticed, for he told her to make a selection of paper and go back to her desk; he would follow with the rest. A few minutes later he put the loaded box on her desk, and emptied it item by item.

Spread in front of her was the new stationery. But still she worried, wanted to shield the booty—how else to think of it? At the same time, why would Neil, who, after all, had taken items from the cupboard for himself, want to get her into trouble? Trust: such a

69

Western value and regarded as a virtue in this country. Never would it be for her.

Again, Neil saw how anxious she was, and again he reassured her: she should have been introduced to the stationery cupboard on her very first day. He co-opted the other Merridale artists for confirmation. They all nodded and smiled and offered encouraging comments, and finally she concluded they simply could not all be in league against her.

The stationery cupboard was, she decided, one of the wonders of Australia, perhaps of the entire Western world. How she wished she could share it with her mother. A cupboard from which you could take what you wanted, the supplies of which were constantly replenished. It reminded her of an old Russian fairytale in which a bowl of food never emptied, no matter how much was eaten.

For twenty-five years she had lived in a society where you took what you could get; you took because you were always in need, you took because tomorrow things might be worse. When she arrived in Australia, she took the clothes, she took the shoes and food, she took the cinema and concert tickets, she took the two-for-one deals at cafés and shops, she took because tomorrow conditions might worsen. And when they did not, when the food spoiled in the fridge and the milk turned sour, when the clothes hung unworn and the entertainments became too plentiful, she learned to restrain herself. But it felt unnatural to refuse such abundance.

Sally, one of the artists at Merridale's, was a very big woman; privately, Galina thought of her as fat. One day, Sally confessed she never had the feeling of fullness, that the only way she could stop eating was to make herself stop when her plate was empty, or after a small second helping, or when her companions had finished their meals: she made herself stop before she was satisfied. This was how Galina felt about Australia's abundance.

While Neil removed trees and replaced them with low-slung bushes, Galina spent the afternoon shading—dots on this wall, cross-hatching on that, zigzags on the roof—each type of shading selected from a special catalogue of marks. The work required little thought, yet it occupied her entire attention. It was nearly six o'clock when she again found herself in the street. The cool change had not arrived.

She arrived home slick with perspiration. Her sandals had chafed, and there was a blister on her smallest toe. She stripped to her underwear, and grabbed a jug of cold water from the fridge; she did not bother with a glass as no one else would be drinking from it. Wisps of hair had escaped the plait; her neck itched, and she swiped and scratched, then leaned over the sink and emptied the rest of the jug over her head.

She straightened up and let the water run down her neck and over her shoulders. Within seconds her bra was soaked: if only she were as porous to Australian life. The day had brought no unforeseen difficulties; the only unexpected happening, her introduction to the stationery cupboard, should have brought only delight. Yet she felt miserable and, as hard as it was to admit, lonely. No denying it any longer: she was lonely.

She wondered if she had been too tough on herself, that the independence she had demanded had been self-defeating. Or perhaps it was more dire than this: that she would never adjust fully to life here, that she was simply too Russian for Australia.

She opened a folder lying at the back of her worktable. There was the Australian man's card, this Andrew Morrow who was the reason she was now living in a country the very existence of which had never entered her mind before he had bumped into her.

Too Russian? So use it, she told herself, be a Russian. Work out what you need and take it.

Andrew Morrow's card was in one hand and the telephone receiver in the other. Theirs had been an accidental meeting two years ago. He might not remember her, and even if he did, he had a life here—family, friends, girlfriend, perhaps even a wife. What need would he have for a lonely Russian treading the slippery slopes of immigration?

She replaced the phone in the cradle and stood staring through the window at her patch of garden. What was the worst that could happen if she were to call him? The very worst? That having been reminded of who she was, he told her to fuck off? (Australians were champion swearers.) Compared with her experience of the past couple of years, this would be tantamount to swatting a fly.

She picked up the receiver again, and dialled his number.

5

UNSTUCK BUT NOT UNDONE

Andrew Morrow put down the phone. It was the Russian girl, Galina Kogan. After all this time. The phone had rung, he had let it pass to the answering machine, he heard his abrupt, uninviting message followed by a drawn-out silence, and in that moment something alerted him, something insisted he take the call. He jumped up, his cup crashed to the floor, he lunged for the phone. And there she was, Galina Kogan, hesitant and apologetic, reminding him who she was—as if he could have forgotten after her starring role in his thoughts and imaginings these past couple of years. She was here, in Melbourne, the real Galina Kogan, and living just a short distance away.

The phone call had been mercifully brief. They arranged to meet the following Saturday for an expedition to the Queen Victoria Market; he would pick her up at nine and they would travel on the tram together. Saturday, just four days away: too short a time to contrive a reason for cancelling, too long to prevent his nerves from hitting fever pitch.

He rolled himself a cigarette and went up to the roof. Under the radiant sky, with Goddy pattering beside him, he paced and smoked and replayed the phone call. Had he said anything inept? For that matter, had he said anything of consequence? He wondered how long she'd been in Australia, and why she was contacting him now. He suspected she was lonely, that she didn't specifically want him, she just needed someone, anyone, for company. As to what he might want from her, *in real life*, he had no idea: within a few weeks of their first and only meeting, it had ceased to be relevant.

Only four days to prepare. Ninety-six hours to work himself into a state of terror. His heart was racing, his mind was a riot, he was already in a state of terror. All the conversations he had imagined now seemed empty, and any new ones he quickly dismissed as puerile or gobbledegook. He tried to calm himself. With so much to see at the market there would be little need for talk; it would be like going to the movies. But they would not be sitting in the dark, they would not be silent, and it would be nothing like the movies. What on earth had he done?

Galina hung up the phone. What on earth had she done? She should have waited, as she had numerous times before, waited for the loneliness to ease. Be a Russian, she had told herself, seek out what you need. What about Russian resilience? She should have gone for a walk, she should have forced herself to work, she should have telephoned Zara or one of the Soviet Jews. Or she could have sought solace at the cathedral—the Catholic or the Anglican, it made no difference; all churches, she had discovered, were havens for the lonely. Surrounded by the glorious windows and the silent statues, she could have settled in a pew and waited for the loneliness to slip into solitude. But she hadn't gone to the cathedral and she hadn't worked, she'd been impatient and foolish. She held nothing against Andrew; she was happy to see him, but not as a solution to her weakness.

There were four days to prepare for the visit to the market. Andrew said they could buy food and later make themselves a meal—either at his place or hers, he did not specify. Galina had heard about this market, and expected she would enjoy the expedition, despite the circumstances that had brought it about. But as a novice cook, she would not enjoy cooking with a stranger. Yet when Andrew suggested they prepare a meal together, she had not hesitated. This, she decided, was a measure of her desperation. What on earth had she done?

Two years had passed since her mother had died, two years since Andrew Morrow had toppled her in the street, yet Galina thought she had retained a clear image of him; but at exactly nine o'clock the following Saturday morning she opened the door to a stranger. In her memory his hair had been white-blond and closely cropped, but this man's hair was golden and fell past his shoulders in lush, Jesus-like waves. And the body, bulked out by the sheepskin jacket he had worn in Leningrad, was now slender, even thin, and he was just a couple of centimetres taller than she was, and not the two-metre man of her memory. He was wearing jeans and a sky-blue, tie-dyed T-shirt, and he was unrecognisable.

He stood outside her door, arms dangling in the awkward space of an Australian greeting. Russians were lavish kissers, and in Italy you shook hands, but here the men seemed at a loss to know how to greet a woman. In exasperation, she held out her hand. He grasped it — gratefully, she thought.

She slipped on her jacket, grabbed her shopping bag, and they walked to the tram stop along the main road bordering the cemetery. The weather was mild with a cool breeze; cottony clouds bulged white and motionless in the astonishing blue of the Australian sky. She buttoned her jacket and wondered if Andrew, with his bare arms, was cold. He seemed nervous — although what he, at home in his own city and in charge of this expedition, had to be nervous about, she could not guess. As they walked, he asked the usual predictable questions: how long she had been in Australia, how long she was planning to stay. A year, she answered to the first, and forever to the second, even while hoping for the questions she most wanted: '*Why* did you come?' and '*How* are you faring?'

She was grateful for the arrival of a tram. She took a window seat—she nearly always managed a window seat on these Melbourne trams—and gazed through the glass at the passing scenery. They travelled in silence; if she'd been less aware of Andrew, she could have pretended she was alone.

And then they were at the market. It was huge, it was astonishing, it was marvellous. Filled with people and surprises, it was how she imagined a carnival might be.

'If I was not seeing this with my own eyes, I would not believe it,' she said. 'You must show me everything.'

Her dark eyes were sparkling, her whole face was alive; she was a joy to watch. Andrew wondered at this unguarded delight of hers. Was it attributable to her Russianness and a direct result of her former deprivation? Might it be typical of any migrant? Or was it specific to her, Galina Kogan? That she could be from London, Nepal, Palermo, or Palm Springs and she would still display such exuberance. Whatever the explanation, it was captivating—*she* was captivating.

He started their tour in the fruit-and-vegetable section. They entered the area and Galina immediately stopped, right in the middle of the main walkway. Quickly, he guided her away from the stream of shoppers to one end of the open-sided shed so she could observe undisturbed.

The air was cool, and plump with summer fruits; pigeons flapped beneath the roof beams, and sparrows darted from one side of the shed to the other; people laden with bags and shopping trolleys jostled together in the aisles. There was the clarion call of stall-holders spruiking their bargains, of parents shouting at straying children, and bursts of laughter trumpeting above the general noise. Galina stood at the end of the shed, transfixed by the extraordinary sight. So many times in the past year she had been struck by the plenitude in Australia, but nothing could compare with this. There must have been a hundred stalls in the section, each piled high with fresh, unbruised produce. It was heavenly: the colours, the appetising smells, the good cheer.

As they walked the aisles, she noticed Italian and Greek names on the placards above the stalls, and quite a few Asian ones, too. Perhaps these were the Vietnamese boat people she had heard so much about; she was on the verge of asking Andrew about this when she noticed a Russian name above one of the vegetable stalls. The elderly vendor was talking with an equally elderly customer, and she lingered over some potatoes in order to listen. It was not Russian she was hearing but Yiddish, a language she did not herself speak but quite a number of Soviet Jews did. She was tempted to try some Russian on them, but though she was sure they'd understand, her nerves failed her.

Sometimes the crowd was so dense, she and Andrew couldn't move — not that she cared, there was so much to see. One stall sold only berries, another potatoes, a third displayed several different varieties of mushrooms. She bought some dark-brown ones: she would make Russian comfort food for their meal, a buckwheat kasha with mushrooms, which should offset cooking with a stranger. And Andrew bought an avocado — for their lunch, he said (how many meals did he intend they eat together?) — before guiding her into the delicatessen hall.

This area was even more fabulous than the fruit-and-vegetable section: an entire building of delicatessens. If only her mother were here. The smell was luscious with cheeses and sausages, smoked meats and pickles. They started down the first aisle. Standing outside one of the stalls was a woman with a plate of cheese. The cheese had been cut into small cubes and she was offering them to passers-by. Some people helped themselves, others declined, and no one was giving her any money. When she and Andrew drew near, the plate was held out to them.

'Go on,' Andrew said. 'Take a piece.' And when she hesitated, he added, 'These are samples. They're free.'

While she stood there dithering, other people were helping themselves, so she did too, although moved away quickly. The cheese was delicious, and she wondered if you were allowed to go back for more; but with another woman just up ahead offering little biscuits covered with a pink cream, she decided not to risk it. The pink cream was a caviar dip, Andrew said. Again she hesitated, and again Andrew said she should help herself, that these were samples. The pink cream was even more delicious than the cheese.

There were many more vendors in the deli section who were giving away their food. Andrew occasionally tasted something, but she took everything on offer, even while perplexed at such largesse: didn't these people want to make the best profits? At least with the two-for-one deals at cafés and shops, the owners were earning some money; these deli people were getting nothing.

She noticed that most of the stall-holders in this section were Italian. 'So it is true,' she said to Andrew, 'Italians are the main immigrant group here.'

Galina's words caught Andrew by surprise. He'd gone out early to buy the Saturday papers to find topics of conversation; he'd been particularly pleased to find an article about the USSR under Gorbachev. 'What's your take on the current situation in the USSR?' he had imagined asking, an excellent open-ended question that would keep her talking with only an occasional prompt required from him. But now she was asking about Italians and immigration.

He swung the shopping bag over his shoulder, shoved his sweaty hands into his pockets, and gathered some words together. He told her there were many Italian immigrants, particularly in Melbourne, but they were probably outnumbered by Greeks. Melbourne, he said, was the third-largest Greek city in the world. It sounded like a boast, which was not his intention at all.

'We've a large Chinese community too, they've been here since the gold rush, and of course there's the new Vietnamese population. And Jews, they came after the war.' He looked around. 'A lot of Jews used to have stalls here at the market. I expect they still do.'

Had he guessed she was Jewish? But how could he? Russians would recognise Kogan as a Jewish name, but he wouldn't. Should she tell him she was Jewish? And quickly dismissed the thought: there was absolutely no reason why he needed to know.

They stopped at a deli that specialised in salted and smoked meats. Hanging from hooks were sausages that looked very much like *sosiski*. She made a mental note of the location of the stall: she'd return by herself to investigate these *sosiski* lookalikes. For now, she bought some bacon for the kasha, and at another stall, Andrew bought a loaf of bread. He then led her into the seafood area.

She was from Leningrad, she knew about seafood. Meat might not be available, and oranges and bananas could disappear for months, but there was always fish: pickled, salted, sometimes even fresh. But a glance at the very first stall was sufficient to prove that her understanding of fish was like an infant's understanding of the world. Behind the glass were large, shallow trays, each filled with a different type of fresh fish: white fish, pink fish, whole fish, fish portions, and not a herring to be seen. And oysters arranged in lines next to piles of mussels in their shells, and bright-pink cooked prawns — she read the label — a mountain of them spilling into the adjacent tray.

'Have you ever tasted prawns?' Andrew asked.

She shook her head, not shifting her gaze from the display.

Andrew checked his wallet, and then bought eight large ones to eat with the avocado.

'It's a special occasion,' he said.

And immediately wished he'd remained silent. It was a special occasion for him, the first outing, perhaps even a date, with a girl who'd previously been confined to his fantasies. But was it special for her? And he decided as he watched her that it was. This trip to the market had been an inspired choice.

They wandered slowly through the fish section to the meat department. Galina would stand in front of a particular display for a long time, sometimes with a frown as if she could not quite believe what she was seeing, but mostly with a delighted smile; on a couple of occasions she actually laughed aloud.

There was something extravagant about her, he decided, a largeness of personality, an inexhaustible enthusiasm. Galina Kogan was ... oceanic. And again he wondered whether it was connected to her Russianness, or whether it was unique to her. (And could she be separated from her Russianness anyway? Not everyone was as schizoid as he was.) Whatever the reason, her joy was more abundant, her curiosity more intense, her vision more sharp, her delight more fulsome. Even when they left the market, she was still thrilling to the wonders of the place. To be so at ease in the world, he was thinking, even when the world was not your own, was something he had rarely known.

He hefted the shopping bags over his shoulder, and they set off towards the tram stop. With no vehicle in sight, he was about to draw on his list of prepared questions when his attention was caught by a drunk reeling on the opposite pavement, shouting to the skies and gesticulating wildly. Other pedestrians were giving him a wide berth, some even crossed the road to avoid him. He was an unusual drunk, it seemed to Andrew, dressed as he was in surprisingly neat and respectable clothes. Nonetheless, he was relieved that the man was on the opposite side of the road; drunks made him nervous, their being so out of control. He feared for them, feared for himself as well.

Galina, too, was watching the drunk man, surprised to see here a scene so commonplace back home. She was wondering whether her reaction meant she had separated from Leningrad more completely than she'd realised, or, having learned how different life was in Melbourne, anything shared by the two places now struck her as an anomaly, when the man suddenly lurched forward and fell into the gutter. The traffic was banked up at the intersection. The lights would soon change. He needed to be hauled off the street. She started forward, but Andrew yanked her back. She shook herself free, turned to him, and was thrown for a moment by his expression. 'What are you frightened of?' she asked, more an accusation than a question, and went again to cross the road, but a man and a woman were already helping the fellow to safety. She watched them guide him to a seat; he was so drunk he could barely walk. The couple were talking to him, then the woman wrote something down and hurried to a phone box. The man kept a hand on the drunk's arm to keep him from falling off the seat.

Andrew, too, was watching, although not really seeing. He felt such a fool.

'You looked so scared,' Galina said. Her voice was quiet, her face overwritten with curiosity. 'This man can hardly stand on his feet. The only person he will hurt is himself. What is so frightening to you?'

Andrew had no answer. The drunk was small and slight: even if sober, he could not have done any harm. Andrew shrugged. 'I'm not much of a drinker,' he said. 'And I try to be in control.'

She was staring at him, she must think him ridiculous. He should have kept silent.

'That makes us alike,' she said with a laugh. 'We both prefer to be in control.'

The tram arrived, and they boarded it. In the silence during the short trip, he floundered in his foolishness. He needed to be alone; lunch now was impossible; he could freeze the prawns; they could eat avocado another day. He grappled for excuses, but with his mind in disarray, nothing was making sense.

Galina, in contrast, was trying to make sense of him. Her circumstances demanded a strength that made empathy an indulgence, yet she found herself feeling for him—not sympathy, but kindness

81

and a certain understanding. She could see he was as discomforted in his accustomed life as she was in her new one.

It had occurred to her that the easiest solution to the difficulties she faced as an émigré would be to find an Australian man and marry him. It would also be an out-of-character solution for one who prided herself on her independence. Nonetheless, the temptation remained: marriage would provide a passport to Australian life, and it would strip a good many of the stresses from her days.

The marriage solution had not prompted her telephone call to Andrew, desperation alone had been responsible, but as the tram trundled past the university and sped more smoothly along the tracks beside the cemetery, the possibility surfaced. He would be an easy catch, the sort of man who would love more than he was loved in return. The thought flickered and just as quickly died. Andrew was not a man to use. And besides, he was an artist, and she respected artists.

'I would like to come to your studio.' The words were uttered without forethought. Quickly she added, 'I would like to see your work.'

They had disembarked and were standing in the street at the northern end of the cemetery. Andrew was still in a quandary as to how he might escape, but at the same time he was desperate to see her again. A visit to his studio was not what he would have chosen, but under the circumstances it would have to do. He managed to nod his agreement, said he would call to arrange a time, and then, pretending he had forgotten about their plan to eat together, extended his hand to say goodbye in the European fashion. She leaned towards him and kissed him in the Russian one.

He sorted through their purchases, handed one of the bags to her, and stepped into the street. He wasn't looking, he wasn't seeing, and she grabbed his arm and pulled him back, just as he had done with her earlier. Although she had better cause. There was a stream of traffic, a huge cortège travelling alongside the cemetery in the slow rhythm of mourning. The cars turned from the main thoroughfare into the side street where he and Galina were standing, heading towards the northern entrance of the cemetery.

The two of them watched the procession. Eight, nine, ten—Galina was counting silently as the cars passed—seventeen, eighteen, nineteen, and still the cars kept coming, their headlights flatly yellow in the bright Australian light. The funeral was clearly for a very important person, she was thinking, an official of some sort, perhaps a government leader. It was almost Russian in size, although not in style. For a large state funeral at home, the procession would be on foot, with musicians tolling out a plangent patriotic refrain, and there would be a huge crowd of onlookers. Ordinary Russians like a good state funeral, not simply for the time off work and an excuse to drink, but as an excellent opportunity to mourn their own squeezed lives. As for the dead official, there was usually little grief felt for him.

Here in Melbourne, the trail of cars with their black-clad mourners was still crawling along the broad thoroughfare and turning at the corner. There was something mesmerising about the scene, like a moving frieze.

'Russians,' she said, keeping her gaze on the cortège, 'are experts at big funerals.'

Andrew looked at her, wondering what he might reply. But there was no need for him to speak, Galina Kogan was far away. He wanted to be away too. He raised his hand in farewell and set off down the street, leaving her to her thoughts.

Slowly, Galina set off in the other direction, and a couple of minutes later she arrived home. She dumped the bag of produce on the table, and sank onto the couch. And there she remained, stilled not by nostalgia nor by indulgence, but the sheer force of the past.

6

LIFE AND DEATH IN THE
SOVIET UNION

There had been rumours, but now it was official: after twenty years at the helm and twenty years of ill health, General Secretary Brezhnev was dead.

Galina had never known life without him; a toddler when he became leader, she had just turned twenty-one. His image graced each of her classrooms, it was posted on walls and shop fronts, it headlined the TV and newspapers. But now bull-faced Brezhnev, with his grizzled eyebrows and his slack skimpy lips, was dead.

Her mother had always been scathing about him and damning of life under his leadership. The food he promised never appeared, the goods that would have made life easier never materialised; only the military forces and the nuclear arsenal expanded, and the space program, too. But what was the use of sending men into space if people on the ground didn't have enough to eat? These things Lidiya said in private to Galina, who had learned from her earliest years that what was said at home stayed at home. Brezhnev filled her mother with rage. The Soviet Union wasn't poor. There was money enough to squash the Poles when they became too independent, and the Czechs when they became too Western, money enough for all manner of emergency. So there must be plenty of money for ordinary people to have better lives.

'We're told all the time that things are getting better. That steel production is up, food production is up, oil production is up, new apartments up, factories up, electricity plants up. Everything is up, yet our pathetic lives sink ever lower.

'Things are getting better? Not a chance. It's just *pokazukha*, window dressing.' Lidiya shook her head in disgust. 'There may well be people, poor deluded people, who will genuinely mourn our recently departed general secretary, but I'm not among them.'

The funeral for Brezhnev would be held in Moscow, but the entire Soviet Union would mark his passing. Schools, offices and factories would close, and everyone would have the day off to mourn the great leader. Lidiya proposed they make the best of it with their own funeral feast.

'Ours will be a farewell-and-good-riddance feast,' she said. 'Although I can't imagine his replacement will be any better.'

So it happened on Monday, 15th November, 1982, that Galina and her mother spent much of the day in front of the TV, with an array of delicious food. The dead man meant nothing to them, and the movement of the funeral was ponderously slow, yet something was compelling them to watch.

'We Russians have an unhealthy tolerance for punishment,' her mother said wryly.

But it wasn't some undesirable national trait that kept Galina watching, it was the event itself. From the very beginning, with the cameras gliding over Brezhnev lying in state in the cavernous hall of the House of the Unions, it was a spectacle. Dead Brezhnev was perched atop a gargantuan pyre decorated with red flowers and a thicket of greenery. A small orchestra was playing to one side, and numerous sombre officials were hanging about, looking like they needed some occupation.

'All these men guarding the great leader,' her mother said. 'As if anyone would want to spirit him away.'

Then came the procession itself: guns, machinery, flowers, banners, bands, medal-bearers, and masses of men in military dress, all of them bulked out in grey coats and wearing their silly peaked caps. Galina had seen men like this before, she'd seen state funerals before, but Brezhnev's was the biggest show of all.

Once the procession was underway, the cameras panned between the proceedings and the huge crowds lining the route.

'I wonder what bribes were given to those people to make them forfeit their day off,' Lidiya muttered.

Galina, too, was focused on the crowd. 'Seems that few women took up the offer.'

'Women have more sense than men,' her mother said quickly. 'They certainly have less time.' She helped herself to another spoonful of creamy mushrooms. 'The women who have to cook and clean and care for children, and hold down jobs as well, they don't mourn this man.'

It was a perennial complaint of her mother's that all the revolutionary promises to women had never been fulfilled. When Lidiya was a child back in the 1930s, women were already assuming the double burden of domestic labour and outside employment. 'It was too much even for a Soviet superwoman,' she said. 'If a woman believed in her work, then the domestic sphere suffered; if she didn't, by this time many women lacked the heart and the resources to make a proper home. Cooking was a drudgery. Life was a drudgery.

'Stalin, Khrushchev, Brezhnev, these leaders come and go, but the hardship for Soviet women endures.' Lidiya nodded at the TV screen. 'No sensible women would mourn this man.'

This was probably wishful thinking on the part of her mother—not that Galina had a better explanation for the lack of women mourners. It was certainly not the cold that kept them away: after a series of wintry days the weather had actually improved. Indeed, if you believed in God you'd think he was personally managing Brezhnev's farewell. For this man, who throughout his life could never have too much pomp and ceremony, there would be no rain or snow on his final parade.

They tried to slow their eating to keep pace with the funeral. This was a mighty challenge for her mother, who always gobbled her food — a lifelong hangover, she said, from the starvation years of the *blokada*. After the mushrooms, they started on the smoked fish and the pickled vegetables. The most plodding, most leaden version of Chopin's funeral march was playing — enough to turn you off Chopin forever, Galina was thinking, and she went to check on the *pirozhki* heating in the oven. Filled with meat and not their usual potato, this was her favourite of the feast food.

She returned to the couch with the *pirozhki*, and settled again in front of the TV. It was said that Andropov would be the new leader. Andropov, like all the Soviet leaders, was old, and he'd been a member of the power elite for as long as she could remember; there'd be no change if he were in charge. He was standing in the centre of a group of dignitaries observing the parade. Leading the legions of military men was the pillar-box-red coffin, borne aloft by a gun carriage, and towed by an armoured tank so small Galina wondered if it had been made specially for parades and funerals. There followed a multitude of wreaths, each arrangement so large it required two men to carry it.

Her mother was laughing. 'It looks like an unfixed forest, like mobile Birnam Wood in Shakespeare's *Macbeth*.'

Following the forest of wreaths, there were forty or fifty military men, each carrying a miniature red cushion on which was displayed one or more of Brezhnev's hundreds of medals. Then came huge battalions of soldiers and navy men and other military officials, many of them marching in a slow-motion goose-step, their arms swinging similarly slowly.

'I bet they're aching all over,' Galina said.

Lidiya did not respond. She had stopped eating. She was staring at the TV screen. The camera had zoomed in on the medals and their bearers. Brezhnev was known to prize his medals; even when dressed in civilian clothes, he would always have one or two pinned to his lapel. Galina assumed that to be a medal-bearer at his funeral was a special honour, given only to trusted members of his inner circle. She was thinking how absurd they looked, these block-shaped, heavy-featured men, each carrying a delicate red cushion, when her mother spoke in an odd, strangled voice.

'I know him,' she was on her feet and prodding the TV screen. 'That one there,' she said more loudly, pointing to one of the medal-bearers. The camera shifted to the crowds lining the street, but still Lidiya stood, her finger on the screen. 'I know him. I'd know him anywhere.'

The procession continued, the voices of the commentators tolled on, the music played. Her mother stood motionless by the TV; it was hard to know whether she was distressed, or confused, or just plain surprised.

Lidiya turned around slowly. She looked as if exiting a dream. 'That was my brother,' she said, marking each word with care. 'That was Mikhail. There, on the TV, one of Brezhnev's medal-bearers. My brother, Misha.'

She returned to the screen. Galina could see her willing the camera to return to the medal-bearers.

'Misha must be,' Lidiya was frowning, 'he must be sixty. That would make him twenty years older than my father was when he was taken away. Twenty years older and a good deal fatter, yet such a strong resemblance.'

Galina had met this uncle only once, a dozen years earlier when he'd turned up at their old home at the *kommunalka*. He'd arrived without warning, he'd taken what he wanted, and he'd left never to return.

'He's done well for himself,' Lidiya said softly.

Now Galina watched, too. She had always wanted a brother or

a sister, so to have a brother from whom you were estranged made no sense to her. But when Mikhail had appeared all those years ago, her mother had just wanted him gone.

'Trust me,' she had said at the time. 'Trust me to know what's best for you.'

Now Lidiya poured herself some of their special Armenian brandy; she tossed it down like vodka, and immediately poured another. Galina remained silent. The funeral plodded on. The brother appeared several more times. To her, he looked like any other high Soviet official: fat, neckless, bovine, old. That he resembled *dedushka* Yuri, the grandfather she had never known, the father to whom Lidiya remained devoted, was hard to comprehend. What had happened all those years ago? What had happened to make her mother hate her own brother?

When the funeral was over, Lidiya stood up and crossed to the window. She stared down into the street. It was dark outside, and her figure was reflected in the glass: one hand shaded her eyes, and her mouth was tight. Galina wondered if she was crying and wanted to go to her, comfort her, but why would her mother be standing over there unless she needed to be alone? At last Lidiya turned and came to the couch. She reached for Galina's hands.

It was time to talk of the past, she said in a soft voice. It was time for Galina to know the full story. The words came slowly, as if she were still unsure of the right course of action.

Lidiya had often spoken about her own paternal grandparents, the cigar-making grandfather and the embroiderer grandmother, and her maternal grandparents, both of whom had been tailors. But about her own parents, Vera and Yuri Kogan, she had been largely silent.

'This was a calculated decision,' she now said. 'I thought it was a cruel mother who'd saddle her child with a spoiled biography.' She shrugged. 'I still do. But there comes a time when you need your history. You need it to explain your country, and you need it to explain who you are. It's time,' she said. 'It's time to know where you've come from.'

The story of the Kogan family went back a long way, as Russian stories tended to do—before Stalin, before Lenin and the Revolution, before the 1905 uprising, before the Crimean Wars, before the tribe of Alexanders and Nicholases, before great Peter himself, right back to the famed rabbis of Prague.

'But I'll start in the early 1890s,' Lidiya said. 'With my own grandparents, your great-grandparents.'

She settled back on the couch, and her voice assumed a storytelling lilt. 'My grandfather was a cigar-maker and my grandmother an embroiderer. They were considered useful Jews, and so were permitted to live in St Petersburg.' Lidiya reached for a framed picture and handed it to Galina. 'They knew how fortunate they were—their lives being so much better than those they'd left behind in the Pale. And they *were* fortunate, in every respect they were fortunate, except they had no children.'

Galina studied the young couple in the picture. They looked so serious, or perhaps they just looked sad, this couple that were unable to have children.

'For years they longed for a child, and for years they were disappointed. Then, just when they'd given up hope, my grandmother found herself pregnant.' Lidiya was smiling. 'Their baby would be Yuri, my father, your grandfather.

'In Russia's long history there have been bad times, worse times, and the very worst times. This period when my grandmother became pregnant counted among the worst. People would notice her condition and say it was a terrible time to be bringing a baby into the world, people with four, five, six children of their own. Some would say there was never a good time to bring a Jewish baby into the world, but my grandparents were overjoyed.

'My grandfather and grandmother were good at their crafts, but there was never enough work nor enough people able to pay. Life for them in St Petersburg might have been better than in the Pale, but it was still tough. Cholera was more common than a full stomach, and typhus more tenacious than ice in winter. Then, in 1891, with the pregnancy well underway, a new deportation occurred. St Petersburg Jews were dragged from their rooms, they were rounded up in the streets: no warning, no explanation, no time to pack up lives that had taken root over decades, no opportunity to calm the children, care for the elderly, or collect provisions. Amid all this, my grandparents, who had thought they would remain childless, were convinced of a miracle. That they escaped the deportation was another miracle. And when their son was born, they named him Yuri, a good Russian name to take into a future where, according to their hopes and dreams, everyone, including Jews, would be equal.'

Yuri Kogan grew to be a strong boy, in every respect he was strong except his eyes. This boy, who loved reading and writing, and who particularly loved numbers, wore spectacles as thick as window panes. Rich Petersburgers were installing the new electricity in their homes — light as dazzling as a hundred candles, so it was said — but for the Kogans, electricity was as remote as the stars. They heard of a way to make an oil-lamp burn more brightly by inserting a strip of tin to spread the flame. It helped, and Yuri's poor eyesight did not matter quite so much anymore.

For hours on end, young Yuri would sit at a bench in the glow of his special light, blond curls falling over his face, a pencil in his grip as he explored the patterns in numbers. So exceptional was his skill in maths that no quota against Jews could keep him from the *gimnaziya*.

It quickly emerged that Yuri embraced all learning; whether literature, languages or philosophy, he mastered everything he tackled. With a book in his hands, he could forget he was hungry, he could forget he was cold, he could forget that the soles of his shoes had worn through to the cardboard, and his best friend had sickened and died. Learning supplied him with all the pleasures and experiences lacking in his own meagre life, and there was simply no stopping him. Although the bullies at school did try.

No one, he quickly discovered, likes a clever kid, particularly a clever Jewish kid. There were bruisings, and plenty of them, and nasty taunts, some of which he didn't even understand. Eventually he found the perfect solution: appeasing the school bullies with cigar ends collected from around his father's cutting machine.

He studied hard, but when his parents talked about the great socialist revolution, he put his schoolwork aside to listen. This utopia, which would provide work, food and reliable shelter to all Russians, would most certainly come. And how wonderful it would be for the Kogans, and all people like them.

Life now, though, was not fair. Yuri saw the huge palaces where rich people lived in warm rooms, waited on by vast numbers of servants. He heard about tables laden with food, and whole rooms just for sleeping. He gazed at bejewelled churches with spires clad in gold, and fat priests wrapped in ornamental robes. He saw rich children swaddled in furs and coddled by nurses; rosy-skinned and chubby-cheeked, these children had less in common with him than would a mouse. Where he lived, babies died and children sickened, teeth were agony, cuts festered, he was always cold and meat existed only in dreams. With the perennial pogroms against the Jews, with the *Ruskoye Znamye* pumping out anti-Semitic vitriol day after day, with the rich in their palaces and the poor squashed into rickety rooms, life was definitely not fair.

What was it about his country, about Mother Russia, that made living so hard and death so easy? And when he asked his parents, he always received the same answer: the revolution would change everything; the revolution would bring a good life to all.

The failed uprising of 1905 brought a few minor changes, but didn't result in fewer rats and more food, nor less cold and better health, at least not for the Kogans. By the time Yuri was a student at university, conditions had actually gone backwards. Yuri buried himself in mathematics and tried to ignore the hardships, but not even he was immune to a raft of new Jewish statutes running to nearly one thousand pages that impinged on every aspect of life—including university study. There were reduced quotas for university entrance, and when enrolled, there were quotas to sit for exams. So a Jew could attend the classes, could do the work, and at the end of the course be denied the examinations and the subsequent credentials. Yuri kept his head down, he pushed himself harder, he wanted to believe that as long as his work was appreciated he would be safe.

With quotas to practise certain professions, quotas for hospital admissions, quotas for cemetery plots, quotas for practically everything, other Jews were not so fortunate. Most of the new statutes struck Yuri as plain ludicrous. Jews were permitted to sit on juries, but couldn't act as foreman. They could be members of a military band, but not lead one. Jewish soldiers from other parts of Russia could pass through St Petersburg, but weren't allowed to spend their furlough in the city. When his own girlfriend, Masha, together with many of her friends, registered as domestic servants in order to keep their residency in St Petersburg, these absurd laws came disturbingly close. 'What happens if the authorities discover you're not a maid?' he asked. Masha shrugged, she would deal with it if it happened. And then she laughed. 'I could have registered as a prostitute like my cousin Rosa.' Yuri did not laugh. What was funny about prostitutes and maids gaining residency, when a doctor or a lawyer could not? What was funny about young Jewish women registering as maids and prostitutes in order to finish their studies?

He managed to hold his place at the university, he managed to do his exams, he managed to graduate as the top student in mathematics, he managed to get a job teaching at the university, and that's where he was working when the war with Austria and Germany broke out. Suddenly, ethnicity didn't matter anymore. Whether you were Russian, Jewish, Armenian, or a hermit from Azerbaijan, if you were fit enough to fight, you fought for Mother Russia. And Yuri wanted to fight — what young man didn't? But even if his eyesight had been perfect, his maths would have kept him away from the front line.

Wars need the numbers men. Yuri counted troops, horses and vehicles, and shifted them across the map; he measured out metres of barbed wire, and distributed them across the battlefields; he mobilised uniforms, boots, weapons, tobacco. Throughout those brutal years, Yuri, together with fellow mathematicians, moved the men and the necessities of war. And he counted off the dead and wounded too — staggering numbers of his fellow countrymen. As the numbers soared, he blamed the czar and his aristocratic military men. And he longed for the people's revolution.

He thought it couldn't come soon enough, but when the revolution finally did happen, it couldn't have been at a worse time. Only later did he realise that it was precisely because life couldn't get any worse that the revolution happened when it did. Russia was losing the war with Germany. The enemy was in striking distance of Petrograd. All the usual hardships were rampant — hunger, cold, disease — but now millions of war casualties, soldiers and civilians alike, were added to the toll.

It is 1917, February, during the Russian winter, when the first uprising occurs. The rouble, already harshly devalued, plunges still further. Food is scarce, fuel is scarcer, and transport is a memory. You have some potatoes, you swap them for fuel; you have your mother's pendant, you swap it for boots. In March, the czar abdicates; the Romanov dynasty is finished, and the aristocracy of yesterday flees. Yuri has longed for this day, but it is impossible to rejoice when daily life is such a grind. He goes to his job because, revolution or no revolution, the war continues. Meanwhile the search for fuel becomes all-consuming. Palaces are plundered, churches are burned, mansions are looted. Into the stove go gilt chairs, carved bedheads, ornate picture frames, rare books; the spoils of the czars are keeping the Bolsheviks from freezing.

Hardship, pain, misery — it seems to Yuri these are infinitely elastic. You think you are experiencing the worst, whether of hunger or cold or enemy attacks, you think you can't take any more, but conditions do worsen and you do manage to survive. The European war drags on. Cholera and typhus are rife, influenza is simmering, babies are dying, children are starving. Only lice are thriving.

'People could learn a great deal from lice,' he remarks to his mother one night when he arrives home to find their place reeking of *karbolka*, and his mother on her hands and knees scrubbing.

Yuri and his parents are hopeful, as are so many people, when Kerensky assumes the leadership of the provisional government. But daily life does not improve; there are simply too many factions, each advancing a different program for the new Russia. So they are relieved when, after a few more tumultuous months, the Bolsheviks assume power and the provisional government is dissolved. Lenin promises 'peace, land, and bread'. It's a rousing cry amid the dirge of war and deprivation.

'The worst must surely be over,' Yuri says to his mother one night.

The two of them are huddled over the *burzhuika*. Yuri had managed to scavenge some fuel, but the stove gobbled it as if it were famished; now any warmth is more imagined than real. With his father stretched out on the divan, sleeping, Yuri keeps his voice low.

'Now the struggle must surely cease.'

It doesn't. The glorious revolution segues into civil war. Russians are now killing Russians, and within the provinces, the bloodshed is further ramped up by ethnic and religious attacks against Armenians, Jews, Poles—all the usual targets. So much hatred and anger and resentment across all of greater Russia, even a committed Bolshevik like Yuri finds himself wondering how many more deaths it will take to bring about peace and prosperity. He estimates the number of dead so far to be at least nine million, surely enough in anyone's terms. As for the future, he wants to work for the revolution, but the universities are in upheaval, and now that Russians are killing Russians, no one wants mathematicians counting the dead.

Throughout the cities and countryside, the Whites, the Mensheviks, and the Bolsheviks are fighting, each group against the others, and all of them against the Jews. In the pogroms of 1918 and 1919, two hundred thousand Jews are killed across the land. The Kogans are devastated; this is not the revolution they had hoped for. During the harshest winter in living memory, death attacks on several fronts: starvation, civil war, racial hatred, disease, and the fiercest cold.

And then, without warning, Yuri's luck changes. He is given a job as a demographer in the newly established ZAGS: the Department of Registration of Civil Statuses, responsible for births, deaths, marriages, and other population statistics. At last, he'll be working for the new Russia. And his luck doesn't stop there: in the same month he starts at ZAGS he meets Vera. He knows from the very beginning that she's the one for him. A teacher of English language and literature, she's warm and spirited, strong and funny, and like him, she is ethnically Jewish. So certain is he that their future lies together, he could have proposed within days of their first meeting. But for the sake of propriety and the pleasures of courtship he delays. A few months later they marry. There are those who think they should wait—these are, after all, the toughest of times. But he and Vera say their marriage is for the revolution, it is for the future. They move in with his parents, into a pocket of space partitioned off by a bookcase and a curtain of newsprint. Two years later their baby son, Mikhail, joins them in their cubbyhole.

Like all young Bolsheviks, Yuri and Vera have always believed that come the revolution, all aspects of daily life would improve. But the new revolutionary society seems not to be working as it should, and many, indeed most hardships remain unchanged. They rationalise that it is, after all, only the earliest of days in a social program that is radical in every respect; that they must try to curb their impatience and, most of all, they must trust in Lenin. So when Vladimir Ilyich introduces his New Economic Policy they opt for a positive stance, even though they have some concerns. The new regulations under the NEP allow for a limited amount of private enterprise; the government hopes that concessions like this will fire up Russia's economy. Yuri and Vera talk quietly together in their corner of the *kommunalka* while little Misha sleeps beside them; they wonder whether any level of private ownership can exist without resulting in inequality and exploitation. In the end, like most of their Bolshevik friends, they decide to accept the risks for a measure of peace and stability.

And life does improve. Food and material goods become more plentiful, buses and trams are more reliable, and there is even the possibility of a place of their own. So many positive changes as a result of the NEP, yet they hear of bourgeois excesses, they see over-consumption by a few to the detriment of the many, and they know there are people who are profiting over and above their needs.

The revolutionary state will eventually be built, they have no doubt of this, although they now realise it will take a good deal longer than they originally thought. Their trust in Lenin remains inviolate; it never occurs to them he won't see the revolutionary transformation to its conclusion. So when his death is announced in the winter of 1924, it initially makes no sense. The great revolutionary leader dead? It's not possible. He's only fifty-three. He's their leader. He wasn't even sick. And when the truth does finally bite, they are heartbroken, all the people are. Their grief over Vladimir Ilyich is compounded by their fears for the revolution: with so much still to be done, the great and glorious future is in peril.

Their mood remains sombre, their fears will not settle. They're aware of skirmishes among the potential successors, but the details are shuttered off from ordinary people. When Stalin emerges as the new leader, their anxieties ease. They know Stalin has a special understanding of the workers; he's a committed revolutionary, a man of action, and he's young. They hear rumours that some among the powerful are unhappy about the new leader, and that Lenin himself did not choose Stalin as his successor, but in a country where rumours blow through the landscape on the daily winds, Yuri and Vera choose to ignore them.

Their support for Stalin is vindicated when he announces his five-year plan. This strategy, with its large-scale collectivisation of farms in rural areas and industrialisation in the cities, will reverse the compromises made to private ownership by the NEP and, at the same time, restore the ideals of the revolution. With his plan, Stalin promises that the Union of Soviet Socialist Republics, established just a few years earlier, will be the envy of the world.

Vera's second pregnancy coincides with Stalin's announcement. Both within the Kogan home and further abroad in the vast Soviet territories, there's reason for optimism. In 1928, in the early days of the five-year plan, Yuri and Vera's daughter, Lidiya, is born. She arrives early by a full month, and is taken from the maternity hospital to the city shelter for premature children. For five long weeks, the longest of her life, Vera says, mother and infant are separated. When the baby is finally permitted to come home, Vera vows there will be no more separations for her family: the four of them will enjoy a long and fruitful life together in the new Russia.

In the years to come, Soviet lifetimes will prove precariously short. But for the moment, everyday life has improved for the Kogans. Yuri holds a senior post at ZAGS, and Vera is working at the new Institute of Languages; like other party members, their positions appear to be secure. Best of all, they have been given a place of their own. In a building not far from Yuri's parents, they have been allocated what they regard as two rooms, but because the partition separating the two areas does not reach the ceiling, officially the space is designated as a single room. Two for the price of one, they joke. Within the rooms they have partitioned off smaller spaces, using bookcases and other furniture. The kitchen down one end of the passage, and the bathroom and toilet down the other are shared with only three other families, all of whom appear to be good and friendly folk. The wallpaper is only lightly marked, the *burzhuika* burns well, and their window faces south. And while there are ancient stains stretched like stormy clouds across the ceiling, it is a negligible failing when everything else is so favourable.

Perhaps because of Lidiya's shaky start in life, or perhaps because Vera is more confident with a second child, she raises Lidiya differently from Mikhail. Despite the party's insistence on exactly five feeds per twenty-four-hour period, Vera feeds Lidiya whenever she thinks she's hungry; she picks her up whenever she cries, and she lavishes cuddles and kisses on her even though the party forbids such behaviour as unhygienic. Vera ignores practically all the party stipulations regarding the emotional hygiene of the Soviet baby.

'I'm the mother,' she says to Yuri. 'I know what's best for our child.'

In all other respects, however, she and Yuri remain good party members, though not without their concerns — different concerns now for these different times. Enemies of the people exist in what seem to be extraordinary numbers: priests, kulaks, bourgeois elements of all kinds. And despite what the party says, food shortages are worse than ever. Many is the night when Yuri and Vera go to sleep hungry, and they know their circumstances are better than most. When their doubts intrude too loudly, they have to remind themselves they are making history, that nothing like the Bolshevik state has existed before, and with so much needing to change, of course there will be occasional setbacks.

Huge posters adorn the streets and buildings. Some warn against enemies of the people, others depict industrious workers with complex machinery, most display the greatness and goodness of Stalin. A large number of the posters portray happy workers on collective farms, with lush fields of grain, carts laden with vegetables, and animals fatted for eating. So much produce in the posters, so little food in the shops.

Vera and Yuri know that as educated people and party members, they are not the target population for the posters: they don't need convincing of the necessity for change. But still there are many that give them pause.

'These posters, they're so —' Vera searches for the right word.

'Banal?' suggests Yuri.

'No.' She is shaking her head slowly. 'Not banal. They're exaggerated. They push the point too hard. They're verging on the comical, the absurd.'

They've stopped in front of a poster they've not seen before, although at five below with a fierce wind raging they'll not be stopping long. The poster seems more incongruous because the main figure, a happy boy of twelve or thirteen, is wearing short pants and a light shirt. This smug, summery youth fills half the poster. The other half is taken up by eight male heads, eight villains with evil expressions, each wearing a distinctive and readily identifiable hat. Among these enemies of the people are a monarchist, a capitalist,

100

a Menshevik, and an anti-Bolshevik general. The caption reads: 'It is a happy citizen who is acquainted with these types only from books.'

'It's no different from a cartoon,' Vera says.

'Exactly, and that's why it'll reach a good many Russians. It's clear and simple and strongly pictorial.'

'Maybe that's the problem,' Vera says, adjusting her scarf and hat so only her eyes behind her spectacles are visible. 'What appeals to many Russians does not to us.'

'Us?'

She has moved to another poster. It portrays an assortment of happy, healthy workers: miners, industrial workers, farm labourers. Presiding over the group is a proud, paternal Stalin.

'Where are we?' Vera says, nodding at the poster. 'Where are the intellectuals?'

Yuri moves closer, his arm presses against hers. 'I don't think that pictures of solemn, bespectacled men and women huddled over books would provide the right impression of our revolution,' he says quietly.

Vera removes her own fogged-up glasses, rubs them with a gloved thumb and replaces them. She peers more closely at the poster.

'We're never in the pictures.'

'Does that matter? After all, we don't need convincing.'

'But we're workers too.'

'These poster people represent an ideal, something for ordinary citizens to strive for during these unsettling times.'

'So these happy Soviet citizens,' Vera points at the poster, 'they don't really exist?'

'Hush,' Yuri hisses. 'Hush.' He grabs the offending hand, and pulls her away.

Collectivisation is the centrepiece of Stalin's five-year plan: huge farms with new equipment for more efficient production and greater yields. No one would challenge the benefits, but the implementation is testing the entire country. Stories of rich kulaks abound: their illegal trading and private ownership, their hoarding of grain that rightfully belongs to all the people, their refusal to work for the common good. These rich peasants are being rooted out and imprisoned, their land and livestock confiscated. Many have been executed.

Six months later, Yuri and Vera are standing in front of another poster, this one displayed outside a bakery. The corners have curled and the colours have been blanched by flour and sunlight, but the picture remains very striking. Most of the poster is taken up with a gargantuan female farm-worker painted in shades of red, and carrying a rake in her right hand. Her other hand is stretched out in warning, a stay-away gesture to a priest and two kulaks—three tiny grey figures who scarcely come up to her knees. The caption reads, 'There is no room in our collective farm for priests and kulaks.'

'There seem to be so many of them,' Vera says to Yuri. 'Not priests, but kulaks. How can there be so many rich peasants and all of them enemies of the people?'

Yuri hushes her, as he needs to do increasingly in these testing days. But as reports multiply of the huge numbers of kulaks arrested for wrongdoing, it is hard not to question.

As for the good peasants, there are shocking rumours: millions of them have died of starvation, and entire communities have been wiped out. There is a scattering of ghost villages across the land.

'Not even the old aristocracy with all their greed and violence could claim such high casualties,' Vera says.

The political leaders talk of the need to bear hardships now for the better future ahead. But as the number of dead mount, the cost exacted by the future seems shockingly high.

And yet it seems the leaders are right again. By the mid-1930s, after the hard years of collectivisation and the worst famine in living memory, the scaffolding of the new Soviet state is in place. The people are told of huge productive farms in the countryside, and of large-scale industrialisation in the cities. They hear of the successes blared through loudspeakers, they read about them in newspapers, they see them emblazoned across posters. The leader's speeches are full of them. And they also hear that the whole world is watching the Soviet Union, that proletarians across the globe are uniting, that International Socialism will soon be realised. With so much at stake, it comes as no surprise to Yuri and Vera that Stalin orders the All-Union Population Census. Stalin wants hard proof of his successes.

Yuri and Vera should be gratified that their long-held ideals have finally been realised. But — and they could never have predicted this — they are no longer the confident revolutionaries they once were. They haven't lost their faith in socialist principles, but they can't, like many of their neighbours and colleagues, ignore the contradictions. There are power failures and gas leaks, they ride to work in rickety trams, people are cold and hungry, shops are empty of goods, tuberculosis is rampant, school-aged children wander the streets, and drunk men lie slumped in doorways.

'They're twisting the language to make us believe lies,' Vera says to Yuri at the end of another weary day.

The Kogans have finished their dinner. The dishes from their meal are stacked up ready to be taken to the kitchen for washing; Lidiya is reading and Mikhail is doing puzzles. With the children close by, Vera keeps her voice low.

'They're lying to us, Yuri. We're told that happiness is living in the Soviet Union under the protection of our great leader Stalin. But look at the reality.' She takes a deep breath, and the words pour out of her. 'We live in a room with four people and share a bathroom with fourteen. It's been months since we last saw a piece of fruit. Our shoes are reinforced with cardboard and our socks are a tangle of darning. The electricity is unreliable; for hours at a time we're reduced to using candles, and the supply of candles invariably falls short of the demand. In the battle between a heated building and the freezing months of winter, it's the winter that always wins. The faucet in the bathroom has been broken for six months, and there's no indication it'll be fixed any time soon. I've spent a fair percentage of the past year queuing for goods that have often disappeared by the time I reach the top of the line. No matter that we feel demoralised and miserable, this, according to our great Soviet leaders, is happiness.'

Yuri is about to speak, to placate his wife. But Vera is not finished.

'I've no complaint against the Department for Agitation and Propaganda. After all, there's nothing wrong with persuasion, not when the message is right. But what if persuasion takes a form that obfuscates the truth? Even deliberately deceives?'

Snow is still on the ground, the river is still under ice, and heaped across the river's frozen surface and creating a weird, other-worldly vista are icy hillocks now grey in the grimy air. The cityscape remains locked in winter, but already the days are longer, and at seven o'clock it is light outside. Yuri twists around and pulls the curtain across the window.

Vera is speaking quietly, but her distress is quite clear. 'How would we know?' she continues. 'After all, if propaganda is effective you don't recognise you're in its grip.'

He shakes his head slowly, he has no more answers than does Vera. What they both do know is to keep their doubts to themselves. There are spies at work, spies in the kitchen, spies on the stairs, spies on the trolley bus, spies in the shop queues. People denounce others before they themselves are denounced. People denounce in order to prove their loyalty.

Yuri, like so many mathematicians, is recruited to work on the All-Union Population Census. In what appears to be grand work for the society he has long believed in, he buries his small doubts, and he's determined to convince Vera to do the same with her larger ones. He tells her that the census, ordered by Stalin himself, will prove the success of the revolution.

Throughout 1936, Yuri is absent from Leningrad for weeks at a time, working in Moscow with other mathematicians and social scientists preparing the census. This huge enterprise, they are told, will be a triumph for socialism: it will reveal the extent to which living standards have improved, it will provide scientific proof of the success of Stalin's reforms, and it will boost the people's faith in the revolutionary project. Hundreds of thousands of volunteers have been recruited for this mammoth national undertaking.

After one sojourn in Moscow, Yuri returns home full of excitement. 'I've seen Stalin's handwriting,' he tells Vera and the children. 'Corrections, in his own hand, on one of the drafts of the census. That's how committed he is to this project. Our General Secretary takes time out of his busy schedule to edit the questions.'

It is summer. The days stretch long into the night, the Leningrad winds are softer, and according to Yuri, there's a mood of optimism throughout the country. He is convinced that Stalin would not be putting so much faith in the census unless he knew it would prove the success of his reforms.

'If he knows so much,' Vera the pragmatist says, 'then why do we need a national census at all?'

Yuri laughs. 'Hard data is better than hearsay. And besides, there are foreigners to convince. Communism is for the world, not just for Russia.'

Vera is not laughing. 'You're sounding like a sloganeer yourself.'

Misha glares at his mother. What would she know about the real Russia? What would she know about anything, holed up at her institute with her students and her translations? He's proud of his father's work. His father is working for Comrade Stalin, and when he's older he, Mikhail Yuryevich Kogan, will work for Comrade Stalin too. In the meantime, he's determined to be the first of his Pioneers group to be invited to join the Komsomol, and then, in another couple of years … well, he has plans.

Not that he's been unhappy as a Pioneer. He's loved the rules and rituals, the games and other activities, and best of all he's loved being part of the struggle to liberate the labouring classes of the world. A year ago, in probably his greatest triumph during his time as a Pioneer, he was promoted to events secretary at the Pioneer Palace. This would have been an honour wherever it might have happened, but everyone knows that the Leningrad Pioneer Palace is the best in all of the Soviet Union. Their palace really is a palace, the former Anichkov Palace, where the last czar was born.

Within a few months and not long before census day Mikhail is a new member of the Komsomol. He puts himself forward for every task, he can't do too much — although he needs to be careful, there are whispers, jibes, about the young, pushy Jew. Not that he's aware, he's happier than he's ever been. He plans to take on leadership responsibilities at the first opportunity, and while he is not in the top academic level at school, he consoles himself with the thought that Stalin wasn't a top student either while the traitor Trotsky was. Mikhail is planning his future. Stalin has surrounded himself with powerful people, many of whom have been drawn from the military or the NKVD, so there's much to recommend both options. Most of his friends want to be mechanical engineers attached to industry, or construction engineers involved in Stalin's massive building projects, but Mikhail wants a bigger canvas: he wants to take part in shaping the entire country.

Lidiya has been a member of the Octobrists since she was seven. She doesn't want to recite the rhymes they're forced to learn, she doesn't care for the games they're told to play, and she doesn't like the songs that make up the Octobrist musical canon. She says it's all too childish. With another eighteen months before she's old enough for the Pioneers, she is refusing to attend her Octobrist group. While Vera, more than Yuri, has some sympathy for her daughter's position, she knows there's no place for defiance or independence in today's Russia.

'How can our children be so different?' she says to Yuri one evening after a particularly trying day with Lidiya. 'Misha could be a poster boy for Soviet youth.' She sees Yuri is about to interrupt, and quickly continues. 'He'll be fine, he wants to fit in, he wants to do everything his country tells him. It's far more difficult for our daughter, with a mind of her own and an imagination that owes more to Krylov and H.G. Wells—'

And now Yuri does interrupt. 'Our eight-year-old daughter is reading H.G. Wells?'

Vera laughs. 'Not yet, but it won't be long. She took my English copy of *The Time Machine* from the shelf and was curious about the script. After I explained about Cyrillic and Latin scripts, she wanted me to tell her the story of the novel.' Vera shrugs. 'What could I do?'

Census day is now just weeks away. Everything is in place. Printing presses across the nation are clacking away, and forms are stacked and packed, ready to be sent to far-flung regions. An army of enumerators has been trained to conduct the census, tens of thousands of staff have been recruited to tabulate the answers, and hundreds of statisticians are on hand to analyse the data. Everything is running to schedule, yet now Yuri is worried. He's more worried than he's ever been.

The problem is Stalin—not that Yuri voices this to anyone other than Vera, and even then the words feel like traitors in his mouth. Stalin has made it very clear that he expects the census to portray a citizenry whose belief in the revolution is rock-solid. It will show that no one wants or needs religion anymore; indeed, so convinced is Stalin of the success of the campaign against Russian Orthodoxy, he's insisted that a question about religious affiliation be included for the first time on a national census. Stalin also expects the population of Russia and the Soviet Republics to come in at an absolute minimum of one hundred and seventy million — he actually expects it to be much higher. The population figure is, he says, of the utmost importance. It will provide hard evidence of improved diet and living conditions, as well as better health services and housing; it will reveal an increase in the birth rate and a decrease in the infant mortality rate, and, most importantly, it will demonstrate the success of collectivisation and industrialisation, his signature policies.

Yuri has done some preliminary figures based on the 1926 census, and there is good reason to worry. If there had been no campaign against the kulaks, if there had been fewer enemies of the people, if instead of famine and cholera there really had been better housing and hygiene, it is possible the population might stretch to one hundred and sixty-seven million — still short of what Stalin expects. And with disease, overcrowding and sanitary conditions as bad as ever, Yuri fears there will actually be increases in infant and child deaths, and a seriously blighted birth rate. The scientist in him welcomes the census to set matters straight, but the Russian in him tells him that the science of the All-Union Census has acquired a political agenda.

A mere forty-eight hours after census day, and Yuri knows he has been right to worry. The population figure will fall well short of Stalin's minimum. But as bad as this is, it is not the only concern. On the census forms, unambiguously defiant, citizens in their millions have described themselves as Christian. (And whose decision was it to include a question about religious belief?) There's the population problem and the religion problem, but equally shocking is that the census has given voice to the disgruntled whispers that have rustled

108

through Soviet life for so long: in the margins of the census forms citizens have vented their discontent. Complaints and insults, anger and criticisms dirty the perfect results that Stalin requires — the perfect results the enumerators should have elicited. The census is a disaster. The people higher up are informed. No one wants to tell Stalin, no one wants to be the bearer of such news. But of course he must be told.

The All-Union Census of 1937 is immediately buried. Over the next several months the data is collected in secret, analysed in secret, and locked away.

'Why bother to keep it at all?' Vera whispers to Yuri, one morning, in menacing 2.00 a.m. wakefulness.

Yuri shrugs. 'Perhaps Stalin has another use for it. Or perhaps he'll prove the people don't know what's good for them. Perhaps he has plans to discredit the census with a follow-up study.' None of which Yuri believes; he's a mathematician, he knows the results are correct. It's impossible to predict the General Secretary's actions, but what is beyond doubt is that the data as it now stands undermines the Great Leader's work.

While the census data is analysed and stored where no one can see or destroy it, those who have worked on it, particularly those in positions of responsibility, are far more exposed. The repercussions are felt almost immediately. In the first weeks after the census, several workers in Yuri's division disappear. He is surprised at the choice of these targets.

'They were middle-level,' he says to Vera. 'None was involved in the framing of the census.'

'But perhaps they were among the first to identify a problem with the results.'

It's another long night, Mikhail and Lidiya are asleep. Yuri and Vera are huddled together by the stove, trying to find patterns, reasons, explanations — not that reason has ever enjoyed top billing in explaining the workings of the Soviet leadership. Outside, winter rages. The window rattles, the wind howls, ice dashes against the glass.

'These are only the first arrests,' Yuri says softly.

The dark days grind on. Yuri is desperate to sever ties with the census and return to his old demography work. But without permission — and he won't ask, won't draw attention to himself — he must remain where he is. As one of the senior officers on the census, it is his task to apportion the questions to be analysed. It has come down from on high that if each analyst sees only one question, they'll remain ignorant of the general thrust of the results. This is nonsense, but nonetheless Yuri, like everyone else, plays his part in the deception. The work is cloaked in secrecy; all those employed are aware that even a whisper could jeopardise not simply their livelihood, but their life. People are being arrested all the time, and as one of the leaders both in the planning and the analysis of the census, Yuri knows it's only a matter of time before they come for him.

Whether at home or at work, these are perilous days. Yuri and Vera are watchful on the stairs, they're watchful in the street, they're watchful on trams and buses. Out in public, their conversation is empty; in shops, where informers are rife, they're silent. Even where they believe themselves to be safe, they speak in whispers. Their voices became more and more hushed as the days stretch out of winter.

The essence of terror, the *terror* of terror, is helplessness. Yuri and Vera know there's a disaster heading their way and there is nothing they can do to stop it. The NKVD always comes at night. Yuri and Vera hardly sleep anymore, and when they do, they never properly undress. Just that week, Vera packed the winter bedding away in the trunk. The bed is strangely flat, their own bodies making only the slightest mounds.

'It's not just me in the firing line.'

Yuri is warning Vera — not that she needs reminding — that when one member of a family is taken, others are likely to follow.

It's the price exacted by the state, and the cost of the better future. Vera is not one of those disenchanted Bolsheviks who cast a sentimental and distorting gaze back to the czars. But this, she says, what they have now, is not how it was supposed to be.

Lidiya feels the tension at home. Her mother is nervy, and her father, whom she hardly saw during the busy months leading up to the census, is now home every evening, often earlier than her mother. She watches him sitting in his armchair, a book face-down on his knee, his forehead crinkled with worries. She wishes she could think of something to make him feel better. Her brother seems unaware that anything is wrong; he is full of the Komsomol. He talks incessantly of new friends and experiences, the drills and exercises; he boasts that Komsomol members are being recruited to hand out flyers and put up posters; they're even being used for crowd control. He says Komsomol members are told to keep their eyes and ears open; enemies of the people, he says, are everywhere. None of these tasks appeals to Lidiya, and she hopes that by the time she reaches Komsomol age the tasks will have changed. Misha spends less and less time at home; sometimes he stays away all night. 'On Komsomol business,' he says.

Like all Soviet children, Lidiya knows about Pavlik, the most famous Pioneer of all. A few years earlier, Pavlik and his younger brother were murdered by kulaks. After the deaths, it emerged that Pavlik had informed on his own father. Pavlik not only became a martyr to the great Bolshevik cause, but he was held up as a model for all children, a boy who was such a good Pioneer that he put his country ahead of his father.

Lidiya would never do as Pavlik did. Always she will be child to her parents first and a Pioneer or Komsomol member second; she cannot imagine a life without her mother and father. She is sure her brother holds a different view. Increasingly these days, Misha makes her uneasy, and she is relieved when he is not at home.

111

It is a mild night in mid-May when they come for Yuri Kogan. The air is still, the sky brilliant with stars, the moon a delicate sliver. Two vehicles pull up in the street. The stutter and burr of the dying engines is loud in the tranquil night. In the *kommunalka* everyone hears, everyone fears, for in the tumultuous times of 1937 this is not the first time the NKVD has come. Once, the Kogans might have felt safe in the knowledge that those who were taken must have erred in some way, but that was before the census.

Yuri and Vera are not asleep, they hear the cars in the street. As doors slam, and rough voices rise through the calm night air, they leap out of bed. They pull on their shoes — they're already dressed — and wake Lidiya. She requires no explanation and quickly dresses herself. They hear voices and the clatter of boots on the stairs. Misha is already dressed; he's standing at attention in full view of anyone entering the room. The footsteps stop; they've reached the third floor. Vera takes Lidiya by the hand, and they stand together in front of the window in a direct line to the door. Yuri positions himself on her other side and calls to his son. Misha doesn't move; he holds himself apart from the family. All four of them stare at the door. The steps draw closer. The boots stop. Fists strike the wood.

Lidiya has only just turned nine, but for the rest of her life she'll remember every detail of that terrible night, lodged in her mind as a series of discrete snapshots. There are five men standing in a semicircle around the open door. Three take charge of her father, three huge men to escort her *papochka* to goodness knows where. The other two will remain to collect evidence.

Her father is protesting, his voice shaky. 'I'm a member of the party, I work for the party. I believe in our great Motherland. The General Secretary has my loyalty. I love Comrade Stalin. I've done nothing wrong. There's been a mistake.'

Lidiya wants to run to him, hold on to him, drag him away from these men. She believes her father, he never lies. But the men are unmoved. 'The party doesn't make mistakes,' one of them says, using exactly the same words she's heard from her father's lips.

'It's a mistake,' he says again, reaching for Vera's hand. Her mother doesn't need to be told. She knows, like Lidiya knows, but it makes no difference to the officers.

Her parents kiss, her father's hand strokes her mother's cheek. He then turns to her. He lifts her up and holds her tight; his cheek is rough, he smells of tobacco and bedtime. And if she'd known this would be the last time she would ever see her father, would she have held on longer? Asked for some special words, or offered him some of her own? Snuggled into his neck so as never to forget the feel of him? The regrets will come later, but for now everything is smothered in fear and hope. Her father puts her down and approaches Misha to embrace him. Misha stops him with an outstretched arm. Her brother does not smile, he does not speak, his gaze flits to the watching officers, he wants them to notice.

Her father certainly does. He shakes his head slowly, and looks very sad. He turns to her mother. 'I'll be back soon. The party knows I've done nothing wrong.'

The big men hustle him through the door. 'A mistake has been made,' he says from the passage.

The two remaining men ransack the Kogan home. They pull books from shelves, and clothes from racks; they haul cartons from the high compartments, and drag bags from cupboards; they break bowls and plates, they toss ornaments aside. The floor disappears beneath the wreckage. And through it all, her mother is saying: there's nothing to find, we are good Soviet citizens, we are party members.

They have a sack into which they put books and papers; in another sack they put the valuables: a kiddush cup studded with colourful stones, a small brass menorah that belonged to Vera's parents, Yuri's new boots, Vera's amber ring, Lidiya's doll. They pick up Mikhail's soccer ball, but after glancing at the stern, silent boy, they put it down again. They take and take, and at last they leave.

There is laughter as they clatter down the stairs. There's laughter as they enter the street. Lidiya stands at one side of the window, hidden by the curtain. She sees the light from their torches leaping and dancing across the building opposite; she doesn't understand how torchlight can be so scary. She sees the men toss one sack into the back of the car and take the other into the front. She sees quite clearly the Kogan family kiddush cup: while one man holds the torch, the other tries to prise the stones loose.

The car won't start. The coughs and complaints of the protesting motor rise high above the street and enter the despoiled space of Kogan family life. There are raised voices and curses, and more spluttering from the car engine. In the end the men are forced to push-start the car. At the street corner the engine kicks over, they jump into their seats, slam the doors, and disappear.

Every morning for the next three weeks, Vera Kogan goes to the Big House with provisions for her husband and questions for any official who will speak to her. The queue is long, some days she does not reach the top of the line. She will never know if Yuri receives her parcels. Every evening and long into the night, she calls on friends and colleagues of her husband, most of whom are reluctant to speak to her, much less offer help. Vera writes letters to party officials, she writes to the local Soviet deputy, she writes several times to Stalin himself. At the same time, knowing that she, too, could be arrested, she needs to make plans to keep her children safe.

Misha wants nothing to do with his father's arrest. At fifteen, he might still be a child to his mother, but this is a boy who stubbornly knows his own mind. The morning after Yuri is taken, Misha slips out of the flat carrying a box of possessions. He leaves a note for Vera—not to allay her anxiety, so Lidiya will come to believe, but to stop her from attempting to find him. He writes that he will be staying with Komsomol friends, older fellows who will see to his welfare.

As always, Lidiya takes a different approach. She tries to reassure her mother with hugs and soothing words, she stands in line at shops, she helps prepare their meals. The other women who share the kitchen assiduously ignore both mother and daughter. They have their own families to protect.

Lidiya might well be old beyond her years, but at nine years of age she still needs looking after. Vera goes to see Marya, an old friend of her own mother. There are no grandparents, she explains. Nothing stands between the children and an orphanage if Vera is arrested. Neither she nor Yuri are enemies of the people so they should be released within a short time. While she says this without hesitation, she knows nothing is certain in these precarious times.

Marya needs no convincing. She packs a bag, and moves in with Vera and Lidiya. Should they come for Vera, it will be Marya, born more than sixty years earlier, a woman of the old school who secretly believes that despite the greatness of Lenin and Stalin, God in Heaven is far greater, who will look after Lidiya—and Mikhail, too, should he return.

Another night, and more boots in the passage, this time marching towards Vera. They check Marya's passport and push her aside; they glance at Lidiya and push her aside too. It's Vera they want. Two men take her away; two others remain for a perfunctory search. When they've finished, they pause in the open doorway, turn to face Marya and Lidiya, make a threatening gesture, and leave.

Mikhail does not return. Neither does Vera nor Yuri. It's just Marya and Lidiya alone in the rooms at the *kommunalka*. Later, Lidiya will discover that her father was shot within days of his arrest. Her mother takes longer to die in the freezing plains of a Siberian labour camp. The official cause of her death is tuberculosis. It is more acceptable than exposure and starvation.

Four months after both parents are taken, nine packages

115

addressed to Yuri in Vera's handwriting are delivered to the *kommunalka*. These are the parcels left by Vera at the Big House to be passed on to her husband; the fresh food has been removed, and each parcel neatly resealed. The return of the parcels is code that Yuri is dead. The sick irony of this occurs to Lidiya only when she is older: that here is a regime which commits murder as frequently and as inconsequentially as an eye-blink, but could never be accused of petty theft.

In these days of terror, it is common to see grandmothers caring for young children. These poor mites suffering the loss of their parents are now forced to hide their grief, for the taint of parents condemned as enemies of the people flows through to the children. Marya instructs Lidiya that if asked about Vera and Yuri, she is to say they are away, doing important work for the Soviet republics. Lidiya has to appear happy, she must behave as if the parents she loves have not disappeared, she must stifle her great sorrow.

There come to be two epochs for Lidiya: the time before her parents are taken and the time after. In the new era, her parents are gone, her brother is gone, food shrinks to kasha and cabbage, clothes are patched, and shoes are improvised. And who does she blame? She blames Stalin, 'the best friend to all children', and she will never forgive him.

There is no hope. Forced to live her life in the negative, Lidiya nonetheless attends school, she does her lessons, she plays with her classmates. She does exactly what is expected of her as if nothing has changed, as if her days are not scarred by loss.

'We have to be careful,' Marya says, as she cuddles the child in her ancient arms and promises never to leave her.

And although Lidiya wants her mother, wants her so badly that her whole body hurts, she knows she has to be brave, she has to be grown up.

It has been decided.

Twenty-two years later, Lidiya herself became mother to a daughter. She looked down at the infant and swore she would protect her from all harm. For the first decade of Galina's life, Lidiya never spoke of her own parents, and for the next decade only sparingly: she was determined to spare her daughter the penalties of a spoiled biography. By the time of Brezhnev's funeral and the glimpse of Mikhail, Galina was no longer a child, and what little faith in the Soviet system remained to Lidiya after her parents were taken was killed off during the war. There was such inhuman suffering when Leningrad was under siege, such neglect from the central authorities, that Lidiya emerged from those nine hundred days decanted of any patriotism or desire for it. So when Mikhail appeared on the TV displaying the rewards of a life without a spoiled biography, Lidiya broke her silence.

By the time Galina left the Soviet Union, the story of her mother's family had been told and retold. She had stored it in the safest chamber of memory, where it lay with a strange and quiet volatility. Through the many retellings, her mother's history, so powerful and vivid, had become her history: the threat of those times, the fear, the terrible loss of a mother and a father, the shocking betrayal of a son and brother. And she, too, had come to hate Mikhail.

The story had expanded since Galina had come to Australia with all she had read about Soviet Russia. She'd been appalled to learn what the great revolution had cost the Russian people — the deliberate starvation of entire communities, the millions of deaths, the lies of the leaders. It was like suddenly discovering that a parent or a sibling, someone very close to you, was a vicious killer. And even if only a fraction of the claims were true, Soviet society had been, and probably remained, monstrously cruel, and Soviet leaders possessed of as little regard for its citizens as the wind had for the clouds it pushed around. She used to believe that in order to remain sane in a repressive regime, memory was forced to discard what it simply could not bear to hold. But the fact was, her own mother and people like her did not forget. Perhaps forgetting was the exclusive prerogative of the perpetrators, providing them with a well-oiled gateway to a guiltless future.

Here in sunny Melbourne, Galina saw happy faces and carefree children; there was freedom and opportunity in this country, but most of all there was an absence of fear. Yet she was all too aware that she, a Russian Jew, was formed by Russia—the Russia of her lifetime and the earlier Russia of her mother and grandparents. She might well be surrounded by freedom and delight, but she carried her past with her. It was as if she were inhabiting two lives simultaneously, and much of the time they were not an easy fit.

To know her past was to go some way to knowing her, so perhaps it would help if she were to share it with some Australians. Andrew perhaps. Take him back as a guest through the Brezhnev years to Khrushchev and her own birth, back to Stalin, the war, the terror, the revolution, back to the beginning. This, she might say to him, this is how I came to be who I am. She considered this only for a moment before letting it go. She suspected that to speak in Australia of her past was as impossible as it had been in the Soviet Union.

7

LANDMARKS OF A LIFE

A few days after their trip to Victoria Market, Andrew telephoned Galina—not to arrange a visit to his studio as she had expected, but to invite her to his parents' place for dinner.

'It was my mother's suggestion,' he said.

Inviting strangers to your home and feeding them was a Russian gesture, not an Australian one, and Galina wondered why the mother would invite her. What could she possibly want?

'She thought you might welcome a home-cooked meal.'

As so often happened in this new life, Galina didn't know what she *wanted* to do about this dinner invitation, nor what she *should* do. Exasperated with herself—why did everything have to be so complicated?—she decided to take the invitation at face value.

'Thank you,' she said. 'Tell your mother I am happy to accept.'

Andrew proposed a number of dates. Galina chose an evening a couple of weeks away to give herself time to prepare—not that it helped, because when the day finally arrived she was more rattled than she would have thought possible. It was a simple dinner, she told herself, and while it was at an Australian home with strangers, she had managed far more difficult situations in the past. She needed to calm down.

Andrew said he'd pick her up early to show her some of Melbourne—'My Melbourne,' was the way he expressed it—and at exactly five o'clock he arrived. She had bought a new dress for the occasion. It was a colourful Asian design, light and pretty, and typical of what Australian girls were wearing this summer; she had teamed the dress with a pair of red sandals. (She had tried the thongs so popular here, but the bit between the toes might have been a tree trunk, for all the discomfort it caused.) As soon as she opened the door, she realised she would need a jacket; the sun was still bright but the wind had swung from north to south and it was quite chilly. Too bad about the summery casual Australian look she was aiming for. She had given up on her hair, having first tried it loose (it reminded her of a giant dandelion), then half of it tied back (like a giant dandelion half blown away), then a plait (too Russian), and a bun (too severe), and in the end bundled it loosely in a clasp at her neck. She grabbed her coat from the hook—not what she had planned at all—and locked the door.

Andrew, stiff and silent during the walk to the car, started talking before she had belted herself into the seat. He talked as if he couldn't stop. Today, less than an hour ago, a lone gunman had marched into the central post office and killed eight people.

'Here, in Melbourne, in 1987, for God's sake. We're not fighting a war, we don't have ethnic disputes. Yet eight people are dead. The gunman, too. Jumped from a window. It's a massacre. Eight innocent people. Random targets.'

His words were boiling over. It was hard to make sense of them.

'Listen,' he said, turning up the volume on the radio.

There was mayhem in central Melbourne. Witnesses to the tragedy spoke in staccato gasps, a relay of shock, horror, and incomprehension.

'We're turning into America,' Andrew said, manoeuvring the car for a right-hand turn into Hoddle Street. His words seemed squeezed through a too-small throat. 'And just a few months ago a young guy, younger than me, pulled out a gun and killed several people, just up the road from here.' Andrew jerked his head to the left.

'What motivates someone to act like this? Such senseless violence. Although does any violence make sense?' He paused as a driver cut in front of them. 'What makes these guys think it's okay to kill? Kill randomly. What is it? A sense of power? Uncontrollable anger? Insanity?'

At which point, Galina had to interrupt. 'Do not use the insane excuse.'

She spoke more sharply than she intended, and immediately saw his confusion, his hurt, too—his was such a transparent face. Quickly, she explained how in Soviet Russia labelling someone insane was a method of silencing and removing dissenters. 'There was a time,' she shrugged, 'I expect it still continues, when mental asylums in the Soviet Union were full of dissidents, all of them as sane as you and I.'

'All right then, not the insane excuse —'

But she hadn't finished. 'Tyrants from Caligula to Hitler, and Stalin too, are often described as insane. When you label someone mad, you release them from responsibility. But these men know exactly what they are doing. Brutality, it seems to me, is a distressingly common human attribute.'

It was a conversation stopper, and whatever Andrew had planned to say was left stranded. The radio station was still covering the massacre; more onlookers were being interviewed, and specialist commentators consulted. After a while, Andrew turned the volume down.

'What makes a sane person,' he paused, 'or rather what makes a sane man—it's always a man—think he has a right to kill a whole bunch of strangers who've never done him any harm?'

Andrew seemed so upset that Galina wondered if he'd known someone killed at the post office. She was about to ask when he spoke again.

'Do these appalling acts, these lone-men massacres, happen in your country?'

The irony did not escape her: she might wait weeks for someone to ask her about Russia, and when finally a question is pitched her way, it lands in territory she'd prefer not to enter. She was framing an answer that would shift the conversation to more neutral ground, some sort of disinfected version of Soviet killings, when he turned towards her and she saw a man struggling to understand what was to him utterly incomprehensible. She wanted to comfort him, to lay a gentle hand upon his arm; instead, she clasped her hands together and attempted an explanation.

'Our massacres are different,' she began. 'Our massacres tend to be committed by our political leaders, not rogue gunmen. And the deaths are likely to be in the thousands, even millions.'

She was aware of a skirmishing of emotions: shame because these atrocities happened in her country, anger and resentment that she and all ordinary Soviet citizens had been so thoroughly duped, and bewilderment at the warped morality that would permit fellow Russians to act in so barbaric a manner. She was filtering information, wondering what details would best bring the topic to a close, when Andrew solved the issue for her.

'That's my old school,' he said, pointing to a huge place on a hill.

It looked like an English castle, replete with turrets and battlements. As if he had guessed her thoughts, he added, 'It's known as "The castle on the hill".'

The place looked extremely grand. 'Your parents must be very rich.'

He shook his head. 'No. We're what we in Australia call middle class.' He paused before adding, 'It's a government high school for boys.'

She gazed up at Andrew's school, and felt a twist of envy — nothing to do with the grandeur of the place, it was its mere presence. She couldn't pass a school and say 'That's the school I attended'; she couldn't identify an apartment building and say 'That's where I grew up'. She couldn't point to the granite embankments of

122

the Neva where she watched the ships, or the Tauride Palace where she went for the children's concerts. Without her own landmarks, her Soviet self, still so dominant in her, became impossible to share with others, and what they saw was an amputated version of who she believed herself to be. There were times when she felt a stranger even to herself.

Leningrad landmarks, experiences and friends explained who she was and how she had come to be this way. Forced to live detached from all that had formed her, she had tried so many ways of melding her Russian experience of self with the Australian one she was struggling to construct. After a while, she suspected her Russian connections were somehow sabotaging the nascent Australian ones. So a few months ago, like a pumice applied to calluses on the feet, she had rubbed and scraped at her Russianness. She rationed her time with other emigrés, she shed most of her Soviet clothes, she restyled her Soviet hair, she applied less make-up to her Soviet face, she removed throatiness from her Australian speech and installed articles into her English sentences. She shed, she rubbed, she scoured until she was sure that if she were seen walking in the street or shopping at the supermarket, she would be taken for an Australian.

All of it had been futile. A year after arriving in Australia, and nearly two years since leaving Leningrad, she was coming to believe that home was to identity as blood was to the body. Yes, she had her own home at the saddlery, a domicile, a physical sanctuary; but home in the sense of identity, home in the sense of belonging, still eluded her here in Australia. She felt adrift in some never-never land, caught between the familiar yet no longer possible, and the new and far-from-secure.

How different it would be if her mother were with her and they could, with their shared past, tread this slippery sprawling present together. And again she found herself wondering, as she had so many times before, whether the loss of her mother was shaping all the other losses. She wasn't missing Leningrad, she was missing the city she had lived in with her mother. She wasn't homesick for Russian, she was homesick for conversation with her mother. She wasn't pining for Russian food, she was pining for meals with her mother. She wasn't suffering the absence of landmarks, she was suffering the absence of her mother. She wasn't struggling in foreign Australia, she was struggling with foreign grief.

She glanced at Andrew and wondered if he would ever be the sort of friend with whom she could discuss these issues. In different circumstances she would have allowed herself to hope he was, but now she did not grant herself that kind of licence. It would, she believed, save her from future disappointment.

He had made a U-turn, and it seemed to her that he was heading back the way they had just come. After a couple more kilometres and a few more turns, he was parking alongside the Botanic Gardens.

'Here's my favourite place in Melbourne.' He was blushing. 'Excluding my favourite mosaic places.'

She had visited these gardens with Zara and Arnold. So different from gardens at home, there were flowers in both winter and summer, and such a variety and lushness of growth that she wondered if there was something other than heat to make the Australian air so much more productive than the Russian variety. Zara and Arnold had favoured the huge multicoloured camellia section, and the azaleas, too, whose blooms were so abundant they glazed the entire bush with colour. Andrew, in contrast, headed straight to the oak lawn.

There were oak trees at home, both in the city and the nearby countryside, and several times she and her mother had made an autumn visit to Tsarskoe Selo to see the colours. These oaks at the Botanic Gardens were huge by comparison—an introduced species, according to Andrew, but they clearly thrived in the Australian climate. She should take lessons from oaks.

'This is my favourite tree,' he said, stopping by one of them. It was not the largest, nor the most shapely. 'Look.' He was pointing at the exposed roots. A hollow about the size of a man's fist had formed, and it was filled with rainwater. 'I've seen birds drinking here,' he said.

Not sure how to respond, she chose silence. He, too, remained silent, and a minute or two later led her back to a path, around the lake and up a steep, green slope on the far side of the gardens.

He guided her to a seat high on the hill. 'This is the Hopetoun lawn,' he said. He liked it because, being so far from the café and kiosk, it attracted fewer people. 'Yet from this spot you can see over the lake and across the gardens, all the way to the suburbs beyond. On a clear day, you can even see the mountains at Melbourne's eastern perimeter.'

Apart from an elderly couple seated on one of the other park benches, and a few of the glamorous Australian magpies foraging in the grass, they had the area to themselves. Andrew rolled a cigarette and lit up, while she, acutely aware of the evening ahead, took the opportunity to ask about his parents.

He did not look at her as he spoke, rather gazed out over the gardens. She had noticed that he seemed to prefer a point in the middle distance when he talked.

He began with his father, a businessman. 'His name's Leonard, and he owns a company that manufactures library supplies: metal drawers for catalogue cards, shelves for books, storage units for tape cassettes, trays for documents, display cases, dividers for the shelves.' Andrew shrugged. 'Pretty much everything for the modern library, except the books and documents.'

In all the time Galina had spent in libraries, she'd never given a thought to library supplies. So many jobs that are rarely considered: the removal of smells from animal hides, cleaning dust and dirt from tram tracks, and, closer to home, drawing designs on sewing patterns. She could create a children's book — yes, that was an idea — called 'Special Jobs', or 'What Do You Want to Be When

You Grow Up?'. Cinema-screen cleaners and ice-cream churners, gem polishers and street poets, there was no shortage of contenders.

'In truth,' Andrew continued, 'my father would prefer to write books than house them.' Andrew now turned towards her and, with lowered voice, said, 'My father has an artistic temperament.'

'So why did he not become a writer? What happened?'

'His own background happened. My grandfather in particular.' Andrew gave a wry smile and returned his gaze to the lake. 'When my father revealed his ambition to be a writer—actually, a poet, which was even worse—my grandfather said the only money to be made in books was in publishing them, selling them, or storing them, and certainly not in writing them. And even though my father left Perth and his family while still a young man, a good many of my grandfather's beliefs travelled with him.' Andrew paused, and in the silence a flush filled his face. 'My father capitulated to his own father. He's not a fighter, although he did put up a tremendous battle when I told him I wanted to be a mosaicist. For a while he turned into his own dad.'

Mindful of the passing time, Galina asked, 'And your mother? What does she do?'

'My mother, Sylvie, had the brains to do anything. But in her family, girls, particularly pretty girls, didn't pursue a career.' He sighed. 'She's a housewife.'

'No other job?'

Andrew shook his head. 'She was working in the Myer depart-ment store'—Galina's favourite shop!—'when she met my father. She married at nineteen. That's what girls did in the 1950s.'

'Then you came along.' But as soon as she spoke, she realised this could not be the case. Andrew was twenty-seven, a year older than she was, which gave him a 1960 birth.

'I was their final attempt after several miscarriages,' Andrew said. He was about to say more when he checked his watch. 'If we're going to walk the circuit of the gardens, we should start now.' He smiled. 'We mustn't be late. My mother is a domestic queen; she's *the* domestic queen. Right now, she'll be putting the final touches to the culinary counterpart of a collection of Old Masters.'

At that precise moment, Sylvie Morrow was in the act of breaking and entering a derelict house in the next street to her own. The dinner preparations were complete, Andrew and his new girlfriend were not due for another hour and a half, and, most crucially, this might be her last chance. She'd had a hunch about this house from the moment it went up for sale. And even if her hunch were nothing other than a strong desire to add to her letter collection, it didn't matter. Hunch or hope, she had to investigate.

Affixed to the rickety fence was a placard, WHELAN THE WRECKER IS HERE. Sylvie had noticed it that morning when driving home with the shopping. There was as yet no demolition equipment on site, but she'd been given due warning. The gate was half-open and wedged tight in a tangle of rubble and grass; with a quick glance up and down the street, she slipped in.

The once-beautiful garden was in ruins. How sad old Mrs Payne would be. Not that Sylvie had known her, in this neighbourhood people kept to themselves, but she had nodded to her a few times and complimented her on the garden. It had been one of the district's best, with an exuberant array of bulbs and annuals, a raised circular bed of roses in the middle of the lawn, and mature camellias, hydrangeas and rhododendrons lining the fences. Daphne bushes and gardenias had been planted close to the front gate, and when Sylvie was passing, she would pause to take in the season's perfume.

All that was now gone. Brambles and vines had invaded, sticky sprawling webs clasped the bushes like hairnets, leaves drooped with dust and thirst. It was fortunate she didn't share Leonard's spider phobia, Sylvie thought, as she picked her way through the tangle towards the front door. The garden was so out of control, she doubted she could be seen from the street; but even if she were, no one would guess she was about to break in. Leonard wouldn't believe her capable of doing anything out of the ordinary, much less something illegal, while Andrew saw her exclusively as over-protective mother and devoted wife. As for anyone else, she was Sylvie Morrow, wife of Leonard Morrow and mother of Andrew, a good resident of this good neighbourhood. Respectability: it was a perfect alibi.

The house had been empty for almost a year. Sylvie had attempted to slip in on previous occasions to search for forgotten letters, but each time there were people around, either in the street or in neighbouring properties. Then a few months after the house was sold, squatters had moved in, and they'd stayed until recently. With Andrew's Russian girlfriend coming for dinner tonight, she wished she had tried harder earlier.

Mrs Sophie Payne had been over ninety when she'd died. For sixty years she had lived in this house, first with her family, then just with her husband, and for the last twenty years alone. During the Great War, before she was married, she had served overseas as a member of the Australian Army Nursing Service. Sylvie had learned this one Remembrance Day, several years ago now. She was walking the dog, when she saw Mrs Payne returning from the dawn service with a poppy and service medals pinned to her coat, and the two of them had stopped to talk.

Born into an age and a milieu when time was put aside each day for correspondence, Sylvie was sure Mrs Payne would have kept letters. And if her family had been a loving one, they would have discovered these letters after her death and cherished them. But her family was far from loving. (People kept to themselves in this neighbourhood, but the rumour network was well-oiled.) There were two ageing children who had not spoken to their mother, nor each other, for years; they would not be interested in their mother's correspondence.

The house had been sold to developers, and soon after the auction the adult children had arrived with vans, trailers and helpers. Just one weekend, that's all it took to dismantle their mother's long life. On the two mornings, the ageing son came; in the afternoons, the ageing daughter. Sylvie had taken the dog for multiple walks that weekend in order to observe the activity. Despite their estrangement, the son and daughter had behaved remarkably alike. They tossed what they didn't want on the front lawn, that smooth swathe of green that Mrs Payne had tended almost to her dying day, and they trampled through her flowerbeds. They had no care for what their mother had cared about, they had no care for their mother; they took what they wanted and left.

Months passed. Weeds ravaged the flowerbeds, and straw strangled the lawn; spring bulbs choked in the rubble, and the camellias gave up the ghost; the guttering sagged, roof tiles slipped, windows were smashed, and curtains ripped by the shards flapped in the wind. The house was following the old woman into the ground.

Sylvie stepped with care onto the rickety verandah; some of the floorboards looked rotten, while others had already collapsed. Names and obscenities had been carved into the wooden verandah posts. Such senseless destruction, she thought, and wondered what pleasure, what benefit, it could have brought the culprit. She stopped in front of the door, and picked burrs off her slacks with slow deliberation. She was about to commit a criminal act, it was not a comfortable prospect. Then common sense kicked in: You're taking from no one. Whatever remains in this place will soon be destroyed. Just get a move on.

She turned back the sleeves of her cardigan, stepped forward and tried the door. It was locked or perhaps stuck, but the wood was ragged, and a shove would probably have smashed it in. She twisted around: she could just see the street, so decided to try the back door. It, too, was locked. She leaned her shoulder against it and gave a nervy push. The hinges broke, the frame cracked, and the

129

door collapsed with a shattering crash. She didn't dare move, didn't draw breath, counted off the seconds, but no one appeared. With a final glance to left and right, she entered the house.

The place was putrid. No old-lady smells of 4711 cologne and mothballs, no dry-grass scent of old-lady crêpe dresses, the stench here was savage. She clamped a handkerchief to her face as she picked her way through the squalor. Bottles and cans and old food wrappings jutted out of a topsoil of cigarette butts and animal droppings. And so many cast-off clothes strewn through the rubble. Abandoned clothes, abandoned people, abandoned house, she found herself thinking. She stood by a glassless window in what might have been a den or a child's bedroom, removed the handkerchief from her face and sucked in the fresh air — although not for long. A pile of clothes a metre from where she was standing reeked of life experiences utterly alien to her own, and she shoved the handkerchief back into her face. Using the toe of her shoe, she pushed aside some of the muck to reveal the carpet beneath. Years ago, she had discovered letters mixed in with an underlay of newspapers, and ever since had been alert to the possibility. Here the floral pattern was smudged in grime, its texture that of stale camembert. The thought of touching it made her flinch.

She made her way up the central passageway, past a mattress blotched with livery stains, past empty cans and broken glass, past crawling insects, past ripped and twisted clothes. She looked into the rooms as she passed: more filth, more rubbish.

At the last room on the left, at the front of the house, she stopped in the doorway. This room was very different from the rest of the house, as if whoever had squatted here had been trying to make a home. The floor was clear of rubbish, the window still retained its glass, the mattress was relatively clean, and a tall wardrobe stood along one wall. There was a chair draped with a rug crocheted in granny squares; the rug had been darned, it had been cared for, and on the windowsill stood a small mirror in a pink plastic frame.

Sylvie felt a surge of fellow feeling for this unknown person striving to create a home. And sadness, too. What had brought him to this? What had happened to him?

Or *her*. Perhaps these attempts at domesticity were the work of a woman, perhaps even a mother with children. And if Sylvie had known there was a woman here, would she have offered to help? She wished she could say with certainty she would have, but there was something fearful in her, fear of these poor, homeless people who were so different from her. Yet what could they do to her? She had the home, she had the social position, she had the respected husband; she, Sylvie Morrow, was protected. Sometimes she really despised herself.

It was with an effort she returned to the job at hand. She pulled on rubber gloves, and lifted up a corner of the carpet to reveal proper underlay, not newspaper. The carpet was newer than she'd first thought; there'd be no letters to be found there.

That left the wardrobe. She opened the doors carefully in case of mice, but only a single lethargic black moth emerged—one life she'd saved. She created a makeshift ladder from three drawers: a risky tower, but the only way she could reach the top shelf.

At first she could see nothing. She held to her precarious perch while pushing the door back to let in more light. She was sure she saw something now, something solid beyond the dust balls and shards of paper, a package in the back corner, yes, a package about the size of a book. She returned to one of the back rooms to retrieve a stick she'd noticed there. Up the wobbly ladder again, she manoeuvred the package towards her.

It was a cigar box, the Henri Wintermans brand, a pretty box made of lightweight wood, highly decorated with tropical scenes and gold medallions and embossed writing, a special box for precious possessions. She felt a fluttering of excitement; even before she lifted the lid, she knew.

Inside were several airmail envelopes, each with the stamps

carefully removed, each spongy with multiple pages. They were addressed to Miss Sophie Herbert, and sent by a M. Lucien Barbier in Lyons, France. The handwriting was an attractive, straight up-and-down script with a hint of italic style. Sophie Herbert must have been Mrs Sophie Payne's maiden name.

Sylvie was not surprised to find the letters—she would have been more surprised and sorely disappointed if she'd found nothing. She lacked a gift for music like that displayed by her sister, she'd been deprived the gift of words possessed by her husband, she had only a fraction of the artistic gift of her son; instead, she'd been given the highly specific and largely useless ability to sniff out letters. Not much of a gift perhaps, but she'd made the most of it.

She slipped the cigar box into a plastic bag, and hurried from the house. Once in the street, she quickened her pace and arrived home with forty-five minutes to spare, ample time to ensure everything was perfect for the dinner ahead.

It was exactly seven o'clock when Andrew and Galina pulled up outside the Morrow home. At a glance, maybe her real estate experience was paying off, Galina took in an old-style house with the decorative brickwork that struck her as distinctly Moorish but was, so she had been told, very English. There was a bay window at the front, and above the verandah, a fringe of the lacy wrought iron so common on the older dwellings here. It was a pretty house, built close to its neighbours but not attached to either of them. This was an important feature when considering inner-suburban dwellings, her colleagues at Merridale's had told her, and extraordinary to someone who had lived with shared walls, shared staircases, shared kitchens, shared bathrooms, shared noise. Like all the homes here, the Morrow dwelling struck her as huge. She doubted she would ever become Australian when it came to housing.

They entered a small garden via a wrought-iron gate, and were approaching the house when she felt Andrew's hand on her arm. Just as quickly he withdrew it with an embarrassed apology.

'I should mention Winston,' he said. 'Winston Yeung, company secretary and second-in-command of my father's business. He often joins us for family dinners.' Andrew lowered his voice. 'He may have already arrived.'

She was pleased there would be another guest, it would remove some of the attention from her.

They stepped onto the verandah, and she was immediately struck by the floor. It was covered with intricately patterned tiles, in a colourful and elegant design. Galina pointed to it. 'Was this the trigger for your choice of career?'

He smiled. 'If it had been, my parents would have sold up immediately.'

It really was a beautiful house, with the iron lacework, the decorative tiling, the small, mature garden, the heavily carved front door. And bordering the door in two long, narrow panels were leadlight windows of such an original composition, a Mondrian-Kandinsky hybrid, Galina thought, not without humour. Very original indeed.

'These windows? They are not old like the house?'

Andrew nodded. 'That's right. My mother made them.'

'Then your mother is an artist, not a housewife.'

'No, she's a housewife with serial passions. Her leadlighting phase was about ten years ago. Before that it was philosophy and life-drawing. At the moment she's attending Shakespeare classes, or perhaps it's Dickens.' He gave a wry smile. 'And there are her continuing passions for me and my father.'

Galina was about to insist on the artistic merit of the windows, when the front door opened to reveal a large smiling man with a tiny dog tucked in the crook of his arm.

'Butch,' the man said, nodding at the dog, 'heard the gate open.'

This was Andrew's father. This was Leonard Morrow.

Once they were inside Leonard plopped the dog on the ground, embraced a furiously blushing Andrew, and then stood back to be introduced to Galina. There was no uncertain greeting with him; he shook her hand firmly, gave it an extra squeeze before he let it go, and told her how very pleased he and his wife were to meet her at last. At last? What had Andrew said about her? But with the three of them heading down a passage towards the back of the house, there was no time for wondering. Sylvie Morrow was in the kitchen arranging food on a large platter. As soon as they entered, she pushed the plate aside, washed her hands, kissed her son, and to Galina's surprise, hugged her. She smelled of food and hairspray.

Andrew was right about his mother: she was very pretty. She wore her hair in the blonde, flouncy style that so many Australian women favoured; her make-up was light, her shoulder pads sat exactly as they should beneath her blue-and-white striped top, her figure was perfect. The resemblance between mother and son was striking. They had the same golden hair and big blue eyes, the same perfect Cupid's bow on their perfectly symmetrical mouths, the same slender, erect bodies, and even similar facial expressions. But whereas Andrew was tall, his mother was tiny. Galina noticed a small stepladder stashed in a corner of the kitchen, necessary if Sylvie were to reach the high cupboards—although, given the abundance of cupboards lower down and a walk-in pantry as well, it was hard to know why she would need the high storage. There was not one, but two sinks, and a bench long enough to house four stools. She wondered, as she often did, if these Australians realised how lucky they were.

Like so many women here, Sylvie looked young for her age, in her early forties, Galina thought, but she must have been at least ten years older. In Russia, people looked the age they were; though what was the norm: these young-looking Australians, or the older-looking Russians? Around Sylvie's neck was a string of pearls, on her wedding finger was a gold band and a diamond-and-sapphire ring, on her other hand she wore an opal, not one of those bland milky opals, but a dark stone with gorgeous oily lights like the black opalescence on the canals at home. Everything about Sylvie was neat, coordinated and attractive. Domestic queen indeed.

Leonard was asking what she'd like to drink. There was a glass of white wine on the kitchen bench which Galina assumed was Sylvie's, and even though she would have preferred something sweet, she said she would have the same. Leonard poured a glass of wine for her and a Scotch for himself, then went to stand next to his wife. He was so much larger than she was, a bear with a faun, Galina found herself thinking, yet they seemed to fit comfortably together. Leonard had his arm around his wife's shoulders; his nails, Galina noticed, were uniformly shaped and clean—but then everyone's nails here were clean. Sylvie looped her arm around her husband's waist. He stepped closer to her, she leaned into him.

Galina tried not to stare. Most of her mother's friends were, like Lidiya, women without husbands, and Zara and Arnold had displayed the modesty expected of observant Jews. Galina was fascinated by this husband and wife of thirty-plus years, their arms around each other, so publicly affectionate, so obviously loving. It was surprisingly moving.

Leonard was what the English call dapper. His hair—thick, wavy, and greying—sat neatly on his skull; his pepper-and-salt moustache lodged impeccably above his mouth; his jacket lapels lay smoothly against his body; his grey-and-maroon-striped tie hung straight down his torso. He was wearing a lemon-coloured shirt beneath a grey blazer; his dark-grey trousers looked as if they'd been freshly pressed. Leonard Morrow could slip into one of those gentlemen's clubs she'd read about in English novels, sip his Scotch, and look perfectly at home.

Sylvie was herding them into the lounge. She had a surprise, she said, and wanted them arranged so she could make a grand entrance. Leonard was consulting his watch.

'Winston will be here any minute,' he said. 'Shouldn't we wait?'
Sylvie shrugged, 'It's up to you.'

Galina was thinking it was surely Sylvie's decision given she was
in charge of the meal, when the doorbell sounded and a moment
later a small, young Asian man in a dark suit joined them. This was
Winston Yeung, company secretary and family friend, and perhaps
one of the Vietnamese boat people she'd heard so much about. She'd
been told that this group of refugees had done extremely well in
Australia, and certainly Winston as a company secretary would be
testament to that. But as soon as he spoke, his cut-glass vowels and
well-modulated phrasing suggested a more British background.
And so it turned out to be: Leonard introduced Winston Yeung as
Hong Kong Chinese.

'I hope you explained I'd be late?' Winston said to Leonard after
the greetings were over. And to the rest of them, 'I've been meeting
with the auditors.'

At which moment, Sylvie made her grand entrance bearing a
large platter. She was beaming. 'A special entrée to celebrate Galina's
first visit to our home,' she announced. '*Zakuski*,' she said to Galina.
'Hors d'oeuvres,' she said to everyone else.

The platter was laden with Russian food.

'I went to a specialist Russian delicatessen,' she said. 'In
Carnegie.'

Galina knew this shop. She had been there with other émigrés,
but not since she'd moved to Carlton. Carlton and Carnegie were
on opposite sides of Melbourne.

'It was such an adventure,' Sylvie said. And addressing Galina,
'I'm happy to go again, if you'd like.'

Andrew, blushing from scalp to shirt collar, reached out and
put a restraining hand on his mother's arm. The poor sensitive boy,
Galina found herself thinking, and sent him what she hoped was a
reassuring smile. Far from feeling pressured, she thought Sylvie's
actions endearing. She could imagine her own mother behaving in a

similar fashion if she had brought a boy home for a meal.

'The other customers in the shop insisted I tried everything before I bought.' Sylvie was laughing. 'Some of it was very strange to an Australian palate. They told me about the various foods, as well as Russian food traditions.' She paused. 'I wonder if there's a sociology of food. There ought to be.'

'Perhaps you'll begin the study,' Leonard said, looking fondly at his wife.

She dismissed his suggestion with a shrug and a grimace, as Leonard knew she would: she never gave herself enough credit, no matter how much he praised her. Although she certainly was enjoying her Russian surprise. She gave each of them a small plate with a fork, and a paper serviette decorated with those Russian dolls, the name of which he could never remember. And then she passed around the food, rather like a happy magician conjuring up surprises. Andrew, in contrast, was staring at the platter, a perplexed expression on his perpetually blushing face. As for Winston, he was perusing the food with studied interest; but, given his preference for simple, fresh produce, Leonard guessed he was being polite. Sylvie, on the other hand, being wrapped in her own pleasure, saw only pleasure.

They ate the foreign food, or rather they explored it, and whatever Sylvie's motives, the adventure—for it was an adventure—turned out to be a success. They tried several types of smoked fish and meats, a couple of salads, and a range of pickled vegetables, all of which Leonard thought tasted much the same. Galina provided a commentary on the food. She began so quietly and hesitantly he feared she was as shy as his son. But soon she was regaling them with stories, not just about the food, but of the life she had left behind: the shops, the queues, the empty shelves, the Russian people's extraordinary inventiveness when preparing meals with few ingredients. She talked about celebratory food, and identified several items on the platters as belonging to this category, much to Sylvie's evident delight.

Galina talked freely in excellent English, but uttered nothing personal: for all she said, she might never have had family or friends. As for her relationship with his son, a relationship so significant she'd crossed the world to be with him, there was nothing in her behaviour to suggest any intimacy between them. Indeed, there was something unreadable about her, and a guardedness too—possibly essential qualities when negotiating the perils of Soviet life, but out of kilter here in relaxed and open Australia. Not that he was in a position to criticise circumspection, he who was such an expert in it.

It was well after eight when they went into dinner. The Russian food had been so salty that Sylvie brought a jug of water to the table, an American custom she normally deplored. She had cooked a leg of lamb with roasted vegetables, green beans, mint sauce, and her excellent gravy—Australian food to follow the Russian entrée, she said. Galina, he was pleased to see, displayed a healthy appetite, surprising in a girl these days, particularly one with a good figure.

There was a pleasing bigness about her, a 1950s movie-star type of fullness, and not a trace of the stodgy, pasty Slavic looks he tended to associate with Russian women. This girl had a presence. It was not just her size, but her unusual colouring: the olive skin with almost-black eyes, and the surprise of honey-coloured hair. He liked the way she styled it, soft around the face and caught loosely at the nape with a clasp. She really was an attractive girl.

He ate his meal, Andrew ate his, Winston ate his, and Sylvie plied the girl with questions, a battery of questions about her impressions of Australia, her decision to emigrate, her family and friends, her future plans. He knew Sylvie was genuinely interested, she was chillingly polite when she was not, but the girl was no more forthcoming now about her personal circumstances than when talking about the Russian food. She needed rescuing.

He interrupted Sylvie with a request for a second helping, and then turned to his son.

'I ran into your old friend Graham Carter the other day. At my accountant's.'

Sylvie was filling his plate with a second serving as large as the first. He caught her eye, gestured that she stop, and turned back to Andrew.

'Odd how people turn out. Graham was such an unusual kid, and now he's rising up the ladder at Featherstone & Peak.'

He saw the smile rise to his son's face at the mention of Graham's name, then quickly disappear. Perhaps this was not the best of conversation topics, after all.

'Graham was my best friend at school,' Andrew explained to Galina. After a long pause, he added, 'Perhaps the best friend I ever had.' Leonard thought he detected a note of resentment in his son's tone. 'What happened to Graham was tragic.' Andrew turned to Leonard. 'It's too bad his father wasn't as amenable to his artistic ambitions as you were to mine.'

Amenable was not how Leonard would describe his actions. He'd strenuously opposed Andrew's choice of career, any concerned father would have done the same. He wanted his son to have a good life, a secure life. In any one generation, there might be one or two artists of renown, while the rest grow bitter, and are forced to confront their failure every day. He didn't want that for his son.

Leonard knew his was not a totally disinterested view; after all, if not for his own father he might have pursued his dream of becoming a writer. But with struggles enough for any man, he now believed his father had been right to steer him into business. As he believed he'd been right to try to dissuade Andrew from a career in art. But when he realised Andrew was not going to change his mind — clearly the son was made of stronger stuff than the father — he withdrew from the fight. To this day though, he remained unconvinced of the long-term viability of Andrew's being an artist. But — and this was crucial — he would never have done as Graham's father did.

'Graham's life would make excellent material for a Russian novel,' Andrew said to Galina. 'A modern-day Dostoyevskian tragedy.' He drew in a deep breath. 'Would you like to hear the story?'

She smiled and nodded, and for the first time Leonard thought he detected a warmth in the way she looked at his son. As for Andrew, he rarely took the floor voluntarily, so perhaps being with Galina gave him confidence.

'Graham and I went to high school together,' Andrew began. 'We were both good students with a particular interest in art. The school encouraged us.'

'I remember.' Leonard heard the sharpness in his voice.

He and Sylvie, and Graham's parents too, acknowledged their sons' artistic abilities, but they praised their sporting and academic achievements as well. Both sets of parents took what they believed to be a balanced approach. So when Graham announced to his parents at the end of his intermediate year that he intended to be an artist, they were not concerned. The boy was young, they said. He had two more years of high school; he'd change his mind. But over the next two years, Graham's resolve actually strengthened, bolstered by success in student art competitions and his art teacher's encouragement.

'I could draw, I could paint, I had a talent,' Andrew said. 'But compared with Graham, I might have been doodling. Our teacher couldn't do enough for him. Never had he had such a gifted pupil.'

'You're being too modest,' Leonard said, and might have continued, except Andrew silenced him.

'No, I'm being truthful. Graham *was* exceptional.' Again, he directed his words to Galina. 'The textures he achieved were unbelievable. He used brushes and palette knives, he used his hands. He was fascinated by colour, layering colour, heaping colours onto the canvas. His paintings were lush, rhythmic, organic.

'Then one day in our final year it all came to an end. Graham didn't appear in class. His space had been cleared, his paintings had been removed from the art-room walls.

'He was absent from school the next day, and the one following. At the end of the week, with final exams just a month away, it was announced he wouldn't be returning to school. Graham was unwell, the teacher said, and would be studying for his exams at home.

'On the Saturday, I went round to his place. It was mid-afternoon and he was still in his pyjamas. He looked a mess, he reeked of neglect — all of him except his hands and nails which were clean of paint. The first time in years.

'Apparently, Graham's father had shown several of his paintings to a collector, a man who, according to the father, knew about art. The collector assessed the work as good, but not first-rate. Not in the class of Fred Williams or Arthur Boyd. Not in the class of John Percival, whom, the collector said — and it was not meant as a compliment — Graham was clearly trying to emulate. Not good enough, Graham was told by his father. "You'll never amount to the best," he said, in a final cruel stroke.'

Andrew looked very solemn. 'For all his bravado on canvas, Graham was not a strong character.'

'Or perhaps,' Leonard suggested, 'he lacked the necessary drive, the courage too, to be an artist. Talent's not enough, you know that yourself. Nothing I did or said could dissuade you from your decision. You were driven.' Leonard shrugged. 'You still are.'

Andrew was nodding gently. 'Who knows what it was with Graham? He was seventeen, and his father ground his heels into his dreams. And now he's an accountant.'

There was a brief pause before Leonard added, 'I can't say he looked unhappy.'

'Such a life,' Andrew said, more to himself than anyone else, 'such a life would extirpate the imagination.'

The blow struck without warning. It was his son's arresting utterance — about a life that would not just extinguish the imagination, but bring about a far more violent annihilation. Leonard

141

wanted to leave the table, consult a dictionary, make sure he understood what 'extirpate' meant. Although he knew exactly what it meant—he was dissembling even in the privacy of his own mind—what he wanted was to be left alone to think. The words had not been said about him, yet their effect was acutely personal. He was a businessman who had once wanted to be a poet; he was a husband and a father with singular tastes; he was a man who lived every day with secrets. He knew all about a life in which a significant part of the self was stifled, even excised.

He glanced at Galina. She was the first girl Andrew had ever introduced to them; she might well be Andrew's first girlfriend. She had left her home and country to be with Andrew; she was more than likely going to marry him. As much as he might want to be alone, Leonard knew it was out of the question. At that moment, Winston met his gaze and gave a barely perceptible nod. It was a gesture of support to Leonard Morrow, father, husband and businessman, and not to Leo Morrow, who had always straddled two worlds.

Perhaps, in order to live with other people, some essential aspects of the self always need to be extinguished, Leonard was thinking. Desire, ambition, even country, as in the case of Galina and Winston. No one can do everything they want, nor can they have everything they desire. Every choice made is another denied.

Galina, too, was reflecting on Andrew's odd utterance. She did not understand this word 'extirpate'. But Andrew's artist friend, she understood. It would have been better if this Graham had been born in the Soviet Union: his talent would have been recognised, and he would have been sent to a specialist art academy where his gift would have been nurtured. And no one would have waited until he was seventeen. Fifteen-year-olds, ten-year-olds, seven-year-olds, five-year-olds, if they were truly gifted were put where their gift could blossom. She did not see tragedy in the story of Graham, she saw ignorance and stupidity. Surely it was obvious that when it came to artistic ability, the art teacher had the authority, not the boy's father nor the father's art-collecting friend.

Such a life would extirpate the imagination, Sylvie was thinking, or, as in her own case, force it underground. It was an uncomfortable thought for someone who had no reason to complain about her life. But how else to explain her passion for letters written by strangers? How else to explain her breaking and entering of a few hours back? Others might look at her and see a kind but limited sort of woman, but with a letter in her hand, her imagination was let loose. With a letter in her hand, she was unstoppable.

She looked around the table; the conversation had lapsed, and everyone seemed absorbed in their own thoughts. She caught Leonard's eye and gave him a nod. In a rousing voice, he suggested they move to the living room. Once they were settled with coffee and chocolates the talk fired up again. The gunman at the post office was on everyone's mind, in particular, what might have motivated him.

'Perhaps some people are born bad,' Winston said.

'Or they hunger for power at any cost.' This from Galina.

Sylvie was convinced the gunman's upbringing shaped his actions. 'Violence, deprivation—anything but love and acceptance.' She turned to her son. 'He looks to be about your age, Andrew. At twenty-seven, you have a career, family, friends, a girlfriend.' She smiled at Galina. 'But this man, what does he have? A gun and grievances, and 100-proof anger.' She shrugged. 'Ours is not a fair world.'

'It's certainly not a fair world for those killed by him,' Andrew said.

'Perhaps he's just insane,' Leonard said. At which point Andrew, after glancing at Galina, jumped in to compliment Sylvie on the meal. Galina, too, voiced her appreciation, and Winston added, 'Hear, hear.'

Sylvie merely shrugged: she was a housewife, and housewives cooked.

Leonard leapt to her defence. 'Don't underrate yourself,' he

143

said. 'You make leadlight windows, you attend adult-education classes, you're a volunteer driver, you knit and sew, you're a huge reader, and'—he looked triumphant—'there's your letter collection. What other housewife collects letters?'

Not her letters, Sylvie was silently pleading, not in front of this stranger, not in front of Winston. She put a playful hand over Leonard's mouth, although she was feeling more plundered than playful.

Leonard shook her off. 'You should show Galina that Russian letter you've never had translated.'

Galina looked intrigued. 'You collect letters?'

Sylvie nodded. She didn't dare speak.

'Letters written by strangers?'

Again, Sylvie nodded.

'Show her, darling,' Leonard said.

Sylvie heard the pride in his voice, but it was not what she wanted, not when it involved her letter collection. Although to protest would reveal how much the letters mattered, and she had no desire to expose herself any more than had already occurred.

So it happened that a couple of minutes later, Sylvie was making her way towards her little workroom at the top of the house, with the Russian girl following, to show what had been seen by no one except Leonard, and even with him it was just the occasional interesting acquisition like the Russian letter. And in that instance it was the stamp she had wanted Leonard to see, a stamp depicting happy women picking lemons. It was dated 1951, the year he had moved from Perth to Melbourne, the pivotal year that ultimately led to his meeting her. She couldn't explain why, but she believed in the happiness of the lemon-pickers and the happenstance of the date, and she wanted to share these with Leonard. Now she wondered if, in fact, 1951 had been a happy time in Russia. The girl would know, but she didn't want to encourage her.

There were times she had shown Leonard a letter because of

the curious handwriting, or the plush paper, features she knew would interest him, but the power of letters to reach across time and country, the stories they told, and all the lives and possibilities they triggered, these remained hers alone. She shared the twin desires common to all collectors of wanting her collection to be admired, but, at the same time, feeling compelled to protect it—and not just the collection, but the passion of the collector, too, the naked heart after all—from people who would damage it by indifference, or derision, or outright contempt.

And what would this girl think of her letter collection? This girl from a culture so foreign it was impossible to assume or predict anything, who might well fade out of Andrew's life before long—although she hoped this wouldn't be the case. What to think about this stranger now following her up the stairs to the room into which no one but she entered, her own private space from the time she and Leonard had bought this house? In the early days, her use of the room was assumed to be temporary, but miscarriage after miscarriage meant it remained hers. Leonard, too, had his own private retreat in what should have been another child's bedroom; Sylvie went in there to clean, but did so with eyes averted. Not that she thought Leonard harboured any significant secrets; he was simply not that sort of man.

Leonard had offered to swap his room for hers, given his was far more comfortable and within the main flow of the house. But that was the crucial factor: in her eyrie she was far removed from the domestic domain, far removed from everyday life. She would climb the creaky stairs to the solitude of her room, and work on her letters—transcribing, cataloguing, or searching for background material. Or she would read, hours every week spent in the pages of books. And sometimes she would just sit, her hands idle, her mind conjuring up other lives—fully imagined companions, if she so desired—while her own life lay quietly to one side.

When Andrew was a little boy she had read him Enid Blyton's

Faraway Tree books. These stories told of a group of friends who climbed to the top of a magic tree, where they entered fantastic places and had gripping adventures. Mounting the stairs to her room was like climbing her own faraway tree; her letters provided the adventures.

Perhaps all housewives superimpose dreams on their plain-Jane lives. This was not something Sylvie had ever discussed with her friends, nor would she. They were, like her, living uncomplicated lives with normal happy children, and steady dependable husbands. If they had problems, she assumed they would do as she did and keep them in-house. And just as she used letters to escape domestic drudgery, she expected her friends had their own outlets.

Her collection had started by accident, perhaps most collections do. She had found her first letter pressed between the pages of a second-hand book she had bought during her third pregnancy. This was her Latin pregnancy: Latin poetry, in translation, to distract her from her hopes and fears. (The first pregnancy was all joy until the miscarriage; the second pregnancy was her Henry James one, with only two of his shorter novels finished before the miscarriage occurred.) She'd enjoyed Latin at school, and Virgil, in particular, seemed the right sort of guide and protector for this new pregnancy. As it happened, the second-hand book that yielded her first letter was not Virgil, but a collection of Propertius's love poems, a beautiful old book with a spongy maroon leather cover and gold-rimmed pages. The letter marked a poem called 'Gone', a short poem that began, 'The girl I loved has left me.' Two lines of the poem had been marked in pencil: 'love's king of yesterday becomes by fate/ Tomorrow's Fool. That is the way of love.'

The letter was dated October 23rd, 1926, and had been written to 'My Darling' by 'forever your Edward'. But he wasn't 'forever her Edward' because, according to the letter, he would not be seeing My Darling again. He wrote that he could deceive his wife no longer, and while it broke his heart 'nevermore to see, hear and hold

146

My Darling', he felt he had no alternative. There was not only his wife to consider, a good woman who had done nothing to deserve his disloyalty, but there were also his three children, and his ageing mother. My Darling must have doubted his sincerity, given where she had kept the letter and the lines of the poem she had highlighted, but Sylvie had no doubts. She thought 'forever your Edward' came across as a self-justifying, self-pitying cheat. She guessed that My Darling was not his first indiscretion, nor would she be his last. In fact, he was probably dismissing My Darling not to make amends with his family, but to make way for My Darling's replacement. But he would have been found out, of that, Sylvie was sure. And he would have ended up paying for his lies and deceits.

A single letter, and she had become psychologist, priest and storyteller all at once. A single letter, and she was captivated. She had always been drawn to letters—not just the pleasures of receiving them, but the *concept* of letter-writing, that very particular intimate, secret, and enduring communication. And she thrilled to the covertness of letters, like someone whispering in your ear, *your* ear and no one else's.

As exciting as that first letter had been, it would have gone no further if she and Leonard had not decided to replace the flooring in the kitchen. She was pregnant again, and reading Virginia Woolf. (It was more auspicious, she thought, to read a female author during pregnancy, although perhaps better to have chosen one with children.) The plan was to finish the flooring well before the baby arrived. The old lino was the same grey-green monotony that covered so many floors in the 1940s and 1950s. The new lino was very striking: a black background with bright rectangles in primary colours, forming interlocking squares—striking and, compared with other kitchen floors she'd seen, rather daring. The work began with the removal of the old flooring. The underlay comprised the usual newspapers, not from the 1940s or 1950s, but the 1930s.

During the short period, just a couple of hours, before the

papers were removed, Sylvie crouched down and read the floor.
The top layer was mustardy with age, and stained with mysterious
splotches, but the lower sheets were well preserved. She was shuf-
fling through the pages, reading headlines and paragraphs, when she
spied some handwriting, almost completely covered by a page of
newsprint. She moved the newspaper aside to reveal a letter written
on blue onion-skin paper. She scanned the contents, then knowing
the floorer would soon be returning, quickly lifted and stacked all
the sheets of newspaper. She found several more letters: some, like
the first, written on blue onion-skin paper, others covering both
sides of high-quality, no-longer-white parchment, but if she held
the pages up to the light, she could still make out the watermark.
By the time the floorer returned to remove the underlay, she had
completed the job: old papers arranged in neat stacks for him to
take to the incinerator, while she took possession of the letters.

She lost the baby, and began her letter collection. And she did
not stop, not even with the pregnancy that produced the miracle of
Andrew—the George Eliot pregnancy, and another female author
like Virginia Woolf without children. (As were the Brontës and Jane
Austen and Emily Dickinson. Someone with the education and the
ability should investigate this disturbing pattern, Sylvie thought.) As
her son grew, so did her collection. Now, after nearly thirty years,
she had over two hundred letters, all in English except the single
Russian letter with the 1951 stamp of the happy lemon-pickers. For
the first time she wished she had not collected that letter, or rather,
had not shown it to Leonard. Her letters, a subtle larceny that did
no one any harm, were her own business.

Posted on the wall in her room was a quote from the poet
Byron: *Letter writing is the only device for combining solitude with good
company*. The observation greatly appealed to her, even more so with
her extension: *Reading a letter is the only device for combining solitude with
good company*. So what was she now doing, traipsing up to her room
with this girl in tow?

She stopped on the narrow stair: she couldn't go through with it. She twisted around and looked down at Galina. Her expression must have said it all, for Galina reached up and placed her hand on the bare skin of her wrist. 'Perhaps another time,' the girl said. She turned and led the way back down the stairs into the body of the house, and Sylvie followed, the print of Galina's hand sparking on her skin.

An understanding had passed between them.

To fill in time they lingered in the sitting room, the everyday room that housed the TV and stereo, and, on a circular side-table, an array of photos. Sylvie, her heart still pounding, attempted to restore herself. 'We're so happy you're here,' she said, pleased to hear the warm, motherly tone in her voice. 'Andrew has told us all about you.'

Again, Galina wondered what exactly Andrew had told them, and then decided it really didn't matter. She turned her attention to the photos. They showed Andrew as a baby, as a toddler, as a schoolboy, as a youth; they showed him as the man he was today; they showed him against a backdrop of different places and different interests. Andrew liked the beach; Andrew liked animals; Andrew liked the company of his parents. There were photos of people Galina assumed were the grandparents, and photos of Leonard and Sylvie with friends, photos with Andrew, and several of the two of them alone. The largest photo in the display was a framed portrait of Sylvie and Leonard on their wedding day, the petite bride in a patterned white satiny gown with a long train, and Leonard in formal clothes, looking like a Hollywood movie star.

'What a handsome couple,' Galina said, holding up the photo. She smiled. 'You still are.'

Sylvie gazed at the familiar picture, and it occurred to her, for the first time, how deceptive photos can be. They capture just a moment, a snapshot, in what are usually complex and on-going situations. And even the moment itself is distorted for the camera:

149

Turn this way, tilt your head, clasp your hands, say cheese. Not that this picture actually lied — she had been happy, and it had been a happy day. But the girl in the picture had anticipated a future very different from that which had eventuated.

8

A GOOD MARRIAGE

It was the autumn of 1955 when Sylvie Stirling met Leonard Morrow in the menswear department of the Myer Emporium. Sylvie was nineteen years old and employed at the busy Revlon counter. (Her preference had been for the book department, but the personnel manager had said it would be a waste of a pretty face, and assigned her to cosmetics instead.) Leonard, six years her senior, was about to buy a controlling share in the library-supplies company where he'd been working for the past four years. There was a meeting scheduled for the following day when the deal would be finalised, and to mark the occasion Leonard had decided to buy a new tie. He was oscillating between a maroon check and a blue stripe when Sylvie returned from her lunch break. She walked past him, slowed down, and without thinking, turned back and offered to help.

She took both ties, and standing on tiptoe, draped first one then the other around his neck. Her fingers grazed his skin, that sensitive spot just above the collar, and bliss bombs bolted down his spine. When she decided on the maroon—it was the more attractive pattern, she said, and it also complemented his colouring—all he could do was nod. It was only as she turned to leave that he managed to find his voice. 'Would you meet me? After work? For a drink? Or tea, if you'd prefer?'

Sylvie had never before approached a strange man, and she certainly had never shoplifted one—the term she always used when describing their first meeting. In the normal run of her life, she presented as a nicely brought-up middle-class girl. She was a loving sister to Maggie, a devoted daughter to her warm, sweet-tempered mother, and a patient one with her hard-to-please, impatient father. She was popular, she was pretty, and while she was cleverer than girls were expected to be in the 1950s, she was adept at dampening down her intelligence. Presenting a calm and cheerful disposition, despite her difficult father, despite the disappointments of life, despite her fears of A-bombs and H-bombs, Sylvie Stirling was in all respects a young lady. So she was even more surprised than Leonard when she approached him in the Myer menswear department.

'Let me help you,' she said.

Leonard heard the words and took in the speaker. She was small, elfin, in fact, with fair hair tied in a ponytail, and the largest, bluest eyes he had ever seen. Luck, having shunned him for the first twenty years of his life, had been his constant companion since moving from Perth to Melbourne. Friends, a great job, and now this bombshell of a girl.

Their courtship began that very evening. He took her to the ladies' lounge of a hotel of which even the strictest parents of a well-brought-up girl would approve, and over a Pimms for her and a beer for him, they started to get to know each other.

Her parents were from New Zealand; they had moved to Australia when she, the younger of two sisters, was six.

Leonard was the younger of two brothers; his parents had moved from England to Perth the year before he was born. Then, four years ago, he'd crossed the continent to Melbourne.

'Both of us are Melbourne immigrants,' he said.

Sylvie wouldn't have cared if Leonard were from outer space, she was already smitten. He was large and good-looking, with thick hair and a lush moustache — rather like Clark Gable, she thought. A businessman who wrote poetry, he was a man of practicality as well as passion. She'd been denied the stimulation of university study, she'd been denied the excitement of an independent career, but everything about Leonard Morrow struck her as stimulating and exciting.

Sylvie fell in love with Leonard innocently, romantically and very quickly. He seemed so grown-up, so worldly. And he was a great reader — not of fiction, but of biographies and poetry. She loved to hear him talk about famous people: their work, their love affairs, their bad behaviour. Most extraordinary of all, this businessman-poet wrote poems especially for her, a quartet of sonnets he presented as a gift on their eight-week anniversary: 'First Meeting', 'First Date', 'Falling in Love', 'Our Future'.

She felt herself changing under his influence. He loosened her up, opened her to new possibilities, gave her the courage not simply to question accepted modes of behaviour but actually to challenge them. On their third date, he took her to see Alfred Hitchcock's *To Catch a Thief*. When they stood for the national anthem, she reached for his hand; she'd never been so brazen, nor so subversive. (Was it treason to be physical with a man during the national anthem?) She sidled closer to him until the entire length of her body was touching his; a florid tingling zigzagged through her until the last note of 'God Save the Queen' faded to silence.

If she was like this after just two weeks of knowing him, a future with Leonard Morrow promised a life beyond anything she had ever hoped for. She couldn't believe her luck.

Nor could Leonard. He'd had plenty of girlfriends before her, though nothing serious. He wasn't a natural at intimacy; it was not something of which he'd had much experience, and certainly not within his own family. Indeed, there was little he had learned from his family — the perfectly adequate family, he would admit — that would assist him in the future he aspired to. His parents, along with

153

his older brother, Freddy, had migrated to Perth in search of a better life. And from their point of view, they had found it. It was Perth-born Leonard, the only member of the Morrow family to be a true Australian, who was the odd one out.

Leonard and his older brother could not have been more different. Freddy was athletic and outgoing, the ideal Aussie lad. He left school at fourteen and started work at Morrow & Sons, Electrics, first as his father's apprentice, and later his partner. As Perth grew from a town to a city, Morrow & Sons was much in demand. Freddy married a Perth girl, they bought a house in the same suburb as the Morrow parents, they had three Perth children spaced two years apart. Freddy and Perth were made for each other.

No such congenial coupling occurred for Leonard. He failed to develop any interest in sport, a serious blight in a sports-mad nation. He grew into a boy with abundant desire, but confined by Perth-sized opportunity. His nerves lay exposed, and were always threatening to expose him. He couldn't explain why he was so sensitive, but over the years he learned the art of self-protection — not through fight or flight, but through disguise and camouflage.

By the age of ten and enrolled in fourth grade, he was a fully fledged actor in a life of his own crafting, and while it was an effort, mostly he managed. Terrence, his best friend and soulmate, made it easier. Terrence, whose dreams like his own stretched beyond Perth, understood him and watched out for him. During weekends and holidays the two of them played endless games of make-believe. They would travel to faraway countries, to other planets, even other galaxies. And they crafted their own private utopia, an existence without parents, without brothers and sisters, without school, and most of all without Perth. In Perth, Terrence was Terry, and he was Len or Lenny; in the life they wanted, Terrence would be Terrence, and he would be Leonard or Leo, a name that would sit very nicely on the cover of the books he planned to write one day.

He and Terrence discovered biographies around the time they started high school. These books led them into the bohemia of Paris and London, Bloomsbury and Montmartre. Nothing was out of bounds in these places, indeed, outrageous behaviour was expected. Unfortunately, Leonard was too self-conscious to embrace the Perth version of bohemia, should it even exist, though he would have been happy if it were to reach out and embrace him first. Terrence had other ideas. He wanted to be an actor, and he needed Experience. He was willing to try anything, and Leonard, in time and with a little persuasion, would have joined him. But he was denied the opportunity. Suddenly, Terrence was leaving Perth, he would be living in Melbourne. His father had a new job. The two boys swore eternal friendship. 'I'll come to Melbourne as soon as I can,' Leonard promised. 'And in the meantime we'll write.' The boys hugged each other—not the done thing, but in such distressing circumstances they didn't care.

At first they exchanged letters almost daily, then weekly, then monthly. Before the first year had passed, apart from the occasional postcard, the correspondence had petered out. But not Leonard's desire to join Terrence in Melbourne.

By his late teens, the writer he had long aspired to be had undergone refinement. Now he wanted to be a poet—not a Banjo Patterson balladeer, but a poet in the tradition of the nineteenth-century English romantics: Keats, Shelley, and Wordsworth. A poet and perhaps a filmmaker. Or a choreographer of Hollywood musicals. Or maybe an actor like Terrence.

Of all the poetry he read, it was Wordsworth's *The Prelude*, the early sections in particular, that best captured who he wanted to be. He longed for solitary walks through the English woods and fields; he dreamed of the delights of being a young poet in Cambridge surrounded by like-minded friends. *The Prelude* brought him respite from his ill-fitting life.

Who knows the individual hour in which
His habits were first sown, even as a seed?
Who that shall point as with a wand and say
'This portion of the river of my mind
Came from yon fountain'?

At times of confusion, or irritation, or dissatisfaction, Leonard would recite these lines, convinced that one day being a misfit in Perth would either make sense to him or cease to matter. It would help if he knew exactly what it was he wanted. If asked — and now that Terrence was gone, no one did ask — he would say he wanted LIFE and he wanted FREEDOM, and yes, writ large. But as to the content of that life and the expression of that freedom, he could not say.

His first job on leaving school was not the electrical apprentice-ship at Morrow & Sons his father had argued for, but an usher at Perth's Capitol Theatre. He managed to convince his parents that this was a short, albeit indulgent detour on his journey towards a proper job. He believed it himself; if not, he would not have found the strength to oppose his father. He loved the job, not for the ushering but for the films and musical theatre he saw for free. And he liked the nightlife, the streets after dark, and the days to do whatever he fancied. He burrowed into the poetry shelves at the State Library, discovering passionate and anguished Europeans — Rilke, Rimbaud and Baudelaire, and the New Yorkers, Robert Lowell and Frank O'Hara. These poets revealed the life he wanted, *la vie passionelle*, peopled with poets and painters, actors and intellectuals, blacks and Jews.

In Perth, to refer to someone as an intellectual would be as insulting as calling them a fairy. As for knowing blacks or Jews, this was the sort of not-quite-respectable notion he could toy with only in the privacy of his mind. And New York? It was no more likely than the moon, or at least not yet. He felt himself to be in training for the real life to come. He read a little fiction, he read a lot of poetry, he devoured an enormous number of biographies, and he wrote poems. He liked to walk and daydream, he loved films and Hollywood musicals, and he harboured vaguely defined ambitions to be a proper poet.

He was twenty-one, and the author of a collection of poetry in manuscript, when he packed up his possessions and crossed the country to begin a new life in Melbourne. It had all happened so quickly that for the first year in his new home he kept wondering how he had managed it; but as work and friends took up more of his time, he decided just to be grateful he had. Terrence was long gone, to London or the Côte d'Azur, or somewhere equally exotic; but with his life filling fast, Leonard did not miss him. Four years later, his collection of poetry had been put in a drawer, he was about to become the managing director of his own company, and he met Sylvie Stirling.

For a different sort of man, the move from Perth would have been the opportunity for a slash-and-burn reinvention, but when Leonard arrived in Melbourne he was a wild child of the Romantics only in his hopes and dreams. Within ten years of marrying Sylvie, he had become a successful businessman, a loving husband, and a devoted father to Andrew. He may well have chosen to live three thousand miles away from his first family, but in his Melbourne existence he remained highly susceptible to paternal suggestion and the mainstream values that had marked out his upbringing. What had changed was his acceptance of this sort of life. It suited him. He loved his wife, he was content with family life, the business was thriving. He realised, even if others didn't, that he needed these outward hallmarks of stability.

Less visible was the man of complicated appetites with a conflicted soul. His beloved Wordsworth wrote: ... *there is a dark/ Inscrutable workmanship that reconciles/Discordant elements, makes them cling together/In one society*. He knew discordant elements all too well;

he knew how they fought one another, he believed that over the years they had been reconciled to some extent, and he'd accepted that life would always make difficult demands of someone like him. But there was one aspect of his existence that remained clear and uncomplicated, and that was his love for Sylvie. Sylvie and his marriage were bedrock.

So much happens in a marriage that changes can occur without either partner really noticing. Some of the changes are desirable, others less so. With the less desirable ones, by the time you do become aware of them, it's often too late to reverse them. This was how Leonard had come to understand the physical side of his marriage, perhaps the only failing of his and Sylvie's otherwise excellent partnership. The problem began quite early, related, he believed, to the pregnancies and miscarriages, rather than any dwindling interest in her body. Nevertheless, he was pleased when a business acquaintance admitted, in an alcohol-fuelled moment of honesty, that his pregnant wife had been a sexual turn-off for him. Don't worry, the man had said, the baby comes, her shape returns to normal, and if you can persuade her not to breastfeed, you'll be back doing it in no time.

But for Leonard and Sylvie, the baby never came. There were just the miscarriages, and the urgent times in between with all their pressures and longings. For they both wanted children. He pushed himself to perform loving sex — he was sure Sylvie didn't notice — but more and more it was a performance.

They were told of a medical procedure for women with a history of miscarriages. Sylvie opted to have it with what would be her last pregnancy, the one that produced Andrew. During the pregnancy Sylvie took things easy. Very easy. Lots of cuddling, lots of affection, but nothing vigorous, and certainly not sex. She apologised to Leonard, she really felt very bad about it. But he reassured her there was nothing to worry about: this was their baby, and they were both looking after it.

Andrew was born two weeks early, a strong and healthy baby. While Leonard knew that the subject of sex would eventually arise, for the time being he and Sylvie were filled with the joys of their miracle baby, and exhausted by the common stresses of first-time parents. And poor Sylvie suffered a barrage of post-partum complaints. She kept apologising for not being sexually active, and he kept reassuring her there was nothing to apologise for. She was sleeping badly, too, not just the baby and the night-time feeds, his snoring was keeping her awake. It was a reluctant confession, he had to drag it out of her, but immediately he moved into the spare room.

Once out of the marital bedroom, all the love he felt for his wife found ample physical expression. In the kitchen, on the couch, strolling through a city park, he wanted to touch her, to hold her. Feeling her in his arms brought a great sense of comfort, and an intimacy too — different from sex, deeper and more meaningful, he thought. They would cradle their baby in their linked arms, and he would experience an explosion of gratitude. This was his family.

The love and physical closeness Leonard felt for Sylvie only increased as Andrew grew. His favourite time of day was after dinner, with Andrew asleep, and he and Sylvie on the couch holding hands, while they listened to the wireless or watched the TV. When they were at a restaurant with friends, he insisted on sitting next to her rather than the usual splitting-up of husbands and wives. He liked to be connected with her no matter where they were.

They were viewed by their friends as a loving couple, and so they were, in every respect except the matter of making love. Leonard, it seemed to Sylvie, had accepted their situation — if not mentioning something could be taken as acceptance — but she was puzzled, increasingly so, as the months and years passed. By the time Andrew started kindergarten, Leonard was still in the spare room.

Sylvie would have liked to discuss the issue with one of her friends, but such things were not talked about, not in her circle; and while Maggie might have some answers, the topic was too embarrassing to raise with her sister. Sylvie knew there were books that might enlighten her; she'd actually seen one at the local library called *The Pleasures of Married Love*, but had been far too self-conscious to borrow it.

The fact was she loved her husband and she adored being a mother, and while she might wish for a little more of the passion she found in films, in the top forty, and in the novels she read, she had little to complain about. And there was plenty of physical affection between her and Leonard; indeed, her friends commented on how Leonard couldn't keep his hands off her. In most respects she was happy, of course she was, yet she couldn't avoid a growing sense she was missing out on something, a basic human experience that was exciting and highly pleasurable. But then she was also missing out on tertiary education and a paying job. This was life, as her mother always said, and you can't have it all.

Although she had thought she might have it all with her marriage to Leonard. Not strong enough to buck the system herself, she believed that Leonard already had, that this poet-businessman would bring his bohemia into the marriage, or take their marriage into bohemia. It hadn't happened.

It was understood, though never discussed, that there'd be no more children after Andrew. He was their miracle baby, and it was best not test their luck. Once Andrew was in kindergarten, Sylvie volunteered her services as a driver for the Blind Institute, and by 1966, when Andrew entered first grade, she was giving her services to the blind two days a week. But what she really wanted was a proper job.

In an ideal world she would be a librarian or a teacher, but both professions required training, and first her father and then her marriage had put an end to that. When the local pharmacist advertised for a half-time assistant, she broached it with Leonard. His response didn't surprise her: there was no need for her to work, he said, and he preferred it if she didn't. If she had persisted, he might have relented, but she knew how seriously he regarded his role of provider, and she didn't want to undermine it.

Except in the matter of sex—and who knows what goes on in the bedrooms of others?—her life looked much the same as that of her friends. But she felt unsettled—not all the time, not even the majority of the time. She would tune in to the hit parade while shelling the peas or making the beds, and sing along at the top of her voice about love and longing and breath-taking embraces and kisses. Sometimes when listening to a song, something strange and unrecognisable gnawed away at her; occasionally, she found herself in tears. It was as if the songs discovered parts of herself of which she was unaware.

And then there were the novels she read. Elizabeth Bowen, Edith Wharton and Henry James all wrote about worldly women who lived passionately—and suffered the consequences. But these characters lived life to the full before their fall. They *thrived*. And in more contemporary novels, she read about girls and women who travelled abroad and held their own in the world of men, who lived as freely as men, women like Doris Lessing's Martha Quest and nearly all of Christina Stead's women. These novels absorbed her, like films did; but unlike films, when she finished a novel, the characters seemed to shine a hard light on her own life. The books nurtured her dreams while simultaneously fuelling her restlessness.

The years passed, Andrew grew, she was busy, and she was happy enough. Days, even weeks would pass without a flicker of dissatisfaction, and then something would happen to trip her up, and she would think life had sold her short. It was in one such mood, in the winter of 1975, that she took herself off to Monash University to attend an information afternoon for prospective mature-aged students. It was a Saturday; Leonard and Andrew had gone to the football and wouldn't be home for hours, and she was fed up.

Prime Minister Gough Whitlam had introduced free tertiary education for all, and many married women were taking up an opportunity denied them when they were teenagers. Sylvie thought it unlikely she would be joining the flock, but attending this information day was making a stand for herself, demonstrating a bravado that in the general run of her life was not required, but which discontent had pushed to the surface.

After twenty years of marriage, her life was not much different from her mother's. The psychedelic sixties had passed her by; the personal growth-and-development movement of the seventies was passing her by; women's liberation was changing the lives of many women, but not hers; more women were entering the work-force — even her sister, Maggie, now had a good job. And what had she achieved? Her home was perfect, her appearance was perfect, her sponge cakes were perfect; but an organised cutlery drawer and nicely styled hair made a mockery of the woman she had hoped to be when she married Leonard. She would soon be forty. To be so old with so little to show for it.

She knew the mood would pass, it always did, but now, today, she needed to step out of her ordinary life and do something different. She consulted the street directory, and set off towards the university. Before she'd gone even a short way, she knew the information pro-gram wouldn't pull her out of the doldrums. She was already worried what Leonard would think if he were ever to discover what she was doing, and anxieties about the event itself were also muscling in. She had never been to this university, nor the newer one in the far-distant northern suburbs. As for the original university, the University of Melbourne, she'd only been on that campus for non-study reasons: once to see a play, and another time for a concert with her sister. Universities were well outside her daily round.

As a girl, she had longed to go to university, and her parents didn't hide the fact that if she'd been a boy they would have considered it. But as far as they were concerned, university was a waste of money on a girl heading for marriage and children. When she reminded them that plenty of married women with children had worked during the war, her father was quick in response: after the war the men returned and took up their jobs, and the women returned to their homes to take up theirs. When the matriculation scores came in, Sylvie was still arguing with her parents: she'd come dux of her high school, so surely they'd relent now. But she could have topped the state and it would have made no difference.

During the forty-five-minute drive to the campus, all the excitement she had associated with university as a girl converted to anxiety in the soon-to-be-forty woman. And yet no one was forcing her to attend this event. She could turn the car around and head home, bake a cake, visit a friend, prepare the dinner, return to life as she left it. But she didn't want to go home. She didn't want her old life.

There were signs at the university directing her where to park, and more signs guiding her to the venue. The noise reached her first, and seconds later she entered a large foyer. There were about a hundred women standing around talking, including many who looked even older than she was. Along one side of the space were information officers seated at trestle tables, and on a nearby windowsill were stacks of pamphlets. Sylvie gathered a selection of these, and retreated to the far side of the room. There she stood, taking it all in.

She was sure she was not alone in thinking that the life she led was the normal life. Of course she knew, as everyone did, that there were people who were poor and doing it tough, and others who were unimaginably rich; there were Chinese people whose lives were different, and Greeks and Italians who were different again. There were country people and city people, and childless couples and others with large families. There were famous singers and film stars, and women's libbers and people against nuclear disarmament—so many lives different from your own, yet you nonetheless persist in assuming that yours is the normal life. And then you find yourself in a situation like this where no one seems to be like you, and there's no assuming anything anymore.

Women stood in clusters of two or three, only she seemed to be alone. She felt so self-conscious, so uncomfortable, she was tempted to leave; but if she couldn't manage an information session, how would she manage an actual university course?

Someone handed her a green flyer. It listed specific information sessions at the various faculties to be conducted over the coming month. So she didn't have to stay, she could return another day. *But you're here now*, she said under her breath, and forced herself not to move. She concentrated on her breathing, softened the muscles in her neck, and focused on the green flyer; in a few minutes the nerves that had threatened to send her home eased. She slipped the green flyer into her bag.

A voice over a loudspeaker asked everyone to move into the adjacent lecture theatre. She went with the crowd, and once in the theatre made her way up to the top row. She couldn't slip out easily from here, but it was also the least noticeable part of the auditorium. Over the next thirty minutes she heard about the arts: histories, languages, sociology and anthropology. And English courses that taught all the literature she'd ever wanted to read. She heard about the sciences, she heard about law and social work. She heard about the help given to mature-aged students, the special study guides, the counselling services, even a crèche. She heard about part-time study, and special assessment consideration for mature-age students. She listened to it all, and the more she heard, the more she realised she couldn't do it. She didn't have the courage. She would be judged, and she would fail. It was too late for her. She wasn't like these other women, and they weren't like her. None of them looked scared, none looked in a panic. The past was the past. Chasing out-of-date dreams was foolish, and crafting a future on stale dreams was plain futile. She couldn't be the girl she once was. She wasn't that girl anymore. It was a madness to have come.

And besides, what would she do with a university degree? Leonard wouldn't want her to have a job, and even if he did, no one in their right mind would employ a middle-aged woman. If she wanted to study English literature, she could do it privately, just as she'd read privately all her life, just as she'd collected her letters privately. No assessment, no judgement, no one looking over her shoulder. It was too late for her. She should never have come.

More than ten years later, the day after Galina came to dinner, Sylvie decided to create a file of letters specifically for public viewing. If ever again she was forced into showing her collection, she would have a selection set aside expressly for this purpose.

Leonard was at his usual Saturday-afternoon golf game, and with several undisturbed hours ahead of her, Sylvie began sorting through her collection. Slipped inside the envelope of one of her early acquisitions was the green flyer from the mature-age student event. She unfolded it and held it up to the light, a foreign piece of paper which, over the next minute, rather like a rediscovered old photo, not only became familiar but summoned up that afternoon of long ago.

She was surprised to find she had kept the flyer, and kept it hidden. Indeed, she had hidden the whole event almost as soon as it had happened, shoving it in a shadowy corner of memory eventually to be forgotten. For some people, she supposed, the very discomfort of that experience would have sparked changes that would shape a future very different from the past. But far from being a trigger for change, that strange, disquieting afternoon had actually reinforced the life she had chosen.

So why had she kept the flyer?

She had always shied away from change: her life now was fundamentally the same as her life then. But what she really wished *now* was that she had made some changes back *then*. She wanted another shot at life. She wished she'd gone to university and studied literature; she wished she'd become the teacher she had long wanted to be; she wished she'd written about the power and intimacy of letters. She wished all the changes she'd like to benefit from now had been made long ago, leaving her with the same comfort and security she currently enjoyed, but a little more stimulated, a little more satisfied.

It would have helped if she were more like her sister, more resilient, more adventurous, more independent. Maggie completed her university degree and joined the public service; she now held a senior position in the Department of Labour. Her sister had taken a courageous leap, and had reaped benefits. And the Russian girl, too, also resilient, also adventurous, had wrought changes greater than anyone Sylvie knew.

She closed her eyes and rested her head on her hands. Outwardly, very little might have changed, but she felt more restless than ever before, and bothered by longings for something different, something more. The possibilities that had stretched before the nineteen-year-old girl who'd married Leonard Morrow had been so vibrant, but now it seemed as if, one by one, the lights had blown and not been replaced. She wondered if it was the plight of all women born in the 1930s to gather more and more regrets with the years, regrets fertilised by later generations of girls leading lives that she and her contemporaries wouldn't, indeed couldn't, have dreamed of.

She wanted to be as happy as she once was — not that she knew anymore what would make her happy. And why did she, or anyone for that matter, believe they had a right to happiness? Did the Russian girl? Did the vast majority of people? And it occurred to her that happiness, like beach holidays and a full purse at the supermarket, might well be a luxury, the privilege of the privileged.

She returned to her task, eventually selecting seven letters and slipping them into a manila folder; she marked the file with a red asterisk, and placed it on a shelf. Leaning back in her chair, she gazed at the liquidambar through the small window set in the roof. The leaves were still fresh and young, and brilliantly green at this time of year, and the sky beyond was chocolate-box perfect, with plump white clouds suspended in a smooth azure blue. Gradually her regrets receded, and the niggling complaints too. After a few minutes, she straightened up and reached for Mrs Payne's cigar box. She'd had a quick look this morning while Leonard was taking a shower; now, with a whole afternoon ahead of her, she could read the letters properly.

Sylvie had several love letters in her collection. She also read the published love letters of famous people—at this very moment a volume of Keats' letters to Fanny Brawne was on her desk—but nothing quite compared to these letters from the Frenchman Lucien Barbier to Miss Sophie Herbert. There were fourteen letters in all: the earliest was dated 1918, the latest 1920. She read them through in chronological order and pieced together their story. Sophie and Lucien had met in Egypt, when he was stationed with his French battalion and she was an army nurse. Their love had fired up quickly in the urgency of war, and it continued once Sophie returned to Australia. The three earliest letters had been sent to a London address, and all the others to Glen Iris, a suburb not far from here.

Lucien Barbier was a passionate, expressive man, even in a language not his own. And he was a poet, too, just like her own husband had been. What would she give for a new sonnet from Leonard now? One of Lucien's letters, the fourth, and the first to be sent to Sophie at the Melbourne address, was nearly all poetry, a lovers' duet in a poetic form called haiku. Not having heard of haiku before, she consulted the encyclopaedia and learned that it was an old and revered form of Japanese poetry, with a strict form of three lines comprising a total of seventeen syllables, with nature and the seasons being favoured themes. Structure, brevity and depth: it seemed like a perfect combination.

'*Ma chérie*,' his letter began:

I have made a copy of our 'Lovers' Duet' for you. How lovingly, how passionately we serenaded each other that night in the café. Only a month since our first meeting and see how we sing. You were so quick to dismiss your efforts, but my heart still quickens with your words. And see how we travel the haiku seasons. We are unstoppable. I have the originals with me now, the stack of drink coasters we used, one for each of our haiku. They are among my most precious possessions. And when we are together again, as surely we will be, I will give them to you and you can be the custodian for the rest of our days. But for now a copy, yours on the right and mine on the left.

LOVERS' DUET HAIKU

Your eyes smoke like ice.
Outside traffic warmly glows.
Why do I shiver?

> Above the chill wind
> I lean into your coal gaze
> and burn in white heat.

Autumn comes slowly,
the turning leaves take their time.
Why does my heart speed?

> Time's knowing thighs lock
> just memory now and sleep.
> You said you'd not leave.

The Spring moon grows huge
through the dark flowering trees.
I am missing you.

> Hear my budding voice
> it bursts and beckons to you.
> Come sink in my tune.

My song is restless.
The battle makes my skin itch.
My lover is deaf.

You must learn to hear.
Run wildly from the battle
I await you here.

The brooch I gave you
for our first Autumn birthday
is now at your throat.

Charred I am, you hurt.
Golden hands crisp at the edges
crease me till I cry.

To see you always
I would invoke Hell eagerly
and call and call.

Can words conquer all?
The quick the cold the bitter?
Answer me my love.

Words often fail me
Those fast frustrating symbols.
My eyes speak clearer.

Your claws burn red welts
they speak clearly to my skin.
Lie hot next to me.

I lie in your arms
and know your heartbeat so well.
My own heart knows bliss.

If Haiku can bend
like a branch in a chill wind
Why my love not you?

I will bend if you
take my love in all seasons.
Hold this in your heart.

In chill and in warmth
Our eyes would know only sun
My lover, my life.

Sylvie's heart is pounding, as if these haiku are for her. She reads again, this time aloud. She reads as Lucien, she reads as Sophie, she feels the hot tension, she feels the new love. And she marvels at such passion. She wonders what happened to Lucien and Sophie. The letters end as they begin, full of love and plans for their future together. What kept these lovers apart? And in her mind's eye, she sees Sophie's mother, Mrs Herbert, a pillar of the eastern suburbs, a woman who would never welcome a foreigner into her family, much less a Catholic one. She sees Mrs Herbert walking to the letterbox to collect the mail, there to find in the bundle an airmail letter addressed to her daughter. Mrs Herbert checks the sender details, she breaks open the envelope, she reads the letter, she realises what her daughter is up to, she determines to stop it. She destroys the letter and all the ones that follow.

Poor Sophie doesn't understand. She rereads Lucien's old letters searching for clues. She pines for him, she plans to go to Lyons, see him, persuade him of their love. But as the months of silence stretch into a year, she decides that Lucien must have met someone else, someone close by, someone easier. When her mother arranges with her friend Mrs Payne to introduce her to Mrs Payne's son, Sophie acquiesces. She doesn't care what happens to her now. Mrs Payne's son courts her; it helps ameliorate the pain. A few months later, he proposes; a few months more, they marry.

It is a shocking betrayal by a mother, Sylvie thinks. She would never do such a thing to Andrew — and girls don't come much more foreign than Galina. But even if Galina were from a tribe in Outer Mongolia, as Andrew's chosen she'd be Sylvie's too. Love is not such a common commodity that you'd toss it away.

As it happens, she likes Galina, admires her too. How can she not? The girl has lost both parents, has fled oppression, is living in a foreign country, is speaking a foreign language, is supporting herself financially, physically and emotionally. This girl, half her own age, has experienced so much. Sometimes it seems to Sylvie as if life, the full-flavoured kind, has brushed past her on its way to juicier game.

She is grateful for the wisdom of maturity, but it seems to be making a mockery of some of her earlier choices. The fact is, you can be immersed in a type of life, as she has been, and so captive to it that you don't realise its limitations, how confining it is. Even worse than not questioning, you don't even see the need to question. The years pass, and it's not that you have regrets, it's not even that you can say how things should have been different. Rather, it's like that old song of Peggy Lee's: *Is that all there is?*

9

OLD SOVIET, NEW AUSTRALIAN

Galina is at Finland Station. In her pocket is a ticket for a train travelling to the West. She is carrying two huge suitcases, one in each hand, and on her back is a bulky hessian bundle that rises high above her head. The weight of the luggage is enormous, and she wonders how she will make it to the train. The station hall is packed, the crush and smell are overwhelming. She pushes through the crowd, it is so hard to breathe; everyone is concerned with their own business, no one offers to help. Up ahead she sees the doors to the platform, they're open, and she feels a blast of fresh air. The people behind press her forward. She draws closer and closer, squeezes through the doorway, and finally emerges on the platform. The cold hits her; inside her clothes the sweat freezes on her skin.

In front of her is a long train. Passengers are walking down the platform; once they find their carriage, they disappear from view. There is no shelter and no one is loitering. Overhead the clouds are thick and low, the wind cuts her face. The platform is black with ice and filth; she's not wearing her winter boots, so must walk with particular care. The train has many carriages, each displaying a number, and she is glad to see hers is one of the closer ones. She hefts her bags to the carriage door; there's an impossibly high step to mount, and her spirits plummet. Suddenly a man materialises and lifts her bags onto the train; he stashes them in the space provided for luggage, then leaves before she can thank him. She sinks into her allocated seat, relief filling her like warm milk. Nothing can stop her now. Other passengers enter the carriage; no one acknowledges her, no one so much as glances at her. She checks the time: only ten minutes before the scheduled departure. A woman seated behind her says, 'Soviet trains always run on time.'

A man in uniform appears and asks to see her ticket. 'You're in the wrong carriage.' He nods in the direction of the front of the train. 'You should be up there. Carriage three.'

She pleads with him. There's not enough time. She wants to keep this seat. The officer's not listening, he orders her to move.

She collects her luggage and steps down from the train. There are eight minutes till departure. The carriages are long, the platform is icy, the bags are monstrous. She is running on the slippery surface. The luggage grows heavier and heavier, the train grows longer and longer, the seconds tick faster and faster. She can't see the numbers on the carriages. She's still running when the train starts to move. Hands reach down, they grab her, the suitcases have disappeared, she wakes up.

It takes a moment to orient herself. Not Leningrad, but Melbourne. Not Finland Station, but her saddlery. Her breath draws quickly. Her neck and shoulders ache. The pillow has fallen to the floor. Dawn is not far off and the sky is lightening. She can hear birds and the distant rattle of a tram. She leans the pillow against the wall and props herself against it. How many borders must she cross? How many bloody borders?

Galina was homesick. Here in her own place, with a cupboard full of food, a rack of bright clothes, a kitchen and bathroom all to herself, she was lamentably and ineluctably homesick. She supposed she had been aware of it for some time, like grit underfoot as she negotiated the roads of her new existence, but now it was demanding her full attention. She, Galina Kogan, was sickening for home.

The mood had crystallised after her visit to the Morrow home. Sleep had turned traitor, and concentration had deserted her. And there was a throbbing in her left temple which threatened a migraine that never came, the persistent threat more wearisome than the full-blown pain. Why such homesickness should strike her now, two years after leaving Leningrad, was difficult to explain. Although the possibility occurred to her that as she'd become more settled in Australia, she may have relaxed her guard; and with reduced defences, the pangs that had long been contained romped in. She was grateful to her new country, profoundly so, but this did not lighten the loss of the old.

Osip Mandelstam wrote of an 'inch of blue sea'; Galina longed for an inch of Russia. She shuffled through various colours in search of the best to portray the Russia of her yearnings. Soviet Russia would never possess the freedom she associated with blueness, and whiteness was far too pure for the country she had left behind. Purple? Lilac? Yellow? Green? None was right. What word, what image could describe her abandoned, yet longed-for sweet Russia?

And that was it. Sweet. She longed for an inch of sweet Russia. She longed for snow and ice and the first spring buds. She longed for the weak wintry light and summer's white nights. It was only now, after a separation of two years, that she realised the degree of comfort derived from familiar surroundings, and the stresses that accrue when you are perpetually confronted with strange and new customs. It was only when you find yourself limping along that you learn, perhaps too late, what constitute the absolutely crucial elements of your existence. She longed for familiar streets and buildings, she longed for the crush of the Metro and the smell of the waterways, she longed for her friends and colleagues, and she particularly longed for her Russian language.

And she longed not to feel any of these longings.

Here in the West, people referred to the in-built obsolescence of household appliances. Might there be an in-built obsolescence to homesickness? And an in-built obsolescence to grief, too? Might there come a time of a kinder memory that exacted neither longing nor loss?

Whenever she was in company, she strove to maintain the outward appearance of a textbook émigré. This involved an acrobatic combination of grateful new Australian with critically informed ex–Soviet citizen. But now it felt as if two entirely different species had set up home in the single environment of her body, and both were competing for memory, habit, allegiance, and the thrum of her rudderless heart.

She couldn't continue this way. She needed to make some changes.

She had thought she would assimilate more quickly if she kept herself separate from other Russian émigrés; now she wondered if she would ever fully assimilate, and, more especially, whether she could tolerate all the losses if she did. What seemed distressingly clear was that her choices—a type of self-annihilation, it now occurred to her—had made her exile total and absolute. She needed other émigrés to connect her with home. And it would help to see Zara and Arnold more regularly; they were, after all, the closest she had to family in this country.

It was no mystery to her why the Morrow evening had been the tipping point. Andrew and his parents existed in the *fullness* of their lives: past and present. They drank from crystal that had come from Sylvie's grandmother; they ate with cutlery that had belonged to Leonard's parents; there were photos on display of Andrew from infancy to the present day, and pictures of the more than three decades of the Morrow marriage; there were anniversary and birthday presents on show, and an array of souvenirs from their travels. And if they so desired, the Morrows could point out biographical landmarks: shops, schools, hospitals, houses, beaches, bridges, countless places that said, *This is how I came to be me.*

Then there was the ease and closeness in the Morrow gathering, most evident with the husband and wife, still so loving after more than thirty years together; but it was also there in their grown-up son, and the friend of longstanding. A few hours with these people had unpicked her disturbingly fragile foreigner's cladding.

There were, she was discovering, so many impossible pairings in the existence of the émigré. While gathered with this family in their home, Galina was soaking up their warmth and closeness while simultaneously being aware of what she was being forced to live without. Warmth and absence; gratitude and loss; resilience and despair. So many impossible pairings. Even émigré and immigrant. To the Soviets she was the former, to the Australians the latter, but to herself she was both. Always this double life: an old Soviet and a new Australian.

Even her work had suffered in the wake of the Morrow dinner. The current batch of sewing designs should have been finished last Friday, but following a nervy phone call to her boss, the deadline had been extended beyond the weekend to the end of business today. Even so, with two entire pattern packets not yet started, she worried she'd miss the new deadline. It would help if she could eat, but food had turned hostile. Her stomach ached and groaned, as if it had been invaded by a typhoon—or a Leningrad wind.

And suddenly she was laughing, the movement stretching muscles stiffened by misery. A Leningrad wind blustering in from the Gulf of Finland, this scourge of Petersburgers had blundered into her Australian life. The absurdity of it, the absurdity of her circumstances. And from one moment to the next, the breath went out of her misery. 'Enough,' she said aloud to the empty room. 'You need to grow a thicker skin.'

Misery comes so easily, she was thinking, but being so unpleasant, only a fool or a masochist would give it the upper hand. Perhaps all dynamic lives are propelled by paradoxes and uncertainties; after all, perpetual smooth sailing is not a great builder of character.

She crossed to her work area, switched on the lamp, and laid out her materials exactly as she would have back in Leningrad. Her Australian table was larger than her old one, but with a similar pale wooden surface; her art materials were much the same, although far easier to come by here. Of course the work was different, but she'd adapted to that. The most significant and disturbing difference was Lidiya's absence. In the evenings, after days spent in their respective jobs, the two of them would work, Galina at her table and, an arm's length away, Lidiya. They were well aware that their sixteen-hour days revealed a work ethic that was not typically Soviet — with the obvious exception of the black market, which operated at full throttle around the clock. The old joke *You pretend to work, we pretend to pay you* still elicited, if not a laugh, then a knowing groan.

She had almost finished one of the pattern packets when the phone rang. So engrossed had she been, it took a moment for her to surface, and the caller had to repeat himself.

It was Leonard Morrow.

After a brief greeting, he launched into the purpose of his call. 'I don't know if you're needing extra work, but if you are, I might have something for you.'

His company was in the process of putting together a new catalogue. They would be using photographs for the actual products, but they were wanting some illustrations of library scenes as well. 'To provide a more creative aura.' He paused to pull on his cigarette. 'Might you be interested in doing the illustrations?'

With the sewing patterns and her real estate job, Galina was earning enough to meet her needs and save a little as well. Nonetheless, she worried that a slump in real estate would see her out of that job, and the new computers might render her obsolete in the sewing-pattern business. So she thanked Leonard for thinking of her, told him that yes, she was interested, and arranged to meet him at his office the following Friday. Not that illustrating catalogues for library furniture, for real estate, for any merchandise come to that, was what she wanted as a career. But it was good interim work until she gained an entrée into publishing, and a return to book illustration.

As far back as she could remember, Galina had wanted to be a book illustrator. It was the marriage of words with images in her childhood books that had first ignited her interest. There were books that were all words, and other books that were all pictures, but comparing these with the combined books was the difference between living in a *kommunalka* and having your own flat, or hearing a single aria as against the entire opera. She knew at a young age that she wanted the flat, she wanted the whole opera.

Her mother never worked on children's books, which was a great disappointment to Galina, as Lidiya was allowed to keep the books she translated. But as it happened, her own favourite picture books were those that had belonged to her mother when *she* had been a child, way back in the 1930s and 1940s. Some of these books had been so loved that the covers were frayed and faded, and pages had been torn; but in a way Galina couldn't explain, that made them even more precious. On the inside cover of most of these storybooks, written in a grown-up's hand, was her mother's name and another name as well.

Galina was young, not much more than three or four, when she first asked about the other name. 'What does this say?'

Her mother had remained silent, it was clear she didn't want to answer, which made Galina even more curious. So she asked again. This was when she learned her mother had an older brother, Mikhail.

'Where is he?'

Her mother shook her head. 'Gone, disappeared, a long time ago.' And then, to put an end to the questions, she added, 'We'll never see him again.'

Galina wanted to know more. She kept asking, she kept pushing, and only when she realised how much she was upsetting Lidiya did she stop.

Some years later, when Galina's own artistic talent was already apparent, her mother explained why these old books of hers, the picture books of the 1920s, 30s and 40s, were so special.

'When I was growing up,' she said, 'enemies of the people were said to be everywhere—in schools, on farms, in the army, in the factories, and most especially among artists and writers.' She lowered her voice to a whisper. 'When everyone's frightened, when everyone's suspicious, it's very easy to make mistakes.'

Her mother paused, and Galina guessed she was thinking about her own mother and father.

'People had to be very careful, and this was the case in every aspect of Soviet life, but far less so when it came to children's books.' And now she was smiling. 'It was as if anything intended for children wasn't to be taken seriously; certainly it couldn't do any harm to the great Soviet state. So the sort of surveillance that happened in other aspects of creative work was far less rigorous in the case of children's books. When it became too dangerous for great writers like Mandelstam to write openly for adults, they wrote stories for children instead.'

She gathered a few more of the children's books and spread them across the table. 'Many of the books I had as a child, many of the books you like best, were written by the best writers in the country and illustrated by the best artists.' Again she smiled. 'Writers and artists, composers too, will always find a way.' And in the quietest whisper, she added, 'Fairytales, fantasies, allegories can be very powerful, despite what our leaders think.'

Everyone has days that start out ordinary and finish as exceptional, and this winter's day in Leningrad when Galina was ten years old and learning why her mother's children's books were so special was one such day. She and her mother were having their whispered conversation when there was a knock on the door. The buzzers at the front entrance had been broken for months, so anyone could enter the building and make their way up the stairs.

Her mother went to the door. Galina, still seated at the table, heard a man's voice, she heard her mother's voice, she heard the door slam, and then a volley of angry words. She twisted around and saw a strange man standing in front of the closed door. He was tall, and bulked out in an army greatcoat. The ear flaps of his *ushanka* were tied back, revealing a thick reddish-brown fur; it looked so soft and warm, it might be fox or even sable, and there was more of this plush fur on the lapels and collar of his coat. His boots were black leather and they looked new. Such luxurious clothes, and so different from the man himself. His face was bloated and covered with bristles, his eyes were red and sloppy like a bloodhound's, and when he removed the hat, his hair was plastered to his head. He reeked of tobacco and unwashed body. His stench quickly filled the room.

Her mother looked to be in shock. The man, however, seemed entirely at ease. He turned to Galina and walked towards her; she automatically stood up. A book fell to the floor with a loud slap.

'Say hello to your Uncle Misha,' he said to her.

Lidiya quickly collected herself. She grabbed Galina by the arm, and held her close.

'No uncle of hers. And no brother of mine.'

She told the man to leave, she told him never to return. He did not move. Her mother then ordered him to leave. Galina thought she sounded ferocious, but the man wasn't at all scared. He appraised the room, his gaze settling on grandfather's old armchair. Lidiya said she could feel her father's presence whenever she sat in it.

'Some things,' the smelly man said as he made himself comfortable, 'some things don't change.' He stroked the armrest with his pudgy hand. His fingers were fat like sausages, and there was grime beneath the nails.

A moment later, Lidiya half-pushed, half-carried Galina to the door and hurried her up the passageway to where her friend Natalya lived. Lidiya whispered that everything would be all right, that Galina was not to worry; when the man was gone, she would come back and fetch her.

The hours dragged like days. Galina didn't want to play with Natalya, not while her mother was shut in with the fat, smelly man; she didn't want to eat the food Natalya's mother prepared, not when her mother might be in danger. Every time she heard footsteps in the passage she ran to the door, and each time the footsteps did not stop. It was after supper when her mother finally collected her. She looked tired and very sad.

Their own room was freezing. 'I needed to clear the air,' Lidiya said as she closed the window. There were changes which Galina saw immediately. The leather satchel that had belonged to her grandfather was gone; so too his pipe and clock. Other items from her mother's childhood—a small painting, an enamelled dish, a silver cruet set—all things that Lidiya had said were precious, had disappeared. And so had the man.

'And he won't return,' Lidiya said. 'He took what he wanted.'

He seemed to have taken something of Lidiya as well. Months were to pass before she grew the missing parts back again.

The man did not take the children's books. That night, her mother did not come to bed until late. In the morning, she saw that the name Mikhail had been blackened out in every single book.

Galina had brought the picture books to Australia. She now took them off the shelf and spread them out on her work table. She was an illustrator of children's books, so why was she spending her time drawing houses and frocks? She owed it to herself, to her mother too, to pursue her ambitions. She would accept Leonard Morrow's job if he offered it to her, but at the same time she would start sending samples of her work to publishers. She'd been in Australia long enough to stop treating it as a temporary stopover to somewhere else. This flitting between the abandoned past and a fragile present might well define the state of exile, but she had to struggle against it; she had to try harder.

She worked steadily and quickly, and by two o'clock had completed the final two patterns. She took a tram to the city and dropped the finished work in to the office. She then decided to take the rest of the day off—an Australian long weekend or, given it was Monday, a case of Mondayitis. She set off through the small streets and bluestone lanes that crisscrossed the city centre. With their tiny cafés and shops, the walls splattered with graffiti, and the smoke-stained bricks—some still punctured with iron rings for tethering horses, with their metal delivery chutes tunnelling down from the pavements, and wafts of delicious food mixed with the stench of rubbish bins and stale urine, these lanes revealed a life stretching way back to when the city was first established. 'Marvellous Melbourne', according to the histories she had read.

It was still marvellous to her. These narrow streets and lanes with their jostling life reaching back through the centuries were, she was thinking, a collage of history and memory. And an image came to mind, a picture showing cars and trams and modern pedestrians hovering over a past of horses and coaches and people in period dress. Perhaps there was an illustration to be done, or a series of illustrations. Or perhaps, and the thought was immediately enticing, there might be a book here, a book about this city so different from Leningrad. The stories a city can tell. When Melbourne meets Leningrad, what each might disclose to the other about their landmarks, their housing, their food, their celebrations. What, for example, might Leningrad's waterways and the Gulf of Finland have to say to Melbourne's brown Yarra and Port Phillip Bay? And what about the different music and street life, the different weather, the different vehicles, the sports and clothing? It would be a project to bring her past and present together, a picture book: *When Melbourne Meets Leningrad*.

The following Friday was pleasantly warm. Leonard Morrow's business was located in a light-industrial area about three kilometres from the saddlery, and with just a small folio to carry, Galina decided to walk. She felt vastly different from the caged squirrel of a few days back. She had already sent off samples of her work to two different publishers, she'd compiled a list of features comparing Leningrad to Melbourne, she had even completed some sketches for the project. She arrived at Leonard's factory feeling refreshed and relaxed, but well aware of her priorities. This job, if Leonard decided to give it to her, would be a one-off.

She gazed up at the building—no mistaking she was at the right place. Stretched across the roof in large capital letters were the words MORROW & SON. Had Leonard so counted on Andrew to join the business that he'd cemented it in the company name? And if this were the case, Andrew's fight to be an artist had been a struggle against far more trenchant parental forces than a simple argument about making a living.

Leonard's factory was situated on the corner of a lane. It was a two-storey, cream-brick building at the front, with a single-storey addition behind. A smallish concern, she thought—but small compared with what? Soviet industry, where all the factories were gargantuan? How long would it take, she wondered, before she acquired new standards of comparison? Not that she wanted to lose her Russian experience, she just didn't want it to dominate. She wanted to choose when to apply it. And why not? Choice was, after all, one of the West's major gifts.

A small laugh escaped: a little self-mockery would save her from being a miseryguts. And with this came another snort of laughter. She loved the blunt, irreverent Australian additions to stiff-upper-lip British English. 'Miseryguts' was a favourite, and, she noted with satisfaction, perfectly executed in the present context.

She smoothed her hair and straightened her dress—the same dress she had worn to the Morrow dinner, she suddenly realised, but nothing she could do about that now. She entered the building and followed a sign directing her upstairs to the office. There she was greeted by the receptionist, a good-looking woman of about forty. She wondered if Sylvie minded Leonard having such an attractive assistant, then quickly dismissed the thought: she'd never seen a closer nor more compatible couple than the Morrows.

As the receptionist picked up the phone to buzz Leonard, Winston Yeung appeared. He approached with his hand outstretched.

'Welcome to our world,' he said with a smile

He smelled heavenly, an aftershave cologne more floral and less piercing than Australian men tended to favour—not that she would complain about any cologne: she loved the way men smelled here. As she shook his hand, she breathed him in.

'Leonard apologises. He was planning to show you around himself, but he's running behind and asked me to do the honours instead.' Winston checked his watch. 'By the time we've finished, he should be free.'

Regularly when she was growing up, Galina, like all Soviet children, toured factories to witness firsthand the power and might of Soviet industry, but Morrow & Son was the first privately owned factory she had ever seen. It was so clean, both the building and the machines; even the workers looked clean. Different areas were designated for different functions, including an entire section for welding. As they walked through the factory, Winston revealed his familiarity with the workers by asking one man about his wife, another about a forthcoming baby, and a third—Asian, like Winston, but maybe one of the new Vietnamese she was yet to meet—whether his family had joined him yet.

'It's a big enterprise,' Winston said, indicating the scene before them. 'Ten times larger than when Leonard took it over.'

'And the son?' Galina asked.

Winston laughed. 'A mythical beast. Australians like family-run companies. Grandfathers, fathers and sons all working harmoniously together.' He paused a moment. 'Although, for many of us, this company does feel like family. Most employees, both in the office and on the factory floor, have worked for Morrow's for years. I'm one of the new boys.' And again that sweet smile. 'I've only been here a decade.'

Galina was interested in his background; all newcomers to Australia interested her, particularly those like Winston, who appeared to have adjusted well. She learned that both he and his brother had been sent overseas for their university studies, the brother to America and Winston to Australia. 'It was insurance for the future,' he said, and explained about the return of Hong Kong to China. 'At that time no date had been set, and while many Hong Kongers hoped it would never happen, my parents thought it best to be prepared.' His expression was serious and suddenly he looked a good deal older. 'And they were right. We now know Hong Kong will be returning to the Chinese in less than ten years. That we don't want to be part of mainland China doesn't matter one jot, it's been taken out of our hands.' He shrugged. 'Actually, it was never in our hands.'

Since the announcement of the handover date, there had been a massive exodus of businesspeople, as well as lawyers, doctors and other professionals. 'It's been a significant loss,' Winston said.

'And your parents?'

'They're still in Hong Kong, and that's where they'll remain. They're too old to move now. But they visit here, and they visit my brother in Chicago, and of course we go home regularly.'

'Australia is full of exiles,' Galina said quietly.

'No. No.' Winston shook his head. 'I don't see myself as an exile. I go back to Hong Kong whenever I want. I could go back and live there if I chose. But the life here suits me better.'

And that was the crucial difference. She didn't have a choice. When she received her exit visa to leave the Soviet Union, she forfeited any right of return. Ever. But there was something else. Imprinted in the semantics of exile was a desire to return, and the assumption that when things had improved, you'd be permitted to return. She'd seen refugee camps on TV, huge tented cities established for people seeking sanctuary from persecution for a few months, perhaps a year, before returning home. But ten years, even twenty years on, there was a second generation of displaced people in these camps, and they, like their parents, dreamed of a time when it'd be safe to go home.

Perhaps you stopped being an exile when you no longer wanted to return home because you *were* home.

'Where is home for you now?' she asked Winston as they made their way back to the office.

He did not hesitate. 'At the moment it's here, Australia. But as soon as I return to Hong Kong, my home is there.'

They arrived back in reception just as Leonard exited his office. He greeted her with a kiss. 'Have you eaten lunch?'

She hadn't, but neither did she want him to feel obliged to buy her a meal. He silenced her protests. 'We can talk business over a sandwich at my local café.'

It was indeed local, only about twenty metres up the street. Leonard ordered his 'usual'—a hot roast-beef sandwich with English mustard—and she settled for a home-made meat pie with tomato sauce. She'd taken a great fancy to the Australian meat pie; so Russian in consistency, carbohydrates and salt, she suspected that the original recipe had come from the kitchen of a Russian Australian.

The business was settled quickly. She had thought she was to be interviewed for the job, but Leonard simply flipped through her folio, pausing at some of her work for Merridale Graphics—'I occasionally see Ralph Merridale at the commerce club'—asked a couple of questions, and the job was hers.

Leonard laid out the roughs for the catalogue, and took her through what he was after. 'Four pictures,' he said, 'painterly, and portraying a variety of library users sitting at our desks, in our carrels, browsing our shelves, searching in our catalogue drawers. And one of the pictures needs to feature teenagers in school uniform as we want to increase our penetration into the private-school market.'

They discussed style and size, they settled on a timeline, and by the time their food arrived, the business was finished.

The café was crowded with workers on their lunch break, and there was a steady stream of people entering for takeaway food and coffee. Despite the surrounding bustle, Leonard remained focused on her. He asked about her family, about Leningrad, about her time at university; he asked about her life in Australia and the adjustments she'd had to make. There were, as far as she could see, no ulterior motives driving his questions, so she let herself talk freely. He would glance up now and then at a loud noise or a burst of laughter, but his gaze quickly returned to her. Other male patrons would be distracted when an attractive woman walked in, would track her progress from door to counter or to a table, and might continue with their blatant staring even after she had sat down; this sort of behaviour was so common among Australian men that Galina had come to expect it. Now what drew her attention was its absence. And it was not because Leonard was old — the Australian male gaze seemed not to weaken with age — but because he was interested in her and what she was saying.

However, after fifteen minutes of responding to his questions, she was feeling uncomfortable. Her experiences this past year in Australia had shaped her preference for asking questions rather than talking about herself — a quality she shared with Andrew, she had noticed. It was not simply that Australians rarely asked her questions, her own questions had been essential to help her navigate through the ever-changing Australian maze.

187

Back in the Soviet Union, understanding people and knowing what made them tick was simple. You all lived with the same restrictions and deprivations; you all wanted the same things, feared the same things, valued the same things. But with each new person here, she needed to discover their current, that absolutely fundamental source of their being that revealed their loves and desires, their biases and beliefs, their struggles and pains, their successes and losses. Questions had been essential.

She now asked Leonard about his family in Perth, about the business, about his sports and hobbies. Leonard answered politely, but briefly. She found him strangely opaque. He seemed to live behind his face — an attractive mask, particularly given his age, but revealing very little.

Ever since Andrew had mentioned that his father wrote poetry, she had been intrigued to know how the businessman and the poet cohabitated. Now seemed an opportune time to find out.

'Andrew has told me about your poetry,' she began. And opting for an oblique approach, 'Are you familiar with our great Russian poets?'

Her question caught him by surprise, and suddenly the unreadable face slipped into focus. She saw his discomfort, his eye contact faltered, and in the long silence that followed she found herself wishing she'd not broached this subject.

Then he returned his gaze to her.

'No,' he said, 'not the Russians, though I did see Yevtushenko perform a few years ago.' There was a pause, so drawn out she was thinking the poetry conversation might be over, when he began again. 'My favourite poet when I was young was Wordsworth. Because of *The Prelude*.' And more quietly, as if it had just occurred to him, 'I suppose he's still my favourite poet, though I've not read him in years.' He leaned forward, and in his normal voice asked if she knew *The Prelude*.

She'd heard of this poem and intended to read it. But with so much else to read for her Australianisation program, it was not a priority. 'It's on my long-term reading list,' she said.

'*The Prelude* provided me with a vision of utopia when I was growing up in Perth,' Leonard said, a vague smile hovering over his face.

Like all Russians, Galina knew all about utopia. Soviet dogma thrived on utopian promises, how it was necessary to suffer now for the glorious future to come. And while you learned through bitter experience that utopia never came, that it was truly a 'no-place', an imaginary place, how much worse daily life would have been without its possibility dangled before you.

She'd long wondered whether for every utopia there was a dystopia lurking in the background. She now suggested this to Leonard. 'And perhaps not in the background; it might actually be your ordinary daily life.'

He nodded, thoughtfully, it seemed to her, so she went ahead with a more personal question. 'In your case, what dystopia was Wordsworth's *Prelude* working against?'

She saw him hesitate, and silently encouraged him. But he must have thought better of it. 'We can return to utopia another time,' he said in a businesslike manner, and gestured to the waiter for more coffee.

'Now then,' he said, once again the urbane older man, 'Andrew tells me that Soviet citizens aren't as enamoured of Gorbachev as we Westerners are.'

She didn't want to change the topic, but Leonard, the adult, the person paying for lunch, had the greater authority. But still she was annoyed. Well, if he wanted Gorbachev, she'd give him Gorbachev.

'I think the West is blinded by what it regards as Gorbachev's Westernness. If he is not so different from you, then it is easier to relate to him. And if he is not so different, then you assume that his freeing-up of the Soviet system is spelling the end of communism and a transition to democracy.' She sounded as if she were giving

189

a lecture. But Leonard had asked for it. 'Because Gorbachev wears Italian suits and has an elegant wife does not mean he is not a committed communist whose primary allegiance is to a strong and enduring Soviet Union.'

She was speaking too bluntly, and with an implied criticism of Westerners; she should stop, but it seemed she couldn't stop. 'Even if Gorbachev wanted to bring the Soviet system to an end—and I do not believe for a moment he does—it will take far more than one man to do that. The system has been in place for seventy years, it has shaped every aspect of life, and it has shaped desire and expectation too. Its roots go very deep. Democracy for the Soviet Union is a Western dream. It's *your* dream.'

She was about to move on to the subject of a free-market system within the Soviet context, how everyone wanted an easier life with ready access to material goods, but they had come to rely on the state to look after them, when she saw Leonard's gaze shift to the door. A man, much the same age as herself, had entered the café. Slender and athletic, dressed in slim-fitting black jeans and a tight black T-shirt, he might have been a ballet dancer. His hair was dark and curly, his face was pale and angelic, his eyes were huge and dark. He was a truly beautiful man.

Leonard's gaze alighted on him momentarily and then flicked back to her. He was trying to listen to her, trying to concentrate, but his gaze was pulled back to the beautiful man waiting at the counter.

Leonard's gaze could not help itself.

10

OWLS OF THE DESERT

Leonard rolled over and propped himself on an elbow. With his free hand he pulled the sheet over their hips.

'What do you think of Andrew's Russian girlfriend?'

It was the day after Galina had come to the office.

'I like her.' And after a pause, 'But it's what Andrew thinks that matters.'

'It's not an easy question for a father to ask a son.'

'Patience, Leo, patience. For as long as Andrew keeps seeing her, you can assume he's interested.'

Leonard lay back and closed his eyes. He had to stop worrying about Andrew. He wasn't a child anymore—another couple of years and he'd be thirty. And it wasn't as if he had anything really wrong with him: he wasn't blind, he wasn't deaf, he had no chronic illness, no degenerative disease. He was just shy. He was also achieving a name as an artist, he was financially independent, he travelled widely, he had friends and now even a girlfriend. To any impartial observer, his son was a successful young man.

Leonard drew in a deep calming breath and exhaled heavily, as if that might dispel his over-protective-father tendencies. This past month had been hectic, the period before Christmas always was, so exhaustion was probably contributing to his concern about Andrew. How greatly he'd love to stay right where he was, but he knew he couldn't; they were going out tonight. He propped himself back on his elbow.

'You need a haircut,' he said, brushing a stray hank of hair from the broad forehead.

Winston's face assumed a wry smile. 'And you're showing your age, Leo. The world has moved on from short back and sides.'

Winston always made light of their age difference. It had never bothered him, and when they first got together, it hadn't bothered Leonard either; in fact, Winston's youth made him feel better about his own age. But as the years mounted up, he had dwelled on the issue more and more, and now at fifty-seven, with skin sagging and body shape changing, he wondered how long he'd stay attractive to thirty-three-year-old Winston.

'If only you could see your expression.' Winston was laughing. 'You look like there's been a death in the family.' He reached for his arm. 'Even at eighty, Leo, even at one hundred, you'll always be my extremely attractive lover,' and pulled him down to the bed again.

A few minutes more would make no difference, Leonard decided, and settled back with Winston's head on his shoulder. He stroked the smooth familiar skin, and felt his own body relax.

He had occasionally wondered if he might be using the age issue to deflect from more serious issues like cheating on his wife and having sex with men. But the truth was he'd never seen himself as cheating on Sylvie. He loved her, and would always love her; what he did with Winston, or any man for that matter, had nothing to do with his marriage. As for sex with men, from the time he was a schoolboy in Perth it was something he'd always done, an aspect of who he was, and part of the man Sylvie had married; like his tendency to ingrown toenails, he had lived with it all his life and accommodated for it. Some of the men he'd met over the years had accused him of being in denial. He wasn't. He was not a homosexual, he was not hanging out in any closet; he was a married man, a family man, who liked to have sex with men.

It made his life a little more complicated than other men's, he was prepared to concede that, or perhaps differently complicated—after all, plenty of men had secret indulgences; but whether complicated or not, it felt normal to him. In his younger years, he'd cruised with bravado; he'd had fun, and it certainly added a bit of sparkle to an otherwise workaday existence. Since meeting Winston, his life had been far more sedate with only the occasional opportunistic adventure. He wasn't using age to deflect from other issues. He was fifty-seven, he was ageing, and that made a difference.

'So many of my generation won't get to your age,' Winston now said.

The head on his shoulder suddenly felt leaden. Winston was obsessed with AIDS, he couldn't leave the topic alone. AIDS intruded on all their Thursdays and Saturdays. AIDS was spoiling their time together.

'Can't you forget the AIDS business for just a couple of hours?' Leonard said. He didn't bother to conceal his irritation.

Winston pulled himself up and sat cross-legged on the bed. His skin was smooth and hairless, his body boyishly slender. An *ephebe*—the word popped into Leonard's mind from some long-ago reading. But while Winston might look like a boy, he wasn't sounding like one.

'I hate the way you refer to "the AIDS business", Leo. It's a disease. And it's killing men like us.'

Leonard, too, sat up. He pulled on a shirt, no need to advertise his age, and tried to find a way out of the conversation he knew was about to happen. He and Winston had argued about the AIDS business dozens of times, and on each occasion he had tried to placate Winston with the facts: the men who were dying of AIDS were active homosexuals, deeply embedded within a gay sub-culture. He and Winston were not. Winston only had sex with Leonard, or at least that was what he said, although Leonard had wondered about his regular visits to the Richmond pool; but whatever he did he would do it safely. As for himself, he was married, and should he have a casual encounter these days, it was always safe.

Winston was so terrified of AIDS he'd attended an information session run by a gay men's health group. Leonard had refused to go. 'I'm not like them,' he'd said. Winston returned with information about services and support groups; he also brought news of an HIV test newly available to those at risk.

'We're all scared,' he said now, drawing the sheet around him. He recited a litany of pain, as if Leonard had not heard it all before: diarrhoea, a raft of opportunistic infections, rare cancers, ugly skin lesions, weight loss, muscle wasting—'Some of these men look like inmates of Changi'—organ failure, dementia, blindness.

'It's a punishing disease, Leo,' he said, with an emphasis on 'punishing'.

Everyone was affected, but the arts community in particular had been decimated. Even the conservative press was reporting on this now, thanks to Rock Hudson and, more recently, Liberace. 'There'll be no ballet or theatre or opera unless a cure is found.'

'And did your gay men's health group mention when that might be?' Leonard heard the sarcasm in his voice.

'You can't simply dismiss this, Leo.'

Leonard thought Winston unduly pessimistic. He regularly reminded him there were many female victims of AIDS in Africa, children too, and he did so again now.

'But here it's called the gay plague,' Winston said. 'And I think that's more relevant to us.'

'Us'. 'We'. He hated the way Winston blithely included them in what was happening. But rather than protest, rather than getting bogged down in the same old discussion, Leonard put an end to it by removing himself from the bed and going to the bathroom.

Back in the bedroom after a quick shower, he rummaged around in his drawer for fresh underwear and socks. ('This is your drawer,' Winston had said, years ago. 'So no excuse for untidiness.')

'Does Sylvie still believe you're playing golf on Saturday afternoons?'

The question surprised him. In all the years of their Saturdays together, he could not remember Winston ever asking about this. 'Why wouldn't she?' Leonard was gathering up his dirty clothes and putting them into Winston's laundry basket. 'She thinks I shower at the clubhouse—which of course I would do, if ever I played golf.'

He wanted to lighten the mood before he left, and jokes directed at his obsessive cleanliness usually did the trick. But not this time.

'Asia doesn't have the same AIDS problem as Australia or America,' Winston said, as he saw Leonard to the door. 'Asia has been spared.'

Sylvie was standing in the living room ready to leave when Leonard walked in. She was not happy.

'I asked you to leave golf early, Leonard. The Barkers invited us for drinks. Remember? Drinks at their place before we go to the restaurant. And they're expecting us,' she checked her watch, 'in eight minutes.'

Of course Sylvie had reminded him, but somehow the details had failed to register. He hated upsetting her, and especially after he'd been with Winston. It brought the two parts of his life uncomfortably close.

'I'll be quick.' And on the way past he gave her a hug. 'Sorry.'

Fifteen minutes and an apologetic phone call later, they were in the car on the way to the Barkers'. Fortunately, Sylvie had a very sensible gauge of what was worth being annoyed about, so her usual sweet temper was already restored. If she'd been a man, Leonard thought, she would have made an excellent politician. He had made this observation just a couple of weeks ago, the night Galina had come to dinner, and the girl had been quick to point out that with a handful of women already in the House of Representatives—'Nine, to be exact'—Sylvie could become a politician without requiring a sex change.

This was not the only occasion that evening, nor during their lunch together, that Galina had produced information about Australia of which he was ignorant. 'How do you know that?' he had asked yesterday when she made a reference to the Petrov case.

'Immigrants have to construct firm ground under their feet, or else they can easily drown in all the newness,' she had said. 'So they have to be better informed than ordinary citizens.' The situation was further complicated by something she called 'unskilling'. 'For émigrés like me, the qualities that kept us afloat in our old country do not work in the new. We find ourselves unskilled.'

Galina was a wise young woman. He really hoped that something lasting would come of her relationship with Andrew.

'I've been thinking about Christmas,' Sylvie said, stretching her arm along the back of his seat and letting her hand rest on his shoulder. 'Winston as usual—you've asked him, I hope.' Leonard nodded. 'Maggie, and whoever of her children happen to be around, and,' there was a brief pause, 'Galina. I'd like to invite Galina.'

'She's Jewish,' Leonard said. 'Well, I assume she's Jewish.'

'Not so Jewish that Christmas would be a problem. I think she'd like to come.'

'Have you asked Andrew?'

'It was his suggestion, although I'd already thought of it.'

Leonard welcomed a variety of guests at their Christmas table: family, friends, and, from the time he joined the business, Winston.

'It's an excellent idea,' he said. 'I hope we haven't left it too late.'

'I think Andrew raised it because he suspected she had nowhere to go. But that's not the reason I'm asking her. I want her to come, I like her.'

Leonard nodded, and they settled into a comfortable silence, and would have continued that way if not for the billboard, just a few minutes from the Barkers' house. It was enormous, it was unmissable. It displayed a still shot from that dreadful TV advertisement about AIDS: ordinary people, women and children as well as men, huddled together while a terrifying Grim Reaper knocked them down like skittles.

Winston harped on and on about AIDS, Leonard wished he would leave it alone, but with this Grim Reaper campaign there was no avoiding it. The traffic lights turned red, leaving Leonard stopped near the huge accusing sign. He hated this campaign, and he hated this poster; he turned away.

Sylvie, in contrast, was staring at the billboard. And when the lights changed and Leonard drove through the intersection, she turned her head to hold it in view a little longer. Then she uttered words that chilled him far more than the Grim Reaper.

'Leonard,' she said, 'I hope you're being careful.'

Sylvie had not planned these words. In truth, the knowledge that minted them was so buried, so untouchable, she could not say how long she had known. There are secrets in every marriage, invisible crevices you skirt around as you eat together, socialise with friends, go on holiday. You see a shadow, you know to swerve, you become sure-footed, an expert at avoidance. But once the words have been uttered and the knowledge exposed, it can't be buried again.

As the ghastly sign slipped out of sight, Sylvie registered a sickening distaste that might have blown into full-strength revulsion if she were someone else, or, for that matter, if Leonard were a different person. She looked at him. He was driving with determined concentration, lips pressed together and eyes not blinking. His moustache, she noticed, was silvery in the night light. This was Leonard. He was her husband. As for this knowledge? It had been incubating their entire marriage.

She knew that in 1962, Leonard was reading Walt Whitman; in 1963, he read W.H. Auden; in 1964, Cavafy; in 1965, Lorca. Leonard was a poet, she reasoned, so of course he would read other poets. In 1966, he read Alan Ginsberg; in 1967, Siegfried Sassoon. She knew that most of these poets were homosexuals, maybe all of them were. There was an unmarried uncle of her mother's, a grower of orchids, who was said to be 'that way'. He'd always struck Sylvie as not much different from other men. And Leonard was her husband; they had a son. She did not think you could be homosexual and married.

She knew that on each of their beach holidays, Leonard took long walks by himself. She knew that Leonard preferred to take his business trips without her. She knew there were days when he would shove his dirty clothes deep in the laundry basket, rather than leave them on the floor for her to pick up. She knew where his gaze was drawn when they were at the beach, at a restaurant, or walking down the street.

She knew, perhaps she had always known, and this knowledge had infused her marriage, it may even have shaped it — the lonely bed, the lavish affection, the single child. Leonard hadn't changed, but with the Grim Reaper threatening from suburban streets, it was the world that had changed, and what had previously been hidden had been forced into the light.

Yet everything suddenly felt different. It was as if a sour, polluted air had been let in. She felt sick, and with each passing moment, she felt sicker. When she looked at the man driving the car, she was filled with rage; the shoulder beneath her hand had turned to slime. Everything had spoiled. *She* felt spoiled. It was immaterial that the taint had always been there; now that she acknowledged it, everything was different. And AIDS made it so much worse. What he did with his body, what dangers he exposed it to, was bad enough. But Andrew greeted his father with a hug and a kiss, and she sipped from Leonard's glass, she handled his soiled clothes.

She pulled her hand from his shoulder and rubbed it against her thigh. Her husband was attracted to men, and he might have AIDS. It was hard to know which was worse. But even with her mind raging against him, she knew which was worse. She might well be angry and disgusted, she might well detest this aspect of Leonard, but she had always known.

AIDS, however, was quite another matter.

She unwound her window and leaned into the rushing wind. She imagined opening the door and leaping from the car, the scrape and tear of gravel, lying alone on the side of the road. She did not move. The wind thrashed her face, it battered her hair. At this particular moment, she hated her husband. Yet she had known all along who and what he was. But AIDS was new. AIDS was different.

She closed the window, wanting to be sure he would hear. She spoke slowly, each word a threat.

'I hope you've been careful, Leonard.'

It was the Monday before Christmas, the factory was winding down, and Leonard was not at work. There were chores to be done at home. Nothing particularly urgent, rather, he hoped his mere presence would show Sylvie nothing had changed, that he was still the loving husband he'd always been. He couldn't talk to her, not about these issues, so no reference had been made to the Grim Reaper billboard, or anything remotely related to it. Dinner with the Barkers had proceeded much as usual, but yesterday Sylvie had been quiet and withdrawn. The silence between them was now deep and dangerous. He tried to ignore it, to act normally, but nothing was normal anymore.

He was terrified she would leave him.

Monday was the day she changed the sheets, and he could hear her in the laundry. There was the jagged clack when she twisted the dial of the machine, the clunk in the pipes as the water entered

199

the bowl, and then a pause. And now she's back in the hallway. He expects her to go into one of the bedrooms to make the bed with clean sheets, but instead she is continuing up the hall, she's heading this way. He wants her to join him if she's preparing to forgive him, and to ignore him if she's thinking of leaving.

She's standing in the doorway. He stiffens for the worst.

'You haven't answered me, Leonard. Have you been careful?'

He can't meet her gaze.

'I insist on an answer,' she says. 'If you've endangered me, or, God forbid, our son, I need to know.'

He can feel how angry she is, and chillingly controlled.

Still not meeting her gaze, he assures her that she and Andrew are entirely safe. 'I give you my word.'

'Your word means nothing to me now.'

The cruel and punishing statement hits right on target.

He speaks in a rush. 'It's not what you think.'

'Then what is it, Leonard?' Her words are cut from ice. 'What exactly is it?'

How to talk about something you've never talked about? How to say the unsayable? But he has to try. 'I love you, Sylvie, I always have and I always will. This makes no difference to how I feel about you. It's never made any difference. It's irrelevant, totally separate from us and our marriage.'

She is staring at him; her face is hard and blank. 'I wouldn't call it irrelevant,' she says quietly. 'No, definitely not irrelevant.'

'But no husband and wife share everything.'

'This is not a hobby, Leonard. It's not golf, or chess, or collecting letters. This is who you have sex with.' She stands silent and staring a moment longer, enough time for her words to take effect, then she turns and leaves the room.

Let her be angry, he is thinking, let her get it out of her system, then maybe she'll soften and forgive me. (But forgive him for what? For being himself?) He feels like a trespasser in his own marriage, but at least he still has a marriage. He has to bide his time, sit it out, remind her by his actions why they've been happily married for over thirty years. He wants another thirty; he can't imagine life without her. And what would life be like for her without him? Has she thought about that?

He walks into the living room. Months ago, she asked him to sort through the LPs and tape cassettes, and get rid of those they'd acquired on CD. Better he had done the job when first she asked, but now, when he's desperate to please her — as if that might counter the far greater pain he's caused — it can't do any harm, and it's the sort of all-consuming, mindless task to silence his worries and fears.

He has a new double CD of Handel's *Messiah*, bought especially for this year's Christmas, and he decides to listen to it as he works. His own largely unmusical parents always played the *Messiah* on Christmas morning, excerpts on a stack of 78s that later gave way to a double LP. It's one of the few habits of his first family he has carried across to his second. Now he lifts out the first CD — he still marvels at this miniature technology — and slips it into the machine.

He settles on the floor and turns his attention to the shelf of records. He sings along to the *Messiah* as he separates the LPs into 'keep', 'discard', and 'undecided'. He is totally absorbed in the task, but at some point he must have stopped, for he finds himself hunched in front of the shelves, his hands idle, and he's crying. The soprano aria 'He Shall Feed His Flock' is playing. *Come unto Him all ye that labour, come unto Him, that are heavy laden, and He will give you rest*. Leonard tries to smother his sobs, and then he changes his mind, twists around fully so his back is pitched to the room, and lets the tears flow. The muscles in his neck ease; he feels stress escape in the wake of tears. At the same time, he's aware of a bleak and pervasive sadness.

He is a man who, in a single day, can pass from loving husband to decisive businessman to sex with a stranger to helpful father. It's as if he carries within himself an invisible machine, like a front-end loader. He'll enter a situation, and *scoop!* The aspect of him required to perform in that situation will be plonked in the foreground, while the rest is left in the pit below. And then another situation, *scoop!* and a different aspect of him will be carried aloft and placed in the central position. Sometimes, and today is a prime example, he wishes the front-end loader would lift the whole damn lot of him, drive to a sea cliff, and dump him in with the sharks.

Whoever he might be, however, there is one immutable fact: he's a man who loves his wife. So pull yourself together, he tells himself, and be a husband. He finishes the records and is starting on the tapes when one of his favourite arias, 'He Was Despised', fills the room. The tears begin again. This time, he retreats to the bathroom.

Sitting on the cold hard edge of the bath, sobbing quietly, the strangest sense comes over him. His younger self rises unbidden from memory, the boy he used to be, living with his family in Perth. It's Christmas morning, summer holidays, and everything is possible. Hope and opportunity march in unison, and so many wonderful dreams just waiting for maturity to make them a reality. He feels it now, crying in the bathroom, he feels all that possibility. And he knows he's crying for the loss of that boy for whom a thousand roads beckoned. And he's crying, too, for the ageing man approaching the future with his face averted, threatened with a lonely dead end.

Sylvie is at the other end of the house. She's in a turmoil. She can find no solutions to her shattered life, she can't even say what she *wants* to happen. She's a woman without options and preferences, a woman without desires.

It's best, she decides, to keep busy. It's best not to think.

Monday is sheet-changing day. She starts in her bedroom, and, as usual, Butch with a ball in his mouth scampers in for the bed-making game. He leaps on the bed as she is removing the sheets, and she orders him down; he stands by the bed following her every movement until she has fitted the lower sheet, then jumps up again. Again she orders him down. He makes a nest in the quilt piled on the floor, and watches with an unwavering gaze while she shakes out the top sheet and tucks it in with hospital corners. Finally, she tips Butch off the quilt, fluffs it over the sheets, smooths it down, and invites the dog up on the newly made bed. And there he perches, eager for some ball-throwing. But instead of their usual game, Sylvie sinks down next to him. Butch, sensing all is not well, settles sphinx-like beside her, his head resting on his paws.

So this is what her life has become, Sylvie is thinking, games with the dog as she makes the bed she sleeps in alone, more games with the dog as she makes the bed in which her husband sleeps alone, this same husband who at the moment she wishes would disappear for a few months—enough time for her hurt and disgust to dwindle, enough time for her to make some sense of what has happened and construct a new future. Of course she feels betrayed, all wives would. Leonard has betrayed her and lied to her for their entire marriage. But not for the first time, she reminds herself that though she might be better informed now, Leonard has not changed. He's still the same man she met and fell in love with, and, as hard as it is to admit it, if he had been a different sort of man she might not have been attracted to him in the first place.

Given enough time, she can deal with disgust and betrayal, but more difficult is her sense of having been short-changed—by Leonard, certainly, but more so by their marriage. Their long marriage has allowed him freedoms denied to her; their long marriage has been far more generous to him than it has been to her.

Christmas came and went. Despite the strain between them, Sylvie and Leonard managed. Thirty years of a good marriage provided a sturdy foundation, and the rituals of the season produced a slew of safe, familiar, and time-consuming tasks. The larger than usual group for Christmas lunch, with Galina as a first-timer, also helped.

They saw in the new year—1988—as they usually did, at the same beachside house they rented with Maggie. Andrew joined them for a few days, as did a parade of Maggie's children and friends. They were rarely alone, and when they were, they treated each other with care. The days were filled with hours on the beach, long walks, and raucous picnics and barbecues; most evenings they played a new game called Trivial Pursuit, played it endlessly and uproariously. By the time they returned home, Sylvie and Leonard had an acceptable excuse for wanting peace and quiet.

They spoke when necessary, always politely, but mostly in different keys. During the day, they went their own ways; in the evenings, they filled the silences with light and forgettable rented videos containing little romance and even less substance. Butch occupied the couch alone, while the two of them sat on opposite sides of the room in single armchairs. When Leonard decided to return to work earlier than usual—some large orders to attend to, he explained to Sylvie—she wasn't fooled about the real reason, nor was she sorry. She felt helpless in the current situation. Helpless, tattered, and old.

Leonard just wanted things to return to normal. He hadn't changed, so why should their life be turned upside down? If the wife of a wealthy man were suddenly to discover that her husband's money was ill-gotten, would it make her appreciate their lifestyle any the less? Sylvie had been happy with him; theirs had been a happy marriage; without his extramarital wanderings he would not have been the easy, congenial husband she had long loved. According to this private logic, they should simply move on from the ructions and return to how they had always been. In reality, of course, he knew this to be pure fantasy.

Every day, he left for work at his usual time, but only spent a few hours at the office. If it was hot, he went to the gallery or the State Library, otherwise he walked. While he paced the streets and gardens his troubles were muted. He heard the birds, he felt the breeze, he saw the trees, he admired the flowers, and he recited poetry under his breath, half-remembered lines of old favourites. *The Prelude* returned to him, the first time in years. He recognised the joy of the poem, and the exuberance of the young man; but in an odd and painful way, the poem and its young man felt separate from him, connected as if by a thread, but not actually part of him. Was this to be his life from now on, he wondered. To be separated from all that had once nurtured him? Poetry? Work? His wife?

His walks began to sour, and he started to spend more time at the office. At the end of January, when Winston returned from Hong Kong, Leonard was again working his usual long days.

'I'm so happy you're back.' Leonard had to restrain himself from leaping across the desk and hugging him. 'I've missed you so much.'

Winston had arrived home the previous night, too late even for a phone call. They hadn't seen each other since Christmas.

'It feels like you've been gone for months,' Leonard said, moving around to the front of the desk. He could feel the pleasure stamped on his face—a sharp contrast to Winston's serious expression. 'Aren't you happy to be back?' And when there was no answer: 'Winston, is there something wrong?'

The two men were standing in reach of each other. Winston took a step backwards. He shook his head slowly. 'I'm not staying, Leo. I'm moving back home.'

'But home is here.'

'I don't feel safe here. I'm returning to Hong Kong.' He paused before adding, 'Permanently.'

'But you can't just leave.'

'Don't worry, I'll put everything in order for my replacement.'

'I don't mean the business. What about us?' Leonard could not believe this was happening, not after ten years, not with his life already in pieces.

'I don't feel safe here,' Winston said again. 'AIDS is everywhere. It's in the papers. It's on the radio. There's no escaping it. For all you hear about AIDS in Hong Kong, it might as well not exist. Of course it does, but not in the plague proportions it is here.' He pulled a tissue from his pocket and swiped at his eyes. 'I can't manage it anymore, Leo. I can't.'

'But we're fine, we're safe.'

'I don't feel safe here anymore,' said for the third time.

Not a religious man, Leonard nevertheless found himself thinking of Judas, his betrayal uttered three times. Absolute and immutable.

'I'm sorry, Leo. But I've made up my mind.' Winston sounded so cold, he might have been a stranger. 'Two weeks' notice from today.' He withdrew an envelope from his breast pocket and put it on the desk. Without meeting Leonard's gaze, he turned and left the office.

11

UNCHARTED WATERS

The summer dragged on, with day after day of baking heat. Every so often a rough southerly would blast in, the sky would darken, and the temperature would plummet ten degrees in ten minutes. A cool day or two would follow before the heat flared again.

Since Leonard's return to work, peace in the household had become less of an effort. They had not discussed what had happened, Sylvie suspected they never would. And besides, what would Leonard say? He loved her, he didn't feel as if he had betrayed her, he believed these acts of his had no impact on his marriage and family life. And while she was inclined to believe him, they certainly had an impact on *her* marriage and *her* family life. The irritations that had niggled over the years had now ruptured. Her comfortable life no longer gave her much comfort.

It was in this mood, on the evening of a cool change with the rain beating down, that Sylvie telephoned Galina to suggest lunch together the following day. She'd not seen the girl since Christmas, and had no particular reason for seeing her now; but then perhaps she didn't need a reason—for this or anything else she might want to do. Her husband followed his inclinations, so why shouldn't she?

Galina sounded delighted. 'Your call is such a coincidence,' she said. 'I was about to telephone you. To invite you here, to my home.'

Galina, it emerged, wanted Sylvie's opinion—not about cooking or furnishings or where to have her hair cut, but about her work. Galina had made a picture book. 'And I cannot know if it is good or bad.' There was a long pause with an audible intake of break. 'I have called this book *When Melbourne Meets Leningrad*.' She explained that her paying jobs went into recess over the Christmas–January holiday period. 'So I have been working with no interruption.'

Sylvie said she'd be honoured to see her work. 'Although I know nothing about art, Galina.'

'Galya, please, it is my familiar name. But you are a mother, and you will have seen many picture books for children.'

Sylvie was about to say her picture-book days were long in the past, then decided not to argue. She wanted to spend time with Galina, and she was surprised, pleased too, that anyone might ask her opinion of anything beyond the domestic.

The following morning, after making the beds and tidying the kitchen, cleaning the bathrooms and polishing the furniture, after baking an orange cake to take to Galina's and fixing a scheduling problem for the drivers at the Blind Institute, Sylvie headed across town. Thirty minutes later, she was parking in the street bordering the cemetery. The grassy verge that separated the cemetery from the road had been energised by the recent rain; so too the gracious old elms. She stood a moment, her face raised skywards: she could smell the trees, she could smell the greenness. And the sky was a miracle. The centre of the dome was leaden, but closer to the horizon the grey blanket had puffed into lush white dollops; as she watched, the clouds parted to reveal a wedge of blue so brilliant it was as if the sky itself had been washed. Seconds later, the blue was gone in a whoosh of wind, but closer to the horizon another crack was opening up. The sky was a changing miracle; if only, she found herself thinking, life were equally vibrant and varied.

She crossed the road and, following Galina's instructions, walked up the lane. She felt a nervous excitement, that special eagerness when travelling somewhere new—London, Paris, or the home of a Russian émigré in Melbourne, Australia. Sylvie couldn't migrate to Sydney or Perth *with* Leonard, much less cross the world alone. This girl had courage and stamina enough to face the most taxing trials. Sylvie wished she had a little more of both herself.

But for what? The question came to her unbidden. What would she do with more stamina? And what with more courage?

Once, she had wanted more of life than being a stay-at-home wife; once, she believed marriage to Leonard would bring her more. But now? She strove for perfection in the things that did not matter. Her house was spotless, her linen was folded with military precision, her biscuits never crumbled, her cakes never failed. Even her own son referred to her as a 'domestic queen'. But if Leonard, or any man for that matter, were to be living like this, he'd be said to be wasting himself.

She was not a women's liberationist, women like her were not, but the lives of women certainly needed an overhaul. If she'd been born ten years earlier, she might have found full-time home-making satisfying; if she'd been born ten years later, she might have managed both marriage and career. As it was, she was caught between the demands of her daily life and the desires of her daydreams. She would gaze out the kitchen window as she kneaded pastry, peeled vegetables, or pulled gizzards from a chicken, and she'd let her mind wander far from the view in front of her. It was a trick that simultaneously saved her and, she now suspected, kindled her dissatisfactions. Fuelled by the novels she read and the letters she collected, her imaginings rendered her life even more prosaic than it was.

Despite those early aspirations of hers, she had, in fact, driven the middle lane throughout her married life, steering clear of any real challenge or change. Whether this was a failure of courage or a capitulation to circumstances, she did not know. But as she stood outside Galina's door on this cool summery morning, she was aware of the allure of change.

She smoothed herself down, and was about to knock when the door opened.

'I thought I heard you,' Galina said with a smile, and guided her in.

The floor had no covering, neither carpet nor lino, and her sandals scraped harshly on the bare concrete. She noticed that Galina's feet were clad in embroidered felt scuffs, and wondered if she should remove her shoes.

'At home, we would have a spare pair of *tapochki* for you to wear,' Galina said, looking down at her own footwear. 'Leave on your shoes. It is the Australian way.' She shrugged, as if to suggest this was just one of many changes she'd been forced to accommodate.

While Galina made tea — 'Proper tea in a samovar' — Sylvie looked around. In truth, she went searching for Galina. She crossed to the open glass door leading to a tiny courtyard. Outside were tomato plants growing in pots, and hanging baskets with geraniums. An odd choice, Sylvie thought, geraniums being one of her least favourite flowers.

'I see you are admiring my tomatoes,' Galina said. 'Tomato juice was a staple of our school lunches, and it turned me off tomatoes forever. Then Andrew gave me some home-grown ones, and now,' she was laughing, 'I have become a convert.'

Sylvie moved over to the workbench, where an array of painted pictures was displayed. These were for Galina's book, she guessed, *When Melbourne Meets Leningrad*. At the back of the bench was a framed print of Trafalgar Square, and pinned to the wall above the work area were postcards of paintings. She walked over to the bookcase. Here there were four framed photographs: one of a young Galina wearing a red kerchief and standing alongside a woman who, Sylvie assumed, was her mother; another of the mother alone; a third, much older photograph of what might be the mother with her own parents; and the last, a quite recent photo of mother and daughter. There was no image of a father figure. Next to the photos was a pretty enamelled teaspoon, and a well-worn wristwatch that had stopped at a little after 8.35.

Everything looked as if arranged to a pattern, but then she'd noticed a superstitious side to Galina. At Christmas, as they were moving into the living room after the meal, Galina had tripped, and made an elaborate gesture in the air, 'To propitiate the gods,' she explained. 'Otherwise next time I might really injure myself.'

'I thought Soviets weren't believers,' Sylvie had said.

'Sometimes,' Galina had replied with a smile, 'it is wise to be cautious. You Australians have an expression for this: two bob each way.'

Sylvie squatted down to look at the books. Most of them were Russian, and some looked very old. There were also a number of Italian books, and an entire shelf of English books—classics mostly, including, to her delight, a copy of Wells' *The Time Machine*. She leafed through the pages; it was a beautiful edition with marbled endpapers. She turned to Galina.

'This was one of my favourite books as a child.' She felt herself smile at the memory. 'I longed for my own time machine.'

'So you wanted to have adventures?'

She nodded. 'I suppose I did.'

'And have you?'

For the briefest moment Sylvie was tempted to open up, but of course it wasn't possible, not to this girl. She might well be a relative stranger—so much easier to unburden yourself to a stranger—but she was also Andrew's girlfriend, perhaps even her own future daughter-in-law. She returned the book to the shelf, and shifted the conversation to safer ground.

'How did you choose what to bring?'

Galina poured the tea and brought the glasses to the table. The question was left hanging, and when Sylvie repeated it, Galina brushed it aside with a brief answer that mentioned hope and guess-work. It was her picture book she wanted to talk about, this book she had created even though she had not really intended to.

'It was the tremendous heat that made me do it,' she said with a laugh. 'It was too hot to go outside.'

She collected the pictures from her desk and put the stack on the table. The sheets were unbound; she turned over the top one so Sylvie was looking at the facing pages of an open book.

Each page was A4 in size and painted in bright colours. The style was realistic, even hyper-literal, rather like Henri Rousseau, Sylvie thought. There were pairs of pictures on facing pages, each titled in a natty crimson print. A Melbourne beach scene was paired with a Leningrad park in winter, waterskiers with snow skiers, a Melbourne tram with a Leningrad trolley bus. There were pairs of buildings: the Melbourne Exhibition Building with the Catherine Winter Palace, Flinders Street Station with Finland Station, St Isaac's in Leningrad with St Paul's in Melbourne, an Australian cream-brick house alongside a Soviet apartment block. Within a single pair of paintings, Galina had incorporated many more differences: in the beach scene there were sea gulls picking at chips, and children playing beach cricket, and a jar of Vegemite on a picnic rug, while in the corresponding snow scene there were children ice-skating, a steaming samovar seen through a frosty window, and ducks waddling across a frozen pond. Other paintings depicted single objects on facing pages: Australian beer was paired with Russian vodka, pasties with *pirozhki*, a bayside kiosk with a kvass cart, boots with thongs, scouts with Pioneers, and teabags with a samovar.

Sylvie took her time over each pair of pictures. They were colourful, clever, and, to her admittedly untrained eye, very skilful.

'Your book is wonderful,' she said at last, looking up from the pages. 'Every picture is a beauty.'

The girl was on the edge of her seat. Sylvie put a gentle hand on her arm. 'You need to resign immediately from real estate drawings and sewing patterns. You're an artist, Galya.' She turned back to the pictures. 'And an educator too. Teachers and parents will love this book. It's perfect for visual perception, for developing cognitive skills, and such a rich source for discussion.'

Galina reached across the table and hugged her. 'I knew you were the right person to ask.'

An avalanche of questions followed. Galya asked about the choice of certain pairs and the inclusion of certain objects. She asked about the art, too, and it soon became apparent that what she was wanting was reassurance.

Sylvie grasped the girl's hand. 'I would want to buy this book, Galya,' she said firmly. 'And,' she gave the hand a squeeze, 'I may be able to help you.'

One of the volunteer drivers at the Blind Institute was the wife of a publisher. 'I'll speak to her and she'll speak to her husband, and if everything goes according to plan, he will ask to see your picture book, he'll love it, and he'll want to publish it.'

Again Galina threw her arms around her. 'You have made me so happy.'

'I can't promise anything.'

'I understand.' Galina drew back. She was smiling. 'Seems Australia has its own version of *sistema*,' she said.

Suddenly Sylvie grabbed her basket. 'I forgot the cake!'

'This is not a problem. We can eat it for lunch.'

'You can't just have cake for lunch.'

'Why not? We can eat what we want.'

For the umpteenth time recently, Sylvie asked herself who made these rules she had obeyed for so long? And, more crucially, who would care what she ate for lunch?

Galina made coffee — 'Coffee is better with cake' — proper coffee in a pot on the stove, and not the instant powder Sylvie used at home. While it brewed, they talked about Galina's garden. Sylvie asked about her choice of geraniums.

'I like the bright colours of the flowers, and there is such a big variety. But as well,' she was smiling, 'geraniums are commonly mentioned in the English novels I read back in Leningrad. They are in window boxes and garden beds, they are even made into hedges. You do not like them?'

'I don't much care for their smell,' Sylvie said. 'And I suppose I've let the smell block out their attractive qualities.'

A breeze from the courtyard wafted over them as they drank their coffee and ate the cake. Galina broke the silence.

'What sort of work would you choose, if you could do anything at all?'

What immediately struck fifty-two-year-old Sylvie was the tense Galina used: not *What would you have chosen if you could have done anything?* but *What would you choose?* Meaning *Choose now*. Galina's English was too good, better than the average Australian's, for her to have made a mistake.

As a child, Sylvie had wanted to be a doctor, but girls didn't become doctors, so when asked she would say she wanted to be a nurse — and wife and mother, of course. She also wanted friends and adventures like Dorothy in *The Wizard of Oz*. A couple of years later she wanted to be like Jo March in *Little Women*, and in another year or two, Elizabeth Bennet in *Pride and Prejudice*, but these remained secret desires. After reading a book about Madame Curie, she wanted to be a famous scientist, and during the period she learned ballet she wanted to be a ballerina like Margot Fonteyn. More realistic ambitions formed once she reached adulthood, like wanting to be a teacher. But now? Common sense and maturity had erased all the old desires, and as a woman deep into middle age, the fire of her imagination was pretty much burned out.

Clearly, Galina thought otherwise. She was leaning forward, her head resting on her hands, waiting for an answer. Sylvie felt unnerved by the question, probably because she *did* have a desire, a long-held desire as unrealistic as wanting to be Jo March, Elizabeth Bennet or Madame Curie. Galya was moving her head in a faint, encouraging nod; everything about her was telling Sylvie to trust her.

'I've always wanted to write about letters.' Her voice was quiet, as if it might minimise the desire.

Galina looked confused. 'You want to write letters?'

It took an immense act of will to confess again. 'No, I want to write *about* them.'

'This concerns your collection of letters?'

Sylvie nodded, couldn't speak, wanted to withdraw the words and return them to secrecy. 'It's silly. Just a fantasy. We all have fantasies, don't we?'

'Yes,' Galina said, 'we do, and they are not to be treated lightly, certainly not where work is concerned.' Galina put her hand on her stack of paintings. 'Most new work emerges from daydreams and fantasies.' She smiled, a sweet, encouraging smile. 'So,' she said, 'you want to write about letters?'

What did she have to lose? It was a dream, and what could this girl do to a dream? So Sylvie let it spill out. How she'd always been fascinated by letters. 'As a little girl I thought it was magic how mail, coming from far away, would end up in your letter box. I imagined letters flying through the sky, high above the clouds, swarms of letters that would swoop down and land in a special letter field. And the postman would collect them and deliver them to everyone's home. Magic.'

And there remained a sense of romance—the adult's magic, after all—attaching to the post: the walk to the letter box, the lifting of the lid, the peering inside, and leafing through the bundle for the postcards and proper letters.

'Every letter is a pocket-sized package of a person,' she continued. 'You find disappointments, fears, desires, events, relationships, work. You find faraway places and strange practices and unknown pressures. It's all there in the words and sentences, and of course in the spaces between the lines.'

Long ago, it occurred to her that she seemed to know more about the strangers in her letter collection than she did about her friends. And the letters seemed to know more about her. These letters written by strangers to other strangers spoke directly to her, they seemed to be written for her. If not for this quality, she probably wouldn't have bothered with a collection.

Galya was waiting for her to continue, and Sylvie, realising how much she wanted to talk about this passion of hers, how greatly she wanted someone to be interested, decided not to stop.

'Letters are written without artifice,' she said. 'The writers of most letters, and certainly the ones in my collection, have no claims to posterity, most of them wouldn't even know what posterity is. Yet they're so revealing. I can read a letter, and know the writer.'

How much more should she say, she was wondering. But if collectors of Victorian underwear can talk about their collections, and collectors of glass eyes, too (she'd heard both interviewed on a recent radio program), surely she could divulge her reasons for collecting letters.

She drank some coffee, drew in a deep breath, and started afresh.

'Reading's an intimate business,' she began.

This long-held belief of hers, never before uttered to anyone, now sounded ridiculous. But Galya was nodding, she seemed to be agreeing. So perhaps it was not so stupid. Or maybe it was something everyone already knew.

'Please continue,' Galya said quietly. 'Please.'

'Reading, it's an intimate business. Just you and your imagination connecting with words that have come from the author's imagination. And this intimacy is, I think, enhanced in letters. The "I" of the letter-writer speaks and connects directly to you, the letter-reader. You and only you. You and your experience. You and your longings. You and your disappointments. And suddenly you're not alone in your most personal and private thoughts.'

In a way she couldn't explain, her letters acknowledged her, they recognised her—much like an absorbing novel did, although in a more personal and targeted way. She wanted to get under the skin of this process, to learn its dynamic, to understand why it was so intense. This was her reason for wanting to write about letters.

'I get to experience other times, places, people, emotions through letters. And while it might be vicarious, it doesn't feel that way. I feel … remade.' This was no exaggeration: the letters provided her with the lives she'd never lived, never *would* live. 'My letters give me a self that, to be honest, is far more interesting than the housewife, cook and volunteer of my usual life.' She smiled. 'I suppose they give me freedom.'

Again Galina was nodding, she seemed to understand, which gave Sylvie the courage to continue.

'Then there's handwriting. You're reading something direct from another's hand. You're touching their hand — that's how it feels to me. And I particularly like letters that are hard to decipher. You have to pore over these; it's the intensest intimacy.'

There it was again. Intimacy.

Whether it was a galloping hand that hurled words across the page, a tidy hand, or a crabbed hand, the manner of writing supplied the same sort of emotional texture that music did to a film. One of her letters, written by a woman to someone she identified only as RO, started neatly in an even, cursive script; but several pages later had disintegrated into a drunken scrawl, just two or three words to a line, and the paper splotched with ink, perhaps even tears.

'And how much more precious does a letter become — not to me, the collector, but the original recipient — when the writer of the letter has died. Think of it: for the wife who lives on after her husband, the man whose brother has passed away, the woman who's lost her best friend, *death does not alter their letters*. I think that's profound. You're able to sit by yourself reading your beloved's words, savouring them, responding to them, just as you did when they were alive. Death, which changes almost everything, leaves letters untouched.'

She wondered if Galina had any letters from her mother.

There'd probably been no reason for them to write to each other: they lived together and rarely travelled. But for Galina's sake, she hoped there were.

'And then there are published letters written by famous people. How extraordinary that an ordinary housewife like me can be privy to the thoughts and ideas and everyday yearnings of people like Winston Churchill, like John Keats, like Somerset Maugham.

'Histories are removed from the action, and historians are at great pains to be clear about what *they* think happened and why. Diaries are often choked with emotion. But all letters are communications, all letters speak to someone, all letters invite the reader into the heart and mind of the writer. There's something deliciously clandestine about letters. I love everything about them.'

At last she forced herself to stop. Of course Galina wasn't really interested, she was listening out of politeness. Sylvie ought to apologise, dismiss her rantings as nonsense. But before she could say anything, Galina spoke first.

'You say you want my book? Well, I want yours,' she said. 'Your book about letters. What is stopping you from writing it?'

The dishes? The vacuuming? The darning? The driving for the Blind Institute? Her lack of ability. Her lack of courage? Her fear of failure?

'Just do it,' Galina said. And, as if she could read her mind, she added, 'No one need see the work. No one need know you're even writing it.

'What are you waiting for, Sylvie?'

The day following her visit to Galina, Sylvie began her letter project. She didn't think in terms of a book, people like her didn't write books; 'project' provided exactly the right weight. Almost immediately there was a changed atmosphere in the Morrow home. In this uncertain phase of their marriage, Leonard, usually the dominant of the two, was quieter and more reflective, while Sylvie was in full voice. After dinner, rather than sitting in silence watching TV, Sylvie now shared her latest thoughts and ideas about letters. Leonard lent her his volume of Coleridge's letters, and a leather-bound edition of the Barrett–Browning correspondence. He showed himself to be an attentive and constructive critic, with knowledge pertinent to her project.

Just like the Leonard of old, Sylvie found herself thinking. Not that she forgot their troubles — his were not transgressions easily forgotten — but she was grateful for his help, and grateful, too, for this reawakened connection to the man she had married.

And Leonard was grateful for anything that made these miserable days pass more quickly; grateful, too, that his wife still needed him. He couldn't bring himself to tell her of Winston's return to Hong Kong; he did not trust himself to talk about Winston at all. Life was a doleful affair, and his wife and her new project made it bearable.

1988 advanced slowly, each month marked with a swag of bicentennial events — new roads, new schools, renovated town halls. After yet another plea to Winston went unacknowledged, Leonard advertised and appointed a replacement: a woman accountant in her fifties, with past experience in small business. The transition was effected with surprising ease. And at home, because of Sylvie's letter project and their nightly discussions, he allowed himself to hope that his marriage might recover.

In March, they talked about the narratives attaching to letters.

'But whose narrative is it?' he asked her. 'The writer's? The recipient's? Seems to me that for every letter — personal letters, not official letters — there are several possible interpretations.'

In April, they moved on to epistolary novels. There had been an extraordinary number written. He ploughed through Richardson's epistolary novel *Pamela*, because Sylvie wanted to discuss it with him. He was happy to oblige, happy to do anything she asked. Not that the book appealed. Much of the time, he said, the letters didn't read like letters at all, just various narrators telling a story in letter form, in which they themselves, as characters in the story were rendered invisible. He baulked at reading *Clarissa*, but he guessed, given its size, he was not alone in that.

'Imagine,' he said one evening, 'a world without letters.' It was the last day of April, a rare Saturday night when they had decided to stay home rather than join friends for dinner.

'It'll never happen,' Sylvie said. 'Even in the caves, people were leaving written messages for each other—or for the future. Although perhaps prehistoric man's sense of time, of past and future, was different from ours.' She smiled. 'Now that's a thought.' And looked quite pleased with herself. 'I think we're programmed to write, and we'll never lose the need nor the desire to communicate in that deeply meaningful and private way. And besides,' her blue eyes were shining, 'who would willingly forfeit the great romance of a written correspondence?'

He wondered how different things might have been if he and Sylvie had written letters to each other. Not only in the past, but now, with their troubles. Would it be easier to write in a letter all they seemed unable to say to each other. And would this be what he wanted? One evening not so long ago, she had shown him a quote written by a Geoffrey Scott, a quote she'd copied down years earlier without a note of where it originated. *To dip the quill in ink is a magical gesture: it sets free in each of us a new and sometimes a forbidding sprite, the epistolary self.* Perhaps letters offer too much freedom. And once written and sent, you can't take any of it back, you can't rub it out.

She had certainly got him thinking, was forcing his mind to work in a way it had not done for years. One evening, she joked that they were turning into a couple of old blue-stockings with their bookish discussions. He was unsure what to make of her comment. Yes, there was a new togetherness and shared intellectual interests between them, but weren't blue-stockings always female? And was she therefore suggesting she now regarded him as an old woman? He didn't dare ask her to explain; he'd already brought too much negativity to their marriage and had no stamina for any more.

The mood at home picked up even further when Galina was offered a publishing contract for her picture book, *When Melbourne Meets Leningrad*. Engineered by Sylvie who, even after all these years, could still astonish him with her capabilities, he and Sylvie, together with Andrew and Galina, had celebrated the signing of the contract at a new restaurant in the city. With a series of city-meets-city picture books already under discussion, the publisher had decided to fast-track the production of this first title. The four of them had celebrated that too, with another dinner at a different restaurant.

Then there was the relationship between Galina and his son.

'They're seeing a lot of each other,' Leonard said to Sylvie one Saturday in May. The long, hot summer had finally faltered, and they were taking a walk together on a cool Saturday afternoon.

Sylvie nodded. 'But it'd be premature to read anything too significant into it. Andrew says very little, and Galya talks of him warmly but not really like a boyfriend.'

A couple of months earlier, Galina had told them why she had left Russia. They now knew she could have gone to Canada or America or Israel, but had chosen Australia because of her chance meeting with Andrew. So while she had not come to Australia specifically to be with their son, he was, nonetheless, the reason she was here. And the two of them did seem close, and to be growing closer.

'Could you ask Galina directly about their relationship?' Leonard now asked.

He could not bring himself to call her Galya. She hadn't invited him as she had Sylvie. He knew she was closer to his wife, even more so since the introduction to the publisher, but still, he thought he and the girl had forged something significant. Now, before Sylvie had an opportunity to answer his question, he asked another. 'What does Andrew call her?'

'He calls her Galya.' She started laughing. 'And the not-so-short but apparently very affectionate Galinochka.'

Andrew and Galina were at that very moment on one of their regular excursions. Adventures, Andrew called them, and in the months since Christmas he had delighted her with a range of destinations. On this particular Saturday he had promised an unforgettable day at a picturesque town on the Surf Coast. 'It'll be a day for the senses,' he said, 'with scenery to rival anything I've shown you before.' But when, after a ninety-minute drive, they parked in a shopping area that looked no different from a Melbourne suburb, Galina couldn't help but think this adventure might be Andrew's first failure.

The place was called Anglesea, and yet another Australian place name pilfered from the British Isles. She loved the lyrical anarchy of Ballarat and Moorabbin, Yackandandah and Maribyrnong, Koo Wee Rup and Nar Nar Goon, Warrnambool and Woolloomooloo. Anglesea, Torquay, Hastings and Brighton simply could not compete. Either the founding fathers lacked imagination, or they were just plain homesick. Not that she'd feel more at home if she lived in Leningrad, Australia; it would be like living in a pool of mockery, your nose rubbed in the differences every single day. More than mere place names was needed to repair the rupture of migration.

So here they were in Anglesea, Australia, a special place, according to Andrew, but as far as she could see, displaying little of interest. She had worked late every night this past week, with several sewing patterns to finish before her contract officially terminated. Then, two days ago, requests had arrived for changes to *When Melbourne Meets Leningrad*—apparently beer, vodka, and kvass carts were not considered suitable for Australian children. She didn't mind, she had plenty of ideas, but making the changes was surprisingly unnerving.

Looking about her, she doubted she'd find a restorative in this place.

She and Andrew had seen so much together these past months. With Godrevy curled on a rug in the back seat, they had driven to the Dandenong Ranges for the flashy parrots, to Warburton by the river to search for platypuses, to Phillip Island for the plump koalas wedged in the forks of trees, to famous flower gardens and eucalyptus forests. They'd seen giant earthworms and fairy penguins, and quaint places like a house clad entirely in shells. After each adventure they would return to the city and have dinner together, either at a restaurant or at her place with takeaway food.

These excursions had been crucial to what she regarded as her Australianisation program. Not so much what she saw, although that always delighted, but the fact of them. You decide to go somewhere and you go. No permission required, no car to find, no petrol to source, no money to worry about. While many of the West's freedoms found her dangling helplessly between an array of choices, this freedom of movement was a freedom she embraced.

And then there was Andrew, her companion of choice. It was now almost six months since she had first contacted him, and she knew nothing about his girlfriends, if indeed there were girlfriends, and she had met none of his friends. At their regular dinners with Sylvie and Leonard, they treated her as Andrew's girlfriend, but as for Andrew himself, there was nothing in his behaviour to suggest anything other than friendship. He had never tried to kiss her, he had never made any move towards her. Although she had her suspicions. She saw the way he looked at her, the warmth in his expression, the pleasure he took in her company.

No such doubt existed when it came to her feelings for him. He was her *blizkiy drug*, her soulmate and dearest companion. A neighbour gave her a bag of home-grown vegetables, and it was Andrew she shared them with; her contract from the publisher arrived, and she wanted Andrew to witness it and celebrate its signing. When there were mice in the saddlery, she relied on Andrew to solve the problem. With exhibitions, concerts and films, Andrew was her preferred companion. And she loved his weekly excursions; he crafted them like mystery adventures, providing just enough information so she wore the right clothes, but not enough to spoil the surprise. When confronted by flocks of parrots, or panoramic views, or ancient gum trees, or a lyrebird (Yes! Once a lyrebird scuttling across a bush track), she would marvel at the surprise, marvel at this Australia, and marvel at her good fortune to have such a friend. So, as she stood in the ordinary Anglesea shopping strip, she assumed there must be more to this place than was immediately apparent.

'This way,' Andrew said, and with Godrevy pulling ahead on the lead, they crossed the road to the grassland by the river.

Blasts of wind gusted up the waterway; she buttoned her jacket and thrust her hands into her pockets. As she walked with Andrew along the bank, she noticed a few ducks and gulls—nothing special in the way of birds, nothing special about the river either.

The surprise of Anglesea came upon her in a background growl that grew steadily into the crash and rumble of the ocean. She quickened her pace, and soon they were standing on a broad exposed beach; it was weirdly exhilarating to pass in a few minutes from a nondescript town and a nondescript river to this magnificent seascape. She stood in the bluster beneath the puckered sky, and absorbed the hugeness of it all. The dog, released from his lead, was running in delighted circles, the ocean was a fury of foam, the waves rolling up the beach toppled over one another in a riot of spray. Beyond the beach and lining the curve of the ocean was a succession of high, buckled cliffs.

'This is wonderful,' Galina shouted, the words lost even to herself in the ruckus.

Andrew cupped his ear and she stepped closer, put one hand on the right side of his neck, and spoke directly into his left ear.

Standing together, the only people on the beach, standing firm in this glorious bedlam, he feels her, he feels her breath on his ear, her lips brushing his skin. A shudder passes through him. If only time would stop now, he is thinking. But soon she's pulling back, she's turning up the collar of his coat, she's patting him down, she's letting him go. And even as she's stepping away, he's willing her to stay close. Keep touching me. *Keep. Touching. Me.* But already she is striding ahead with Goddy bouncing about her, both of them heading in the wrong direction. He runs to catch up with her, grasps her arm and turns her round. 'This is the way,' he shouts. He's still holding her arm just above the elbow. How to stay like this? Then in a fit of exasperation, he slips his hand past her elbow and there they are, linked together. She gives his arm a press—whether shiver or affection, it's impossible to know—he adjusts his pace to hers, and the two of them are walking arm in arm along the stormy beach. She seems totally relaxed; he, on the other hand, is all at sea. What he needs is a direct line to a romance expert, Lord Byron perhaps, or, better still, Don Juan himself. (Was he a fiction of Byron's, or did he really exist?) He needs some more experienced, worldly man to tell him what to do. Although he knows exactly what to do, that's not the problem. It's the doing it.

'Antarctica is just over there,' he says, pointing to the horizon with his free hand. 'I've always wanted to live in a lighthouse on Antarctica.'

Neither Don Juan nor any experienced man would say anything so stupid. Galina's gaze remains fixed ahead, and he dares hope she didn't hear. His parents, friends, even Galina herself, know he has an interest in lighthouses, in much the same way as other people are interested in mountains or monuments. But as a sanctuary for a stifled psyche? That remains his secret.

Galina stops, and turns to face the unruly sea. 'Are there lighthouses on Antarctica?'

So she did hear.

He shakes his head. Better not to speak.

'Perhaps we should build one,' she says, with a smile.

A few minutes later they are standing at the southern end of the beach. 'Over there,' he says, nodding at the outcrop of land, 'beyond that point is a beautiful lighthouse: Split Point Lighthouse, or the White Queen as she's fondly known. It's isolated, as you'd expect, but it's also unusually dainty, and, to my eye, oddly vulnerable perched up there on the edge of the cliff.'

He describes the slender white tower tapering to the red crown at the top, and the fine black window slits cut into the column; he *creates* the lighthouse for her. And a smile plays across her face, as if she were truly seeing it, and she squeezes his arm, still linked to hers.

During the past few months, in the privacy of his mind, he has resorted to the cosmos to describe her. She is out of this world; she is heavenly; she's a fiery comet; she's a shooting star. And now here, on this Australian beach, with the roar of the sea and the awakened sky and her arm firm against his body, *here on earth with him*, how brightly does she shine, how greatly does he love her.

That evening, they bought fish and chips, and took the food back to Andrew's studio. He had tried to dissuade her, but she insisted: they always ended up at the saddlery, she said, and it was time for a change. He said his place was a mess; she said she didn't mind mess. He said his place was cold; she said she was Russian, she knew about cold.

'I *have* been to your studio before.'

And on those occasions he had spent hours preparing. He had swept the floor of tesserae, he had tidied up books and magazines, he had vacuumed dog hair from the furniture, he had removed most of his lighthouse pictures (as if an obsession could be so easily downgraded to an interest), he had thrown a blanket over the stained couch and a makeshift tablecloth over the scarred table, he had purchased flowers and arranged them in a jar tizzed up in tinfoil, he had stocked the fridge with drinks and bought an array of food to nibble. Yes, she had come to his place, but on those occasions he had planned, he had organised.

'It looks just the same as usual,' she said, as they entered the studio that evening.

Galina set out the fish and chips while Andrew fed Godrevy. Then he joined her on the couch, and together they ate their meal. The only cold drink he could find was a single stubby of beer, and they passed the bottle between them. Galina felt relaxed and contented after their perfect day, and pleased to be here rather than her place.

There was something intrinsically romantic about Andrew's studio, that the artist might wake in the middle of the night with a bright idea and go straight to work. It was the romance of creativity, Galina decided, and while she supposed her saddlery provided the same for her, she didn't think of herself in the same artistic terms as she did Andrew. Émile Zola was a foreign writer readily available in Russian, and Galina had read his novel *The Masterpiece* as a student. It was this book more than any real experience that had created for her the life of the artist. Andrew's studio, although far more spacious than the studios in Zola's novel, was in other respects similar. (While there was much she did not know about the West, Galina had been surprised at how much she actually *did* know from the novels she had read. Such a cheap and ready source of knowledge, it was surprising no one ever mentioned it.)

They ate, they passed the bottle between them, Galina relaxed, and Andrew fretted. He worried she was not comfortable, that she'd prefer to be in different company, that he could think of nothing interesting to say, that there wasn't more alcohol to loosen his tongue. And then, out of the blue, it occurred to him that while his whole mind was focused on her, it was not really on *her*, it was focused on his worries *about* her, which meant he was missing out on her now: Galya with him, in his home, on his couch.

Andrew wanted so much to happen with her; he wanted today, he wanted next week, he wanted next year, he wanted his whole life. Though surely, if there'd been a chance of her falling in love with him, she would have done so by now. As for himself, only a fool or a masochist would fall in love where there was no chance of reciprocity. She was beautiful and interesting and creative and talented, but all these qualities could be enjoyed in a close friendship. And while he longed to touch her, hold her, kiss her, make love to her, sleep with her, wake up next to her, he could deal with these longings—was already dealing with them. He needed to shift Galina into a more realistic perspective; he needed to remove her from the centre of his longings.

The problem was he didn't want to.

They finished their meal, and while he cleared up and made coffee, Galina took herself to the far end of the room where the pool mosaic lay finished. The work stretched in brilliant blueness for close on four metres. She had seen this work at various stages of its creation, but this was her first sight of it completed. She knelt down and ran her hand over the sparkling water.

In high summer in Leningrad during the white nights, a sheer ethereal blue floats over the streets and squares, the gardens and waterways. It creates a sense of enchantment, as if you are moving through a dreamscape. As unlikely as it was, Andrew's pool reminded her of Leningrad's white nights. She felt an almost irresistible urge to lie down on the mosaic and rest in its exquisite blueness.

Andrew returned to the couch, and Galina pulled herself away from the pool to join him. They sat in silence drinking their coffee. Andrew was waiting for her to say something about his mosaic. Hadn't she liked it? Or did they have nothing to say to each other? Or perhaps this silence might be described as companionable. And in the end he decided, uncharacteristically for him, to opt for the more favourable alternative. And why not? The evening was progressing well, better than he could have hoped for.

Then it all blew up.

'We are so lucky to have art,' she said, breaking the silence and

228

nodding in the direction of his mosaic pool. 'I thank the gods for such a gift.'

His reply came without pause. 'Art never saved anyone.'

Perhaps he intended to be modest, or perhaps he was trying to be cool by promoting a view currently fashionable in some quarters. Whatever the reason, he found himself defending a position he did not believe.

'You cannot think this about art,' she said.

And again without pause. 'Bombs kill. Starvation kills. Torture kills. Natural disasters kill. Art never stopped any of this.'

'But you said, "Art never saved anyone." Do you really believe this?'

The silence that now descended was definitely not companionable. When he failed to answer, she spoke again. 'Have you never in despair looked at a painting or listened to a piece of music or read a poem, and been returned to life?'

Of course he had, he wanted to shout. All the time. But his throat had seized up.

Galina was watching him, she could see his struggle, but on this topic she would not help. Every Russian knows that art saves lives; poetry, music, novels, paintings, all these have saved lives. A million people died in the siege of Leningrad, but the number would have been even greater if not for poetry. Throughout those nine hundred desperate days, so her mother had told her, Olga Berggolts's radio broadcasts encouraged with inspiring words and stories, but most of all it was her poetry that sustained the people. Who knows how many more Leningraders would have died in the siege if not for the poetry of Olga Berggolts, she wanted to ask Andrew, who had probably never heard of the siege of Leningrad, much less of Olga Berggolts. And another story from the siege: a young woman, an artist, starving like everyone else, who made herself paint through a long freezing night, knowing that if she didn't she would succumb to the over-whelming desire to curl up on the floor and let death take her.

This meticulous ability to mute pain—that's what art can do, and Andrew was denying it. Andrew with his comfortable, fear-free life didn't know what he was talking about.

Then there was Shostakovich's life-saving Seventh Symphony first heard in Leningrad during the siege. Andrew probably knew nothing of the great Dmitri Dmitriyevich. The Germans tried to stop the performance, they wanted to silence so powerful a weapon. But they failed and the performance went ahead; recorded and played over the wireless, it energised hundreds of thousands of Leningraders. The Nazis knew what Andrew was now denying: art saves life, art *gives* life. And the reams of literature circulated in *samizdat* in the post-Stalinist years—people risked their life for this art because they knew it would make them stronger. And Anna Akhmatova's *Requiem*. 'Can you describe this?' a woman asked the poet as they stood in the prison lines in Leningrad at the height of the terror. 'Can you describe this?' And when Akhmatova said she could, the woman smiled: people would know of these terrible times. Akhmatova's life was hard. She survived the death of her husband and the imprisonment of her son; she survived censorship and repression; she wrote poetry and she survived.

Galina wondered what had made Andrew say something so demonstrably wrong. Given his own frailties and the fact he was an artist himself, she expected there had been many times when he had turned to art to pull him out of the mire. Of course he must know about the power of art to fortify and save.

At last he was speaking. He was apologising, although not entirely coherently. Then, after another silence, he summoned a fresh breath, heralding a change of topic—a less contentious one, she hoped, or, to use one of her favourite Australianisms, one that was less dodgy.

'Do you think love can save lives?' he said.

The weather, travel, even politics would have been preferable to love, but at least it was a change of topic. 'Well, yes,' she said carefully. 'Love can save lives in the sense of dashing into a burning house and rescuing your children, or getting your mother to hospital when she has had a stroke.'

'I mean the *power* of love, in that more numinous sense that you're suggesting is the power of art.'

She shook her head. 'No. Art speaks directly to you. Its effect is private. No one else need be involved.' The words came slowly, she did not want to inflame either him or her. 'When it comes to saving a life, art works in a very private way. But love always involves someone else. I would not like to think of my survival being hinged to another person.'

'But falling in love —'

And all caution abruptly disappeared. 'Love is too important simply to fall into it thoughtlessly or unwittingly. Love deserves your fullest attention, your clearest consciousness. Love demands a deliberate course of action.' She paused. 'I would not *fall* in love with anyone.'

He was thinking she used English better than he did, better than most native speakers. He was also thinking how instinctively he disagreed with her—and how she'd hate the idea of anything happening 'instinctively'.

Not long afterwards, she rose to leave. He said he'd walk her home; she said she would prefer to go alone.

'Do you forgive me?' he said at the door. And before she could answer, he added, 'Are we all right?'

She nodded, leaned towards him and kissed him briefly on the lips. 'It was only an argument, Andryusha. Of course we are all right.'

He did not believe her.

He'd been such a fool; even as her friend, she surely must be having second thoughts. And what she said about love, it was meant personally, a clear statement she would never fall in love with him.

As for the kiss, that was a kindness, a gesture of pity; so too the intimate Andryusha. He wished he could erase the evening, he wished he lived on a lighthouse far from human company, he wished he were not himself.

His mind raged as he washed the dishes and tidied up, it raged as he took the rubbish out to the bin, it raged as he went up to the roof and smoked in the darkness, it raged when he returned inside. He paced the studio, up to one end and back to the other, up to the end and back again; he gathered some scattered tesserae, added them to his oddments tray, loitered at his workbench, rearranged the containers, straightened his tools, lined up everything with geometric precision, transferred a stack of small picture boards to a shelf.

Then, with his thoughts banging against one another, he retrieved one of the picture boards and walked back to the bench. He cleared a space, positioned the board, sifted through his oddments for sea colours and sunset colours, selected tiles, glass, mother-of-pearl chips, some pieces of stone; he dragged his stool to the bench and sat himself down. And soon he was choosing and chipping, placing and gluing, working freehand to create a picture, impressionistic and colourful. He cut the chips in crescents and ellipses, and set them into a brilliant sunset of waves and swirls. A whirling Van Gogh sky emerged in yellows, oranges, reds, and pearly whites. And rising up and mingling with it were the peaks and eddies of a stormy sea—blues, greens, greys, and a peachy yellow—in the centre of which he built a lighthouse. Every so often he went to the sink to make up a fresh batch of glue. He did not drink; he did not use the toilet. His mind was quiet, his heart was still, his picture grew.

He finished just before dawn. He had created a stormy seascape at sunset with a lighthouse. It was unlike anything he had ever done before. He made himself fresh coffee and went up to the roof. It was a vibrant dawn; the sky was lit with the colours of his painting.

He watched the sun rise. He had survived the night.

12

LIFE'S RAFFLE

Sylvie and Galina had arranged to spend the whole day together, starting with brunch at Galina's local café. They had planned a walk through the cemetery to read the headstones—they're like letters, or rather telegrams, Galina had said with a giggle—before visiting a gallery where one of her real estate colleagues was showing his work. But with her book about to go into production, and a number of last-minute queries to settle, her publishers had insisted she come to company headquarters and deal with the issues face-to-face.

'My publishers are located practically in the bush,' Galina said the previous evening when she telephoned Sylvie with her apologies. 'And they are paying for me to take a taxi—both ways. I cannot guess what it will cost.'

When Melbourne Meets Leningrad was shaping up to be a hit. Not only because the Soviet Union was front-page news, but the idea of two cities getting to know each other through their landmarks and customs had excited interest, not only with Galina's Australian publisher, but also abroad. The book had already been sold into several territories, and a series of city-meets-city books had now been given the go-ahead. Galina's publishers stood to make a pile of money from her first book. Of course they could shell out for a taxi, Sylvie was thinking. Both ways.

'I already have an idea for my next book,' Galina continued. 'I want it to draw on Australian English, *Aussie* English. Pollie, dero, smoko, brekkie, rellies, drongo, and'—a snort of laughter escaped down the phone—'miseryguts.' She paused. 'Do you think I should mention this when I see the publishers tomorrow?'

Galina sought her opinion as no one else did. Sylvie was about to say she had no idea as to the best way of pitching a new book when common sense took over: Galina seemed to be on a roll with her publishers, and her Australian English book sounded appealing. 'Yes,' she said, 'if there's an opportunity to mention it, I would.'

The next day was sunny and clear. In her pre-Galina days, Sylvie would have absorbed her disappointment by baking, or visiting the sick, or sewing a few aprons for the annual Royal Children's Hospital fête. But now she had her letter project, and what a godsend it had been. Sitting at her desk, she could forget about Leonard and her marriage, she could forget about their uncertain future; for hours, she could separate from her usual life, and when she returned to it she felt recharged. Of course she was disappointed not to be seeing Galya, but she was happy for a day of work.

She collected the washing from the machine, and went outside to hang it on the line. It was one of those late-blooming days of May that surprise like an early birthday gift; the sun still had some warmth and there was not a cloud in the sky. She bent down to the laundry basket and stretched up to the line, relishing the movement and soaking up the warmth. By the time the washing was neatly pegged, she had decided to forgo her work in favour of the original itinerary. She would drive to the other side of the city, she'd stroll through the cemetery, she'd have a meal at Galina's favourite café, and she would do all this alone.

She dressed light and bright in slacks and a pale-pink cotton jacket, and in a similarly light mood drove across town to Carlton. She parked near Melbourne University, at the opposite end of the cemetery from where Galina lived. As she locked the car she was struck by the unlikely neighbours: all those bright young people spending their formative years next door to the city's dead. It was a geographical oddity that seemed vaguely perverse.

A moment later she was revising her opinion. Death for most young people is so distant as to be irrelevant. For the students, this cemetery adjacent to their university might easily discard its death-liness and instead become a convenient place for a peaceful stroll or a short cut home, perhaps a lovers' rendezvous. And at that very moment, a young couple, arms around each other, emerged from a side garden and exited via the main gates. As they passed, Sylvie smiled. They did not acknowledge her.

The sun was gently shining, a breeze feathered her hair, the carolling of magpies rippled through the clear languid air. As she ambled along, she felt a sublime serenity. Is this the great gift of the dead? she wondered. That in some mysterious way they infuse you and soothe you with their everlasting rest? She could not remember walking here before, but then it was uncommon for her to take a leisurely stroll anywhere—and why she should be so busy with neither job nor young children, she did not know. Of course now, with her letter project, she really did have something to occupy her. And there'd been more time spent with Leonard recently. He seemed to need it; he seemed to need *her*.

In the months since the Grim Reaper Saturday, theirs had been a ragged and often forlorn time. The revelations had taken them to the edge of a precipice where they had teetered for several weeks, before pulling back—together. While there was much that continued to upset and confuse her, she was absolutely certain she wanted to stay married to Leonard, and equally certain she wanted to keep loving him; she suspected that thinking too deeply about their problems jeopardised both. Lately, Leonard had been ringing her during the day just to chat, and arriving home early from work. Despite the improvement in their relations, he seemed anxious and generally on edge. When she questioned him, he mentioned a large contract requiring delicate negotiations, a contract, as far as she could judge, no different nor more complex from others he had managed, and requiring, she would have thought, more, rather than less time at the office. And some time ago he had stopped his Saturday golf—a pity, as it had helped him unwind. Just this last weekend, when his irritability was testing even her patience, she suggested he return to his Saturday game. He shook his head. Golf had changed, he said; some of the other fellows had left. And, he added, Winston had left too.

She didn't think Winston was a member of his golf group.

And neither he was, that was not what Leonard meant. Winston had left the company, he'd left Australia. Winston had returned to Hong Kong.

Winston Leung, central to Leonard's work life for a decade or more, had left the country with apparently no plans to return. Leonard refused to give any details, but he was clearly upset. Sylvie assumed there had been unpleasantness, which would explain why Leonard had waited until now, apparently months after the fact, to tell her, and why Winston, a member of the Morrow extended family, had not said goodbye to her. Of course Leonard would be suffering, *was* suffering.

She continued her stroll among the dead. Each headstone told a story, many possible stories; in this sense, Galina was right, they *were* like letters. She lingered in front of a grave where a man and woman were buried with their three young children, all having died in a single month in 1893—of some ghastly disease, she supposed. Further along the path was an unmarried woman of forty-one buried for all eternity with her mother, and what disappointments oozed from that sad arrangement.

In another section were two men with foreign names in a single grave, cousins who had died months apart in 1944, both in their early forties. If theirs had been war-related deaths, surely this would have been mentioned on the headstone. Perhaps they had been gangsters operating the black market, two men hated enough to be murdered, yet loved and mourned by their own family. Perhaps they were like Leonard, men with feelings for each other—although she couldn't imagine any family being so free-thinking that they'd accept such a relationship, much less advertise it to the rest of the world by burying the men together.

Many of the epitaphs were very moving—even to tears, in some cases. Such powerful feelings for long-dead strangers alongside her adamantly muted feelings about her husband's … what? His lifestyle? His infidelity? His perversity? There was so much she didn't understand.

It was while she was tramping through one of the more overgrown areas of the cemetery, where headstones were askew and many inscriptions were so weathered as to be illegible, that she came across a Mary O'Donahue, not the first Mary O'Donahue she had seen, but this one a possible match for her Mary O'Donahue.

MARY O'DONAHUE
BORN BALLARAT, 1894,
DIED 1945, MELBOURNE.
AND THE DAUGHTER OF THE ABOVE,
GEORGIANA O'DONAHUE,
1912–1946.

Sylvie had in her collection a 1911 letter written to a Mary O'Donahue at an address in the mean streets of Fitzroy, a letter of sadness and harsh condemnation from Mary's father, also an O'Donahue, from a Ballarat address. Mary had brought disgrace upon the family, he wrote. He prayed for her soul, and he mourned the loss of his only daughter.

Standing at this grave, which might well be her Mary O'Donahue's, Sylvie imagined a sweetheart, unbridled passion, and an unwanted pregnancy. The sweetheart turns sour and disappears from the scene long before the birth of a baby girl, Georgiana. Mary

237

raises her daughter alone. She works hard to support them both, and when Georgiana is old enough she goes out to work too. Georgiana never marries; she dies a year after her mother, both women succumbing well before their time to poverty, hard work, and neglect. It was a common story, with the single peculiarity of the daughter's fancy name. The only Georgiana known to Sylvie was Darcy's sister in *Pride and Prejudice*. Was Mary O'Donahue educated, at least to the extent she could read Jane Austen? A daughter of a middle-class family who might well have made a good marriage, or, with the Great War just up ahead, might have travelled to Europe to work as a nurse on the battlefields, but instead had been condemned for her sins to a hard life, festering disgrace, and an early death?

Sylvie made a note of the location of the grave before moving off in a deliberate search for long-married couples who had died within a short time of each other, exactly as she would like for her and Leonard. She would still choose him above all others, which meant, she supposed, that she was also choosing their unorthodox marriage. It had been a surprisingly compatible arrangement, one enriched by gentle passions. And that was the truth. It had only corroded when she discovered Leonard's secret — a secret that had been there all along.

Equally unorthodox, she expected, was her major passion, her letter collection. She had wondered if her letters revealed a sneaky streak in her; that, rather than being a conventional wife with too much curiosity and a penchant for making up stories, she was simply a snoop and a spy. From early girlhood, she'd been taught that to open a letter not addressed to you was a monstrous transgression verging on the criminal. Yet she collected the letters of strangers, she relished these letters, and she did so without a skerrick of guilt. The writers and recipients of her letters were, after all, long dead and out of life's copyright. They were, she told herself, fair game.

An hour later, with a contemporary letter in her grasp, her certainties about what was fair game had become distinctly ragged. The name of the sender was Mark Asher, and, according to the return address, he lived locally. The letter was directed to a Zoe Asher, at a location a couple of suburbs away. The envelope carried a stamp and was unsealed; Sylvie guessed that the writer, this Mark Asher, was yet to decide whether to send it.

In twenty-five years of collecting, nothing like this had ever happened. Her letters were old, and the lives they revealed were over; this letter was today's news, or perhaps today's woes. And it had just appeared. She had left the cemetery and driven the few blocks to the small shopfront café that was Galya's local. She had sat at a table bordering the window, beyond which was the street. On a narrow ledge about half a metre from the ground, where the window slotted into the supporting wall, someone had left a newspaper. She rearranged her coffee and focaccia, and spread the newspaper on the table. It was not the daily paper with its bicentennial flag-waving and reports of nuclear tests (the Soviets, the French and the Americans were all setting off bombs), but a periodical called the *New York Review of Books*, a couple of months old, dated March 1988. She read down the index, a list of articles about books and authors unknown to her, and written by people similarly unknown to her: Isaiah Berlin, Gabriele Annan, John Gregory Dunne, and no woman writer unless Aryeh Neier was a woman. The titles of the articles intrigued her, and two in particular: 'On the Pursuit of the Ideal' written by this Isaiah Berlin — she wondered if he was related to Irving — and 'The Gorbachev Prospect'.

Before Galina entered her life, Sylvie would have glanced at headlines about the Soviet Union and, at best, skimmed the rest. Now she read every article she came across and, of course, she talked with Galya herself. Her astonishment and admiration over what this young girl had experienced continued to grow. Compared with Galya, she may well have passed her own life in a prettily painted biscuit tin.

Being privy to Galya's courage, however, seemed to be making her braver. Sitting alone in a café, for instance, was something she would never have done before meeting Galya. Too self-conscious, she would have preferred to go hungry. And wandering a cemetery by herself would have been no more likely than a visit to a nudist beach (even that analogy would not have occurred to her six months ago). And she would never have had the confidence to start a project, a proper work project, if not for the girl. And it seemed, as she glanced down at the literary newspaper, that the more she stepped outside her usual life, the more new experiences presented themselves.

She decided to start with the Gorbachev article. It was when she raised the paper to fold the pages back that the letter from Mark Asher to Zoe Asher had fallen in her lap. She retrieved it gingerly between thumb and index finger, checked front and back, and placed it on the table.

With the tip of her finger, she raised the flap of the envelope. She could see a single folded sheet inside—good-quality paper, as was the envelope with its lining of brown tissue. The writing covered both sides of the page. She probed a little deeper: a fountain pen had been used, black ink, spidery script, neat enough, but she guessed not easy to read.

The letter lay in its envelope on top of the newspaper. Sylvie didn't move; her hands gripped the edge of the table. The prohibition against reading other people's mail was wrestling with the ravenous heart of the collector. She stared at the letter, stared so intently it seemed to move under her gaze, willing her, goading her to read it. She lowered her hands, clenched them together in her lap, and directed her attention away from the letter to the view beyond the window. A man was hurrying across the road, heading this way. He slowed down as he approached the café, peered through the window, saw the letter, glanced at her, and a moment later was standing by her table.

'I was afraid I'd lost it,' he said, gathering up the letter and holding it to his chest. 'If someone had found it and posted it,' he was shaking his head slowly, 'I don't know what I would have done.'

He was breathless from stress, or relief, or the dash through the streets. His tie was awry, his collar button was undone, and his copious hair sprang wildly about his face. He was a trim, compact, broad-browed man of about her age, not conventionally handsome, but quite attractive, a middle-aged version of Art Garfunkel.

He stood by the table, the letter still pressed to his chest. Gradually, his breathing slowed and his face shed its distress. He did not move away. Sylvie wondered if he were in a state of shock.

'I was about to order another coffee,' she heard herself say. 'Would you like to join me?' The words slipped out easily, as if she made a practice of inviting strange, stressed-out men to have coffee with her.

He accepted immediately, more with an explosion of breath than actual words, and dropped into the chair opposite. He placed the letter on the table, buttoned his collar, straightened his tie, and made an attempt to tame the pesky hair. The proprietor came over and greeted him by name, took their orders, and then, without any prompting from Sylvie, Mark Asher began to talk. He talked in a way one can only do with a stranger never to be seen again, he talked as if he had needed to for a long time.

It was a sad story. His wife, a woman with a long history of mental illness, had killed herself while he was away for a weekend, his first holiday in years. His daughter, his only child, Zoe, blamed him, not for her mother's illness—he'd been a devoted and patient carer—but for her mother's death. For Mark was not alone on his holiday. Zoe was convinced her mother knew he was with another woman and it was this that drove her to suicide.

The wife had died two years ago. Within a couple of months, Zoe had dropped out of her final year of high school; a few more weeks, and she had left home. Since then she had been living with what Mark termed 'low-life'. He offered an apologetic shrug. 'I don't know how else to describe her new mates.

'But at least she's talking to me now. I've been writing to her regularly since she moved out. Chatty letters with news about friends and relatives. And I write about her mother too. I might include a photo, and once I enclosed one of my wife's handker-chiefs—it smelled of her perfume. It was after I sent the hankie that Zoe finally responded.

'That was about nine months ago. A few more months passed before our first face-to-face meeting, and now we get together for a meal every second Tuesday, and,' he pointed to the letter, 'I write to her on the alternate week.' He let out an audible sigh and swiped again at the unruly hair. 'I let her set the rules. Despite the chaos in which she lives, or perhaps because of it, she insists on order and predictability with me.'

'And the people she's living with?' These were the first words Sylvie had uttered since Mark had begun his story.

'I've never met them, nor am I likely to. One of the guys has actually been in prison.' He was shaking his head in disbelief. 'They're all seasoned shoplifters, none of them has finished high school, and all are on the dole. When Zoe mentions them she seems to be bragging, as if she deliberately wants to shock her middle-class dad.' His face opened into a smile. 'She's certainly succeeded in doing that.'

At the present time, Zoe was working days in a supermarket and taking night classes at a local high school. 'She's always been a high-achieving student, though I expect she's not shared that with her new mates. Then last Tuesday, to my great surprise and pleasure, both of which I tried to hide, she mentioned the possibility of university study next year.' A hesitant, hopeful smile slipped into his face. 'And she put out feelers about coming home.' He picked up the letter and slipped it inside his jacket. 'That's why this letter is so important. I've made some suggestions, the first time I've dared. I need to reread it before I send it, make sure I've said the right thing, struck the right tone.' And with an ironic raising of his eyebrows, he added, 'I suspect I'm still a couple of drafts from the final one.'

'So,' Sylvie said, 'what do you have in mind?'

At the back of his house, he said, were old stables. The ground floor was currently filled with junk, and he used the upper floor as a study—he was an academic at the university. He could shift his study into the house, and the stables could be modified into a self-contained flat for Zoe. Close but separate. If, on the other hand, she'd prefer to live in college, he would be happy to provide any support she wanted. 'I mean for next year, should she complete her HSC, should she pass, and should she decide on university. Not that I wrote any of that.'

He'd hardly touched his coffee. Now he reached for it, took a sip, grimaced, and pushed it away. 'I have to be so careful. In an earlier version, I wrote I'd be happy to pay her college fees, but this was far too intrusive, far too controlling. In the next draft, I wrote something like, "I'm happy to pay your college fees should you fail to get a scholarship."' He was laughing. 'Fail? What on earth was I thinking? I can't be critical about her clothes or lifestyle, so to be critical, even conditionally critical about her studies, well, I'd find myself back at first base.' He shook his head slowly. 'I take more care over letters to my daughter than I do writing academic papers.'

He slumped back in his chair. At last, it seemed he was finished. In the silence, he toyed with his coffee cup, twirling it in the saucer, he rubbed the back of his neck, and then returned to his twirling. Sylvie hadn't coped particularly well when Andrew decided to live on the other side of the city, goodness knows what she would have done if he'd opted for an utterly alien lifestyle. She was wondering if she would have had the patience, the wisdom too, to handle the situation as Mark Asher had done, when she saw him looking across the table at her. He was shaking his head slowly, his lips pressed together, his embarrassment obvious.

'I'm usually reserved,' he said, 'and most especially about personal matters. I can't imagine what possessed me. I've been sitting with you,' he checked his watch, 'for close on thirty minutes, and I haven't even asked your name. I can't imagine what you must think of me.'

As it happened, she thought rather well of him. So much so that when he suggested he treat her to lunch to thank her for being such a good sport, she accepted without hesitation. It was her decision they make the arrangement there and then. And so they did, a week from that day. He invited her to University House and the staff restaurant there. It would be a first for her, as everything about Mark Asher would prove to be a first.

Sylvie was up in her office when she heard Leonard come in from work. Spread across her desk were several pages of a letter, together with the clean copy she was making. She quickly covered the papers with her grandmother's hand-embroidered cloth kept exactly for this purpose (it often happened she was called from her desk without time to put her work away) and switched off the light. She stepped onto the landing, closed the door. And stopped.

Leonard was home early, very early; not only was she in the middle of some work, but after this quite extraordinary day, she wasn't quite ready to face him. Where was it written that a wife must spring to attention as soon as her husband walked in the door?

From the top of the stairs she called out she was busy and would join him in a short while. He called back that she was to take her time, perhaps equally pleased to be left alone. Sylvie re-entered her office and resumed her copying.

She had arrived home with her mind in a riot. She might have read through the 'Pillow Talk' pages of her letter project, or started the next section, titled 'Safe Trespass'—it was to focus on the clandestine quality of letters—but both would have required an intellectual effort that, in her current state, was beyond her. Making a fair copy of a hard-to-read letter was a task with clear and limited boundaries, it was totally absorbing, and exactly what she needed after meeting Mark Asher.

As to whether she would keep the rendezvous next week, she was far from certain, but that would not stop her from the very pleasant pastime of entertaining the possibility.

She took her time with the copying, given the knotted handwriting, she had no choice, and gradually the extraordinary events of the day shifted to a softer beat. She assumed that Leonard was downstairs in his chair, wrapped in his after-work cardigan, his feet up, a Scotch in one hand, the newspaper in the other. It was such a fond and familiar image, one of so many that cemented their long relationship. Their meals were another; and it occurred to her, as it never had before, that their meals provided a perfect illustration of their marriage.

When they had company, she would sit at one end of the dining table, Leonard would sit at the other, and their guests would sit in between; she and Leonard would conduct the evening in a faultless duet, while at the same time exchanging a private commentary in their own subliminal language. When it was just the two of them, they ate at a small table in the kitchen. They enjoyed eating like this, like nursery meals in the books she read as a child. Nursery meals, nursery relationship. But what was wrong with that? It was safe, it was secure, it was full of history, and it had been full of love. As for sex, it was not something women like her were brought up to want; and not knowing what she had missed out on, she'd not felt its absence. Of course sex was everywhere these days: on billboards, in TV advertisements, rocking along in pop songs, at the movies. But she saw films of people climbing Everest, of trekkers crossing the Sahara, and while she was interested, even fascinated, it did not make her want to climb mountains or cross deserts. And the same could be said about sex.

Until today.

Sitting at a window table in a café with a strange man who couldn't stop talking, she recognised a hot, jagged stirring deep within her that was unambiguously sexual. What did she know about her husband? That he had slept with other people, he had slept with men. It had not, in the end, changed the way she felt about him.

And if she were to do the same?

It was an astonishing thought. But the fact was she, not Leonard, nor any of the writers of her letters, she, Sylvie Morrow, was attracted to a man who was not her husband, and she was thinking of acting on it.

Downstairs, Leonard is asleep in his armchair. He is inside a dream.

It is dusk, and he is standing at the top of a street, a ten-gallon drum of oil beside him. He opens a tap in the lower portion of the drum, and oil slides out in a lovely sinuous stream. Like liquid onyx, he is thinking. But too fast, this stream is flowing too fast. He attaches a piece of rubber tubing to the tap, and by lowering and raising the makeshift hose he is able to moderate the flow. He wants a slow, lava-like stream to slide down the street; he wants the edges to be neat, and he wants to be safe. When the oil reaches the lowest point of the street, he adjusts the tubing to reduce the flow to a trickle. He takes a box of matches from his pocket and walks down the slope to the midway point. He strikes a match and lowers it to the oil. The fire shoots away in both directions. The stream is fabulously alight, a gorgeous orange-red-yellow-blue flickering over the slick surface. The fire travels up the slope, and circles the tubing at the barrel's tap, it travels down to make a fiery pool at the bottom of the street.

Leonard gazes at his beautiful creation. 'Lethal' and 'dangerous' do not enter his mind. But the dreamer knows better. The dreamer tries to warn his dreaming self. The flames leap, at first in little skips and hops, and then in a wild dance. By the time Leonard recognises the danger, he is ringed by fire. The heat is tremendous, the smoke is suffocating. He's unable to move, the fire is roaring. He calls for help.

Sylvie appears, she walks swiftly towards him. The flames don't touch her, and she's unaffected by the smoke. She soothes him with her words, she wraps him in her arms, she guides him to safety.

Her arms are around him when he wakes.

13

MANIFEST DESTINIES

After the loveliest autumn, with mild days and crisp nights and trees ablaze with colour, winter had arrived. This was Galina's second winter in Australia. Twelve months ago she was living with Zara and Arnold, she had not yet contacted Andrew, and she was dividing her work between real estate illustrations and sewing-pattern designs. Now she had a place of her own, she was, according to Sylvie, 'a member of the extended Morrow family', and she was about to have her first picture book published.

She felt a good deal more comfortable in Australia, although would not yet say she felt at home. She was coming to think that one's first home holds tight to the role and will thwart any competition. But she was establishing routines, and whole days could now pass without her being tripped up by Australian ways.

On this particular morning, she and Andrew were eating breakfast at her local café. Both were early risers, and after a couple of hours' work, they often took a coffee break together. But today was different: Galina had telephoned Andrew at seven and suggested they meet for breakfast. It was such a lovely morning, she said, it would be a shame not to enjoy it.

So here they were at the café around dawn. The temperature outside was just a few degrees above zero, and there was frost on the grass—enough to give a lovely crunch underfoot. People were entering the warm café as if they were escaping a blizzard. There had been several days of low temperatures, and everyone was complaining about the cold.

Galina was amused by the local reaction. 'I am waiting for a really wintry day,' she said to Andrew as they ate their breakfast. 'Not snow, I know it will not snow here. But cold with an *Antarctic* wind,' she emphasised 'Antarctic' to distinguish it from her far more familiar 'Arctic', 'and the requirement for hat and gloves.'

Andrew felt a rush of pleasure, more for the formality of her speech, which he delighted in, than its content. 'You might be waiting a long time,' he said. And then, for no apparent reason, he asked, 'When's your birthday?'

A smile rose to her face, one of those private smiles behind which lay memories. 'I was born on the cusp of spring, March 23rd. Although often the snow was still thick on the ground and it might still have been midwinter.'

He asked how she had celebrated her birthday in Leningrad. And she told of a special outing, a concert or a film, followed by a celebratory supper at home. There would be the retelling of the past year in highlights, and the forecasting of the year ahead in hopes.

'We took every opportunity to celebrate,' she said.

Fresh coffee arrived, and they both sipped in silence, immersed in their own thoughts. After a time, Andrew put his cup down and leaned across the table. He was looking rather pleased with himself. 'Let's go to the snow,' he said. 'A holiday in the Victorian High Country. We could find a place that's not popular with skiers, and you could wander around and pretend you were in the countryside near Leningrad.'

He seemed so excited by his idea that Galina could neither refuse nor correct him: nowhere in Australia, even if it snowed for a month, even if the eucalypts started soughing in Russian, could be mistaken for Leningrad. But his enthusiasm was infectious, and soon the two of them were discussing dates and destinations, lodges versus flats, skiing, hiking and other activities for their High Country holiday.

The time sped by. A sharp white sun had risen, and people cocooned in clothes were hurrying to work. Galina glanced at her wristwatch, and instantly Andrew fell silent. It took so little to throw him off, Galina thought, and quickly proposed they continue their planning that evening over dinner.

He brightened up immediately. 'I'll bring maps,' he said. 'And I think I have some old pamphlets about the High Country.'

'As you will be supplying the adventure,' Galina said, 'I will supply the meal.'

Andrew hurried home. He had some work to finish, followed by a meeting with a committee from Parks and Gardens, and he would also need to fit in a visit to a travel agent for maps and pamphlets of the High Country. It had been a small lie in service to a good cause. A few uninterrupted days with Galya: the prospect was thrilling. And overwhelming.

The fact was he wanted to see her as often as possible, and he wanted their time together to be perfect. Every single time. Before each meeting he was excited and hopeful, during the meeting he was tense and flustered, and afterwards he felt an abysmal failure.

It probably would be better if he were on a lighthouse somewhere, alone with his dog and his yearnings. He could keep Galina close twenty-four hours a day without making a mess of things. And with his lively imagination, anything and everything would be possible with her. Yet he couldn't be entirely incompetent here, in the real world. Galina was quick to accept his invitations for a meal, for their Saturday adventures; and if he touched her, the sort of touch that couldn't be misconstrued, she never brushed him away. She kissed him on the cheek in greeting and again when departing; she shared the armrest with him at the cinema. But did she know he loved her? And did she have any special feelings for him? After nine months of regular contact he could answer neither question.

For the sake of his own sanity he needed to know. He had considered recruiting Sylvie to the task — she had her own friendship with Galya, the sort of woman-to-woman interaction in which confidences are shared — but his well-meaning, over-protective mother already intruded far too deeply into his life. And besides, he was afraid the relationship between Galya and his mother was more of a mother-daughter connection, in which case the main Morrow attraction for Galya might be Sylvie, not him.

He entered the studio, busied himself with Godrevy, and attended to some mail. But thoughts of Galya would not be silent. Which was why he needed some answers: he simply could not go on this way. Surely it was better to know the truth and risk losing his dreams than to live with so much uncertainty. Tonight, he decided, he would reveal himself tonight. Then immediately changed his mind: he didn't want to jeopardise their trip to the High Country.

He picked up the telephone and dialled his parents' number. He knew he was sending the wrong message to Sylvie, but he needed help, and his mother was always so astute about people. The phone rang and rang. Perhaps he had dialled the wrong number; he tried again, but still no answer. It was not his mother's driving-for-the-blind day, it was not the day she lunched with her sister, it was not her shopping day, and besides, it was nine o'clock in the morning. You could set your calendar by Sylvie — although now that he thought about it, this was not the first time recently he'd telephoned to find her out when she should have been home.

He would have to deal with this alone. He telephoned the travel agency in Carlton. Yes, they said in response to his question, they had material on the High Country. He dithered over whether to pick it up now or after his afternoon meeting, then decided later. He needed to work. He tried some sketches for a new commission, he tried working on a maquette for the same project, he tried some paperwork, but his mind simply would not leave Galina alone. In the end, he gathered up a delighted Godrevy and took him for another walk.

If Andrew had decided to go to the Carlton travel agency that morning, he might have witnessed a scene far more troubling than his turmoil over Galina: his mother with a strange man outside the delicatessen, the man holding a bag of food, his mother grasping a baguette, the two of them talking and laughing, two people who were unmistakeably close. If Andrew had seen them, he might have considered an innocent explanation, certainly he would have wanted one, but the evidence would have been against it. He would have seen that these two, his mother and the unknown man, were intimates—a myopic recluse from outback Australia would have come to the same conclusion. Fortunately, Andrew was out walking the dog when Sylvie and Mark Asher turned away from the shops and made their way to Mark's house for a whole day together.

They had known each other for nearly two months. Two, three, sometimes four times a week, Sylvie would drive across the city to meet him, and on the days in between there were long and often racy phone calls—so racy that a couple of weeks ago she had asked Mark whether they were having phone sex. She was shocked at how easy it was to ask such a question, but then ever since they had met, she had often shocked herself. Respectable, reliable Sylvie Morrow, who had previously known only one man, now had a lover. And she'd not been the innocent led astray by the more experienced Mark. At their very first date, when they met for lunch at University House, she knew exactly where she wanted to end up with him.

Never before had she experienced an irresistible and

252

overwhelming sexual feeling, yet she had recognised it immediately. On that first date, every part of her was aroused: her face, her legs, even the skin of her hands. And when he reached across the table and with his forefinger stroked the soft, inner side of her wrist, her whole body fired up. Sitting on a hard chair in a crowded café, fully clothed with both hands on the table, Sylvie experienced a physical response she would not have thought possible. She ate in a rush—she didn't want dessert, she didn't want coffee. He had a class in an hour. Your office, she said, show me your office. He'd hardly shut the door when she lunged at him, mouth, tongue, hands, she pulled him on to her, she pulled him into her, she didn't give a damn.

Demure, well-behaved Sylvie Morrow had vanished entirely.

Had she been fooling herself all these years? That while she cooked and cleaned and did the laundry, a sex-crazed woman had been huddling beneath the skin, just waiting for an opportunity to leap out. Had she repressed this aspect of herself? And how can a repressed person even know what they are repressing? She supposed she should read Freud, but as one of the correspondents in her letter collection had written, she had already entered 'the dessert phase of life' and she didn't have time for Dr Freud.

It dawned on her, more emphatically than ever before, how very brief is the human span of years. The endless days of youth, the early years of a marriage stretching to a far distant 'till death do us part', the pledging of lifelong friendships, new interests popping up, and countless possibilities beckoning along an endless road to the future: time, like air, is in such lavish supply when you're young. With each passing year you add to the pile of things you want to do. Then suddenly comes the day when the pile of things you want to do has turned into the things you will never do, and 'endless' and 'forever' have been erased from the picture.

In the week between her chance meeting with Mark at the café and their first date at University House, it occurred to Sylvie, as it

253

never had before, that she had no time to waste. She stood at the edge of the precipice, and, with her eyes wide open, she leapt.

At last she understood why people made such a fuss about sex. It was fun, it was engrossing, it was *sexy*. The touch, the smells, the fluids, she loved him all over her, his mouth, his tongue, his hands. She loved what he could do with his body, she loved what he could do with hers. From the beginning, she'd observed a certain modesty with Leonard, through ignorance more than anything else, and when Leonard had not challenged it, she'd accepted it as the norm. Now she discarded all modesty. She would stand naked in front of Mark, she who had never before stood completely naked in front of anyone, and he would watch and appreciate. And when he'd feasted enough (that was his word, 'feasted'), he would step towards her and wrap his body around hers, and she would feel him all over her as they touched and touched and touched. Nothing was out of bounds. 'Let yourself go,' he said. And she did, as if she would never have to account for herself, as if there never would be a day of reckoning.

He was her walk on the wild side. He *was* her wild side. And yes, they made love to Lou Reed. That sexy tease of so many of his songs—she couldn't believe she had missed it before.

Everything she did with Mark was new, and everything was a live wire. He took her to a café located in a narrow lane at the top end of the city. They entered via an unmarked door, up a wooden staircase into an ordinary room, with ordinary tables and chairs, where wine, white or red, was served in tumblers and there was no menu. And throughout the meal he touched her, his hand on her hand, his foot nudging her foot, his knees pressed against hers. They went to a pub where union deals accompanied the downing of beers; with the tip of his forefinger, he removed the froth from her upper lip, and, not even realising what she was doing, she raised her head just the slightest, and sucked his finger into her mouth. They saw a play performed in a building that looked as if it ought to be condemned; locked in the darkness with him, she might well have been naked.

He was a historian, of the modern period. On one occasion, she had sat at the back of an auditorium while he lectured on the Russian Revolution. She found herself wishing that Galya was with her, and in the next moment so pleased to be alone. This lecture, this lecturer, indeed everything about Mark was separate from the rest of her life. Separate but ever-present. She could feel him against her, even though he was at the lectern more than twenty metres away. He was a dynamic and engaging lecturer. She gazed around at the students: she was not the only person who was enjoying Mark Asher.

She'd never had an affair before, she'd never discussed the affairs of others, she had no idea how she knew the protocol, but somehow she did. She knew that affairs had to remain separate from regular life, that they were in addition to that life; she knew you had to keep turning up the heat in an affair; and, crucially, she knew you must recognise when to finish. As for knowing this was an affair: she was a woman in her fifties, she'd been married for thirty-two years, she knew. However, she hoped the end was a good way off.

They had returned an hour before from their shopping expedition, and were sitting at Mark's kitchen table drinking coffee; the remains of their deli brunch were scattered across a teak platter. Sylvie was aware that relations with his daughter were thawing, so much so that Zoe would definitely be moving into the stables once the renovation was complete.

'When do you expect the stables to be finished?' she asked.

Mark stood up and led her by the hand to the large glass windows at the back of the house. He nodded at the stables beyond the courtyard. 'The bathroom is nearly finished,' he said, 'and the kitchen is being installed next week. Painters come in after that. I've suggested to Zoe she might like to choose the rugs and furniture, make the place more her own.' And then, guessing what had prompted her question, 'I don't think Zoe's being here will affect us. She's working and studying. She'll hardly be home, and certainly not during the day.'

They stood gazing through the glass to the stables a few moments more, then he turned to her. She thought he was struggling to say something, the muscles around his eyes and mouth would not keep still, but he remained silent.

'Come to bed,' she said, slipping her arm around his waist. 'Come to bed, my love.'

In her saddlery, not far from Mark Asher's house, Galina was working on her Aussie English picture book. With the Australian vernacular showing a marked preference for the risqué, Galina was thinking it might well be a picture book for adults. Whoever the audience, she was enjoying the work. The hours slid past, and it was early evening when she packed up for the day. With Andrew due in an hour to discuss their High Country holiday, she turned her attention to dinner. There was no time to go to the shops, but she was Russian, and Russians can make a meal out of crumbs.

She settled on an East-meets-West combination: mushroom kasha, leftover barbecue chicken, with a few beans each. She reached for her copy of *The Book of Tasty and Nutritious Food*, and opened it to the kasha recipe.

There had been no question of leaving this tattered old book behind. It had been her mother's, a gift when Lidiya joined the Komsomol. Slipped inside the front cover was a photo cut from *Komsomolskaya Pravda*, depicting the new Komsomol members, with Lidiya, a small grainy figure at the front, marked with an X.

Although Galina knew the kasha recipe by heart, she placed the open book on the bench; she liked having this staple of the Russian home in view while she cooked in her Australian kitchen. She dry-roasted the buckwheat in a pan, chopped an onion, and while it was browning, sliced the mushrooms — three different types bought from a stall in the market because she simply had not been able to choose between them.

Her ability to choose remained at a fledgling stage. If faced with three different types of mushroom, and she had sufficient money, she bought all three. There were two bread shops within walking distance, each crammed with multiple varieties; sometimes it was all too much, and she left without buying anything. While the situation had mellowed in the past two years, she doubted if choice, so attractive in theory, would ever be easy for her.

For a long time she had worried about the quality of Australian food. Food at home might well have been basic and in short supply, but Soviet food was the purest in the world. Here, additives were actually written on the packages. It was Sylvie who set her straight about Australian food labelling, while Leonard questioned whether anyone really could trust the Soviet authorities on food purity. 'They deceived you about so many things,' he said, 'so why not the food?'

The Australian love affair with Gorbachev was continuing. Most of the news items came out of Moscow, but every now and then there were reports from Leningrad, and she would catch a glimpse of a familiar building, or the Neva, or a gathering of people in a square where she herself had once lingered. (Look, she once said, look, *Mamochka*, only to realise she was speaking aloud in her empty Australian home.) She wanted to prolong these segments, and she wanted to silence the TV translator who was blocking out the Russian speech.

It had been a madness cutting herself off from other Russian émigrés, yet, like an alcoholic who cannot risk even a taste of

257

alcohol, so it was for her with Russian: she had deprived herself totally, and locked herself inside English. It was that common state of the émigré, she realised, that when everything is uncertain, you establish rules and rigid coordinates to guide you, even though they might inadvertently undermine your very identity.

These days, she met regularly with other Soviet Jews. Heavy with nostalgia, fats and sugars, these get-togethers moved at a Russian pace. She relaxed in the comfort of speaking Russian and eating the Russian food. She met a guy at one of these gatherings, an engineer from Moscow. He liked her, and she liked him. But while a Russian boyfriend would enrich her private and domestic life, out in the Australian streets and shops, he would only add to her difficulties. She distanced herself, not without a measure of sadness, before anything serious could develop.

The decision might have been different if not for the Morrow family. Now central in her Australian life, each of them was important to her. Sylvie could not replace her mother, but Lidiya's absence had hollowed out a space into which Sylvie could easily enter — not fill, but occupy a portion of it. So Sylvie had slipped in with the greatest ease. But Andrew was the most important. It wasn't just their weekly adventures, nor their meeting for coffee several times a week; he was the one with whom she shared the ebb and flow of her daily life. And then there was Leonard, neither the easiest nor the most important, but surprisingly, the one who seemed to best understand her situation, who was able to recognise that cramping of the familiar self that characterises exile and displacement. Often during dinners at the Morrow home, it was Leonard who would pass a comment or make an aside that coalesced exactly with her experience. And during conversations that involved just the two of them, if she'd not known otherwise she would have picked him to be an exile himself. He had an understanding of the new Australian — he used the phrase 'being on the outside looking in' — that was right on target.

She checked the time. With Andrew due to arrive soon, she put all the ingredients in a pot and set it on a low flame. Everything was on schedule, and if she had been a different sort of person she would have allowed herself a brief relaxation with a glass of wine and the newspaper. But being who she was, she needed to watch over the kasha, make sure that nothing went wrong.

'Connoisseurs of catastrophe'. That summed up the Russian people, even down to cooking kasha. She'd read the phrase not so long ago and it had struck a chord. 'We Russians are connoisseurs of catastrophe,' she said aloud. There are the bad times when the shops are empty and the toilet is broken and the winter is fierce; there are the worst times: the siege, the pogroms, the terror of the 1930s; and the better times: being allocated your own flat, a job at the children's book publishers, a ticket to the Kirov. Bad times, worst times, better times: it is the Russian way. This, she decided, looking around the saddlery, was a very good time indeed.

There was a knock at the door. She checked her watch, Andrew was early. 'It is open,' she said, stirring the pot. 'Let yourself in.'

There was another knock and she called out again. This time, she heard the door open.

'I am attending to our dinner,' she said, without turning around.

She heard the scrape of shoes on the floor. Andrew was not wearing his usual canvas loafers.

Then he spoke. *Pakhnet, kak doma.*

Without thinking, Galina responds in Russian. Yes, she says, it does smell like home. And then she realises: not Russian, not here, not with Andrew. And whisks around.

There's an old man standing by the couch.

'*Galya, ya by tebya uznal gde ugodno.*' Galya, he says, I'd know you anywhere. And then he utters the words so often spoken by Lidiya. '*Ty tak pokhozha na tvoyu babushku.*' You look so much like your grandmother.

She knows who he is. She knows immediately. This man who

was sufficiently powerful to be a medal-bearer at Brezhnev's funeral, this old swarthy man who informed on his parents, this man with his dyed hair and his smoker's voice who neglected his own sister, this man from the Soviet elite who dined on caviar while his own family went hungry, this man is Mikhail Kogan. Her uncle, her mother's estranged brother is here. In Australia. In her own home. His face is roughened by a day or two of beard, his body is stocky and heavy, and emanating from him is that familiar Russian male smell.

She doesn't move. She doesn't know what to do.

He approaches as if to embrace her. She steps back, the stirring spoon clatters to the floor. He picks it up, looks in the pot, shrugs as if to say, have it your own way, and settles himself on the couch.

He's waiting for her to say something, but she is unable to speak.

'I'm here because of you,' he says, breaking the silence.

Still she cannot speak.

'I might have gone to America or Canada, but your mother's friend, Nadya, told me you were in Melbourne.' His speech gives off a whiff of tobacco. 'You are family. I came here.'

At last she manages to speak; her voice is, to her relief, quiet but steady. 'Why did you need to leave? You and Mother Russia got along extremely well.'

He raises his eyebrows. 'You've inherited your grandmother's cynicism — never her most attractive quality. But since you ask, I will tell you.' The eyebrows contract to a frown. 'My country is being ruined. That fool Gorbachev is ruining it. I'm a patriot, I've always been a patriot. I couldn't watch any longer.'

So, he too, had taken the Jewish option. 'Just like you,' he says. He shrugs in that particular Russian way. 'Judaism has caused me only grief. It owed me, and as the best ticket out of the Soviet Union, it was pay-up time. Other Soviet citizens without a finger of Jewishness were using the same means to leave Russia, at least I used what was rightfully mine.'

260

He had been in Melbourne for just two days, and was staying on the south side of the city. Jewish Welfare had consulted their records, saving him the trouble of searching for her.

'They showed me a map. I saw you were living on the other side of the city, a long way from where I am staying.' Again, that Russian shrug. 'It doesn't matter to me where we live.' He pauses. 'Next time, I bring my bags.'

Galina gathers up her full voice, and she lets him have it. She blames him for the arrest of her grandparents, she accuses him of deserting her mother, she attacks him for disloyalty and betrayal, she condemns him for outright cruelty, she harangues him for her own impoverished life in Leningrad.

He watches her closely. He doesn't interrupt, he's quite enjoying himself. It's as if his own mother has returned from the grave. Although why the girl's so angry with him is inexplicable, he's done nothing to her. She blames him for this, she blames him for that; given enough time, she'll probably blame him for Lidiya's death. When at last it seems she's finished, he waits a moment before speaking, to let the anger fade.

'There's no point in dwelling on the past,' he says. 'You know nothing about those times. They were very different, and,' he pauses for emphasis, 'they're over.' He has nothing to apologise for. One survived as best one could in the Soviet Union, an approach her mother subscribed to even if Galina does not. He has done nothing wrong—not that he expects her to understand, but then neither does he care.

'The facts are simple, Galya.' He speaks more slowly now, stressing each word. 'I am family, and I am old. You are young, and you have a duty.'

'And what about *your* duty to family?'

He shrugs. He's not interested in arguing, there's nothing she can say to alter the facts. He takes in her surroundings; she is set up very well, with more than enough space for two. He notices the table laden with work—she's inherited her grandparents' work ethic, he is pleased to see. She will soon adjust to the new situation. He will give her a couple of days to prepare, then he will move in.

Andrew telephones Galina to let her know he is running behind. She does not answer, and he assumes that, like him, she has been caught up with her work. When finally he knocks on her door he is nearly an hour late. He waits a full minute before knocking again. At last he hears the lock released and the bolt slipped back—odd, as she never locks her door when she's home. The door opens just a crack. As soon as she sees him, she opens the door wider, pulls him in, slams the door, and shoots the bolt home.

She looks terrified. Her hair is wild, her eyes are red, her face is pale, her mouth is twisted and stiff. Something terrible has happened, and without the usual internal debate, without any thought whatsoever, he steps towards her and wraps her in his arms.

The story comes out in stuttered bursts: a man, rough, unkempt, young, let himself in. Probably a drug addict. Threatened violence, took money, left.

Andrew reaches for the telephone to call the police.

'No, no. Not the police.' She sounds so distressed. And then, as if she hears herself, adds more quietly, 'What can the police do? The man took what he wanted. Now he has gone.'

Andrew sits her down and pours her a measure of brandy. Galya is usually so composed, so self-possessed, he has never presumed to know what she is feeling. But this girl in front of him is shockingly exposed. The intruder might not have harmed her physically, but he's left her distraught.

Over the next hour she calms down, while he provides comfort and distraction. He asks about the food she has prepared, and insists on being shown *The Book of Tasty and Nutritious Food*. Despite only the flimsiest interest in food preparation, he plies her with questions about this dish and that. It's late when they eat. The kasha is tasty enough — with lashings of butter and a teaspoon of salt, so it should be — but the consistency reminds him of lumpy porridge and is not at all to his liking. By the time he raises their excursion to the snow, she seems to be back to her old self, so he is surprised by her lack of enthusiasm for a plan which just that morning had so excited her.

'It'll be good for you,' he says. 'Separate for a few days from this place. Put today's events behind you.'

It is as if the past couple of calming hours haven't happened. She is shaking her head, her face is sunk in gloom, her entire demeanour suggests these events will never be put behind her. He doesn't understand. He knows she's had a shock, but she has withstood so much worse in her life. Perhaps all the stresses she's borne over the years have mounted up, and the incident with the intruder has somehow tipped her over the edge. Whatever the explanation, she is clearly in despair.

He slides his chair around the table so as to be seated next to her. The squeal of wood on the concrete subsides in a soft, safe silence. He puts his arm about her, holding her without speaking. A minute more, and she lowers her head to his shoulder. He thinks she may be crying, but doesn't try to check: Galya is not the sort of person who would want to be seen crying.

What he does know for certain is she's scared and she's shaken. He offers to stay with her. 'I can sleep on the couch.'

She accepts immediately. 'But come into my bed,' she says. 'Then I will know you are here.'

They both lie between the sheets fully clothed. He wraps his arms around her, she rests her head on his shoulder, and soon she is asleep.

It is morning when he awakes — he'd thought he wouldn't sleep at all. He's lying on his side and she is curved against his back, her arm flung across his waist. For the next hour, he holds her hand to his chest, firm to his beating heart. This is definitely not the time to tell her how he feels.

Two days later, Mikhail Kogan moved into the saddlery.

His arrival wrought an immediate change in Galina. Entombed in a weird sort of numbness, she lost all sense of inhabiting her own body. She did not think; she could not think.

And she was as efficient as a robot.

First she made space for him. It wasn't difficult: the Kogan home at the *kommunalka* had accommodated both her and her mother, and there'd been four people living there when her mother was a child. Now she pushed her bed from the centre of the back wall to one corner, and moved her work table alongside. There was insufficient room for her chair, but she could sit on her bed while drawing—although work was no more possible at the moment than a trip to the moon. She returned to the second-hand shop where she had bought her couch. There she found a sofa bed and a free-standing wardrobe; the sofa was an ugly brown and an impeccable match for her state of mind, the wardrobe was a scuffed and scarred white; a fresh coat of paint would have improved it, but she didn't have the heart for improvements. Her old work space became Mikhail's alcove. She positioned the wardrobe so it acted as a screen between his section and the rest of the room. The sofa bed, her desk chair, and a side-table were installed in the alcove, and any of Mikhail's possessions that were not immediately needed were stacked on top of the wardrobe. The back of the wardrobe was brown masonite; she could have invigorated it with posters, but she didn't.

Detached from all this activity, she was reduced to a puppet. She saw her hands doing the work, they might have been anyone's hands. She lifted, she pushed, she dragged, she stacked, she reconfigured her minimalist Australian space with Russian ingenuity. Not a square centimetre was wasted.

When Mikhail had turned up in Leningrad, her mother had

done what was required to get rid of him. But that was Leningrad. And that was Lidiya and her story. His being here now, in Australia, created an entirely new story. And it was Galina's alone: her story, her problem, her decisions, her life, her future.

It was better not to think.

She settled him into her home and helped him unpack his belongings. His clothes, although creased and grubby, were of the best quality. No patched and darned garments for him, no worn-at-heel shoes, no threadbare, warmth-defying cloth: Mikhail's fine clothes advertised his membership of the Soviet elite.

He shoved a bundle at her. 'These need to be cleaned,' he said.

Briefly her old self revived, and she shoved them back at him.' I will show you how to clean them,' she said.

His anger was quick to flare. This was a man unaccustomed to being opposed, but, like it or not, he was dependent on her — not for money, he seemed to have plenty of it, but for everything else. His English was so poor it would earn him no rewards in the Australian streets and shops, and, as a member of the Soviet elite, he'd had people to take care of his personal needs. Mikhail needed her.

The days and weeks passed, though time itself, without work or friends or outings to measure it by, lost all meaning. Automaton Galina shopped and cooked and cleaned; she tended her little garden, she cleared the rubbish in the lane; when the roof leaked in a heavy storm, she found a plumber and had it fixed. Automaton Galina kept the wheels of life turning.

It might have been different if Mikhail were easier to like, but he ordered rather than asked, he took rather than gave. But could it have been different? Lidiya had hated this man. To like him, even to tolerate him, would be a betrayal of her mother. Yet there was a vague, haunting sense — nothing she could hold on to — that here in Australia the claims of family trespassed where once they would not have dared.

The saddlery reeked of his smoking. When he moved, when

he spoke, when he breathed, it was with a lifetime of cigarettes. He complained constantly. The cigarettes in this country were shit, *gavno*. The food in this country, also *gavno*. The whole damn country, *gavno*. And she wanted to say: Then leave, just leave. But where would he go? Mother Russia wouldn't take him back, and that was, in truth, the only place he wanted to be.

Finding the right cigarettes became a priority: if he was happy while smoking, he would have less opportunity to complain. She took him to a tobacconist, and translated his preferences to the proprietor. They returned to the saddlery with four different packs. The first was the local Marlboro brand, which he insisted was not the same as the Marlboros he had smoked in the Soviet Union; Australian Marlboros were *gavno*, he said, and tossed the pack in the rubbish. He then tried the Peter Stuyvesants, another brand he'd smoked at home — also quickly trashed. She prayed, as non-believers do in desperate situations, that one of the brands would suit. And when Mikhail declared himself satisfied with the English Dunhill (what a life of privilege he must have enjoyed in the Soviet Union), she decided God must be a smoker. She bought Mikhail a carton. A whole carton, she learned, lasted a single week.

He wasn't interested in seeing the sights. Melbourne couldn't compete with Moscow, it couldn't even compete with Leningrad, a city for which he had little fondness; besides, walking tired him. She said they could order a taxi, but he was not interested in taxis. He did, however, allow her to take him to a barber, not to have his hair dyed as he initially wanted, but to have it cropped. She explained that thick grey hair in an older man was considered attractive here, and the appeal to his vanity worked. But little else did. He complained about the food, he complained about the saddlery, he complained about the absence of friends. He absolutely refused to meet her Jewish Russian friends. 'I'm not interested in your *zhidovnia*,' he said, the insult so much worse coming from the mouth of a Jew.

He sat on the green, floral couch, smoking his cigarettes and watching TV. He liked the game shows. And golf, he liked to watch the golf. 'Do you play?' she asked, already planning to sign him up at a club.

Of course he didn't play. How many golf courses had she seen in Russia? He liked the pace of the game, and it required no English. 'It is suitable for me at this time of life,' he said. 'I have earned my relaxation.'

One day she observed him watching an American slapstick movie. He was still laughing when the credits started rolling. The very next day she invested in a video recorder and signed up at the local video store.

She kept him occupied, and that kept her occupied. He watched the TV, he watched the rented movies, he ate the food she prepared, he smoked his cigarettes, he complained often, he never thanked her. But then what did he need with thankyous? As far as he was concerned, she was just doing her duty.

He would sit on the couch and make a mess, he would eat his meals and make a mess, he would use the bathroom and make a mess. He filled ashtray after ashtray. And she cleaned up after him—the couch, the kitchen, the shower, the disgusting toilet. Her life was busted, but she didn't need to live in a pigsty; and besides, cleaning was easy for the automaton niece: the muscles moved, the mind was motionless.

She tried to work, but she had no heart for work, and anyway, whenever she settled at her desk he seemed to want more tea, more cake, more heat, more cool, more cigarettes. The automaton niece always responded.

About a month after Mikhail moved in, she met Andrew for coffee. She had put him off several times, but could do so no longer. She had no idea how she would manage to be her usual self, but when she saw him, already seated at a table, a smile entering his face at the sight of her, she was rushed with a sense of familiarity, of blessed normality. Immediately they fell into their usual chatter. It was such a relief being with him, and she wondered if, with his help, she might manage Mikhail and reclaim some of her old life. It was a brief moment of optimism. Andrew was attempting to make future engagements with her: a movie, a drive to an old homestead recently opened to the public, even the High Country holiday, and suddenly she felt caught. She declined all his suggestions. Not now, not now, she said, wrenching the conversation back to his project for Parks and Gardens, his parents, his dog, his days.

These difficulties notwithstanding, the hour spent with Andrew restored a little of her lost self. She'd had a life, and it was gone. She'd had a future, and it was stalled. Mikhail could live for another twenty years; unless she acted to change the current situation, she'd be resuming life as a fifty-year-old. She needed to give Mikhail a life, so she could reclaim hers. As a starting point, she needed to get him out of the house, and then she might be able to send him on sightseeing daytrips, introduce him to some of the community groups for seniors, find him some friends, shift him.

So she planned an excursion. With so much resting on this outing, the destination was all-important. She considered and dismissed several options. Then it came to her: the food hall at the Myer Emporium. Together with the TV and smoking, eating was Mikhail's favourite activity; he would enjoy the beautiful displays and the huge variety of foods. They would take the tram, they would stroll through the food hall, and they would buy their dinner there. It was perfect.

He resisted, as she knew he would, but she insisted, for the first time revealing her stubborn side. Still he continued to resist, demanding she show some respect. In the end she bribed him: there would be no meal that night unless he joined her on the Myer expedition. Mikhail understood bribes.

It was just before eleven when they entered the food hall. The delicious smells hit her immediately. She loved this place, and the life in her quickened. She pointed out the confectionary, the cakes, the salads, the cheeses; as her voice grew more and more animated, he became less and less interested.

'At home,' he said at last, 'I shopped at the special shops.' He cast a withering glance at her. 'I am not impressed with these foods.'

Her hopes dwindled and then died. He wandered off. She watched him from a distance. He moved slowly, heavily. He was not yet seventy, but his was a Russian age, and he was old and weary.

As was she. She did not bother with the rest of the food hall. There was no point, no point to anything anymore, foolish to have even tried. She guided him outside to the tram stop. They travelled home in silence.

For two years, her Australian life and her Russian past had existed uneasily together, like a tandem bike with differently sized wheels. Now Soviet Russia was not simply shaping her Australian days, but had actually taken over. She was stuck, with neither desire nor energy to get going again.

14

LOVE AND OBLIGATIONS

The seemingly endless winter of 1988 was wearing itself out.

Two months had elapsed since that red-letter day when Galina had agreed to go on holiday with him, a mere eight weeks since the intruder had broken into her home, but from Andrew's perspective everything had changed. While Galya appeared to have recovered from the break-in, she was even more controlled and unreadable than before and, significantly, she was keeping him at a distance. They had met for coffee at her local café and there had been a couple of lunches, but he had not been to the saddlery during the past two months, and all his suggestions for exhibitions, for films, for the Saturday excursions she used to like so much were rejected; indeed, she hardly seemed to give them any consideration, responding with a mechanical no-room-for-discussion refusal. As the weeks turned over, his hopes, fired up by her ready agreement to take a holiday with him, were turning to ash.

'She wants to see me only occasionally and always in public,' Andrew said to his mother. 'She couldn't be clearer about this.'

Sylvie nodded. 'She's treating me in much the same way. The mystery is why she's suddenly changed.'

It was late one Sunday morning, Leonard was out walking, and Andrew and Sylvie were sitting in the Morrow kitchen. A packet of shortbread was open on the table, along with a pot of brewed coffee—a surprising but welcome change, Andrew thought, from the powdered stuff his mother usually served.

'I can't believe the intruder is the sole explanation,' Andrew said, helping himself to another biscuit. 'Something's wrong.' He paused, and when he spoke again it was an unambiguous plea. 'Would you speak to her? Galya sees you as a mother figure, a confidante. My position's far more muddy.'

Sylvie smiled. 'I think that's muddying the obvious.'

Were his feelings so transparent? And were they to Galina? Not that this was his major concern at the moment. 'Will you speak with her? Please.'

He realised even as he spoke, that requesting his mother's help in this, or indeed anything, reinforced rather than loosened her entrenched over-protectiveness. But he was desperate.

However, Sylvie, much to his surprise, was not stepping forward.

'Galya's been through so much these past few years. Then just as she's settled into her new life, an intruder breaks in.' She shrugged. 'Maybe that's the entire explanation. And if it's not, I'm prepared to wait until she's ready to open up. But if you want some answers now, then it's up to you to approach her.'

His mother was right, he knew this even while he was asking her to do his work for him.

'Just make up your mind and do it,' Sylvie said. 'Do it today. When you leave here, don't go home, go straight to her place.'

He nodded. He would. The decision was made, so no need to dwell on it, and, checking the time, no need to worry about it just yet. He poured the remains of the coffee pot into his mug and took a sip. It was cold, and he pushed it away.

'So what have you been up to?' he asked his mother.

'Oh, just the usual,' Sylvie said.

She carried the coffee pot to the sink. With meticulous attention, she rinsed out the grains and prepared a fresh pot. She kept her back turned to her son. Unlike Galina, her face was all-too-readable.

Just the usual, said with polished ease.

She'd always considered herself a poor liar; certainly, that's what Leonard believed, but then he knew rather more about the topic than she did. As it turned out she was rather good at it, which was crucial for a life now manoeuvred with military precision. She planned her lies, she kept them simple, she held her gaze steady when telling them, and just in case she forgot one in the welter of excuses that were now required to explain her lack of punctuality, her forgetting to collect Leonard's dry-cleaning, her not having bought a birthday present to send to Leonard's brother, her not doing any of the myriad of chores that used to occur like clock-work, she kept a note of her lies. Tuesday: lunch with Maggie; Wednesday: shopping with Galya; Thursday: an extra few hours at the op shop, whereas all these times had been spent with Mark. Leonard was so convinced of her being a poor liar, it would not occur to him that she was telling him anything but the truth.

She checked the kitchen clock, and changed her mind about fresh coffee. 'You've decided to talk with Galya,' she said to Andrew in a no-nonsense sort of voice. 'No point in putting it off. And when you do talk with her,' she said, as she hugged him at the door, 'say you were worried about her. She can't take exception to that.'

As soon as Andrew left, Sylvie checked the clock again, made herself another drink, instant coffee so as not to waste a minute, and took herself to the living room. She dialled Mark's number and settled into the couch for a giddy half-hour before Leonard returned from his walk.

Since Winston's departure, Leonard had come to understand the value of exercise. By devouring time and decanting the mind, it provided much-needed respite from a life under stress. During the week he walked every morning and evening, and on weekends he walked through half the daylight hours. He walked so much that Butch, initially thrilled at his master's new habits, now baulked at the front door.

This Sunday morning, with no particular destination in mind, Leonard had set off soon after breakfast. Clad in overcoat and blue beret, he strode briskly and rhythmically eastward. His head ached constantly these days, his poor brain seizing pain as if it were its only friend; it was particularly insistent this morning. After about two hours, he found himself somewhere in Caulfield or Carnegie. The sun glared with a piercing wintry white, he pulled his beret lower, and although he should have been heading back, he ambled on. There had been a couple of spring-like days recently, but today the weather had returned to winter—a relatively mild winter, according to the weather bureau, yet it had felt perpetually cold to him. He had no idea how he would make it to the end of the year, much less the end of his life.

Things with Sylvie had settled, but apart from her letter project, she had little need of him. She had changed these past months, had become more independent, perhaps having decided she could no longer depend on him. She didn't seem unhappy, despite what had happened between them, just different. Andrew hadn't needed him for years. And Winston, who had promised him a lifetime, had tossed him out like old milk.

Every day found him in a perpetual tussle with memory. He knew that if he tried not to think about Winston he would suffer less, but at the same time he wanted to remember all that he once had in order to feel less alone. Perhaps the worst of it was he'd become so accustomed to his parallel lives that, with one suddenly shut down, he felt strange to himself. His routines were different, his emotional world was different, his working days were different; he might well have been exiled to another life.

He was gradually coming to terms with the changes when his

273

old life had intruded in the worst possible way. A man he could hardly remember, a man with whom he'd had a short affair not long before he met Winston, this man was 'doing the right thing' by contacting former sexual partners to let them know he had tested positive for HIV. From the little Leonard could glean during the brief telephone call, the man actually had full-blown AIDS.

Neither Winston nor he had taken the test. Winston had had only a handful of sexual partners in his entire life; as for himself, the men infected with AIDS were promiscuous homosexuals (definitely not him), and bisexuals (not him either). As to what he was: some men frequent prostitutes, others watch porn, others are turned on by women's feet, or knickers, or rolls of fat; he was a married man who was turned on by sex with other men.

He felt attacked on all sides for simply being who he was. He recalled Galina saying that for her, leaving Russia was not really a choice, that she was pushed to act by outside circumstances impinging on who she was. It occurred to him that the real choice for him was the same impossible one as for her: not to be the person he was, not to be himself.

The last leaves dangled brown and dead from the branches, a sheet of newspaper lifted by the wind slapped against his legs, and as he walked, his mind filled with the oddest desire: to be held inside an Old Master — he could see it so clearly — a huge canvas of a family group, all of them wearing Elizabethan collars, and he, the youngest child, forever surrounded by parents and siblings. Forever young, forever loved, forever safe.

Winston was gone and he missed him. He might have AIDS and he was terrified. He was desperate for his wife's comfort but unable to seek it. He felt shockingly alone and fatally unmoored. No matter how far and fast he walked, his past was in hot pursuit, and any satisfactory future was punishingly out of reach.

He had reached a five-way intersection, vaguely familiar, and paused a moment before veering up one of the roads. Immediately he was assailed by the sweet, sweaty hay-and-hair smell of horses. He knew there was a racecourse in the area, and assumed there were stables nearby.

The smell brought a flush of an old happiness, and he slowed his pace better to capture the memory. It was twenty years ago — such a carefree time — and he, Sylvie, and eight-year-old Andrew were on holiday in the UK. For a week they had taken a furnished flat in London's Primrose Hill, and every morning a troop from the Royal Horse Guards would clip-clop past. He would hear the horses long before they appeared at the corner, the hooves sounding crisp and percussive in the still, cold air. As they passed, and for minutes afterwards, there would be that sweet, grassy smell. There had been a groomsman too, who'd added extra spark to that trip. And now the same smell and a deep longing to return to those untroubled days.

He set off again at a pace. There was no point in hankering for the impossible. He might have AIDS, and he had to make a decision about the test. He should be grateful he'd got away with his parallel lives for so long. But he wasn't grateful, and if it had been in his power, he would not have chosen to be this way at all.

He recalled an idea of Yeats' that had appealed when he was a young man writing poetry: *We make out of the quarrel with others, rhetoric, but of the quarrel with ourselves, poetry*. He now wondered whether his desires would have been appeased and the conflicts of his life resolved if he had been a better poet, a more committed poet, like Yeats himself. Far from bringing him sense and clarity, his poetry had been little more than a hydrant for pent-up emotions. These past months without Winston he had written some new verse, the first for years; but fraught discipline and a lack of practice had undermined his efforts, and already with reason enough to despise himself, he had put his notebook away. Poetry wouldn't save him. Perhaps nothing would.

He checked the time. He needed to be heading home, and looked around to determine exactly where he was. Up the slope from where he was standing he noticed a church, Victorian-era, with patterned red brick and a spire. The service had just finished and the doors were open; chill wind notwithstanding, the minister and his wife were outside, greeting the parishioners as they left. The crowd was large and diverse; clearly this was a popular church. But it was not the congregation that drew his attention; it was the intriguing couple at the church door, the minister and his wife.

The minister was dressed in what appeared to Leonard's secular eye to be full ecclesiastical regalia. Over a white cassock hung a creamy cloak heavily embroidered with gold; a large crucifix, a gaudy affair of brightly coloured stones, dangled mid-torso; and draped around his neck was a crimson stole, also encrusted with gold embroidery. But more compelling than the decorative garb was the minister himself: he was fabulously handsome. Tall, with blond curling hair, carved cheekbones, a jaw set in perfect symmetry, and a face so cleanly shaven as to look pre-pubescent, this minister had movie-star looks.

The wife was everything the man was not. Short and stocky with a sensible haircut that might well have been barbered, she wore a blazer over a shapeless skirt. Hers were functional and unfashionable clothes that emphasised her square frame. Her face bore no traces of make-up, and there was no jewellery that Leonard could see. She was as unadorned as her husband was decorative, and as defiantly plain as he was beautiful. If Leonard were ever required to describe a marriage of convenience, this pair would provide the perfect model.

As he watched, a boy and a girl, both of primary-school age, joined them. This then, was the family. The girl leaned against her father, who wrapped his left arm around her and pulled her close. The boy squeezed in between his parents, gazing up at the passing parade of parishioners.

Leonard remained motionless on the footpath until the last of the congregation had drifted away. It was then that the minister turned towards him, and with an arm still wrapped around his daughter, his gaze connected with Leonard's. It was one of those loaded exchanges that Leonard had responded to so often in his long and complex life, an unmistakeable acknowledgement that each recognised the other.

At the same time, a young woman appeared from inside the church. She was tall and slender and androgynous; Leonard expected she was often mistaken for a boy. The wife said something to her husband, then went inside the church with the other woman and the children. For a moment, such a protracted moment, the two men were left alone, locked in each other's gaze.

It was the minister who broke the spell. 'You'd always be welcome here,' he called out, and held Leonard's gaze a moment longer before joining his wife, his children, and his wife's friend inside the church.

Standing alone on the footpath, Leonard stared up at the closed door. He felt a charge of longing and envy. What, he wondered, occurs in front of us every day, what unusual and creative arrangements? This man and his wife were not in exile from God's family; this man and his wife were not exiled from the society of humankind. What deals and alliances will people make in order to live in peace?

The traffic, swollen by the Sunday-afternoon football crowd, inched forward, but rather than his usual impatience on the road, Andrew welcomed the delay. His mother was right: it was up to him to speak to Galina, but that made the prospect no less nerve-racking. He rehearsed several opening gambits, but they either came across as too much about him (*You seem to be avoiding me*), too sharp and personal (*You're not yourself, Galya*), too vague (*There appears to be something bothering you*), or too revealing (*I'm really worried about you*). By the time he passed the football ground, he was still searching for an opening sentence, the traffic had cleared, and he was just a short distance from her place.

He'd never arrived unannounced before, and wondered if he should stop at a phone box and call her. As indecision over his unexpected arrival fired up his already heated anxieties, he tried to defuse the situation by considering what other people would do in this situation. With the problem shifted away from himself, reason found room to move, and reason was clear: it was daytime, and it was the weekend when behaviour tended to be more relaxed, so people might just pop in.

He decided not to telephone.

Eight minutes from the football ground, with green traffic lights all the way, he pulled up in the lane outside Galina's place. At the same time, the clouds parted and a sharp, white sun hit the windscreen. He sat with the engine extinguished until the pale warmth of the sun penetrated the glass and then, his heart pounding and a wad of words pinching his throat, he made his way to her door.

He took a moment to smooth his breathing and then he knocked—perhaps a little too quietly. He counted one, two, three, four, five slow seconds before knocking again. As he waited, he tossed between relief that she was not at home and disappointment that having worked up the courage to see her, he was being denied the opportunity. Then he heard a noise. It was the sound of the safety chain being slid into place, followed by the release of the lock. The door opened a few centimetres to reveal not Galina, but the unshaven face of an old man. Andrew stepped back.

'Yes?' It was just a single word, but enough to expose a heavy accent and a lifetime of cigarettes.

'Galina?' Andrew said, and added slowly, 'I am a friend of Galya's.'

He heard Galina's voice from inside; she was speaking Russian.

He'd never heard her speak Russian before. They'd been friends for more than a year, and never had he heard her speak her own language — nor had this occurred to him until now, he who had given her so much thought.

The man withdrew, the door was closed, the chain was released, and now Galya appeared in the doorway. He was shocked by her appearance. Slumped against the door frame, she looked exhausted and unwell. Even if she'd wanted him to leave, he doubted she'd have the strength to ask.

She moved aside to let him in. The saddlery, too, was shockingly changed. Her minimalist space had disappeared: every surface, every inch of floor, had been put to use. Her work area had been partitioned off with an ugly wardrobe, and there was an additional rack of clothes near the glass door that blocked out most of the natural light. The room was very warm, and stank of cigarettes. Clothed in a khaki shirt and brown trousers, the man stood front-on to Andrew; stocky and thickset, his feet were apart, his fisted hands were on his hips. With his deliberately threatening stance, this old man cut a powerful figure. Galina, in contrast, just stood in the clutter, her eyes downcast, her arms hanging limply, a picture of defeat.

The man had clearly moved in. But why? And who was he? Andrew did not wait for an explanation; rather, responding to Galina's helplessness, he gathered her coat and bag, took her firmly by the arm, and said they were going out — just the two of them. That she didn't protest was testament to her sorry state. She did, however, say something in Russian to the man, who responded angrily, his beefy arms punctuating a torrent of words. Andrew felt her hesitate, but he allowed it no traction and pulled her through the doorway into the lane. He led her to his car, sat her in the passenger seat, and drove to his place. She remained silent throughout the short journey.

He guided her from the car to his couch. He was about to make tea, then thought better of it, settled down next to her, and took her hand. For several seconds there was no response, then tears started rolling down her face. Still she made no sound. With his free arm, he drew her close. When she was comforted, she would speak. In the meantime, he would wait.

It was mid-afternoon when Andrew telephoned his mother. 'Galya's with me,' he said. 'There's a problem, a personal problem, and we could use your help. Could you come over?'

Sylvie explained the situation to Leonard. He offered to accompany her, but he was not one for emotional matters and she suspected he'd prefer to stay home. She reassured him they would manage. 'If things change, I'll call you.'

The cold hit her as soon as she entered Andrew's studio. It was not simply that the cavernous space was impossible to heat, but mostly Andrew did not even attempt it. Galina and Andrew were sitting on the couch; his arm was around her, and a tiny two-bar radiator was glowing in front of them.

'It's freezing in here,' she said.

Andrew laughed. 'We had a bet that within two minutes of your arrival you'd remark on the cold. You've surpassed even yourself.' And turning to Galina, 'Hasn't she, Galinochka?' He spoke so lovingly, so nakedly, that Sylvie felt a stab of anxiety for her son.

The girl raised her head. She looked wretched. The luxuriant features were pinched and arid, her skin looked like putty, her eyes were sunk in deep trenches. A stranger seeing her now would judge her as plain.

'Galya's told me the whole story,' Andrew said, once Sylvie was settled in a chair.

It had taken considerable time for it to emerge. Galya had remained silently crying while they sat together on the couch. When the tears stopped, he had made a pot of tea. The hot drink seemed not to touch her; she swallowed quickly and with thirst.

He refilled her mug, and only then, taking occasional sips, had she responded to his questions. Her speech was rusty, the words issued in jerks and breaks.

'Galya's told me the whole story,' Andrew said again. And just as he was about to relate it, Galina unfolded from her slump, filled herself with air, put a restraining hand on his arm, and began to speak. She explained to Sylvie that it was not a drug-addicted intruder who had barged into the saddlery a couple of months earlier, but her uncle, newly arrived in Australia; two days later he had moved in. She gave a potted family history, mentioning, but not emphasising Mikhail's long estrangement from her mother. She said that from her uncle's point of view, it was irrelevant what he might have done in the past, irrelevant what her mother might have felt about him, and utterly irrelevant what Galina might think of him now. The time was the present, the place was Australia, and he was family.

She shrugged. 'And he's probably right.' Though she did not look convinced.

Andrew believed she owed him nothing. 'The man informed on his own parents.'

'It was long ago, times were hard.' And again Galina shrugged. 'I do not know for certain what he did.'

Andrew couldn't understand why she'd defend him.

'He is family, and he is old.'

And he had acted reprehensibly, Andrew wanted to add. But he kept his thoughts to himself. Even bad family, it seemed, was better than no family at all.

Sylvie had listened without comment. Now she posed a crucial question.

'Imagine,' she said to Galina, 'this is an ideal world where anything is possible. What would you like to happen with your uncle?'

There was a long silence; ideal world or real world, there seemed no way out of her dilemma. Galina felt as if separated from herself;

she hardly felt she was living at all. As for her brain, her active rational mind, it had fallen to pieces. If she were not managing the practical routines of life, the shopping and cooking and cleaning, she would think she was having a nervous breakdown.

Sylvie was repeating her question. 'What would you most like to happen?'

Galina collected a few stray thoughts. 'I suppose I want him out of my place, but living somewhere comfortable where he is looked after.' Even while she spoke, she knew this was impossible. 'I cannot force him to leave. He would never forgive me, and anyway it would not be right.'

She felt utterly defeated; nonetheless, she managed to add, 'I would like my life back.' A long silence followed. 'Are you able to work wonders? Are you a magician?'

Sylvie smiled. 'Perhaps,' she said. 'Perhaps I am.'

'My uncle is no ordinary man.' Galina knew she must warn them. 'He thrived during the most dangerous of times. Compared to the obstacles he has overcome, I am a little pebble.'

'Are you afraid of him?'

She saw Sylvie's concern, and wished she could allay it, but did not have a ready answer. 'He is the only family I have in all the world,' she said at last. It didn't answer the question, but it would have to do.

There was a tension in the air, they all felt it. 'I think we could do with a drink,' Andrew said. He went to the kitchen, and returned with wine and a packet of chips. 'Your favourite brand,' he said to Galya. And then to his mother, 'They are the saltiest, oiliest chips you can buy.'

'They are the most Russian,' Galya said, helping herself.

Once their glasses were filled, Sylvie got down to work. 'We need to provide your uncle with some Australian life that's independent of you. What contact does he have with other Soviet émigrés?'

Galina shook her head. 'This is part of the problem. He refuses to mix with Jews, and they are the only émigrés I know.'

There was a long silence while Sylvie pondered. When at last she spoke, it was with confidence. 'We need to smoke him out.'

Galina did not understand.

'We need to devise a situation where Mikhail will want to leave your place of his own accord. He needs to see that life is better beyond your door.'

A possible solution was soon found. With the aid of the telephone directory and a few phone calls, Sylvie found an ethnic Russian organisation, located in the inner city not far from Galina's place. The centre provided a social forum for Russians living in Melbourne, as well as offering a range of leisure programs and educational courses. Sylvie's optimism about this place was equalled by Galina's pessimism. It had become a struggle, she said, to get Mikhail to leave the saddlery for any reason whatsoever.

'He is not interested in Australia. He was born a Russian and he'll die one, no matter where in the world he might be.'

'Exactly,' Sylvie said. 'And that's why an ethnic Russian club should appeal.'

The possibility of change gave Galina hope. Hope, in turn, gave her strength, but it was knowing she was not alone that gave her courage. Both Andrew and Sylvie made themselves available, over the phone and in person. And while this was easy enough for Andrew who lived close by, it was not for his mother—until Sylvie explained she was doing some work at the University of Melbourne, so was often in the area.

A few days later Galina was ready to approach her uncle. She had bought two Napoleons from a French patisserie (*millefeuilles*, as far as the French pastry chef was concerned, but her uncle need not know this), and over tea and cake, she told him about the Russian club. He said he was not interested in clubs. She emphasised it was an *ethnic* Russian club. She saw a glimmer of interest, and moved her account up a notch. When the glimmer segued into a couple of questions, she let her imagination soar, elaborating on the club's myriad attractions. Five minutes more and Mikhail had agreed to try the club. But not, he said, the cake shop.

'This Napoleon? *Gavno*.'

The following Thursday, early in the afternoon, Galina and her uncle took a taxi to the club. He had dressed with care for the occasion in his woollen suit and a white shirt. His tie was embroidered with an insignia that was unknown to her, but she expected it might be meaningful to the people they were about to meet.

They received a warm and friendly welcome from a man who introduced himself as the manager of the centre. He looked to be around fifty, and spoke a Russian that was inflected with something else — maybe Australian English, it occurred to Galina afterwards. She had worried that their Jewish name might have posed a problem, but Mikhail, having spent most of his life not being Jewish, had gained considerable practice explaining the name away.

The man pointed out two sitting rooms at the end of the hall, a library and events room about halfway down on one side, and a kitchen on the other; he invited them to look around, he'd be in the office if they had any questions. There was a special pinboard for church news (the Russian Orthodox church was just a short distance away), and a large 'what's on' noticeboard in the passageway. Her uncle glanced at these and moved on to the library. From the doorway, he saw two women in their middle years chatting together. Galina could feel him bristling: he wasn't about to spend his time with women, no matter how Russian they were. And when the first of the sitting rooms contained more women, younger and with toddlers, he turned on her, accusing her of wasting his time. Fuelled by desperation, Galina drew on her last reserves of courage, and persuaded him to stay a little longer. And it was fortunate they did, for in the second sitting room was a group of men playing cards, as well as an elderly man seated in an armchair reading a newspaper.

Her uncle headed straight for an array of periodicals spread over a low table; they were a few weeks old, but it didn't seem to matter to Mikhail, who shuffled through them and then pounced on one.

'This,' he said, 'this newspaper I used to read every week.'

The old man in the armchair raised his head. His face was red and round, his body filled the chair; he was one of those jolly plump men who would make an excellent Grandfather Frost. He nodded at the newspaper in Mikhail's hands. 'It's a favourite of mine, too.'

The man introduced himself as Alexei Lebedev, and invited them to join him. After a few pleasantries, he told them he was from Moscow, that he'd arrived in Australia with his family more than twenty years ago.

'So you left when Khrushchev was general secretary?' Mikhail said.

Alexei smiled, one of those smiles loaded with meaning. 'Khrushchev's thaw was not so good for me,' he said.

'In the end it was not so good for him either,' Mikhail said.

Both men found this hilarious.

Their conversation quickly gathered pace. It was one of those exchanges that skipped from here to there as the men placed each other in the Soviet network, and established points of common interest. After a while, Galina slipped out to the kitchen to make coffee. When she handed the cups to the men, even Mikhail thanked her.

Alexei was a widower. 'My children look after me, and they visit often with the grandchildren. But they are not my wife.' His fat face crumpled, and his eyes filled with tears.

'My children want me to sell the house, they want me to move in with one of them. But why, when I have lost my wife, would I willingly give up our home? We lived there for so long together. All our memories are there. It makes no sense.' Then to Galina. 'They worry about me. Like you worry about your uncle.'

A short time later, Mikhail gave her permission to leave. He said he would make his own way home. Galina checked he had sufficient money for the taxi, and that the card with the saddlery address was in his wallet. Alexei stood up to say goodbye. 'Do you mind?' he said, holding out his arms. She stepped forward and he clasped her to his big soft chest. Mikhail had no choice but to embrace her too, yet it wasn't just for show: as he held her close, he whispered, *spasiba*, thank you.

Standing outside on the footpath, Galina felt different. A light breeze blew, the air was enticingly fresh, the sky with intricate ribbons of cloud was a work of art. She unbuttoned her coat and strode down the street.

'It might turn out all right,' she said quietly to herself. 'It may just be all right.'

She walked past terrace houses with tiny front gardens, she passed factories and warehouses and small corner shops. She smiled at a woman pushing a pram, at an old lady walking with a stick, at two boys in school uniform riding bikes on the footpath. Up ahead, she saw a woman, much the same age as her mother, tending an unruly creeper. She slowed down and breathed in the gorgeous perfume. Intense and flowery, this creeper with its messy habit and small innocuous white-and-pink flowers was nothing to look at, but its perfume was sublime.

'Lovely, isn't it?' the woman said. 'You know spring is coming when the jasmine appears.'

A short time later Galina arrived home. While the coffee was brewing she rang Sylvie to report on the success of the visit. Sylvie was not home, so she left a detailed message with effusive thanks. She took her coffee out to the courtyard and sipped it slowly. It was quiet and peaceful.

When she returned inside she went straight to her desk. She took a sheet of paper and ruled a line down the middle, forming two columns:

I don't want to throw him out	I want my life back
He has nowhere to go	I want my home back
My mother hated him	He is family
He is old	I am young
I have a duty	I have my own life

She studied the two columns. One of them, the left-hand side, seemed Soviet in flavour, while the other, the right-hand side, was more Australian. One of them, the left-hand side, reflected the past; the other, she decided, pointed to the future.

'For such a controlled girl, the total collapse when the uncle appeared surprises me,' Leonard said to Sylvie that evening after she played Galina's telephone message to him. They had finished dinner, and were sitting together in the kitchen.

Sylvie was not fooled. 'Galya's tough and strong, not because she's made that way. She's had to construct the steel cladding because she needs the protection.'

Sylvie might well have been talking about him, Leonard was thinking. This business of a well-crafted, sturdy exterior to guard inner turmoils, he'd done that sort of double duty every day of his life, even more so since the phone call from the man he could scarcely remember, the man who was dying of AIDS. Leonard couldn't put it off any longer. He was having the HIV test tomorrow—not simply because of the danger he might pose to his loved ones, nor because he was terrified of having contracted HIV, but because living with uncertainty had now become intolerable.

Deciding to have the test had been bad enough, but where to have it was even worse. Geoffrey, his GP, would have taken blood and sent it away, like he did for blood sugar and cholesterol; but Geoffrey was out of the question as they'd known each other for years. The AIDS council conducted tests, but he certainly wasn't going there. In the end, he contacted an STD clinic he'd used before, and was told they tested for all STDs, including HIV. The receptionist asked if he'd like to make an appointment, or, if he preferred, he could just turn up. He was about to give his real name, stopped himself, had no idea what to do, and rang off. He had a vague memory of having used a false name when he'd attended the clinic before. It was best, he decided, just to arrive in the morning and not admit to any former visits.

Tomorrow couldn't come soon enough; at the same time he wanted it never to come. Sleep was unlikely.

Sylvie stood up. 'I'm going to my office to do some work.'

He reached for her hand. 'How about our going out for supper and a nightcap?'

The suggestion surprised both of them.

'Now?' Sylvie checked the wall clock. 'It's after nine.'

'Why not? If we were younger we wouldn't give it a second thought.'

Sylvie was already on her way to the bathroom to fix her hair and make-up. Five minutes later she was ready to leave.

'I feel like a naughty girl sneaking out after curfew,' she said, linking her arm through her husband's and pulling him close. 'We should do this more often.'

15

CLANDESTINE MOMENTS

The STD clinic was a fluorescent-lit, medium-sheen space with easy-to-clean green plastic seating lining the walls, and greyish-green dappled lino on the floor. It was a generic space, interchangeable with hospital waiting areas, vehicle registration centres, passport application offices, and airport departure lounges. Years ago, Leonard had joked to Sylvie that the ubiquity of green in buildings of all types had resulted from a post-war overproduction of green dye, and, until stockpiles were depleted, both public and private enterprise had a patriotic duty to use the colour wherever and whenever they could. From then on, should they happen to see green walls or floors or furniture, the two of them would exchange a glance and burst out laughing.

No laughter today, and no Sylvie either. Leonard was alone in a place that diagnosed and treated 'communicable diseases'. Communicable diseases indeed. Everyone knew that this clinic did not deal with measles, mumps or the latest strain of flu.

He had arrived at nine o'clock, hoping to be in and out before anyone else turned up, but with seven people already seated in the waiting area, he had badly misjudged. He hesitated in the doorway, but guilt and responsibility, together with the now unbearable torment of not knowing his HIV status, propelled him forward. He approached the elder of two receptionists, and a minute later was directed to a seat with a sheaf of questions to complete.

This was his third visit to the clinic. On the other occasions, it was to treat something he'd picked up—a dose of gonorrhoea the first time, and a nasty seeping lesion the second. As he settled himself in a seat, he recalled his mother's belief that good luck ran in threes; he desperately hoped that bad luck followed a different maths.

When first he'd attended here, he assumed that the detailed questionnaire would eliminate the need for an embarrassing face-to-face interview. He was painfully disabused of this when the questionnaire was used to shape a shockingly intrusive interrogation. Apparently, the state required reporting of certain diseases, including nearly all the STDs, and mandatory reporting itself required a detailed narrative around each occurrence of any of the mandated conditions. On both previous occasions he had experienced the interview as torture. He expected worse today.

Two of the people in the waiting area, much the same age as Andrew, were wearing identical wedding rings; Leonard wondered what possibly could have brought them here. The man was dressed in a suit, the girl in a stylish skirt and jacket; their arms were linked and they were talking together in hushed voices. At one point the wife removed a thread from her husband's collar. It was such an easy, intimate gesture that Leonard thought it impossible that this could be a couple in which one member had brought an STD to the marital bed after illicit sex elsewhere. They looked so close and loving—like him and Sylvie, he supposed. But then, like him and Sylvie, appearances might be deceptive.

This was not the case with the others in the room. There was a long-limbed gaunt man, probably a good deal younger than Leonard, but with a face carved by deep wrinkles, he could have been mistaken for seventy. He had coated his face in thick, clay-coloured make-up, which, rather than concealing the great cracks, set them in greater relief. He was dressed in jeans and a frilly jacket, and on his feet were red stilettos. His hair, bleached the colour of straw, was piled in a nest on the top of his head. He was intent on his nails, removing them carefully one by one, and putting them into a matchbox.

A few seats away was a boy who looked no more than fifteen. He was a dark, sweet beauty, like one of Caravaggio's boys; his eyes were closed, and he was nodding along to a Walkman. There was a women whom Leonard assumed was a prostitute, perhaps the beautiful boy was too, and a buffed and moustachioed man who, judging by his relaxed and animated conversation with the receptionists, was well known here. Leonard touched his own moustache, and wondered if he should shave it off. The last patient — were they all patients? This was not a normal medical clinic, after all — was a man in his forties. Well-groomed, athletic, dressed in smart, casual clothes, and, yes, with a moustache, he was, at this very moment, smiling at Leonard. Surely the man wasn't coming on to him? Here, in an STD clinic? That would be taking opportunism to a sick level. Leonard did not smile back, he had nothing to smile about. He hid behind his newspaper and swore to himself that if the test were negative, he would never enter this place again. Ever.

The plastic seats had arms — to keep us from touching and infecting one another, Leonard was thinking. He nagged at a knob of plastic on the edge of his chair. Bloody touch. Bloody sex. He hated sex. Hated himself. And Winston, he hated him, too, not just for leaving, but for leaving him to do this alone. And if the test turned out to be positive, the punishments would just keep rolling in: the confessions, the exposure, the appalling illnesses, the shame, the pariah status, and of course, the death sentence. He couldn't bear it. Better to call it cancer and swallow a handful of pills. It would be terrible for Sylvie and Andrew, but not nearly as bad as the truth and the end that would entail.

He turned a page of his unread newspaper. A name was called, and the woman who was probably a prostitute responded. First names only in this place, he noticed, or perhaps she was known here, a regular like muscle-man. And he turned another page.

'I'm getting a coffee. Would you like one?'

It was the man in the sports clothes. He *was* coming on to him.

When Leonard remained silent, he added, 'There's a machine in the foyer.'

Whatever the man's motivation, he did seem kind and friendly, and Leonard was tempted. Yet he declined the offer: his actions alone had brought him here, he was in this alone, he had to suffer alone.

After nearly an hour of pretending to be engrossed in his newspaper, he heard his name called, and was directed to one of the consulting rooms. The doctor seated behind the small desk was fortyish, with brown, receding hair, a grey suit, and no wedding ring. Of course, many men didn't wear wedding rings, and Leonard had considered removing his for the appointment, in the same way he had considered giving a false name. But he had determined to do everything by the book. He was so scared, and there was an irrational voice suggesting to him that good behaviour would be rewarded—as if behaviour of any sort could save him now.

With the introductions over, the doctor got down to business. He began with a general medical history, which, given Leonard's excellent health, was completed quickly. The doctor then moved on to Leonard's sexual history, a picking over the past that sounded so sordid: sex in public toilets, in parks, in swimming-pool change rooms, in the swimming pool itself, in sand dunes, in a cemetery. The interrogation delved into his first sexual experience (with a boy at school), right up to and including his years with Winston. There were questions about safe sex, when this began, and whether he always practised it now. The doctor typed all the information into an extremely neat computer. It was much the same size as a milk crate, and a far more compact machine than those the girls used at the office; if the circumstances had been different, Leonard would have asked about it.

With the history noted, questions now focused on the sexual partner Leonard knew to be HIV-positive, the man who had brought Leonard to the clinic today. The doctor requested his full name, and, when Leonard hesitated, noted drily that the man's secret, if ever it was a secret, was no longer. At the mention of the name, the doctor nodded.

'You know him?' Leonard asked.

'*Knew* him,' the doctor replied.

The doctor wanted to know the dates and whereabouts of their affair, as he and his colleagues were mapping the spread of the disease, what the doctor called 'its geography'. And he wanted to know what their sexual practices had been, or, given the length of time that had elapsed, their likely sexual practices. 'We're trying to create a profile of the sort of activity that increases the chances of transmission.' He also wanted to know about Leonard's general health during his time with the infected man, as there was a possibility that the presence of other infections increased susceptibility to the HIV virus.

It was embarrassing, it was humiliating. Every question felt like a condemnation, not because of the doctor's manner—he was businesslike, and showed no emotion—but due to the data itself. Leonard just wanted the interrogation to be over, and thirty minutes later it was. Except for one final issue.

'Your wife,' the doctor said. 'If you test positive, your wife could well be infected.'

'But we haven't slept together for twenty years.' Leonard heard the pleading in his voice.

'And we don't know how long this disease has been around. Although I do concede it's unlikely to have been twenty years.'

It was the only good news in the entire consultation.

'But,' the doctor continued, 'the virus is also transmitted by blood.' He shrugged. 'If you test positive, it's feasible that a cut or a wound could have exposed your wife to the disease.'

There was no good news.

He took Leonard's blood pressure, listened to his heart and lungs, peered inside his mouth, palpated his liver, traced his digestive tract, prodded his armpits and neck and groin, asked about skin lesions, upper-respiratory-tract infections, diarrhoea, anal warts, herpes. He removed the surgical gloves and typed his findings into the computer. Then with a clean pair of gloves he took blood. Leonard watched the procedure, he watched as if it were an operation being performed on someone else. It was the only time during the entire appointment he felt detached from what was happening.

'The results will take two to three weeks,' the doctor said, sealing and labelling the vials. 'How would you like to be notified?'

Leonard gave his direct line at the office, and was about to ask for discretion when the doctor said they were well aware of the need for privacy. They would, if Leonard was unavailable, leave an innocuous message asking him to call back.

It was eleven o'clock when Leonard left the clinic. The sun was shining, the trees were bursting with blossom, spring had definitely arrived—and far too tempting to see this as a good omen. Leonard had parked in a one-hour space; of course there was a ticket on his windscreen. He had known he would be longer than an hour, and he knew the parking officers in this area were ruthless. It was as if he were deliberately courting a manageable type of punishment in order to neutralise the punishment that was out of his control. But for what? Being who he was? Who he had always been? As he pocketed the parking ticket—easily paid, easily dismissed—he wished he had the same control over whatever might be swirling in his blood.

For the next two and a half weeks, Leonard arrived at the office early and remained until late. After dinner, he went for a walk—not his usual solitary hike, he did not want to be alone, but a more leisurely stroll with Sylvie. If it had been feasible he would have liked the two of them to walk out of their life altogether: new city, new friends, new interests, new beginning. Of course it was impossible, and not just the confessions and the practicalities involved, but Sylvie had an aversion to change. The giddy, irrepressible girl who had waylaid him all those years ago in the men's department of Myer had, through the years, become more and more fixed in her ways.

So there was no leaving the life they had made together. But during these long evening walks, they did decide to visit Canberra and see the new Parliament House, and they made plans to renovate their bathroom. They talked about friends, and they discussed the relationship between Andrew and Galina; just being with her made him feel better. They went to the movies, and on a couple of occasions they met in the city for a meal and the theatre. To his surprise, Sylvie delighted in their new practice. 'We'd become far too settled,' she said. And then added, 'It's the challenge of all marriages, isn't it? How to keep them fresh.'

The two weekends were far more difficult. Sylvie had met some people from the university who shared her interest in letters, and she'd made arrangements with them on both weekends. Leonard was pleased for her, he wanted her to be happy, but wished her new friends had not appeared right at this time. In the end, he played golf on the Saturdays, and on the Sundays he went to the beautiful minister's church.

16

YOU MUST CHANGE YOUR LIFE

Sylvie was sitting at the table in Mark's kitchen. A ripe washed-rind cheese oozed onto a board alongside a crispy baguette, and the coffee pot was on the stove. Leonard was playing golf, and she and Mark had the whole afternoon together.

A rally was to be held at the city square in support of Nelson Mandela, and Mark had suggested they might go. Mandela had been transferred from prison to hospital because of a flare-up of his TB, but would be returned to prison on his recovery. The rally was to protest his imprisonment, both past and future. With the exception of the Vietnam moratoriums, when even conservative people with sons of call-up age took to the streets, Sylvie had never been to a political rally.

What do you do when you start so far behind?

That she should steer a steady course her entire life, and only at this late stage diverge onto the road less travelled, was incredible. That she should be a woman in clear sight of old age when first she experienced passionate love was incredible. That she might be washing dishes, peeling potatoes, driving for the Blind Society, baking for the hospital fête, and actually feel Mark's hands on her, feel his mouth graze her neck, his body enfolding hers, his head pressed into her breasts, his legs entwined with hers, his tongue, his breath, his hands caressing her, it was incredible. Before Mark, she'd never made love during the day.

Where to begin when you start so far behind?

If she were to attempt to make up for time lost when she was twenty or thirty or forty, then she would miss out on the possibilities offering now, to middle-aged Sylvie Morrow. Once time was lost, it seemed you were always in arrears. These days, she found Mark in the pages of books and in the daily newspaper; she found him at the supermarket and at the petrol station. The most mundane aspects of her life had been changed by knowing him.

There had been times during the years when she could have screamed with boredom and frustration, but she had stifled those feelings, knowing they'd pass. And besides, she had no good reason to complain, although she did wonder if other wives experienced the same dissatisfactions. She'd recently read an article about the Women's Liberation Movement changing the lives of women. It hadn't changed hers, nor indeed the lives of her friends; the women's movement simply hadn't touched her. But Mark Asher had.

Was any marriage as simple as she'd once thought? How many husbands were like Leonard, men who loved their wives but sought sex with other men? She'd consulted a library copy of *The Kinsey Report*, and learned that 10 per cent of males had sex with other males; this meant there might be as many as two or three men in their social circle just like Leonard. Since meeting Mark, she had also wondered how different her marriage might have been if Leonard had been like other men. There would have been more and better sex, she supposed, and given her response to Mark, that would have made a difference. But what else? And again she acknowledged that perhaps it was Leonard's being as he was that attracted her, that without this odd quirk of nature he would have been far less appealing.

She wondered, too, how many women in strong and enduring marriages took lovers. She'd prefer not to be deceiving Leonard, but, at the same time, she felt surprisingly little guilt, and no sense whatsoever of betraying him. Mark didn't threaten her marriage—her marriage hadn't changed—but the borders of her life had shifted substantially. These days it felt as if there were no borders at all.

She could hear Maggie accusing her of self-delusion, and knowing this, had not confided in her sister. But neither did she feel a need to confide. You confide when you want reassurance, or when you are conflicted; she did not need reassurance, nor did she feel conflicted. She loved her husband, and she had taken a lover.

So much to experience when you start so far behind.

She had always been a keen reader, but with Mark she was discovering vast new literary territories, all of which added currency to her life. He had introduced her to the system of inter-library loans, and she now regarded it as one of the wonders of the modern world. Such delight in collecting a book from her local library that originated from a distant suburb; one of the books she'd ordered had come all the way from Canberra. She found a book called *Letters to Merline* by a German poet, Rilke. She believed it to be wrong, like a literary peeping Tom, to read a famous person's letters whose work you didn't know, so *Letters to Merline* sat untouched while she read a volume of Rilke's poetry. Such charged, singeing poetry. She read Rilke's poetry, she read his letters to Merline, and she fell for Mark Asher; she suspected she was not the first person to have read Rilke while falling in love.

So much to learn when you start so far behind.

Mark was risk and passion, he was possibility made real, he was life writ large at a time when so many of her friends' lives were shrinking. Mark pushed old age to the horizon and then, with a nonchalant shove, toppled it out of sight.

She was passionate about this man who had crashed into her life, and she loved being with him, but as to whether she truly loved him, she could not say. With Leonard, there was no such doubt. Her love for her husband had returned to where it always had been: essential and central. They understood each other and needed each other; they shared a son, plus thirty years of life. Leonard was bedrock.

But Mark tapped into previously neglected aspects of herself, and all of life was richer for it. And Mark was new and different, and for reasons she couldn't explain, she now seemed hungry for change. Even an afternoon tea of a washed-rind cheese with fresh bread was a novelty to one more accustomed to orange cake and Nescafé.

No matter what happened, there was no going back.

Mark spread some cheese on a hunk of baguette and handed it to her. He moved his chair closer, brushed a strand of hair from her forehead, then traced her hairline down to her ear and lightly, slowly around the earlobe. The touch shot down her spine. She shivered.

'Sometimes,' he said with a smile, 'I think your entire body must be an erogenous zone.'

A short time ago, she would have floundered in embarrassment at such a comment, now she just giggled. She swiped some oozy cheese from the side of the crust and sucked it off her finger, then took a proper bite and chewed slowly.

There was a tiny spider moving up the wall opposite. It was approaching a picture, a framed photo of Mark's daughter, Zoe, with her mother, the two of them on a beach dressed in swimsuits, their arms around each other and laughing. As the spider disappeared behind the picture, Sylvie found herself thinking about secrets, perhaps exposed yet not actually seen, like the laughing woman in the photo who, within a few months, would kill herself.

Mark must have seen her looking at the photo. 'She looks so happy—they both do,' he said quietly. 'But Rhonda was struggling at the time; she just wasn't showing it.'

'And yet women are supposed to be so emotional,' Sylvie said, 'and so emotionally undisciplined when compared with men.'

Was this just another myth promulgated about women, she was wondering. Her own experience, and there was nothing exceptional about it, made the case. She'd suffered multiple miscarriages without giving in to hysterics. She'd responded calmly and efficiently when

Andrew had fallen off his bike and broken his arm, and similarly, when he'd fallen from his treehouse and broken the other arm. She'd responded without histrionics through any number of emergencies.

'Women are supposed to be so emotional,' she said again. 'But it seems to me that many of us are experts in hiding our feelings.' She paused. 'And not just our feelings: we've learned how to hide what we really want.'

'Is that what you've done?'

She nodded. 'Until I met you,' she said, and made a wry smile. 'But if you hide what you want and what you feel well enough, and for long enough, your desires end up out of reach—not exactly forgotten, but somehow rendered unimportant, even irrelevant.'

Mark's gaze was still directed at the photograph of his wife and daughter. 'I'm not sure about that. I think what we hide, consciously and deliberately, tends to be truer to the self.'

'But wouldn't that suggest we're ashamed of our true selves?'

He was rummaging in his unruly hair. 'Freud might say that's exactly the case. Or should be the case. The untamed self has to be controlled, even repressed, otherwise we'll all run riot, and civilisation will be doomed.'

'Of course, Dr Freud aside, you could widen the boundaries of what is deemed acceptable behaviour, and thereby allow for a little more diversity.'

'You don't think we'd all become savages?'

She shook her head. 'I actually believe that human beings are fundamentally good, that we're all fundamentally cooperative, and that we all want to build community.'

'My own idealist,' he said softly.

She shook her head again. 'No, that's too simple. I also believe in the human capacity for change.'

She heard the words from her own mouth, words that just months ago would have been no more likely than her speaking Chinese. But she'd come to see life differently. Home with its familiar routines was so comfortable, so secure, but there had to be more to life than a perpetual warm bath.

Open your front door and anything might be possible.

She reached over and let her hand rest on his wrist. Then she pushed the sleeve of his jumper up to the elbow. She brushed her fingertips over the pale skin of his inner arm, slowly, from wrist to elbow. They both watched her fingers on his skin. 'Who would have thought this was possible,' she said.

'This?'

'This love affair.'

'Is that what we are?'

She leaned forward and kissed him lightly on the lips. 'You're the experienced one, you tell me.' She drew back, smiling.

He held on to her. 'Don't stop.' His face was centimetres from hers. 'I don't want you ever to stop.'

Mark was not smiling.

'You know what I'm saying?' And he's grasping both her hands. 'I want us to be together all the time, Sylvie.' He tightens his grip. 'I want a lover *and* a wife.' And to ensure there is no misunderstanding: 'I want to marry you, Sylvie. I want you to leave your husband and be my wife.'

Her stomach is sinking, her heart is thumping, and her brain is shouting, No, not yet. And briefly she wonders if she might stretch this out, have another month or two of Mark. Waver a little, give him reason to hope, *string him along*. A brief moment before the temptation is expunged.

She knew this time would come, has always known, but hoped it would be a good deal later than this. She doesn't want a husband; she has a husband. She has wanted, and still wants, a lover. But it's no good if the lover wants a wife.

He is leaning forward, he is clinging to her, his whole face pressed into a plea. She loosens his grip, and hooks her hand around his neck. She touches the familiar skin and lightly moves her fingers; she must remember the texture of this skin. She draws him towards her and breathes him in; she must remember the scent of him. She holds him against her, his chest, his hips, his thighs; she must remember the weight of him. And she kisses him, slowly she kisses him, and he picks up her rhythm, their mouths together in the supple, cushiony fleshiness of a kiss she must never forget, a kiss that must last forever.

Sylvie missed Mark. She missed him that afternoon when she arrived home hours earlier than expected, she missed him the next day, and the day after. She missed him through all the days and weeks that followed. Perhaps if they'd had more time together, perhaps if they'd had less, it would have been easier. Perhaps premature departures are never easy.

The day after their last time together, she wrote him a letter. Just as he had wanted to be entirely clear about his desires, she needed to be entirely clear about her decision. It was a hard letter to write, not simply because she wished she didn't have to write it, but because despite years of immersion in other people's letters, she'd written very few herself. A single page took a morning to complete—not to her satisfaction, satisfaction played no part in this whatsoever, but a letter that could not be misinterpreted.

She used notepaper that had sat in her drawer for years. The sheets were ivory and lightly textured, with a watermark of a patterned shield. She had chosen an envelope with the same brown-tissue lining that Mark had used in his letter to Zoe, the letter that had brought the two of them together. The gesture would not go unnoticed.

Dear Mark,

In all our times together we never talked about the future, nor did we speak of an ending. We were for now, & as long as we held tight to the present we would continue.

Our being together, this now, was perfectly timed for both of us. If we'd met any earlier, you would have been too tied up with Rhonda's death & your troubles with Zoe, any later, & some other woman would have snapped you up. As for me, my neat & tidy life had already started to fray. You found an opening & dived in.

You have given me more than I ever thought I wanted, more than I ever thought I'd missed out on. As you once said, quoting someone famous, 'Life is not a rehearsal.' I know that now. My future will be immeasurably different from my past because of you. I will live it differently because of you.

You probably think it is foolish of me to end it now. That I could have more, much more, if only I were prepared to take a leap. But if we had discussed the future I would have been clear: I've only ever wanted one husband. I married Leonard for better & for worse, & I married him until death do us part. But it's important that you know I've only ever had one passionate love. I didn't talk about Leonard to you, it would not have been right, either to him or to you. He was separate from you, as you & everything we did together was separate from him.

I expect there were features about my marriage you guessed from my behaviour, but I had neither need nor desire to discuss my marriage with you. However, it was never my intention to deceive you.

Now each of us must forge our own life apart. For me, I go from you having been changed & strengthened, I have been bettered. I hope there'll come a time when you look back at us with the same gratitude & love I feel now.

Perhaps one future day when out with Leonard I'll bump into you. You'll have Zoe on one arm & your new wife on the other, & we'll greet each other with unabashed delight. And when we embrace, as surely we will, we'll hang on just a little too long, before turning away from each other & re-entering our own lives.

Until that time, goodbye, dearest Mark.
With love & gratitude from Sylvie.

Before she could make any more changes, she folded the sheet into the envelope, sealed and addressed it, and left the house. She was sad but calm, and in no doubt whatsoever about what she had chosen to do.

On the way to the letter box, she passed old Mrs Payne's place. There were massive construction works underway, and she was forced to step off the footpath into the street. The old house and garden were long gone, and in their stead were the outer walls of two townhouses. She remembered so clearly how she'd felt when she first read those love letters from Lucien Barbier to Sophie Herbert; most particularly, she remembered their lovers' duet in haiku. How she had marvelled, how she had ached. Never had she known such passion, nor, she thought at the time, was she ever likely to.

She pressed Mark's letter to her chest and continued to the letter box. She stood a while, extending the moment, the leave-taking. Then she pushed the letter through the slot, heard it fall to a cushion of letters below, and made her way back home.

In the brief time she'd been away, Leonard had returned from church. She found him standing at the kitchen sink staring out the window, just like she had done every day of their long marriage. He twisted around when she entered, and must have seen something in her expression, because he walked over to her and wrapped his arms around her. She leaned into him. He was so much bigger than Mark.

She was fifty-two years old, and this was her husband of thirty-plus years, and this, the two of them together, was the deeply forested landscape of their marriage. It was contentment of a kind.

They stood locked together for a long time. It was so silent in the kitchen, and when Leonard spoke she felt herself start. His breath was warm on the top of her head. He was suggesting they go somewhere for the afternoon. 'Like Andrew's Saturday outings with Galina,' he said. 'But for us, a Sunday.'

'And after our Sunday outing,' Sylvie replied without any fore-thought, 'let's go to Europe.'

He laughed. 'This evening? Tomorrow?'

She pulled back, wanting to see his face, this face she was still adjusting to without the moustache, and she wanted him to see hers. 'Soon,' she said, 'I'd like us to go soon. A proper journey.'

'To Europe?'

'Europe or anywhere, as long as it's far, as long as it's different.' And an idea suddenly came to her. 'No one we know has been to South America. We could go there, start a trend.'

She saw Leonard's surprise, saw his confusion: this was not the wife he was accustomed to. What an irony, she was thinking, if her affair was discovered not because she was caught *in flagrante delicto* with Mark — she would never be with Mark again — but because of how she had been changed by their time together.

A moment later and Leonard's frown had disappeared, he was smiling. 'South America?' he said. She heard the intrigue in his voice. And then more firmly, 'South America. What an interesting suggestion. Long ago, I read a suite of poems — wait, I'll find it,' and he dashed into his study, returning with a thin book. It was called *The Heights of Macchu Picchu*. They sat at the kitchen table and looked at the book together. The original Spanish was on one page and an English translation on the facing page. Sylvie had never heard of the poet Pablo Neruda, nor this place Macchu Picchu.

Leonard told her that Neruda was Chile's greatest poet. 'Political poems, nature poems, love poems. Wonderful love poems, unrivalled by any other modern poet. Including Rilke.'

Her husband knew about Rilke? This poet she thought she'd discovered herself?

'And Macchu Picchu?'

'I've seen pictures of it,' Leonard said. 'It's an ancient Inca citadel built high in the Andes, surrounded by stunning, rugged peaks. It's in ruins now, and perhaps because of this, it looks to me more like a great sacred site than a fortress. Ever since reading Neruda's poem, I've wanted to see it.'

'So let's do it,' Sylvie said. 'Let's go there.'

He was smiling at her, lovingly, nakedly.

'I prefer you without the moustache,' she said. 'I see you more clearly now.'

His smile disappeared. 'I know,' he said. 'I know.'

The weight of those words was inescapable. She was deliberating on what to say, when he spoke again.

'Do you forgive me, Sylvie? Can you ever forgive me?'

She didn't forgive him, but that was not the right answer, or perhaps Leonard's was the wrong question. In the long silence that followed, she tried to work out exactly what she did feel. Forgiveness didn't seem particularly relevant to what had happened to them. And how useful would it be anyway? Forgiveness by itself would change nothing. And if Leonard had told her at the beginning that he had these tendencies, told the young, sheltered nineteen-year-old she was, she probably wouldn't have married him. And what a great loss that would have been. He had been a loving and attentive husband, he'd been an involved father, he'd been a good provider. She had loved him for more than thirty years, and she still loved him.

At last she answered. 'I accept you, Leonard.'

He did not move. The room was silent. The second hand of the kitchen clock jerked through the seconds. She saw the tears well up. Never before had she seen her husband cry; men like Leonard didn't cry. She left her chair and moved around to the back of his. She wrapped her arms around his shoulders and held him. She felt him shudder, she heard his deep sigh.

'Tell me about Rilke,' she said.

Across town, Galina and Andrew were admiring the window display of the Readings bookshop in Carlton. Arranged in tiered rows were the new releases, together with the Christmas titles. In the middle of the display was a copy of *When Melbourne Meets Leningrad*.

'What a splendid sight,' Andrew said.

Her first book, published and for sale in a shop; it was hard to believe, despite what her eyes were telling her. And it did look splendid, even to her hyper-critical gaze. Not only its central position in the window, but its eye-catching cover. She had wanted a painterly, impressionistic design, but the publishers had overruled her. And seeing her book among all these other books, she realised the publishers had been right. The cover's style now struck her, not without humour, as a fine tribute to Soviet Realism. The illustration depicted a Soviet girl in her Pioneer uniform framed by the Church on the Spilled Blood, holding the hand of an Australian boy standing in front of a Melbourne tram; the colours were bright, the lines were sharp. Soviet Realism taking pride of place in a Melbourne shop window, and she smiled: it wouldn't have happened without her.

Andrew produced a camera. 'Posterity calls,' he said.

Galina wanted a photo of her book on display, but she didn't want to make a show of herself. Andrew must have seen her hesitate, because he leaned in close and spoke directly in her ear. 'This is a special occasion,' he said. 'A unique occasion. It's your book, your day, and we need to mark it for all eternity.'

He was right, and it *was* what she wanted. She hesitated a moment longer, then let him have his way. He positioned her against the window and took some photos; he asked her to move to the left and took more photos; he moved her to another position and took still more photos. He was taking each picture as if it were a masterpiece, while at the same time interrupting the pedestrian traffic.

'She's a new author,' he explained to passers-by. And, pointing to the book in the window, 'There's her book. Don't forget that name. *Galina Kogan*.'

It would appear that when it came to *her* being in the limelight, Andrew managed to overcome his shyness.

At last he was finished and the camera put away.

'Did you take an entire roll of film?' she asked.

He shook his head. 'Not quite. But I'm happy to finish it off if you'd like.'

He was laughing at her, and she joined in. However, when he suggested they go inside the bookshop to see how her book looked on the shelves, she begged off. She'd had enough. 'Another day,' she said. And then, as explanation, added, 'It is good to spread out your joys.'

He guided her to a nearby café where they toasted the success of her book with cappuccinos and jokes.

'The Soviets might invite you back when your book becomes a runaway success.'

'Success on foreign soil? No, they would not like that at all. This book makes me even more of an enemy in Soviet eyes.'

'So different from Australia.' Andrew was shaking his head. 'When someone hits the big time overseas, having been previously ignored in Australia, he suddenly becomes Australia's favourite son —'

'Or daughter.'

Andrew nodded, 'Yes, of course. Son or daughter.'

Galina recalled Zara telling her about the great Australian cringe. She raised the issue now with Andrew. 'This is like relying on the acknowledgement and judgement of your betters?'

Andrew nodded. 'I'm afraid so.'

'You condemn this?'

'Of course I do. It's bloody 1988. Our generation of Australians must stand up for itself.' He paused. 'All Australians should.'

308

As Galina walked home, Andrew's words resonated, not in the context he meant, but in her own situation. Ever since Mikhail had gatecrashed her life, she had not stood up for herself. He was still living under her roof, he was still eating her meals, he was still expecting her to look after him; he was, in short, still using her to negotiate his Australian life. Initially, all decisions had been beyond her, but with Mikhail's expanding interests through the Russian club, she had regained something of her old self—though not enough, it seemed, to resume her life properly. It was as if she were becalmed, and while the state was not disagreeable, it was largely ineffectual. But now? She had to stand up for herself. She'd put her own life and her own future on ice for long enough. She needed to act.

She had long ago fixed on the solution to Mikhail's housing: Alexei Lebedev from the Russian club. In the three months since their first meeting, Alexei and Mikhail had become firm friends. They met at the club two or three times a week, they'd been on several club outings together, and Mikhail had stayed over at Alexei's place a number of times. Alexei was lonely, his family home was large, he would welcome Mikhail as a permanent housemate. And at Alexei's place, Mikhail would have the space he had enjoyed as a member of the Soviet elite, along with all the Western conveniences he so admired.

When he first visited Alexei's house, Mikhail had returned home full of admiration for the kitchen machines and household gadgets.

'You live like a peasant,' he had said to her. 'No mixmaster, no Bamix, no air conditioner, no microwave. A peasant,' he repeated in disgust.

A long time ago, Sylvie had asked if she were afraid of Mikhail. Galina had not answered, but of course she was. Though what could he do here, in Australia? To her, or to anyone, for that matter? And the answer was clear: nothing, nothing at all. But it seemed that rationality had no authority when it came to her fear. This man had been responsible for his own parents' death, he had treated his sister abominably, he had thrived during the worst of times. This man now lived in her home, he slept metres from where she slept. She should have told him to leave long ago, but she was afraid of what he could do, a fear well founded on what he had done.

She recalled a startling moment in Dostoyevsky's *Notes from Underground* when the narrator, in describing his bullying of a work colleague, said he was scaring sparrows for his own amusement. A lot of Soviet officials scared sparrows for their own amusement; it was a way of flaunting their power while proving their loyalty to the Soviet state and its leaders. It wasn't only what Mikhail had done as a boy to his family; as a member of the Soviet elite he would have scared plenty of sparrows. But he wasn't in the Soviet Union anymore, he wasn't in the power elite. *He had no power*. But for all her reasoning, the fear remained.

One evening, after a pleasant day spent with Alexei, Mikhail had tried to explain to her how it had been—not to make amends, and certainly not to seek forgiveness or excuse himself. 'I have no need to make excuses,' were his opening words. He just wanted her to understand the situation from his point of view.

He was fifteen when he informed on his father. 'When you are young, the world is simple. You believe what you are told.'

Most of all, he believed in Stalin. Stalin could do no wrong. Stalin was truly 'the best friend to all children'.

'Stalin never met me,' he said. 'But I thought he knew me better than my own father.'

'But surely you loved your parents?' Her tone of voice was anything but neutral.

He shrugged. 'I suppose I did, but my allegiance to my country and my leader was stronger. That's how we were taught it should be. That's how I believed it should be.'

He wasn't sorry for what he did, and he felt no guilt. 'I was doing the right thing.'

He explained that once you are inside the system, an insider committed to the system, you don't see it, you don't question it. 'It's your world, your normal world, and it looks after you. I did not need to analyse, I did not need to think.' He lit a cigarette and inhaled thoughtfully. 'It's easy to forget what is inconvenient to remember. Your faith makes you forget, and the rewards for being a good Soviet citizen make you forget. I remember nothing about the night my father was taken away.'

Lidiya, in contrast, had remembered every single moment—like a series of snapshots played in slow motion, she used to say.

Mikhail sucked on his cigarette, vigorously, as was his way. Between drags, he said that if circumstances had been even slightly changed, if this or that or something else had happened, he might have acted differently as a fifteen-year-old. 'But I think it unlikely. Your mother and I were opposites. I loved Stalin, I loved the Soviet system. And the Soviet Union was very good to me. It's not hard to love what treats you well.'

He regretted very little, but he was sorry he hadn't done more for Lidiya. 'It's too late to tell your mother, so I'm telling you instead. I'm sorry. I wish I'd done more for her.'

Lidiya would have scoffed at his apologies. Apologies, she would say, are no good to her now. Apologies don't undo the damage he did; apologies don't make all the pains disappear. If Mikhail had apologised forty years ago, or thirty or even twenty years ago, it might have been different; but he loses nothing by apologising now, he risks nothing. Her mother would reject his apologies, would regard them as empty. People like him would say anything to get what they want, she'd say. They'd lie, they'd distort, they'd cheat. And what he wants now is an easy old age in a country that is utterly foreign to him. And he needs you, his niece, and he'll say anything to bring you onside.

Her mother would probably be right, but somehow Lidiya's judgement didn't hold as much weight in the Australian context.

In fact, it occurred to Galina as she walked home after coffee with Andrew, that all these old animosities don't transport well at all. It's as if they lose muscle during the long journey.

She unlocked the door and entered the saddlery. The smell of Mikhail's cigarettes hit her; she suspected the smoke had seeped into the furniture, into the bed coverings. When he was gone, as surely he would be soon, she would have to wash everything. Actually, there was much she wanted to throw out, and she felt herself smile: how very un-Soviet to throw out anything that retained a skerrick of usefulness.

She poured herself a glass of water and went out to the courtyard. Mikhail was playing cards at the Russian club—not with Alexei, who was babysitting his grandchildren, but with some other fellows he'd met. She'd sent him off this morning with a sandwich lunch, so she didn't expect him home until mid-afternoon. Time enough to work up her courage.

She must stand up for herself. Mikhail must go.

When her uncle first turned up in Australia, she wanted revenge for the suffering he had caused her mother and grandparents. The desire for revenge had now gone. Revenge didn't reverse the earlier wrongs; it changed nothing about those old hurts, nor did it bring justice. No matter what she might do to Mikhail, the losses would still be her losses, the pain her pain. But neither did it seem fair that he got off scot-free. And she wondered if evading punishment was another privilege of the privileged class. Bad, powerful men rarely got their comeuppance.

Whatever happened, she must take her life back.

Next week was the anniversary of her mother's death—three years from the day in 1985 when her old life ended. And since then she had created so much new life: new country, new friends, new work. How much longer would she forfeit her life for this old man, this old Soviet who never gave any thought to anyone other than himself?

She sat on the edge of the planter box. Her tomato plants were growing nicely; she loved tomatoes almost as much as passionfruit and bananas. These small pleasures of her new life. A gentle breeze ruffled the leaves, and she raised her face to the blue Australian sky. She had let him suck the courage from her, but she must build it again.

And suddenly it burst upon her: Mikhail was in her debt. Mikhail owed *her*. Mikhail owed her for the deaths of the grandparents she never knew; he owed her for the neglect of her mother, and for all the deprivations that ordinary Soviet citizens like her suffered while he lived his life of caviar and ermine. *Mikhail was in her debt*. And he was adding to the debt right now; he was taking her shelter and her food, her English language and her Australian know-how.

It was time to make him stop. It was time for him to leave. It was time for her to take her life back.

She considered various strategies, but in the end, with her courage still faltering, she opted for the Soviet way. Mikhail would leave: she would arrange it. She picked up the phone and dialled Alexei's number. The phone rang and rang. She prayed for him to be home. Finally, he picked up; he was out of breath, he'd run in from the garden. She went straight to the point. She said that Mikhail would like to come and live with Alexei. She said that he was too proud to ask for this himself, but she knew for certain it was what he wanted.

Alexei was delighted at the prospect, as she knew he would be. His house was empty, he was lonely. But he was worried about Galina. 'You are Misha's family. You will be lonely now.' And she said it was because she was family that she could act in Misha's best interests. She would manage.

'I want my uncle to be happy,' she said, with convincing ease.

'You are a good girl,' said Alexei.

Together they devised a plan. Most crucially, Misha must never know about this phone call.

'You are a very good girl,' Alexei said again. 'You have made two old men very happy.'

She had been a good *Soviet* girl, that was what she'd been. She had called in her debts at no cost to herself.

17

UNDER THE AUSTRALIAN SUN

The country was burning. Every evening, the television news ran footage of fire devouring crops, bushland and dwellings. Galina saw kangaroos in a frantic leaping from the fury; wombats, echidnas and bandicoots were incinerated in the undergrowth. As for the sheep and cows corralled in paddocks, the poor creatures did not stand a chance.

Her fear of fire was an inherited terror. Her mother had lived through the siege of Leningrad: nine hundred days with the Germans at the gate, no water, no food, no electricity, and death perpetually on the prowl. Lidiya was just thirteen when it began. The cold of those winters was excruciating, she said. People broke up furniture, they broke up buildings, they broke up paintings and pianos to feed the stove; and the cruelty of it was you were never warm. Later it became even more difficult, not simply because of the scarcity of timber, but strength also was in short supply. Starvation, her mother said, shrivels not only the body but also the will.

And then came the fires you didn't want. They broke out in the *kommunalki*, small fires that spread through the dry crackling rooms and passageways. And outside, in a macabre and terrifying light, the constant shelling and incendiary bombs whipped up towering con-flagrations all over the city. Leningrad was burning, and there was neither strength nor water to douse the flames. The siege ended, the war finished, Lidiya grew up, she married and bore a child, but her terror of fire died only when she did. There was ample opportunity for her daughter to inherit the fear.

'There are no fires in the High Country at the moment,' Andrew said as he packed the car. 'And none en route either. I've checked.'

At last they were going to the mountains. It had been Andrew's idea they go in summer. Galina had laughed. 'An alpine resort without snow. What would we do?'

He suggested hiking, picnics, reading, staring into the wild blue yonder, but it was his mention of a temperature a good ten degrees cooler than in the city that convinced her. She had adapted to Australian English, she'd adapted to the food, she'd even adapted to the mysteries of private enterprise, but she doubted she would ever adapt to the Australian heat.

Leonard had lent them his car for the trip, convinced that Andrew's ancient Morris would make neither the distance nor the climb. Andrew had protested, but Galina was quietly pleased. Leonard's car was large and comfortable, with air conditioning and a cassette player. Andrew's car sounded like a lawn mower, and its beige-and-green Bakelite radio functioned better as an aesthetic object than a music machine. Andrew had made a selection of cassettes, a variety of rock and folk as well as a range of classical music that was weighted—she guessed with considerable care—to the Russians: Tchaikovsky, Scriabin, Stravinsky, Rimsky-Korsakov. There was no denying that Andrew was a thoughtful man, and easy company too. Like the brother she'd always wished for. But Andrew didn't want to be her brother, she'd known this for quite a while. Sometime and, to be fair, sooner rather than later, she'd have to tell him there was no romance in the way she felt about him. But when to speak? And how? She didn't want to spoil what they already had.

The traffic was relatively light and they reached the outer

suburbs quickly. A short time later, they entered the rural township of Healesville.

'We should stop for morning tea,' Andrew said, as he drove slowly up the main street.

Galina was laughing. 'But we are less than an hour into our holiday.'

'Holidays require holiday food.' Andrew pulled over and parked. 'And that means cakes from a country bakery, whether you're hungry or not.'

They shared a sticky coffee scroll with lashings of icing and swirls of cinnamon, washed down with a fizzy passionfruit drink. She'd never known of passionfruit until she came here, but they now counted among her favourites. She watched as he rolled a cigarette. A rollie and a ciggie: two more Australian words to add to her list, although given the widespread campaign against smoking here, probably not to her new book.

It was not that she didn't find Andrew attractive, but what she had been needing from him since that day she picked up the telephone and called him, was the reliability of a friend. If there had ever been the possibility of anything romantic between them, the moment had long ago passed.

He finished his cigarette, and they took what he described as a mandatory stroll through the main street, up one side and down the other. There were several handicraft shops selling homespun wool and bulbous pottery, creams and soaps made of eucalyptus oil and lanolin. After three such shops all with similar wares, Galina suggested they stick to the street. She was drawn to the quaint exteriors of the buildings and the village atmosphere of the place. She could imagine herself living here; then realism kicked in: she'd be lucky to last a week before dashing back to the city.

Andrew stopped to buy film, and they returned to the car. As he started the engine, he turned to her with a smile. 'You can now cross Healesville off your "Getting to know Australia" list.'

317

Once they were on the road again, Galina selected a tape of Rostropovich playing cello classics. The music filled the car, that majestic mellowness of the cello. Her mother had loved the cello, as had her mother before her. Perhaps everyone loves the cello: full-bodied, strong, secure, lyrical, but always with underlying gravitas—rather like home, she thought, and friendship, too. She looked across at Andrew. He was sitting erect, as he always did when driving, looking straight ahead at the road. But he must have felt her gaze, because he smiled, and then to her surprise he reached out and squeezed her hand. A moment later both his hands were back on the steering wheel. He was such an odd, endearing mix of a man.

If the cello were the metaphorical musical instrument for home and friendship, what, she wondered, would be the instrument for lovers? And it came to her immediately: electric guitar. Exciting, energetic, loud, blood-boiling, and definitely not restful. This cello was restful, this car was restful, and again she looked across at Andrew, this man was restful.

The last few months had been exhausting: Mikhail's sudden appearance and her collapse—the most accurate way, it now seemed to her, of describing what had happened; then her picture book launched, and with Mikhail's departure, the restoration of the saddlery as her home. It had been a huge task and a heavy one, and she'd been grateful for Andrew's help. It had been his suggestion they put the unwanted furniture on the nature strip. Someone will take it, he said. And he was right. They put the stuff out one evening, and by morning all of it was gone. She found it disturbing that her rejects could be useful to others; she had met no poor people here, but clearly they existed. It was Andrew who reminded her that she had furnished the saddlery with second-hand items, and although she had paid for her various pieces, they were still other people's cast-offs.

Then it was Christmas, her second with the Morrows, but far more enjoyable than last year's. It was not just the festival itself that had been strange that first time; there were the Morrows, whom she had met only once before, and even the food had been problematic. They had all applauded the roasted turkey, but to her palate it was bland. She had thought the seafood would be to her taste, but, with the exception of some smoked salmon, it was not her type of seafood at all; as for the crayfish they all raved about, it was a tasteless, rubbery, sea-smelling stuff that, she suspected, she would never grow to like. For her second Morrow Christmas, she had contributed to the feast with her own seafood platter of sprats, smoked salmon, a variety of herrings, and pickled vegetables. And there were the new guests this year, newer strangers than she was: a business acquaintance of Leonard's who, together with his wife, was visiting from Japan, and Mikhail.

Mikhail had chosen to come with her to the Morrows rather than accept Alexei's invitation to his family Christmas. She had worried how he would cope, and had kept a watchful eye on him. But despite the language barrier he seemed to manage; more than that, he actually seemed to enjoy himself. In the early evening when the party broke up, she and Andrew had driven him back to Alexei's house. He thanked Andrew, not simply for the lift but for the whole day. And he thanked her. 'I had very good time,' he said. And wished her a happy new year in the Russian custom.

There had been so many changes these past few months, but then change seemed to be endemic to Australian life. Big changes like where you lived and worked, and small changes like when her usual brand of honey disappeared off the supermarket shelves due to a company takeover, and she was forced to choose from seven other varieties. And the time her sandals went missing, and when she returned to the shop to replace them, they were no longer available, but a dozen other styles were.

Such small changes, but they could trip her up, she who had negotiated one of the largest changes imaginable. She doubted she would now have the courage to cross the world alone. Although was it courage? At the time, she'd had no idea what was ahead of her. Her mother's death had deprived her of the only future she knew, so in a sense she was already plunged into the unknown before she left Leningrad. Courage surely requires an understanding of the difficulties ahead, but in those dark days she had acted with little thought and even less knowledge.

The cello tape had finished, and she swapped it for ABBA. ABBA was familiar, ABBA was big in Russia. On their concert tour of the Soviet Union it was rumoured that, due to restrictions on the rouble, they had to be paid in oil commodities. She laughed quietly to herself: there was always a solution in Soviet Russia.

A few hours later, Andrew parked outside a small apartment building in the mountain town of Hotham. The flat they had rented was designed for winter, with a rack for skis and an area just inside the front door for wet clothes and boots. The windows were double-glazed and lacked wire screens, which, from the short distance from car to flat, Galina decided were desperately needed. The air was thick with flies.

Andrew took the smaller of the two bedrooms and immediately unpacked. He returned to the living room with two broad-brimmed bush hats, each with a curtain of netting. 'To keep the flies off your face. Out of your nose and mouth too.' He was smiling. 'Once before I stayed here in summer. The weather was perfect, the walking was sublime, and the flies were unbearable.'

It had been a long day and they were both tired. Andrew made a dinner of toasted cheese sandwiches, after which they walked around the town. The place appeared deserted. They followed the roadway to the end of town, then retraced their steps and continued past the flat in the other direction. Up ahead, a hotel was lit up, and voices and laughter reached them through the clear still air. As they drew closer, they saw that a broad balcony was filled with people standing around drinking and talking.

'Obviously the place to be,' Andrew said.

They decided to do as the locals were doing. They bought drinks, carried them to the edge of the balcony, and stood leaning against the railing, gazing out at the mountains. As Galina sipped her drink she imagined these slopes under snow. She missed snow, she missed the cold.

By the time they had finished their drinks the sun had set, and they made their way back to the apartment in the dark. While Galina prepared for bed, Andrew sat on the front steps smoking, a deliberate move of his, she decided, to save them any embarrassment. She called out goodnight and shut her door. He lingered for a while before taking himself off to his room, where he lay himself down and immediately fell asleep.

The following morning, Galina woke at five o'clock. Unusually for her, she stayed in bed, gazing through the window at the rectangle of mauve sky and listening to the early-morning sounds of the mountains. No cars and trams, no helicopters monitoring the traffic; instead, she heard the carolling of magpies and other birdsong, and the soughing of wind in the trees. It was sublime, it was tranquil. She felt her mind slowing — not turning off, she felt remarkably alert, but slipping into a gentle pace which allowed for clear and lucid thought.

Once, in what now seemed to be another life, she had been in the countryside outside Leningrad in January, on an expedition with her Pioneer group. It was a cold day, minus ten or less, and during the early afternoon she had gone for a walk by herself. Fresh snow lay all about: smooth mounds shaped by thick undergrowth, slender pipes traversing the bare branches, and large dollops weighing down the foliage of the conifers. The air was very still. There was that special light of winter — no sun, a white sky, no shadows, and no depth to the landscape. She had walked along a pathway that someone had recently cleared; it was like moving through a black-and-white photo that had been rinsed in blue. As she walked, she was aware of a peace she'd never experienced before. And now on the other side of the world, another January, another countryside, and in summer not winter, she recognised that same feeling. Fully alive and steeped in bliss.

At half past five she roused herself and pulled on some clothes, keen to have her coffee in the peace and quiet before Andrew entered the day. This was nothing specific to Andrew: it had always been her preference to start the day in solitude with a book and coffee.

She walked into the kitchen. The kettle was warm. Surely Andrew had not already emerged? She checked the water level, flipped the switch, and crossed to the window. Outside, the air was filled with a soft pink-grey light — the colour of a galah's plumage, it occurred to her. Perched on a low brick fence about fifty metres from the building, gazing out over one of the ski slopes, was Andrew. He was inhabiting the early morning, the huge awakening sky, the silent slopes. He had the mountains to himself.

She made her coffee and brought it back to the window. She watched him. He did not move, neither did she. How very con-nected to him she felt, the two of them awake when no one else was, a time when the day ahead was a blank page. She sat by the window, he sat on the low fence, the sun rose, the sky brightened, and only when he turned to come inside did she, too, move. She remained in her bedroom reading until seven o'clock, when she emerged as if for the first time.

They walked throughout the day. The sun shone, but not too hot, and the hats protected them from the flies. They followed tracks over grassy slopes peppered with wild flowers; they ate their picnic lunch in a wooded glen, and when they'd finished they walked some more. It was a day marked by contentment, and she decided not to spoil it by raising the issue of their relationship.

On the second morning, Galina woke at quarter to five and rose immediately. She pulled on clothes in the dark and tiptoed in her socks to the kitchen. The kettle was cold. She made herself coffee, slipped on her shoes, and took herself outside to the low fence where Andrew had sat yesterday. She positioned herself in the exact same spot, staring out at the mountains, sipping her coffee. She was willing him to watch her, as she had watched him. She couldn't explain it, was not interested in explaining it, just wanted him to be there by the window, watching. And he was, she knew he was. She felt his gaze on her back, felt the kindest touch in the early-morning stillness.

This presence, Andrew's presence, absorbed a strange seepage from her Russian past as lines of poetry filtered through her mind. Mandelstam's *I have studied the science of departures*, Akhmatova's *The paths to the past have long been closed*, and Mayakovsky, from a poem she loved as a girl, *Surely, if the stars are lit there's somebody who longs for them*. She heard this relay of Russian as she sat on a low fence, with a summery Australian mountain in front of her and the gaze of an Australian man behind. And when she returned to the flat, when she found him standing next to the window, when he turned to her and she saw the smile on his face, when all this happened, her resolve to speak to him again collapsed.

They read through the morning, then after lunch they went for a walk. An hour later, on a path that twisted around one of the peaks, they arrived at an impasse, a rock fall. Andrew sat her down on a boulder while he went to investigate. The minutes passed. She started to worry. Where was he? What had happened to him? She was on her feet, she was about to call, and at that moment he appeared from around the bend.

'I think we can make it,' he said.

He took her arm and guided her over the precarious ground. His touch was firm and secure. And so it remained, even when the rocks gave way to grass, and the worst of the journey was over.

ACKNOWLEDGEMENTS

Special thanks to Jenny Goldsmith, Celia Dann, Dennis Altman, Anna Dedusenko, Tamara Havloujian, Sarah Myles, Jean Porter and Jenny Stephens; also to Robert Dessaix and Maria Tumarkin for clarification of Russian language, and to Anne Mitchell and Meredith Temple-Smith for information on mandatory reporting of sexually transmitted diseases. I am grateful to Ian Lodewyckx, who generously shared his experiences of Soviet Russia, and also to Lara Gelbak, who, unstinting in her help and always creative in her approach, provided a wealth of information about Soviet life.

I am especially indebted to Constantine Danilevsky, translator, editor and friend, who gave of his time and expertise throughout the writing of the novel. And to Mark Rubbo: thank you for your friendship and support over many years.

Lastly, special thanks to my agent, Jane Novak, for her expertise and warm attentiveness, and to Henry Rosenbloom, quintessential publisher for these changing times.